Canaveral Light

A Novel

Don David Argo

To Marie,
I enjoyed meeting you at
the conference — Math is a
great leveler — please enjoy
my novel, a work of love for the
State — Best Wishes,
Don Argo

FSCS
9-4-03

For information address
The Florida Historical Society
1320 Highland Avenue
Melbourne, Florida 32935

Manufactured in the United States of America
ISBN 1-886104-05-0

Library of Congress Control Number: 2001129158

Published by
  The Florida Historical Society Press
  1320 Highland Avenue
  Melbourne, FL 32935
  phone (321) 690-0099
  floridahistoricalsoc@aol.com
Cover Art by J. T. Glisson

Acknowledgments

One man, especially an amateur historian, could never do the historical research for a novel this large. I received help from two of the most knowledgeable of Florida's historians, Edna McDonald of Middleburg and Alice Strickland of Ormond Beach. Mrs. Strickland generously gave me permission to use a scene from her writing that I reshaped into Burnham's soliloquy at the book's end. Vera Zimmerman of Merritt Island helped with finding documents on Douglas Dummett.

The songs of Florida folk singers have always been an inspiration to me, but none more than those of the late Will McLean. I thank Margaret Longhill, Director of the Will McLean Foundation, for permission to reprint Will's poem: *My Soul Is A Hawk*.

James Billie, Chairman of the Seminole Tribe of Florida, shared several stories of Indian lore. I especially thank him for the legend of the bashful star.

Many Florida natives shared stories of the old days of their families. C. W. "Speedy" Watton grew up near Kate Dummett's family at Allenhurst and Shiloh, two communities that no longer exist. He pinpointed their locations for me and led me down into the remains of the old haulover canal. Robert Ragans of Oak Hill grew up on the Dummett Groves and was a fountain of stories about Dummett Cove and Banana Creek. Ray Gingrich of Oak Hill taught me to find the remains and artifacts of history by using old maps. He showed me the sites of Fort Ann, Fort McNeil and Fort Taylor. He led me to the sites of the Dummett homes in New Smyrna Beach, Ormond Beach, and on Merritt Island. These three men have passed on, but their stories will live because they kept them alive. They proved that history is about people, and not necessarily about great events.

Ray Swanson of West Palm Beach is a fifth generation descendent of Mills Burnham and grew up on the reservation of the Jupiter Light. Each of his male ancestors back to Burnham was a lighthouse keeper at Cape Canaveral and his father served at both the Cape Canaveral Light and the Jupiter Light. Ray gave me a "master's degree" education into the workings of a lighthouse. We spent many hours on the Cape fighting through

Florida underbrush and mosquitoes to visit home-sites and graveyards of the Burnham and Wilson families. Ray and his distant cousin, William Tucker of Orange Springs, gave me genealogical trees of their families that were invaluable to this story.

Stories are told but novels are written. My motivation, inspiration and direction in writing came from two of Florida's best: the late Michael J. Shaara, winner of the Pulitzer Prize for Literature in 1975, and Patrick D. Smith whose Florida novels have been nominated for both the Pulitzer and the Nobel prizes.

I was fortunate to be a member of two critique groups who bled red ink over the wonderful words I thought I had written and made me face the harsh reality of writing. Ulys Nickle, Dana Rae Pomeroy, Bev Springer, and Pam Ascanio were members of the first group. Jim Harris, Harrison Reid, Judie Chirichello, Jena Bartlett, and Jan Brink were the most recent assassins of my prose. The late Robert R. Walters, the spearhead of the first critique group, was the man most responsible for any craftsmanship that I may have.

I am grateful to Dr. Lewis N. Wynne, Executive Director of the Florida Historical Society, for seeing the importance of this story and helping to make it part of the heritage of Florida.

This book is for my wife and friend, Kathy, who roamed the cemeteries and wilderness of Florida with me without complaint, and to my children who made it worth doing: Kim, Kevin, Sean and Shaara.

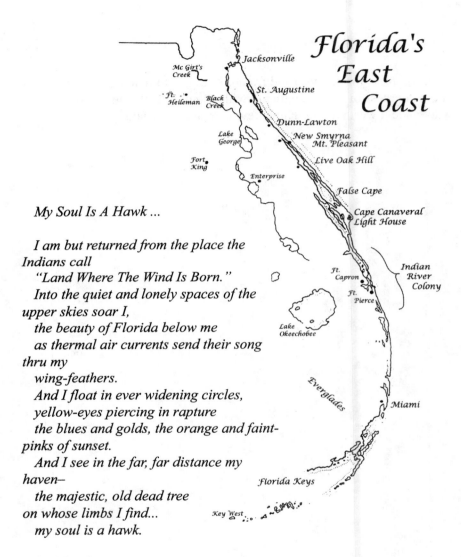

Florida's East Coast

Jacksonville
Mc Girt's Creek
St. Augustine
Ft. Heileman
Black Creek
Dunn-Lawton
Lake George
New Smyrna
Mt. Pleasant
Fort King
Live Oak Hill
Enterprise
False Cape
Cape Canaveral Light House
Ft. Capron
Indian River Colony
Ft. Pierce
Lake Okeechobee
Everglades
Miami
Florida Keys
Key West

My Soul Is A Hawk ...

I am but returned from the place the
Indians call
   "Land Where The Wind Is Born."
Into the quiet and lonely spaces of the
upper skies soar I,
   the beauty of Florida below me
   as thermal air currents send their song
thru my
   wing-feathers.
   And I float in ever widening circles,
   yellow-eyes piercing in rapture
   the blues and golds, the orange and faint-
pinks of sunset.
   And I see in the far, far distance my
haven—
   the majestic, old dead tree
on whose limbs I find...
   my soul is a hawk.

Will McLean
Florida's Troubador
1917—1990

BOOK ONE

1837 — 1838

Chapter 1

Lieutenant Mills Burnham braced his long legs against the bow rail of the steamboat, *Essayons*, and leaned forward to watch a log in the water swim away from the boat. This is a really messed up country, he thought. A river that runs north, and now logs that swim. He smiled as the twelve-foot alligator slipped beneath the surface of the St. Johns River. Log indeed.

He removed his blue campaign cap and carefully wiped the sweatband with the heel of his hand. Looking ahead, he could see the broad mouth of Black Creek cut the western shore. The ship's captain, Fenn Peck, angled the steamboat toward this juncture of creek and river. Thirty yards from a narrow sand beach, Peck spun her sharply away, signaling his first mate to cast off the towline. The barge they towed shot forward under its own momentum and ran aground. Burnham swiveled his head, keeping the barge in view.

Aboard the barge, fifteen soldiers leaned spraddle-legged against their wild-eyed horses. Each man held tightly to his reins with one hand and clutched a cumbersome musket with the other. Two soldiers from the barge jumped into the knee-deep water and carried the towline into the trees, tying it off tightly. The barge swung around with the current and snuggled against the beach.

The steamer churned a wide circle, returning to a point even with the barge. The big paddlewheels ticked over slowly, holding the vessel in place against the current. Burnham watched as the soldiers led their horses into the water and up onto land.

Motioning the mate in to take the helm, Captain Peck left the pilothouse and moved to the rail beside Burnham. "Be seein' you at dawn," Peck shouted to Lieutenant Herbert on the beach, who waved his reply. Peck turned, signaling to the mate to steer the boat away from the bank.

"We'll move into the creek and tie up overnight," Peck said, grinning at Burnham through the stub of a soggy cigar. "The squad'll be sweepin' through a fifteen square-mile area, over toward Doctor's Lake, huntin' for the heathen's campfires. I doubt they'll find one, but iffen they do, there'll be one hell of a bloody fight."

Burnham glanced at the sun—about three hands above the treeline. He pulled a turnip-shaped timepiece from his watch pocket. Four o'clock. Out of habit he gave the stem two turns before replacing the watch. The soldiers mounted their horses and entered a narrow trail into the woods. The forest quickly swallowed them.

The steamer eased into Black Creek. Burnham moved back to his former position in the bow and again braced himself against the rail. The waterway quickly became a tunnel walled in by foliage. Burnham scrunched down to make himself a smaller target, his eyes searching the dense jungle for signs of attacking Indians while his mind feared he might find them. He wondered if every Seminole in the Florida territory could hear the chuffing of the steamboat. With this thought, he moved away from the rail.

He looked back into the pilothouse. Peck had now returned to the helm, holding the spoked wheel with a light touch. The stocky, second genera-tion Irishman wore a brass-buttoned uniform similar to Burnham's but had a Greek fisherman's cap pulled down over his eyes.

In the waning daylight, the steamer finally reached a small jutting point of land a few miles up the creek. Peck eased the boat into the shallows and backed to a full stop. After making the vessel fast to the trees, the crew moved ashore.

Unsure of his role, Burnham stood to one side, awaiting instructions.

"We'll be takin' on a load of wood here from cribs we got hid back in the trees." The captain snorted, spat a soggy wad of tobacco to one side of Burnham's foot. "Welcome to Floridy, Lieutenant. You is now a mule." He chuckled.

Burnham followed the men deep into the forest to the stockpile. Two hours of hard work, most of it after dusk, saw a sizable stack of wood in the engine room. Burnham figured he should be exhausted, but instead was strangely exhilarated by the strenuous labor.

Their task completed, the men gathered on the lantern-lit foredeck for their supper. Taking his cue from the others, Burnham spooned cold grits onto a tin plate, slurping cane syrup over them from a clay bottle. The mate passed out stiff biscuits and slabs of fried, white fatback. Captain Peck issued rations of rum, pausing a moment to speak to each man before moving to the next.

"A man's gotta splice the main-brace whilst he eats," he said while pouring Burnham a cupful. "An old, seafarin' tradition."

Burnham had never tasted rum. The first sip coated his tongue with a thick sweetness. A soft heat filled his stomach, while his ears immediately felt hot and glowing. The combination of tastes gave him a sense of con-tentment. Such a crude meal. Delicious.

After eating, the men sat on the deck looking at the stars, smoking cigars and pipes, talking in the evening quiet. Burnham climbed the ladder to the pilothouse roof and sat next to the first mate. The mate explained to Burnham the plans for the morning. "We'll move back down the creek to meet them sojers, then haul ass for Fort Heileman."

"What if they aren't there? Maybe they'll get in a fight—get held up."

"We wait till midmorning. The agreement is that if they ain't there by then, we leave them and they ride on to the fort." He paused, then fidgeted self-consciously. He lowered his voice to almost a whisper. "You got a woman—and a home?" he asked.

The question took Burnham by surprise. He coughed into his hand to gather his thoughts, then told the mate about his wife, Mary, and their baby, Frances.

When he finished, a heavy silence hung between the two men.

"You got anybody?" Burnham finally asked.

"No." A momentary sadness edged the word. "I ain't never had nobody. Not even no parents." The mate sat up straighter and smiled as he continued. "My life's been with the Cap'n. He's my daddy, my momma, and this boat's my wife and my home."

Again, a silence. Then, quietly he said, "It's really all I ever wanted."

When the men spread around the boat to sleep, Burnham crawled into a wagon he'd found earlier, scrunching down into the softness of a pile of uniforms. He worried about mosquitoes until he felt the fresh, night breeze blowing cool and strong. Lulled by the gentle lapping of water against the hull, he drifted off to sleep.

The mate shook Burnham awake after what seemed only minutes. A moment of confusion clouded his mind before he remembered where he was—on a steamboat in the Florida wilderness. He shook his head in wonder that he should be here, sleeping in a wagon instead of a feather bed...in his New York home...with his wife.

The breeze had died. A fat, white moon hung heavy in the west, peering back at Burnham through a haze of fog while dimly lighting the scene with an eerie glow. Ghostly forms scurried around the deck, making ready to get underway. Below, someone was heaving chunks of wood into the furnace, and the *Essayons* again vibrated with life.

The steamer pulled into the current, headed downstream. The damp fog pressed low on the stillness of the creek, shrouding the creek banks from view. Deck lanterns, fore and aft, illuminated the fog, the light appearing to take on the substance of the mist. The boat seemed adrift in an alien world, alone in the universe.

Burnham moved forward to sit in the cool air, feeling a calm sense of comfort on this peaceful creek. Beads of moisture coated everything he touched. Other than the rhythmic slapping of the bow wave, the only sounds were frogs croaking disapproval of the intrusion into their watery world and an occasional bull gator roaring a challenge from the darkness.

Within an hour, a brighter glow appeared ahead in the east and Burnham began to see details on the bank. Thick, dark forests lined the creek on both sides. Long-legged Ibis stalked like white wraiths in the deep shadows of liveoaks. The creek narrowed and the boat had just entered a tunnel of these overhanging trees when the rattle of gunfire slammed into his senses.

The gunshots stirred the crew like wasps from a knocked down nest. While the men scrambled for their rifles, the Captain signaled for more steam and the *Essayons* bucked into high speed. As they rounded the next bend, Burnham saw the mouth of the creek and the St. Johns.

In moments, the steamer turned a wide arc into the river. At first, Burnham could not attune his mind to the scene opening before him. A frightening moment of panic seized him. The dark forms on the beach were Indians—shooting at dark blobs in the water, blobs that were men—the soldiers. The men, some obviously wounded, struggled awkwardly to keep the grounded barge between themselves and the Indians.

The *Essayons* turned sharply toward the bank. When Burnham realized that Peck intended running the boat between the Indians and the men in the water, he shouted at the crewmen on deck, "Shoot at them. Hurry."

The mate grabbed a hatchet and splintered the lid of a crate lying on the deck. He pulled out a flintlock musket and threw it to Burnham while yelling to one of his men: "Open that other crate. It's got powder and shot."

Burnham caught the rifle and ran toward the portside wheel, crouching below the gunwale. Pulling his Colt's from its holster, he laid the pistol on the deck. The mate slid into position beside him, shoving a powderhorn and a bag of shot at him. "We ain't got no patches or grease. Make do."

As the boat slid toward the slot between the shore and the men in the water, Burnham poured a charge of powder down the musket barrel. Glancing up to check the boat's position, he flinched when he saw a large, half-naked Indian rise from a bush less than forty feet away. Garish streaks of paint smeared his face, shocking Burnham by the closeness of this specter of death. For an instant, he hesitated, unsure of what to do. Then, dropping the musket, he scooped up his pistol and snapped off a shot at the Indian.

The Indian's shot instantly echoed Burnham's. A lightning bolt of pain dug into Burnham's skull and he lost control of his legs. Yet, even as he fell, he saw the hole in the Seminole's forehead. The man lurched forward through the bush and crashed face down into the water.

For almost a minute, Burnham lay still, gathering his senses. Then he rose to his knees, grabbing the musket. He wiped dampness from his eyes with his sleeve. Ignoring the red streaks of blood and the hammering within his skull, he tried to remember if he had charged his rifle with powder. Deciding it would be better to have none than too much, he frantically rammed a lead ball down the barrel, then looked over the gunwale for a target. Not seeing any Indians, he pointed the muzzle toward the trees and pulled the trigger. The pan flashed and a satisfying explosion hammered his ears. He ducked down to reload.

The Seminoles had retreated, moving into the safety of the trees to continue their fire. Their bullets hummed around the boat, splintering wood with dull thunks followed by the shrill whine of ricochets.

The mate screamed, lurched against Burnham, then slumped to the deck. Feeling the steamer stop, Burnham peered over the gunwale. A thick cloud of acrid gunsmoke hung between the boat and the riverbank.

Dropping the musket, he ran stooped across the deck to the other side. The water there was filled with men struggling to stay afloat. Heaving a length of tarpaulin over the gunwale, he tied the end to a stanchion. The men sculled to the tarp, clutched frantically at it, and began to climb. When a man reached the gunwale, Burnham grabbed him, jerked him up and over, then reached for another.

In a few moments they were all out of the water. Stepping over the soldiers sprawled on the deck, he ran to the other side and picked up his musket, yelling at them, "Get up. Grab guns—defend us." The soldiers scrambled across the deck to the open crate, armed themselves, and began pouring a withering fire into the woods.

The boat backed away from the riverbank with agonizing slowness. Then Peck reversed the engine, forcing the paddlewheels to bite strongly into the mahogany colored water. The boat continued its turn and began to move swiftly upstream. Moments later, it churned around a bend and into the peaceful waters of Black Creek.

Burnham let his musket clatter to the deck, then collapsed beside it. Spreading his legs, he dropped his throbbing head forward. Gingerly, his fingers explored his scalp for damage. A shallow groove angled upward into the hairline. The ball had barely cut his skin. Relieved, he wiped the blood from his face, pressing his sleeve against the cut.

Slowly then, he crawled over to the sprawled body of the mate. The man's glazed eyes stared with surprise at the sky. Burnham tore open the shirt, staring for a moment at a small hole blackened with blood just above the left nipple. Dear God, it didn't seem nearly enough to cause a man's death. He pressed his ear against the unmoving chest. There was no heartbeat.

Gazing numbly at the dead man, Burnham sat back, feeling the large muscles of his thighs begin an uncontrolled quake. A cold, watery shiver spread from his gut down across his legs. Along the edge of his reason, his mind picked at the unthinkable fear of cowardice, like fingers plucking at a scabrous sore. This fear threatened to lodge itself within him.

He shook his head, trying to clear his mind, then rose to a crouch and moved around the deck checking the condition of the other men. A body lay crumpled near the front of a paddlewheel—one of the crewmen, as dead and surprised-looking as the mate. The soldiers lay around the deck, groaning, three of them with wounds in arms or legs, wounds that stained their clothes scarlet, but none apparently in danger of dying.

A boy who couldn't be more than eighteen ripped his pants leg down, his young face contorted with horror and pain as he stared at an exploded kneecap. Burnham gritted his teeth. The boy would lose that leg. The kid couldn't have been shot while in the water, so he must have run a long distance with the knee in that condition. Now he couldn't even stand on it.

Only nine of the soldiers had made it to the safety of the boat. Lieutenant Herbert sat leaning against the deckhouse, his head thrown back in exhaustion, his breath coming in long, rasping, sucking sounds.

"Lieutenant, where are your other men?" Burnham asked quietly.

"Scalped by now, I suppose. It was a trap. Damn it—a trap!" Fatigue and despair creased the young face, reflecting the self-incrimination, which must have been churning behind it. "We went in like a bunch of fools and those red bastards cut us to pieces." He lowered his head, shaking it slowly. "My fault—I lost those men."

Burnham scooped a dipper of water from a keg by the deckhouse door. The boy took it and drank deeply, sloshing water down his chin.

Herbert continued. "Dammit, I *saw* them Injuns sleepin' around that fire!" He paused and darted his eyes wildly from side to side. "We charged in, yellin' and firin'. But then the damn place lit up like sunrise from *their* fire. They must have been fifty of them, hidin' in the trees. Some of my men went down on the spot. The rest of us turned and run like hell."

"Take it easy," Burnham said, patting a slouched shoulder. "I'll get water to your men." Finding a bucket, he dipped it into the water keg.

After seeing to the soldiers' needs, he climbed up to the pilothouse to check on Captain Peck.

"What's our losses?" Peck asked.

"Six soldiers," Burnham replied. "Your first-mate and one other."

"Damn. I raised that boy from a pup." Peck brushed his eyes with his sleeve. "Can't be helped now," he said doggedly.

"You need a break. Can't any of your crew steer this thing?" Burnham asked.

"Nay, none of them."

"You reckon they'll follow and hit us again?"

"Who knows how the devils think. I don't suppose they can keep up with us."

A deep silence followed these words. Each man became lost in his own thoughts. Burnham slumped on the bench outside the pilothouse door, and stared blankly at the sun-drenched landscape that drifted past the steamer. All evidence of violence was gone as quickly as the fog, replaced with the bright song of redbirds.

Slender palms bordered the next several miles of creek bank. Occasionally, small groves swept past with orange fruit hanging in stark silhouette against dark green, almost black, foliage. The snowy blossoms of magnolias loaded the air with a heavy perfume. Thick branches of water oak draped with whiskers of gray Spanish moss hung over the banks, stroking dimly concealed reflections into the deep shadows of the river. To Burnham, the biblical Garden of Eden must surely be no better than this, but did these mysterious shadows hide the devils who lived in this Eden? He shuddered at the thought.

Now that he was out of the stiff breeze from the steamer's motion, humidity again drenched his body with sweat. Stripping off his woolen tunic, he folded the sleeves and epaulettes inward, then removed a letter from an inner pocket. Although he had memorized the letter from a score of readings, he gently unfolded it. The words of the last paragraph burned into his mind. *Though distance divides us, our souls are never apart.*

Mary.

He drew his finger lightly across her signature as if stroking her auburn hair and sighed at the empty yearning in his chest. He looked around to see if anyone was watching, then re-folded the letter and slid it back into the pocket. After stuffing the tunic through the handles of his valise, he stepped back into the wind and walked forward of the pilothouse.

The separation from Mary and baby Frances clouded any elation over his new career as a gunsmith. A year or more in the Florida wilderness without them—how could he endure the loneliness? His mind conjured up his last picture of Mary at the wharf, her hand raised. An unmoving little hand in a sad little wave. He blinked sudden moisture from his eyes and turned his face, as if away from the picture, feeling the bite of the wind against his cheek.

Burnham remembered Peck's warning from the day before. "Seminoles, Miccosukee, Uchee—whatever. They be all the same—killers. You'll see. When we go up Black Creek to your Fort Heileman, we'll be close enough to the banks to get hit by arrows—or even rocks if they has a mind to throw them. But these savages has muskets, and they can shoot straight. Our lives be on the line every trip."

Burnham remembered the chill that shuddered through him. Paradise did have its devils.

Now, he felt the old fear stirring deep inside him, the fear of conflict. Even as a child, he had always given in to smaller youngsters rather than confront issues. He always avoided fights, but never understood why. Was it cowardice? And was that the real fear, that he might find himself to be a coward? The shiver of a chill again passed through him, but this time he knew it was down where the fear lived.

Ahead, a raft of baitfish thrashed the surface in frenzied splashes. Gulls hovered above the mad activity, darting in to pluck fish from the churning water. From the far side of the creek five pelicans sailed in a vee low to the whitecaps. Without losing formation, they suddenly pulled up to altitude above the cloud of baitfish, turned into a stall, then crashed headlong into the water. Burnham shook his head in awe. How could they do that without breaking their necks? And why here? Less than an hour ago, only a few miles away, men killed men, but birds keep right on fishing? It didn't make sense. But maybe that's what life's all about. The powerful attack the weak, the wily attack the dull, and those with the advantage win.

He turned to look the length of the boat, wondering if anyone else had seen the spectacle. The deckhands sat on benches in the shade of the main deckhouse, their heads drooping in fatigue. The healthy soldiers were busy caring for the wounded. No one had noticed the birds but him. So, who were the powerful and who were the weak? Who were the wily and who were the dull? The Seminoles?

Would Mary like this country? Would she like living here after the Indian trouble ended? He couldn't imagine anyone not liking it. Could he cope with a land where even nature herself was violent? Could he learn to live here, to succeed and to meet his responsibilities to his family?

After two hours of this calm, his reveries were broken by a commotion from the deck. Burnham rose and moved to the rail. Ahead of the boat, he saw a column of smoke rising above the trees.

"Probably the Hallowes place," a crewman yelled up from the deck. "Damn, I hope not—but it has to be." The man looked away from the spiraling, dark pillar. "They was a wife and three little girls there."

Burnham's hands tightened on the rail while the steamer glided past fields of sugar cane. The motion seemed agonizingly slow, as if the boat itself dreaded the approaching scene. Then, around the next bend, he saw a portion of hell transplanted to this spot on Black Creek.

A two-story frame house came into view, its roof consumed by fire and collapsed inward. Only some stouter timbers remained, thick slabs of hardwood, dancing like black skeletons in the fire's heat. Flames gushed from the lower windows, swept upward along the walls, drawn by a hungry updraft. Off to the side, two outbuildings also burned. All too plainly he could see bodies lying in the yard. Only one seemed to be a woman. He could see no children.

Nothing moved except the flames that greedily sought new fuel for their ghastly appetites.

"Reckon we'll stop?" the crewman asked.

"Iffen we do, I ain't getting off," answered a young soldier. "I done been shot at and missed, and shit at and hit about all I can stand."

Peck held the boat in the center of the creek, maintaining speed. He had no intention of stopping. Opening the forward window he yelled, "Any sign of life over there?"

"None," Burnham answered.

Burnham moved along the rail to the stern, watching the boiling pall of smoke until the trees cut off his view of the macabre scene.

The *Essayons* turned into the South Prong of Black Creek, then slowly backed around the corner into the North Prong. It was warped in to gently nudge against the Fort Heileman dock amidst a flurry of heaved lines. Soldiers immediately rushed aboard to take off the wounded, loading them into a dray along with the two bodies. Shaking his head to an offer of help, Mills Burnham found his valise and walked carefully down the gangplank onto the dock.

Burnham squinted his eyes against the dazzling sunshine reflecting from a road of crushed, white shell. A smoky haze from unseen fires did little to relieve the glare.

The road led from the dock to a large split-log stockade. Trees had been cut to form a two-hundred-yard field of fire around the stockade. The entire point of land between the prongs of Black Creek now contained only stumps and new palmetto growth except for a few large oaks shading several hundred dusty bivouac tents lining the creek. Small knots of enlisted men slouched near the tents, lethargically watching the activity at the steamer.

Burnham scraped his boot across the dock planks. Rough, he mused, but serviceable. Turning to look across Black Creek, he saw several hundred log and plank shacks scattered over a sand hill like a swarm of parasites. He smiled to himself as he thought of New York City. Here he saw no marble, no granite, and no paving bricks for the road weaving through the shacks. It seemed the veneer of civilization did not extend to the Florida Territory.

A young officer strode onto the dock. "Hello, Lieutenant," he said, smiling and offering his hand. "I'm Lieutenant Metcalf. John Metcalf. Welcome and thanks."

Burnham returned Metcalf's strong grip, frowning. "Mills Burnham. Thanks for what?"

Metcalf stood about six feet tall but had to crane his neck to look up at Burnham. "Peck told us about the fight. He said you saved our butts. The soldiers I talked to said you snatched them outta the water like some kinda giant."

"They would have made it," Burnham said. "Peck's got a well-trained crew."

"That's true, but they're followers, not leaders. They couldn't have done what you did."

Burnham felt himself flush with embarrassment. Peeling back a lock of hair sticking to his cut forehead, he let his gaze wander over the dusty shacks sprawled on the far side of the creek. "That place over there looks like a dump," he said.

"That's Garey's Ferry, the town. A pesthole. Civilians dyin' every day from one thing or another—dysentery or whatever." He pointed upstream and looked at Burnham from the corners of his eyes. "That old barge snugged to that cable is Garey's Ferry, the ferry...it's different from Garey's Ferry, the town." He snickered at his little joke.

They began to walk slowly up the road to the stockade.

"Where'd they all come from? The people. Why do they stay if it's so bad?"

"Ain't no place for 'em to go. Last year when the army built this post, people flocked in here for protection. The Seminoles been murderin' settlers wherever they find them." Metcalf stopped and pointed back at the village. "Must be close to a thousand people over there, livin' in about two hundred shacks. Probably three or four sick in nearly every hut."

"I certainly don't need the sickness," Burnham frowned. "The reason I came here was to clear up my lungs. I'd hoped the climate would be good for me."

"Oh, the climate's good, no problem there. Those people are sick 'cause of the way they live. Dump their shit right out on the ground. Fleas and flies everywhere. Probably eighty to a hundred people died there last year in less than a month—measles, cholera, whooping cough—whatever." They turned and continued walking toward the fort.

Sucking fresh air deep into his lungs, Burnham reminded himself that he had rarely coughed in the fortnight since leaving New York on the brig *Perue*. Maybe the salt-laden sea air was curing him. He slid his shirtsleeve up to look at an arm that had been frail and bony like an old man's. Funny how a lung ailment can affect almost every other part of the body. He squeezed his fist. His forearm muscles now had a healthy tone.

They went through the north gate of the stockade. The walled fort, about two hundred paces square, contained blockhouses towering above each corner. Firing platforms, one at ground level and the other about ten feet higher, ran completely around the wall, with ports cut into the logs about every twenty feet. Guards peered over the wall while slowly pacing the upper platforms.

In the northeast corner, a large water oak stood, its limbs carefully trimmed within the walls. Its cool shade relieved Burnham's eyes from the glare of the crushed shell paving the entire stockade. Beneath the tree, a large brick oven and grill faced long, plank tables and benches.

Metcalf pointed to a closed gate in the south wall. "That opens out to the Fort Harlee road, about twenty-seven miles southwest. There's a little town, Whitesville, about four miles south of here. Town's empty though. They all over to Garey's Ferry." Metcalf pointed again at the gate. "We keep it closed. Never know when a Seminole might whang a lucky shot through it."

An extensive, log warehouse stood against the east wall. Soldiers hustled in and out, loading a large freight wagon backed up to the building's steps.

"Officers are quartered in here," said Metcalf. "With you, we now got three officers assigned here permanent. The enlisted men stationed here live in the blockhouses. We maintain about sixty men, mostly laborers, but squads are always moving in here from other forts for layovers. In fact, there's probably nine or ten companies bivouacked here now."

As he walked past the wagon, Burnham looked in and saw powder kegs, about fifty grapeshot cannonballs and several crates of rifles.

"This lot's headed for Colonel Harney down at Fort Dallas on the Mayiama River," Metcalf told him. "It goes out on the *Essayons* to Jacksonville, then by schooner to Biscayne Bay. The war's moving south, thank God."

Metcalf led him up the steps onto a broad, covered porch and into the warehouse. Fenn Peck sat at a desk in a corner talking to a small, bearded man wearing captain's bars on his shoulders. Peck jumped to his feet when Metcalf and Burnham entered.

"Here's Burnham now," Peck said.

The Captain stood up and extended his hand to Burnham. "Lieutenant Burnham, I'm J. C. DeLagnel. Glad to have you with us. It's about time they sent us a qualified gunsmith. And one not afraid to fight, I might add."

Burnham smiled. "I'm your servant, sir." He saluted, then shook the captain's hand. "I don't know what Captain Peck told you, but I was scared to death during that fight...especially when it was over."

DeLagnel looked carefully at the blood smear on Burnham's forehead. "Did our Doctor Wilson take a look at that scalp wound?"

"No sir. I'm sure he's pretty busy with the others, especially that boy with the smashed knee. This is just a scratch."

Captain Peck laughed. "You were lucky, son," he said. "It couldn't have been that Indian's first shot or we'd still be hunting for the top of yore bean."

"Oh?"

"Yes," said DeLagnel. "You see, an Indian measures that first powder charge carefully. Then, when he goes into battle, he fills his mouth with lead balls. After the first shot, he'll guess at the powder and spit a ball down the barrel. Won't even ram. A quick tamp of the butt on the ground sets it and he's ready to fire." He turned to Peck and grinned. "They've seen enough barrels explode from too much powder that they usually underload it. And that little Spanish rifle they get from the Cubans is small-bore. With that, and the way they load it, I've seen balls hit men in the chest and just bounce off."

"I see. Well, I'm thankful I got here alive anyway."

DeLagnel, about forty years old, stood five and a half feet tall, slender and dainty, though straight like a steel ramrod. His dark hair was salted with white. Motioning Burnham to follow, he walked toward the center of the warehouse. "This is it—the *Arsenal of the South*. Your work area is that bench in the cage and you'll bunk in with Lieutenant Metcalf. He'll line you up on our routine, get you settled in. Good luck, Lieutenant."

He returned to the desk and resumed his conversation with Peck.

Burnham looked around the large room. Military ordnance lined the main room of the building: rifles, lead shot, cannonballs in racks, Congreve rockets, and in one crate a mass of rawhide cow-whips. At the south end, a wire grillwork enclosed a separate section containing a long workbench.

Metcalf fished a crusty briar pipe from his jacket pocket. "Gotta go outside to smoke," he said. "Too much black powder in here for comfort." He grinned and led Burnham out the door to the porch.

As Metcalf sat on the steps and began packing tobacco into the pipe, a guard yelled from the upper firing platform.

"Someone comin' outta the woods!"

Chapter 2

Metcalf and Burnham rushed to the western wall followed by DeLagnel and the others from the warehouse. Several soldiers were already mounting the lower platform and peering through the firing ports. The two lieutenants climbed to the top platform, each selecting a port to look through.

"I think it's Dummett," Metcalf shouted down to DeLagnel. "He's about halfway across the plain. If he raises up now we'll know for sure."

"I can understand why he's crouched," said Burnham. "But why would he raise up before he gets to the fort?"

"Cause Dummett plays his own game. He comes in 'cross the field to avoid snipers that might be coverin' the road. If he raises up too soon, he makes a good target for any Seminoles hidin' in the woods. Then, about halfway in, he lets everybody have a fair shot, both the Injuns and us. He don't really care which side gets him."

At that moment, Burnham saw the black-bearded man rise to full height and begin a casual stroll toward the stockade. Of average stature, he wore a dirty shirt and a bandanna tied around his neck. Leather suspenders held up torn pants with the legs stuffed into knee-boots. On his left hip, a holstered pistol hung butt forward. Across one shoulder, he balanced a rifle. As the man drew closer, Burnham saw a knife sheathed below his left armpit. A large knife.

A killing knife.

"Who is he? He sure as hell seems cocky."

"No, not cocky." Metcalf smiled. "Confident. Douglas Dummett. Some say he's the devil and some say he's just mad-dog crazy. I'll tell you all about him later."

DeLagnel walked over to the South Gate and swung it open. "Ho, Dummett," he yelled. "Welcome back."

Douglas Dummett entered the stockade, walking directly to a water keg under the oak.

"Fine day, ain't it?" he said to the cluster of soldiers crowding around him. DeLagnel waited patiently while the man guzzled a dipper of water, with most of it running down his chin. After pouring a second dipperful over his head, Dummett wiped his face with his sleeve and turned to DeLagnel.

"You got some bad information. I checked five miles out from both sides of the road, all the way to Harlee. There's not a Seminole anywhere between here and there."

"I suspected as much," said DeLagnel. "They hit a squad of our men over on Fleming Island, and burned the Hallowes plantation."

"Damn shame," said Dummett, nodding. "Hallowes had three nice little girls. But the injuns'll come back around here. Always do. When I wake up, I'll want some beef if you've got it. I've lived on roots and oranges for two days. Lost my tote going through a bog." He turned and entered the nearest blockhouse, pulling the door shut behind him.

"He probably ain't slept in those two days," Metcalf said to Burnham. "He'll sleep maybe ten hours now, so let's us head on down to the *Essayons*. I got me some work to do."

That evening, after a meal of broiled beef and fried potatoes, Metcalf grabbed two tin cups and led Burnham down to Black Creek. "We gonna go over to Garey's Tavern and lap up a few glasses of rum. You like rum?"

Burnham looked at the cups for a moment before replying. "I've had it once. Can you tell me more about Dummett?"

"Tell you what I can. He's strange, and that's for sure."

As they stepped out onto the dock, Metcalf pointed to the shadows beneath. "That cypress dugout under there belongs to Dummett. He's partial to canoes. I got a skiff here that we use to cross to Garey's Ferry. Old man Garey don't run his ferry at night except for emergencies."

They rowed across the creek, then walked up the hill to a large tarpaper-covered frame shack. Clusters of men stood outside drinking and talking loudly.

Metcalf pointed to a small log building beside the tavern. "Old man Garey's making a fortune," he said. "Sells tons of food and dry goods from that grocery store next door. The settlers ain't got but two choices: buy or starve. The tavern's probably the most miserable you ever seen. The old man rents out rooms in the back. The people in 'em die, and he rents 'em out again the next night—but, damn, his rum is good." He grinned and pulled Burnham toward the tavern.

Shoving through the crowd by the door, they entered the tavern. Immediately, a raucous noise pounded Burnham's ears. Clouds of green bottle-flies circled above a long, oak bar where a line of men leaned on elbows and talked into their drinks. About two dozen tables were scattered around the large room, each surrounded by drinkers. Thick smoke dimmed the scant illumination from the fireplace and a few sputtering candles. The wood smoke, tobacco and mildew permeated the room with a tangy mixture of odors.

After a moment, a wizened little man stepped from behind the bar and pushed through the men between him and the officers. His face had the dried texture of smoked fish.

"Well, Lieutenant," he yelled above the din. "I see you brung me another customer."

After introducing Sam Garey to Burnham, Metcalf rejected his offer of food, ordering rum instead. "A bottle of that stuff ain't likely contaminated," he laughed.

Taking the bottle, they shouldered their way to a long table in a corner. Two enlisted men jumped up and offered their chairs. Thanking them, Metcalf pulled the two tin cups from his jacket.

"They're clean. Always bring your own," he said, swinging a chair around and straddling it. He filled the cups to the brim, downed a large swig and began to talk. Burnham pulled his chair around the table and strained to hear.

"These men spend every night in here. The soldiers ain't got nothing else to do, 'cept maybe visit Mrs. Drew's whorehouse down the road yonder. The civilians figure gettin' drunk in here beats watchin' their families get whittled away by disease."

"I guess a man can become bitter." Burnham looked over the rim of his cup. "Do you ever visit—"

"Mrs. Drew's?" Metcalf arched an eyebrow, then grinned. "Hell, no. She's the best looking woman in the place, and she's uglier than home-made sin." He laughed and took another swig of rum.

"Tell me about Douglas Dummett."

"Most of what I know is common gossip. Some of it he tole me hisself. His old man's a rich planter over on the Hillsboro."

"Dummett didn't look like a rich man to me."

"Don't let nothin' 'bout that man fool you." Metcalf glanced quickly to both sides, then leaned forward and lowered his voice to a conspiratorial whisper. "The man's smarter'n a coon. Talks like us crackers, but he been to college."

He raised up, nodded his head and waited a moment, seeming to give Burnham time to digest the secret he'd just been told. Metcalf then continued as if it were safe to talk aloud. "They say when he was just a kid, he took some slaves down to the Indian River country, built hisself a nice home and planted a big orange grove." He took another hefty gulp of his rum, looking at Burnham's cup.

"You don't like this rum?" he asked.

"Yes, I like it. Very much," said Burnham, sipping at his cup. "I'm just not used to it." He wondered when its warmth might begin soothing the kinks from his body and mind. He took another long sip.

Metcalf brushed a fly away from his cup. "That's it. Have at it, Lieutenant. Cain't hurt you none.

"Dummett weren't smart at everything," he continued. "Married hisself the best looking woman in St. Augustine and drug her down to the boondocks. He spent all his time workin' his citrus trees and coon huntin'. I guess she couldn't stand the lonelies and took to spending lots of time up in New Smyrna."

"He let her go there alone?" Burnham felt his interest rising again.

"Yep, and I 'magine that was his mistake. After awhile, she took up with an army officer, and run off with him to the States."

A fleeting moment of loss filled Burnham, almost as if it had happened to him. He couldn't imagine surviving such a blow. Then he told Metcalf about Mary, alone in New York with the baby. "I don't worry about her that way. She's an honorable woman."

"Well, Dummett's wife weren't. Knocked him into a blue funk. Ain't over it yet. When the Injun trouble started, he helped head up a militia. Made hisself Captain. They called themselves the Mosquito Roarers." He snorted. "Real bad men—they thought. Hell, they was a rag-tag bunch of planters that hadn't never shot at nobody before. And they damn near got Dummett kilt."

"I've never even hit a grown man in anger, yet today I killed one." Burnham frowned, then took a long swallow of rum. "I doubt if my inexperience makes much difference to the dead man."

"I reckon not. But to get almost killed over someone else's stupidity might matter to a live man." Metcalf turned the cup in his fingers. "There's a plantation over on the Halifax River, Dunn-Lawton it's called. It's a sugar cane mill. With the Indians raidin' and all, the white folks quit their river plantations about a year ago. Left lots of stuff behind. Them Mosquito Roarers went to Dunn-Lawton to salvage a large food cache. "When they got there, the place was burnin', but the Injuns had penned up some cattle. The head Roarer, Major Putnam, figured the Injuns would come back for 'em the next day, so he sets up an ambush, postin' men along the river trail, tellin' 'em to charge when he fires.

"At sunrise next morning, when the Injuns get there, old Putnam fires too soon. Turns out they're only a couple of scouts. Rest of the bunch is waitin' down the trail. Dummett, he charges out and shoots one of the scouts. Whilst he's peelin' that one's hair, the other Injun slips in behind him and shoots him in the neck."

"Damn. From behind? Didn't the others help?"

"Hell, no. The other Roarers never roared a peep. Oh, I guess some of 'em did. I heerd of one, James Ormond—real hellcat. Ormond drags Dummett off the trail into the brush and saves him. Them other Mosquito Roarers turns tail and runs, roaring like hell I 'magine." He laughed and paused, again looking at Burnham's cup. "Drink up." He poured himself another cup of rum and then refilled Burnham's.

"Dummett wasn't wearing a uniform today," said Burnham.

"The militia didn't have no uniforms. Just what you saw him wearing. No matter. He quit them fools after the Dunn-Lawton fiasco. Figured he didn't owe 'em nothing. But after his wound healed, he didn't stop killing Injuns. No, sir. He goes his own way and kills 'em where he finds 'em. He don't seem to mind the lonelies, bad weather or bad luck."

"Maybe he *is* crazy."

"No, he don't take no unnecessary chances. He's smart and he's got more guts than a government mule. Cold nerve saves his ass when he gets in a mess, and he gets away with it 'cause he probably don't give a damn if he dies. DeLagnel uses him to track the Injuns, sorta keep up with their whereabouts."

Burnham finished his cup first this time and slid it toward Metcalf. "One more won't hurt now." He thumped his chest and belched. "Excuse me."

The door flew open and Douglas Dummett filled the opening. He now wore a clean but slightly wrinkled broadcloth coat and trim peach-colored trousers. Looking around the room, he spotted them and walked to the table, scooping up a chair on the way. The men in the room melted from his path as if he carried cholera. Dummett seemed unaware of the commotion his entrance caused as he straddled his chair and pointed toward the rum bottle. "May I?" he asked, pulling a cup from his shirtfront. Metcalf introduced Burnham and filled Dummett's cup.

"An honor, Sir," Burnham said, gripping Dummett's hand firmly.

Dummett shook his head and smiled. "I heard about the attack on the boat. DeLagnel says you're a good one to ride with."

"Just lucky," Burnham replied, leaning back in his chair. "What else could I have done?"

"You could have hid. Lots of men would."

Burnham laughed. "Guess I was too scared. I never thought of that."

Dummett roared, "Such modesty."

Finally, the crowd began to thin. The fire died to embers, darkness masking the room's filth. Dancing shadows from the glowing coals made the room seem almost comfortable.

Burnham found the rum going down much smoother now, while they talked quietly about the future after the Indian war ends. Dummett was surprisingly verbose for such a loner. Metcalf raised his head in wonder when Dummett told them he planned to take the job of customs collector for the Port of New Smyrna.

"I've got to recoup some of my papa's losses at Mount Pleasant, our home place. The red bastards destroyed the furniture and the interior walls, but left the shell of the house as an insult to me." He laughed and slapped his thigh. "They didn't know my papa buried several thousand dollars in silver and gold. They did their dance right over it. It has been there two years and Papa's getting short of hard money. About time I fetched it."

Burnham stood, knocking over his chair. "Sir." His voice seemed slippery to him. He adjusted his lips to his tongue and continued. "Sir, if I can be of service to you...in that adventure..." He sat down, crashing to the floor beside his overturned chair.

Dummett lifted him easily and returned him to his chair. "Thanks for the offer. I'll remember it. But right now I have other business." He stood, shook hands again with Burnham, and left the tavern.

Metcalf poured them each another cup of rum and Burnham settled down, sliding forward to the edge of his chair. They relaxed.

Much later, as they stumbled into the skiff, Burnham noticed Dummett's dugout canoe pulled up to the bank. He started to raise a hand to point at it, then toppled back against the gunwale.

"He's still over here. Shouldn't we—"

"He's probably...visiting...Mrs. Drew," Metcalf mumbled.

"Damn," said Burnham as the hammer spring snapped from its recess for the third time and flew across his workbench. He slammed the ancient matchlock rifle to the bench and slid from the three-legged stool. Tired of searching for the elusive spring by the dim glow of the oil lantern, he wandered into the empty warehouse.

In the three weeks since his arrival at the fort, his life had settled into a routine—days spent in repairing rifles and pistols, followed by evenings spent in relaxed conversation with Metcalf. The jaunty lieutenant was a Georgian, a native of Valdosta on the Territorial border. His humorous outlook on everything seemed rooted in rural soil, in sharp contrast to Burnham's more serious views. They enjoyed several evenings of rum and conversation at Garey's Tavern, in defiance of the epidemic sickness on that side of the creek. Dummett joined them sometimes, never appearing to seek their friendship but eagerly accepting it on these occasions.

Burnham had many questions for Dummett about the way life had been before the Indian war began, a time Dummett assured him was peaceful and calm.

This evening, after supper, Burnham had been unable to find Metcalf so he concentrated on converting old Sam Garey's ancient musket from a fusil to a flintlock. It seemed a foolish waste of time. Most of his days were spent converting flintlocks to the modern percussion rifle. The favor would probably go unrewarded, but the old man seemed attached to the rusty old smoker and begged him for the conversion.

Stepping out onto the dark porch, he saw Metcalf hurrying across the compound toward the South Gate, a lantern bobbing at his side. Burnham yelled, "Headed any place particular?"

"Oh, there you are." Metcalf waited for Burnham to catch up. "I figured you'd be over there already."

"Where?"

"That woman? Mrs. Johns? That woman what Dummett brought in here scalped by the injuns and left for dead? They moved her from the dispensary to the Clark house," said Metcalf. "Doc Wilson says she's recovered enough to tell her story more clearly now, and DeLagnel wants us there. Has to write a report. Let's haul it on over there."

As they walked through the dark, Metcalf told Burnham the wild rumors of the woman's care and treatment—she was dying from loss of blood—Doc Wilson had filled her so full of laudanum that she was insane—every soldier who had told Metcalf the tale had some crazy version to share.

"Dummett packed up and left to track the Injuns soon as he could tell from the woman's babbling where she'd been attacked." Metcalf walked faster as they neared the Clark house.

A small crowd of soldiers stood in front of the stately Clark house, apparently the unfolding tragedy holding their interest more than rum or whores. Entering the house, Burnham and Metcalf found Mrs. Johns seated at a table in the sitting room, her back to a small fire crackling in the brick fireplace. Samuel Wilson, a young, civilian surgeon on private contract to the fort for the summer, sat beside her.

Captain DeLagnel sat at the end of the table, a pad of paper, pen and ink in readiness before him.

"Gentlemen," DeLagnel waved the two young lieutenants into the room. "Have a seat."

Burnham stood awkwardly before the young woman. He judged her to be about sixteen, but lines of experience had aged her face. Bright, feverish eyes, large and black as coal, burned into his for a moment from beneath a turban of bandages, then looked down to the handkerchief twisted around her fingers.

Burnham and Metcalf positioned chairs across the table from her.

"Take your time, now," DeLagnel told her. His voice was unusually soft and kind. "Always remember, we only want to help you. You just talk, and we'll try not to interrupt unless something is unclear."

She gave a little nod, then inhaled deeply and began to speak haltingly.

"My husband...Clement...he'd been scared for us to move to a fort... didn't have no cash money and we'd heard how much it could cost...all our eats and whatever. We'd surely end up owin'." She began to cry softly into the handkerchief. "Lord knows, poor Clement worked hard enough this last year trying to clear us outten debt. Wasn't for Mister McCormick letting us work his farm, we'd never made it." She fell silent a long moment, then seemed to pull herself together, looking slowly around the room at the men. But, again, her eyes took on a hardness, like diamonds forged by endless time and immeasurable pressure.

"Back in February or March, we'd heard that the army made a truce with the Injuns. Clement, he heard the army moved 'em all out. Then all the killing started up again. He figured it was just a small band of savages and the army would clean it up. We'd be safe.

"Well, we stayed on the farm. At least we could eat vegetables from our truck patch, if nothing else. We hid in a nearby clearing during the day... slept in a barn loft by night.

"We was digging turnips...I guess it was night before last, in the patch by moonlight. Oh, Lord Almighty," she sobbed into her arm, "I can't believe it even yet. My man...Clement. He fell to his knees before I ever heard the rifle shot. Blood...spread all over his shirt. He yelled for me to run, to save myself. I—I reached for him, but he...I could tell he was dead already...so...so I turned to run, I didn't know where...but I was lifted right off the ground. A horrible, painted savage...shook me just like a rag doll. Laughing...laughing all the time. He threw me to the ground...and grabbed my hair. I felt a knife burn around my head, then...then he ripped my hair from my head." She buried her face in her hands. "I heard it pop when it let go. Dear God, the pain like to of kilt me. I was rolling on the ground when he slammed his knife into my body. I reckon I fainted then."

From somewhere behind Burnham, a cough shattered the stillness like a gunshot.

"I woke up in the darkness alone with my husband's dear, lifeless body," she said, looking up at the men. "He'd been scalped and cut up... you know...down there. I covered him best I could with brush, then got into the woods quick as I could. I felt...weak.

"I was scared the Injuns might've moved up toward Jacksonville, so I headed south...it's...it's wild that way. It was morning when I passed Doctors Lake. I tried to steer clear of any place they might ambush me...just kept going...on...and on." Her eyes fixed vacantly on the table before her.

Doctor Wilson took her hand and held it gently. "Please relax if you can," he said. She looked at him gratefully and a slight smile touched her thin lips for a moment. Then it faded when the pictures reformed themselves in her mind.

"All that horrible day," she finally continued, "I warn't aware of nothin' but the pain...oh, God...Clement was such a sweet boy, but never a growed man lived what was a better man. My mind...as I stumbled through the brush I feared I was going mad...that I might be dying—I was so weak, losing so much blood. I tore off a piece of my dress and wrapped it tight 'round my head. Stuck another wad into the cut in my side, deep as I could shove it.

"About dark I stumbled like a blind woman right into the arms of that white boy who brung me here." She stopped talking and began to sob harshly into the handkerchief.

Burnham sucked heavily, trying to pull air into his tightened lungs. Coughing into his sleeve, he tried to picture Mary in place of that small body across from him.

DeLagnel caught Burnham's eye and nodded toward the door. Burnham tugged at Metcalf's sleeve and the two men left the room.

Outside, Burnham leaned against the porch railing and stared at the field of stars above the treeline to the north. Dear God above, if anything like this happened to Mary—how could he ever ask her to live in this hell on earth? But how could he go back to New York and ask her to live in the poverty destined for them there? Would things ever be different in Florida? They had to be. He had to believe a paradise like this must hold some future for men of vision, men of strength, men with strong women like Jane Johns and Mary Burnham by their sides.

Dusk slowly settled into darkness. Douglas Dummett lay behind a log at the edge of a pond, listening to the Seminoles he had tracked for two days. He had been lying there for over three hours, quietly listening. As the twilight deepened, the evening chorus of cricket chirps intensified. Filtering the lonesome notes of a Will-O-The-Wisp from his consciousness, he focused his attention across the pond to the Seminoles.

The Indians had finished eating and now sat around their campfire. Occasional laughter erupted when one became the butt of another's joke. Their words carried clearly on the damp air.

While listening, Dummett vividly recalled his instant rage when he found the young woman, Jane Johns, and brought her into Fort Heileman, her head swathed in bandages. It took several minutes for her irrational gibbering to settle enough for her to spill her tragic story from her lips. His horror had grown as the woman talked, yet her bravery and fortitude forged within him a deep respect that quickly replaced sympathy. Dummett recognized the ironic fact that his own wife wasn't worth one drop of Jane Johns' blood.

The poor woman will live out her days in agony over the loss of her husband, he thought, but mostly over her affliction. She'll be humiliated forever by the unthinking pity of others. He intended to make these red bastards pay for that humiliation.

Now, from across the still pond, Dummett could hear the Indians settling down for the night, one stepping to the water's edge, bragging about how far he could piss into the darkness. A raccoon snuffled along the ground near Dummett's log, unaware of the man lying there.

At midnight, long after the Indians settled in to sleep, Dummett rose and sat on the log. From sound alone he now had a good idea of the arrangement of the enemy camp, where the sleepers were and where the guard was posted. The Seminoles had chosen their campsite wisely. He couldn't have chosen much better. The swampy pond lay along the southern fringe of their camp, protecting them from attack in that direction.

Even though the Indians had selected an almost perfectly secure site, Dummett intended making them pay for their security with their deaths. The camp would certainly be the scene of their deaths or his.

Laying his weapons along the log, Dummett checked them carefully by the pale light of the overhead full moon. After seeing to the loads, he wrapped the breeches of his rifle and pistol with tanned leather strips, binding them above and below tightly with thongs, tightly enough to shed water, but loosely enough for him to cock the hammers. A six-foot pine sapling, trimmed, with one end sharpened to a point, leaned across the log beside him. He loosened the thong holding his knife in its sheath.

There were four weapons, one for each Seminole.

He strapped the pistol tightly to the barrel of his rifle, then picked up the staff along with two palm fronds. After silently cursing the moonlight, he cautiously eased himself into the water while holding his firearms above the surface. He floated the palms around his head to break up his silhouette. His path was through what should be shoulder-deep water covered with lily pads. He didn't expect discovery.

Dummett spent the last hour before dawn crossing the fifty yards of pond. No matter. After tracking these killers for two days, the hour seemed a small investment. First light would be the ideal time to attack. He would be able to see them clearly enough, yet they would awaken with minds lead-heavy with sleep.

Finally he could feel the mucky bottom of the pond slope upward under his feet. He slithered quietly through marsh grass to dry ground and slowly—very slowly—stood to full height.

He could see that the Indians were situated about the way he had expected. Three of them lay wrapped in blankets around the white-ashed embers of the fire, one no more than ten feet from him. The fourth, the guard, drooped against a tree on the far side of the small clearing.

Dummett cocked the hammers on his firearms. Gambling on the first rays of daylight to blind the sentry momentarily as he opened his eyes, Dummett gripped the spear tightly in his right hand, took two quick steps, screamed, and slammed the sharpened point through the chest of the first sleeper, pinning him to the ground. The Indian gasped desperately for air and reflexively clutched the shaft with both hands, then almost immediately relaxed with a hollow sigh.

Dummett instantly raised the rifle and fired its lead ball into the chest of the guard who had only begun to turn toward him in surprise, a challenge half formed on his already lifeless lips.

The nearest Indian struggled with sleep for an instant, his mouth wide, a guttural animal snarl forming in his throat. Dummett slashed the heavy knife viciously across the strained cords of his throat. Abruptly the snarl became a rattling gurgle. The man collapsed, nearly decapitated.

The remaining Seminole was on his feet, reaching frantically for his rifle. Dummett strode swiftly to his side and, with the pistol still strapped to the rifle barrel, fired its shot into the man's ear.

He stood for a drawn moment, satisfying himself that all were dead, then scalped them, savagely ripping the locks from their heads. He threw the bloody wads of hair onto the coals of the fire, muttering "Go bald into your next life, you bastards."

With the last scalp sizzling on the coals, he rested against a tree. An intense release of tension swept through him. When it calmed, he began to rummage through their totes. In less than two minutes he found what he wanted, threw dirt on the campfire, and stepped to the edge of the clearing. "I bequeath the bodies of these fallen cowards to any buzzards, worms and maggots able to stand the taste," he shouted into the darkness.

The next morning he stepped into DeLagnel's office, reverently laying a blond scalp on the desk.

"Have someone make this into a hairpiece for the lady," he said. " It should fit nicely. It's her own.

Chapter 3

T he months sped by, one after another, as if racing time itself. While the activity at the fort fascinated him in its difference from the Watervliet arsenal, Burnham's interest in his work quickly deteriorated. Long hours of converting old flintlocks into percussion rifles gave him too much time to consider his future in the army. He was also becoming disillusioned with the prospect of remaining in Florida. Scarcely a day passed without units coming in from the interior telling stories of hardship, misery, and death.

The news of Osceola's capture in October excited, and yet enraged, the fort. Hope sprung up that the war would soon end, but the events that followed quickly dashed that hope. Metcalf heard most of the details of the story from a St. Augustine Wagon Master passing through Fort Heileman. Unable to keep it to himself, he ran to Burnham's workbench to pass on the tale. Entering the cage, he tossed a letter to Burnham.

"Wait'll you hear the news. General Jesup's been getting his butt whacked by Van Buren," he said. Burnham stopped his work on a rifle and picked up the letter—from Mary. He considered opening it but quickly decided to wait until Metcalf was gone. While Metcalf talked, Burnham listened, more interested in the letter than in hearing military gossip.

"Van Buren's probably going to get his butt whacked in the next election iffen he don't do somethin' 'bout this war. Van Buren's bound and determined to move every Injun out of Florida to the Oklahoma territory," Metcalf continued. "So, Jesup sent for Osceola to come in under a flag of truce for a confab. And a couple of weeks ago, Osceola did come in. Went to Moultrie Creek under a white flag—took Wildcat with him. General Hernandez and Lieutenant Peyton met with 'em." He paused and grinned. "Our boys surrounded 'em and took 'em easy.

"Hauled 'em into Fort Marion to a cell. But the story goes that Wildcat escaped. Starved hisself a few days, then climbed a wall and skinned through a window a kid couldn't get through. Probably keep the war goin' now for another year or so."

"Whoa! Hold on." Burnham placed the letter aside and finished wiping the barrel of the rifle with a rag soaked in light oil, its pungent aroma filling the small workspace. He leaned the rifle against the bench and replaced his tools into their cases.

"If they captured the chief, how can one Indian keep the war going?" He wiped the oil from his hands with a rag and picked up the letter.

"Well, Osceola ain't no hereditary chief," Metcalf said. "He's just a war chief, and he ain't the only one. He *is* probably the best war general since Napoleon—my opinion for whatever it's worth."

"Yes," Burnham said. "They're very clever in battle. Whoever set up that ambush on Lieutenant Herbert's squad on Black Creek was a sharp leader."

"Right. But Osceola also had the hoodoo on the rest of 'em," Metcalf said. "Since he killed old Charlie Emathla for tryin' to turn in his clan at Tampa Bay, all the rest of the chiefs kind of fell right into line. Been doin' just about everything he tells 'em. It seems when Wildcat escaped, Osceola ordered him to keep the fight going. And the sonuvabitch will do it too. Even when they run smackdab outta lead and powder, they'll probably keep on fightin' with knives and arrows—and then fists. Wildcat's a hell of a lot more rabid than the rest of 'em."

"Where are they now?" Burnham slowly slit open the envelope with his penknife.

"Rumor is that Wildcat's combined his people with old Sam Jones. They've moved farther south for the winter, maybe down near the Kissimmee or the Indian River. Likely getting ready to pour it on in the spring. But we'll be ready for 'em."

Burnham grimaced at the thought that rushed into his mind. He lowered the letter, then stepped from his high, three-legged work stool and walked toward the window. He stopped, looked out the window for a moment, then turned back to Metcalf. "John, I'd like to bring Mary and the baby here permanently. Make a life for them. But I don't see how I can with this danger. Is it ever going to end? How'd it start?"

"Started way back with old Tom Jefferson wantin' to spread the country from the Atlantic to the Mississippi." Metcalf stopped and arched his brows. "But, for Americans only—white people. Maybe from ocean to ocean. Jefferson didn't do nothing 'bout it, but Monroe did. Sic'ed Old Hickory on the Seminoles back in '18. Made things so hot down here the Spaniards was tickled to sell Florida just to get shut of the whole mess. You see, the red man's only in the way of progress."

"But it's their land. I can't see how we could take land rightfully belonging to—"

"Hold on right there," Metcalf interrupted hotly. "The Good Book says the Earth belongs to him what will work it. The Injun don't do that. The land belongs to him what will take it and defend it. The white man's doing that."

"But isn't that what they're doing? Defending their land?"

"It ain't theirs." Metcalf's voice broke as it rose to a near shout. "And the niggers they stole up Georgia way ain't theirs, neither. I ain't sure about namby-pamby Van Buren, but if Andy Jackson was still President, they would be moved west."

Metcalf turned on his heel and walked stiffly from the warehouse. The sudden flare-up so astonished Burnham that he could not call out to his friend. He sighed and turned regretfully back to his letter.

He read for a moment, then jumped to his feet and ran outside. "I'm going to be a father," he yelled.

The lonely guard on the wall glanced indifferently at him and continued his walk.

At supper that evening, Burnham filled his plate and walked over to the table where Metcalf sat alone. Burnham stood in silence for a moment, looking out across the stockade toward the open South gate. Then, gathering his resolve, he spoke. "May I join you?"

"Suit yourself, Yankee."

"John, what the hell's got into you?" Burnham sat his plate on the table and slid onto the bench.

Metcalf looked steadily at him and said, "I guess I thought you'd be different from the others. Or maybe I just hoped you'd be different, and ignored the way it is with ya'll from up north. You really ain't no different."

"Different? How? What did you expect of me? What the hell are you talking about?"

"Nigger lovers. That's what ya'll are. Wanting to set 'em free, without seein' our side of it."

"John, you don't hate them. I've seen you talking to some of the colored soldiers and you're polite to them."

"See? You won't even call 'em niggers. Colored." He snorted. "That's all I've ever heard a Yankee call 'em." He swallowed some food with effort and said, "No, I don't hate 'em. I just keep 'em in their place. They're servants. Down here they've always been servants and they'll always be, irregardless of the way ya'll abolitionists up North treat 'em."

"But I'm not an—"

Metcalf rose, threw his plate in the washtub, and stalked across the stockade. He looked over his shoulder once at Burnham. Then, shaking his head, he wandered over to the open South gate. As Metcalf began to swing the large gate shut, Burnham saw him pause. Then, in a grotesque pirouette, he slowly turned and slumped to the ground. The crack of the rifle shattering the night's stillness seemed almost an afterthought to the bullet's work. Burnham leaped to his feet and ran toward Metcalf.

"Get that gate closed," he yelled. A soldier scampered in behind the gate and began shoving it.

Burnham shouldered into the knot of men already gathered around Metcalf. Dropping to his knees, he leaned down, staring into Metcalf's open, glazed eyes. A large, purplish hole was drilled into the center of his forehead. The back of his head was burst like a splattered melon.

"He's the one always telling us not to lollygag by that gate when it's standing open," a soldier said. Burnham raised his head in sudden anger, but a cold emptiness quickly filled his being. For the first time since coming to this land of sudden and violent death, tears welled in his eyes. He slumped forward and, with quivering fingers, closed Metcalf's eyes and mouth. "Is it really ever going to end, John?" he cried softly, gazing into the face of his dead friend.

The months continued their rapid advance. By the New Year the army began preparing its forces for an all out push to defeat the Seminoles once good weather arrived.

Burnham knew that three forts—Christmas, McNeil, and Taylor—had been hacked from the wilderness for the operation along the St. Johns River, all the way to the newly discovered lakes, Poinsett and Winder. Each new fort became the advance supply depot, moving the power of the operation farther south.

A Major Whiting replaced Captain DeLagnel as quartermaster of Fort Heileman. In addition to repairing rifles that should have been scrapped, Burnham soon found himself packing tools—axes, hatchets, nails, spikes, saws, rope—all the equipment necessary to build forts and bridges. He heard an estimate that more than twenty bridges were built between Fort Mellon and Fort Christmas. Some said the expense of the war had already reached more than the territory cost.

February came, and Burnham felt like a burned out log from his boring routine. Mainly, he was sick of the noise of the place, that background clamor that begins at sunup and continues long after dark. Rattling was the most prevalent racket of an army. Guns and holsters, sabers and scabbards, the buckles of rifle slings, the traces and singletrees of mule-hitched wagons, canteens—even the flagpole halyard. A myriad of rattles accompanied the zing of countless whetstones slicked across the edges of knives and sabers, as if the perfect cutting edge carried a reward other than pride. Enough cutlery was honed to shave the entire camp daily, yet not more than a dozen faces were beardless, and those were more from the default of youth than from the effort of shaving.

Since Metcalf's death, Burnham often found himself thinking strange and uncontrollable thoughts, mostly about the tenuous hold humans had on life. But other notions crowded in, mainly, he suspected, as relief from boredom. Why else should he wonder if one human sense could detect another? Can the ear see color? Dummett had told him he could certainly smell fear. And now Burnham found himself tasting sounds, smelling heat, and seeing odors emanating from the garbage pits and latrines along the creek. Using all the will power he could muster, he forced himself to think of more pleasant prospects.

Three months remained on his enlistment. As yet he hadn't figured a way to move Mary and the baby to Florida. Even if he did get them here, he had no idea how to support the three of them—the four of them. Mary's latest letter said she was now in her seventh month; the child would be born before his enlistment ran out. Maybe he could find some-one's farm to work, like Clement and Jane Johns worked old man McCor-mick's place.

Then, one afternoon, Douglas Dummett returned from one of his excursions, stopping by the warehouse to pick up a new sling for his rifle.

"I'm taking a little trip to recover my papa's treasure cache," he told Burnham. "If you want to tag along, I can clear it with that new Major. I'd sure like the company and it should be fairly safe. I think maybe you could use the break, too; see a little of the country, kinda get to learn how the grunts live away from civilization."

They set out the next morning at sunup on the steamer *Camden*, going down Black Creek to the St. Johns, turning south to head upriver. By late afternoon, they had reached Fort Picolata. After lying over there for the night, the steamer left at dawn, headed south toward Fort Mellon on Lake Monroe. In early afternoon, Burnham and Dummett stood in the bow as they came to a lake so large Burnham couldn't see the other end. The steamer moved out onto the broad expanse glittering in the sunlight and was immediately buffeted by large waves rolling in from the south.

Dummett raised his arm and swept it toward the west. "This is Lake George, 'bout sixteen miles long and eight miles wide—damn near an inland sea. I've seen these combers be larger than swells out on the Atlantic. This old steamer's an ocean-going vessel, fairly deep draft, so she'll ride fine in these seas." He pointed toward the bank to their left. "We'll follow the Eastern Shore till we hit an old Indian trail I know that goes toward the Tomoka River. The Captain knows where to drop us off."

Burnham's eyes stung from the sun glinting off the water, and the skin of his face began to draw tight against his cheekbones. The noonday sun cast no shadows on the *Camden*, and the heat turned the cabins into sauna, so they stayed outside in the bow. By mid-afternoon he was severely sunburned. He was acutely aware of the irony of being sunburned in the dead of winter.

"How much longer do we have to bake in this oven?"

"We're almost there. I used to get provisions from Fort Volusia at the head of the lake and cross over by horseback from there to the Tomoka. But Volusia's abandoned now and this old trail's better for walking." Dummett grunted and pointed toward a large cypress jutting out from a point of land. "This old tree marks the trail."

The lake shoaled rapidly about a quarter-mile from the bank, so the two men were taken ashore in a small dinghy.

When they entered the thick woods, a new world opened up for Burnham. He felt a relief flow into his body, a relaxation he hadn't enjoyed in months. He looked upward at pines growing through the roof of the forest, their tops stretching for sunlight above the intertwined branches of sweet gum, maple, and magnolia. Ancient, gnarled live oaks spread limbs thicker than a man's body more than two hundred feet. Beards of wispy Spanish moss hung in lacy tatters from the limbs, while green Resurrection fern matted their tops.

Damp leaves and moldering humus carpeted the floor of the forest cluttered with an undergrowth of ferns, grapevines, and huckleberries. Although the trees were barren of foliage at this time of the year, the thick interlacing of wood darkened the forest. Decaying vegetation permeated the air with an almost spicy aroma, accented with the fragrant seepage of resin from several lightning-splintered pines.

Skinks and lizards, big yellow banana-spiders and little green treefrogs—living creatures both seen and unseen—scurried noisily through their dense domains. Squirrels quarreled with the two men, barking angrily from their lofty perches at the invaders of their territory.

By nightfall Burnham felt his legs had been borrowed from someone who wore them out before lending them. Every muscle ached sharply at first, then settled into a dull pain that began in the middle of his back and rolled down to feet that didn't want to obey his command to walk.

And the welts of mosquito and tick bites covered his body.

They camped in an open glen beside a small springfed pool. After Burnham gathered dry wood, Dummett arranged several sticks in a star-shaped pattern. He looked up at Burnham, smiled and said, "Not too long ago, I killed some Indians whose camp butted up against a pond. But theirs was shallow; this one's deep." He shaved thin strips of fat pine into the center of the star. "Besides, we ain't going to be stupid enough to sleep here. This fire's just for eating and loafing."

Dummett wadded a handful of dry, black moss into a tight ball and laid it beside the pile. Opening a small tin box, he removed one of several squares of charred cloth, a large chunk of flint and a strip of steel. Burnham moved closer and into better position to watch as Dummett held the flint flat on the cloth with his thumb. With the steel in his other hand, he struck sharply across the edge of the flint, sending a shower of sparks onto the cloth. After blowing gently on the glowing sparks for a moment, he wrapped the moss around the cloth and began waving it smoothly back and forth. In only a few seconds it began to smoke, then suddenly burst into flame. He quickly dropped the burning wad of moss into the center of the logs and fed the strips of fat pine into the small flames. In moments the fire blazed.

"Strip off the clothes," Dummett said. "All of them, including the small-clothes. Buck naked." He shoved the point of his knife into the fire. The tip quickly darkened. Then, slowly, a white-orange glow began to spread down the blade. He pulled it from the wavering flames. Carefully studying Burnham's body, spreading crevices and parting hair, he touched the fiery knife-tip to a tick, chuckling as Burnham flinched.

Through clenched teeth, Burnham gasped, "How come I have them and you don't?"

"Oh, maybe you're just too clean or something," Dummett answered cheerfully while sizzling another tick. "Or maybe it's what I eat: garlic and onions. And the water I drink. I don't know, but you live here long enough and they'll avoid you like the plague. Mosquitoes too."

After double-checking that he had gotten them all, he walked to the pond and thrust the knife blade into the water. "Don't want to lose the temper from the steel," he said as the water bubbled and steamed.

He brought back a handful of black, sticky mud reeking of sulfur. Slathering it on the welts, he laughed as Burnham crinkled his nose. "This'll keep them off tomorrow. Best you get dressed now."

By shoving the logs into the center of the star as they burned, Dummett forced the flames to roar heartily. Soon a hot bed of coals glowed through the ash at the juncture of the small logs. Then he pulled each stick back, allowing the flames to die. Next he thrust four green, forked sticks into the ground as the basis for a rack made of interwoven green sticks. From his tote, he pulled two thick slabs of beef and placed them carefully on the rack to roast slowly over the now whitened, dusty-looking coals.

That done, they leaned back on their blankets, smoking their pipes and smelling the aroma of juices dripping and flaring in the coals.

"We'll enjoy the beef tonight, but we're stuck with white bacon from now on," Dummett said. "You'll like it though. Everything tastes good out here."

Dummett pointed around him. "Well, tell me. What do you think of my country? You realize some of those oaks you saw today have lived more'n four or five hundred years? I bet you'll see some tomorrow that go over a thousand, maybe even two thousand. They must've been here when Christ walked this old earth."

Burnham sighed. "This is truly God's chosen land. No doubt about it. How'd you get to these parts?"

"My papa was a planter in Barbados. The slaves rebelled in 1818, but he escaped and brought us to Connecticut. We couldn't stand the skin-splitting cold up there, so we moved down here when I was seventeen, about the end of the first Indian War. Papa built a sugar mill on the Carrickfergus plantation where we'll hit the Tomoka River in a couple of days. Later, Papa bought Mount Pleasant, 'cross from the village of New Smyrna on the Hillsboro."

"Sugar mill. That sounds like a good kind of life," Burnham sighed. "And working the land. I'd like to bring Mary down, but I'm afraid to with all this Indian trouble. Before this fighting started, did you get along with the Seminoles?"

"Hell, yes! Famously. They were part of our lives, coming and going like family. But that didn't matter. When a few greedy whites stole their land and their niggers, they turned on everyone."

"Friends too?"

"Especially friends, if they figured they were being betrayed. A neighbor of ours, a youngster named John Bulow, was especially friendly with Wildcat, old King Philip's son." He paused and laughed as he stood to turn the meat.

"One day, us Mosquito Roarers went up Bulow's lane to set up our headquarters on his place. Damned if Bulow don't lay down on us with a cannon like he's Don Quixote. Said we weren't about to make Wildcat think he was tied in with the militia. I had to put a rifle to his head to keep him from blasting away at us."

Dummett rummaged in his tote, pulled out two cups and filled them from a small flask of rum. "Old Major Putnam got his revenge on Bulow by making him a Roaring Mosquito—impressed him into the militia right on the spot—then threatened to execute him if he disobeyed orders. When we left, we took Bulow with us. Sure enough, our footsteps weren't even cold when old King Philip and Wildcat came in and torched the place."

"So this Bulow fella was right after all. You called him a youngster. How old are you?"

"Thirty," replied Dummett, getting slowly to his feet. He went to the fire, speared the meat with his knife onto tin plates, handing one to Burnham. "I'm an old man compared to you," he laughed, laying strands of Spanish moss over the rack. "These'll smoke up good and chase the redbugs out, then we'll hang them from your clothes tomorrow. The ticks might think they're spider webs and keep away from you."

They hunkered down and began to eat. Between bites, Dummett continued to talk. "Old King Philip and his clan—Miccosukees, Uchees, and over a hundred of their nigger slaves—hit New Smyrna on Christmas day, two years ago. The Sheldon and Hunter families abandoned their homes and crossed the river to Mount Pleasant. The Indians set fire to Judge Dunham's place, a really nice home, and they were doing their dance around it when a keg of black powder in the cellar went off—blew a bunch of them to hell." He grinned for a moment, savoring the thought.

"A couple of days later, Papa took the girls and the neighbors to St. Augustine. Just in time, too. The Indians crossed the river and wrecked Mount Pleasant. I stopped by there not long after. They'd cut up the beds and scattered feathers and horsehair everywhere. Busted up all the furniture. Hell, they even used Papa's family paintings for target practice—shot arrows through my granddaddy's eyes."

"Through his eyes?"

"Seems strange to us, but the Indian believes a portrait has captured the man, and the soul lives behind the eyes. If he kills the eyes, he kills the soul."

"You said girls—your papa took the girls to St. Augustine. Your sisters?"

"Yeah, more or less. You see, I have four sisters. Three of them are married and don't live at home anymore."

"But you said girls."

"Well, my mother was never in good health after my sister Anna was born, so we were raised mostly by Maum Molly, one of the servants.

Anna's the youngest, a lot younger than the other girls—Mama was getting a little old when Anna was born. Probably that's why she got sickly. Anyway, Papa bought a little girl from a Minorcan in St. Augustine, sort of to have someone for Anna to play with, to grow up with. It was a damn lonely place we lived in at that time."

"Bought a—how can you buy a little girl?"

"Oh, hell. I keep forgetting you're a Yankee. Leandra—that's the girl's name, Leandra Fernandez—she's part nigger, a slave."

"I see. He just bought some woman's child and split them up." Burnham winced as he said that, vividly remembering John Metcalf's reaction when their conversation drifted into racism.

Dummett laughed. "You don't believe everything you heard up north about southerners and their servants, do you? My papa—hell, most men I know—would sell one of his own children before he'd split up a family."

"Then why—"

"The Minorcan, Fernandez, was her papa. He only had the one nigger servant. Got her pregnant. She died giving birth to Leandra. It made quite a scandal in town over him taking a nigger to wife, so to speak. And he didn't have any other women to raise the baby, so he sold her to Papa."

"So Leandra's not really colored," Burnham said. "She's half white."

"Down here, even one drop of nigger blood makes her a nigger."

"Yes, that's what Metcalf told me. But, to me, blood is blood and it's all red."

"Yeah, you're a Yankee all right. And I hope you stay that way. But it doesn't change Leandra. Course, she and Anna were raised almost like sisters—has her own room, eats with the family—even went off to school in Savannah with Anna. She's been told she's Anna's handmaid, but we don't treat her like a slave. They're the same as sisters."

Dummett stood and scooped some ashes into his empty plate and began to scrub it. "Time to leave this place," he said.

After they cleaned and packed their gear, Dummett kicked dirt onto the fire, then scattered leaves over the spot. He shouldered his tote and led Burnham into the woods. After a mile or so, they came to a large oak he spotted when they passed earlier. Its roots resembled gigantic knees rising from the ground. "Pick a spot between two of these here natural shields and scoop out the leaves—don't want to get more ticks do you? We're safe sleeping here," he said.

Later, while a drowsy numbness softly enveloped his mind, Burnham said, "Good night, Old Man," only to hear Dummett snort, "Humph!"

Two more days of steady trudging put them near the Tomoka River. Where possible Dummett chose to avoid the old King's Road that ran from St. Augustine to New Smyrna. It was a safety precaution. "Ain't much harder doing it this way, 'cause you can see the old road is mostly grown over now," he said on one of the few times they crossed it.

The terrain became mostly a forest of pines and hardwoods, that protected them somewhat from a cold drizzle of rain that had begun during the previous night. Dummett stopped and slowly pointed his index finger in a large circle, sweeping his gaze across the trees ahead of them. "I've hunted coon, possum, and deer in these woods for years. To me, it's like some folk's house yard."

"That might be so," Burnham said, "but whose yard is like this?"

"Mine." Dummett paused, then pointed again. "In fact, this once was my house yard. Look there."

Burnham stared in the indicated direction. Through a wall of vines he could make out a clearing. As they approached it, he couldn't believe his eyes. A large house stood, flanked by a barn and five small cabins lined up along a footpath. As they walked toward it, he could see that the house was abandoned and had been vandalized. The roof caved in at one corner and the doors and shutters drooped from broken hinges.

It occurred to him that Dummett might have them stop in the house to shelter from the rain. Burnham shook his head in resignation when Dummett forged on past the buildings. About three hundred yards on the eastern side, a wagon trail ran past the place. Beyond this trail stood a two-story stone building that looked liked Burnham's idea of what an old Spanish mission should look like.

Dummett chuckled and pointed to a cistern near the large building. "My sister got drunk sneaking some rum when she was a tad and fell into that hole—damn near drowned."

Burnham walked around the cistern and stood with hands on hips, staring up at the huge building. He breathed heavily, trying to stall against walking back into the brush. "What was this for?" he asked.

"Sugar mill," Dummett replied. He walked over to the side of the building and kicked one of several large, rusting iron vats lying there. "This was our plantation. I built this mill myself. Course the niggers cut the coquina rock into fitted blocks and did the heavy lifting, but I did the heavy thinking and planning." He laughed and crossed the clearing, striding into the thick, surrounding underbrush.

Burnham took one more deep breath, lowered his head and followed.

As they approached the Tomoka bottomlands, they came to a low-lying swamp of maidencane. It blocked the way to the river that could be seen in the distance, dark gray under the heavily overcast sky. Burnham could see no way through, but Dummett seemed to possess an uncanny sense for finding a path. They continued to struggle for more than a mile through huckleberry bushes and thick palmetto stands, stumbling across rotted logs, then through fields of sawgrass that ripped at them like double-edged knives.

Without warning, Burnham broke out onto the western bank of the river and stumbled knee-deep into the cold water.

The sharp edge of a cold easterly wind sliced across the slate-gray surface of the river, cutting through Burnham's light jacket and nipping his body. He shivered involuntarily, the chill locating itself in the bones of his upper arm, then spreading rapidly across his chest.

But he wasn't allowed to rest. Dummett immediately stepped down into the water with him, and they waded slowly along the mucky bank for several hundred more yards until they reached a hickory tree with skeletal limbs overhanging the water. Burnham could look through its spidery, leafless canopy at angry, gray clouds scudding toward the west. The light drizzle misted through the tree into his upturned face.

Dummett cocked a brow at him, then began to laugh as he stepped back onto the bank. "Hell, you look sadder'n one of my scrawny coonhounds. This rain is good. A Miccosukee don't like the February cold or rain any more'n you do—if there was a Miccosukee around to not like it, which there ain't."

Burnham joined him on the bank, moving over against the bole of the large tree for whatever shelter it provided. "I'm not complaining," he mumbled. "I just—" He stopped when Dummett started pulling rusty-brown palmetto fronds from a pile heaped in the brush about twenty feet south of the hickory. He wasn't sure what was happening, until he saw the dark hull of a boat emerge from the cover. He pushed himself away from the tree and went to help. A few moments later they'd uncovered a twelve-foot dugout canoe. In its bottom, beside a centerboard case, lay a short mast and rigging wrapped in a canvas sail, along with two small paddles.

"This'll take the weight off those tired feet of yours for awhile." Dummett grabbed the upthrust stem of the canoe and began to snake it through the underbrush toward the river. Burnham got behind the boat and pushed.

Letting its momentum carry it into the water, Dummett swung it around as it floated above the sandy shallows.

"A year it has been here, and it's dry as the day I left it. In case you didn't know, the palmetto is nature's best roof." Dummett stepped the mast and began rigging the small triangular sail. "We got maybe twenty miles to Mosquito Inlet, but we've a fair wind. Won't take long to get to the plantation from there. Should be at Mount Pleasant by dark." He grinned. "A nice afternoon's sail."

Burnham smiled ruefully at the bleak promise.

Dummett motioned Burnham into the canoe, then pushed them away from the bank. Using one of the paddles as a rudder, Dummett steered the little vessel toward the middle of the river.

"Deeper water out in the middle," he explained, "and there's less chance of getting picked off from the woods over there."

"Picked off by who? I remember you saying there weren't any Indians around here."

"Well, that's the truth," Dummett answered slowly. "We saw no sign, but that don't mean every Indian around is required to walk across our path. Never pays to let the vision of truth get in the way of reality."

Dummett lifted the paddle to point at a large slough cutting through the riverbank far to their left. "That's Smith Creek. Looks like the only stream outta here toward St. Augustine, don't it? It ain't. Been lots of travelers took it by mistake only to have to backtrack to the haulover. Did it myself once when I first lived here. The haulover is the only way outta this basin to the north. Now, you just get comfortable. We gonna be on this water a while."

Burnham scrunched below the gunwale, settling in against the grainy cypress for the trip. Soon they crossed the Tomoka Basin into the Halifax, sailing through a maze of mangrove islands. Thousands of ducks, pelicans, and seagulls rafted on the placid waters between the islands. The mangrove limbs bent under the weight of white egrets and ibis, making him think of patches of snow. He wrinkled his nose against the rich, musky aroma of guano. It was all so peaceful, so much like a dreamscape. He closed his eyes. Around him the gentle slap of the water against the hull was a soft rhythm playing on his senses—soothing, lulling. He didn't know when he drifted into sleep.

He awoke to the pitching of the canoe. Looking around, he saw the water agitated by a flow of the Atlantic through a wide cut in the barrier island far to his left. "Mosquito Inlet," Dummett pointed out. "We have a couple more miles." The drizzling rain stopped, yet thick clouds low on the western horizon shrouded the sun. "We'll go right on past the plantation to fool any Miccosukees that might be watching from the mainland. Then, when it gets dark, we'll double back."

Less than an hour later, Dummett lowered the sail. At this point the river was about a mile wide, and Burnham had the sensation they'd entered a mystical lake. Against the purplish haze of the setting sun, he saw the dark silhouette of a fort on the eastern bank. Six tall, Doric columns overshadowed its stockade.

"What's that? An architecturally designed fort?" Burnham asked.

"That's Fort New Smyrna. Those columns you see are all that's left of Judge Dunham's mansion, the one that blew up," Dummett replied. "They built the fort about a year ago, but it ain't in use right now. I think we're safest to wait out here in the river until the moon rises. It'll be best to do our work at night."

By midnight the sky cleared considerably, with only high clouds drifting darkly across the face of the full moon. They sculled quietly across to within thirty yards of the eastern bank and followed its dim outlines north for a mile. At a handsignal from Dummett, they turned sharply toward the bank and grounded on a sandbar. Stepping out into ankle-deep water, they pulled up the centerboard and dragged the canoe across the shallows, nestling it among black pilings thrusting upward from the dark water, looking in the darkness like bony fingers reaching for them.

"Well, the house is gone," Dummett whispered. "Burnt to the ground."

Burnham stared intently into the wooded shadows above the bank but couldn't see a thing, house or no house.

With Burnham feeling like a blind man and clutching Dummett's shirttail, they climbed the steep bank, making their way across a narrow, weed-clogged field to a high mound. Six rock steps cut into the slope led to the charred remains of the mansion, seeming to invite entrance into the gutted heart of the ruins.

"We got to work fast," Dummett said, feeling his way in the pale moonlight around the foundation to the rear of the house. Burnham followed, his eyes slowly adjusting to the darkness. He wondered how they would dig with no tools, then saw Dummett begin tossing aside the piled remains of the brick chimney. Dummett was soon digging frantically through the mound of rock and rubble on the ground, tearing at the stones and sticks. In only a few minutes he unearthed a ring of twisted cable. "Give me a hand."

Burnham moved quickly to his side and they both grabbed the cable and pulled upward. At first nothing moved, then a six-foot section of iron plating burst free and Burnham could see down into a vault that appeared at least four feet deep. It was lined with coquina blocks.

"Uh huh," Dummett exclaimed in hushed tones. Leaping into the vault, he began struggling to lift a chest.

"Would you look at this," he grunted. "Papa must have put more in here than he told me." Burnham grabbed the chest and together they wrestled it from the hole. When it was out, they lay back against the rubble heap, sucking air into their heaving lungs, all the while staring at the three-foot long wooden chest.

Finally, Dummett leaned forward and opened it. Carefully, he pulled out the first piece. He handed it to Burnham. It was the serving bowl of a punch set. The piece seemed to glow through a patina of oxide in the moonlight. It was about five inches high and much heavier than it looked. Burnham could make out the detail in the etching. It was incredible. Each line, each curve, each curlicue was precisely tooled in the purest form of silver. "It's beautiful," he whispered.

"But this is what's so heavy." Dummett handed him a leather bag, its weight belying its small size. Dummett took it back. "It's full of Spanish doubloons. There must be twenty of these bags in here."

Burnham gave a silent whistle.

"Now come on. We got to high tail it. Help me close this thing back up."

After securing the lid of the chest, they struggled to haul it to the canoe.

By dawn, they had paddled at least five miles up the Halifax River. Coming to a small island, by mutual consent they pulled over to its lee side to rest and eat a breakfast of cold, jerked beef. But, like a magnet, the chest drew them and once more they opened it. Burnham looked at the rest of the silver—trays of cutlery, forks and spoons, goblets, a teapot—all as richly tooled as the punch bowl.

He picked up one of the bags, hefted it in a hand, and asked, "How much is one of these worth?"

"Each coin's worth about fifteen dollars federal money, and there's thirty-five in each bag." He opened one and poured a bright, golden stream onto the sand, the coins ringing like bells as they struck each other. "You figure it out."

Burnham picked one up, shaking his head. "I haven't seen a piece of hard money since I was a kid. And I don't suppose I'll ever see this much money in one spot again in my life."

"Sure you will," Dummett said, beginning to repack the chest. "The land'll take care of you, boy. It can make you wealthy."

Later, under a sky unseasonably bright for February, a warm land breeze picked up from the east prompting Dummett to set the sail. By mid-morning, many miles of water had slid past. So far, the river was a network of narrow passages between small islands, but it now opened suddenly, with only one large island lying ahead of them. "We're at Dunn-Lawton Plantation," Dummett said, angling the canoe toward the main-land bank. "We can get fresh water here from the well. After that, we might shuck ourselves some oysters."

As the small canoe glided over the first of the shallows, finger-like geysers of water erupted beside them, followed immediately by the crash of musket fire.

Chapter 4

At the instant the first volley exploded into their senses, Dummett yelled, "Run!" and vaulted over the side. Burnham stood, hesitating. It was an instant too long.

A ball slammed into his left shoulder, followed instantly by one tearing through his thigh. Crying out with pain and surprise, he collapsed back into the canoe, a moan of sudden, terrible fear escaping his lips. He felt the canoe vane into the wind. Its mainsheet was still tied to the gunwale and he realized the sail was driving the boat back toward the deep water of mid-river. Desperately, he grabbed Dummett's discarded paddle and shoved it into the water, stabilizing the craft while taking a hurried look over his shoulder.

Three Indians were splashing through the shallows, chasing Dummett. The Indians raised their rifles and fired as Dummett knifed forward into the water and vanished below its dark surface. And while Burnham watched, a chilling sight burst from the woods: a devil on horseback, his naked body streaked with vermilion, his intense black eyes fixed on Burnham.

The horse leaped several rocks on the bank, landing in the shallows, sending a cascade of water sheeting toward the frail craft. The Indian recovered his balance, raised and fired his long rifle. The bullet plopped a small hole in the canvas above Burnham's head.

The canoe was now skimming much quicker, reaching across a beam wind. But Burnham could clearly see breath steaming from nostrils that flared above the horse's driving forelegs—driving toward him. He could see the flying black hair of its savage rider. They were gaining on him.

In one instant the gap between horse and canoe narrowed, and in the next the horse crumpled forward in a neck-wrenching spill. The Indian flew crazily forward, his arms windmilling madly, to sprawl headlong into the river.

The Miccosukee regained his feet and hurriedly reloaded his rifle. Burnham ducked as the rifle spit a second ball into the sail, this time much higher than the first. Two more holes were punched into the canvas before the Indian turned to help his struggling horse to its feet.

Burnham glanced back, looking for Dummett, but all he saw were the three Indians swimming to one of the mangrove islands back down the river.

His mind raced from one vivid picture to the next. Had Dummett died in the fusillade of bullets fired at his back? Had he drowned? Or worse! Maybe he'd been caught and scalped by the pursuing savages? Burnham didn't know what to do. He felt the icy fingers of panic clutching at his mind just as they had after the Black Creek battle on the steamboat. What in God's name should he do? It was impossible to rescue Dummett. It was too late for that. And with his wounds, he'd be no match against the savages. His wounds! Damn, he'd forgotten them. Tossing the paddle aside, he began to check them.

He lay back in the canoe, biting his lip and forcing himself to relax. Forcing his thumbs into the hole in his pants leg, he ripped the cloth downward. Two puckered, blackened holes seeped thin rivulets of blood down his thigh, one in front and one down around the side. They looked worse than they were. The bullet had passed only through the living flesh, missing the bone. His shoulder was another matter. The ball had entered the muscle just out from the collarbone. There was no exit wound; it was still in there. Instinctively, he flexed the shoulder. No bones grated.

He looked back. The Indians had vanished, leaving the river as tranquil as it had been an hour ago. But Dummett was gone. There was nothing he could do about that. Two friends gone—violently—in only a matter of months. He accepted the situation without feelings of cowardice in not returning—nor grief. Grieving could come later. What was important now was survival. His survival. There was nothing he could do but continue sailing north, so with a final check of the sail and mast he lay back to rest.

Two hours later, he crossed the Tomoka basin and came to the end of the river.

Dummett's chest heaved against empty lungs sending shock waves of flame through him. His legs scissored powerfully, driving his body toward the silvery surface above.

He rolled to his back as his face broke free of the river's surface and he sucked great draughts of air through his gasping mouth. A quick glance told him the three Seminoles were fooled by his change of course toward that maze of islands. One more deep breath and he pulled himself underwater again, swimming across the sandy bottom, pulled along by the tide flow felt even here from the distant Mosquito Inlet. Near a small mangrove island, the bottom shoaled quickly, then deepened in the turbulence on its lee side.

He surfaced carefully, his head hidden deeply within the shadows of the twisted mangrove roots at the tip of the island. Small coon-oyster shells gouged bloody grooves in his fingers where he tightly gripped the roots. He listened intently. In a few moments he heard the Indians on the other side of the island. Even though his whole body was trembling with exhaustion, he began to swim quietly away. His arms seemed to gain strength and soon their powerful strokes were pulling the river swiftly past him. Rounding another island, he once more changed course, stroking across the wide lagoon toward the Eastern Shore.

Minutes seemed like hours while he swam. At last, however, he reached a high bank and pulled himself into the cover of dense, shadowy foliage. After checking to see if he was visible to the Indians, he lay still, quietly pulling in deep breaths to fill his protesting lungs and to permit the tiny quivers in his muscles to subside.

He listened intently for sounds of pursuit. The only thing he heard was the wind whistling through the tops of the trees and the water slapping against the bank.

Finally satisfied he had lost the Indians, he rose and ran smoothly across the narrow strip of sandy soil to the ocean beach beyond.

The tangled foliage abruptly gave way to the smooth undulating gracefulness of sand dunes. With a last look back at the dark trees, he began running north through stands of sea oats, avoiding soft patches where possible. After a mile or so, he found a palm frond. He picked it up and dragged it behind him as he moved down to the hard-packed sand at the edge of the surf. A hundred yards or so farther on, he halted to look back. He was satisfied with what he saw. The sunlit surge of frothing sea breaking over the flat beach was washing away his tracks.

For a minute longer he studied the area behind him. The only movement was the sea and a few soaring gulls. He nodded his head, then turned to begin a slow but steady trot, breathing easily to conserve his energy.

As he ran, he considered Burnham's fate. If Burnham had swum toward the small island, he'd have seen him by now, and if he swam toward the north, the open expanse of the river, there was no place for him to hide. That meant the Indians would have caught him by now. They must have caught him. He stopped and looked back at where he'd been, then shook his head. Damn, there was no other possibility.

Losing the chest of silver was bad, but losing Burnham was a catastrophe. He'd been a good man. Damn it! Damn it...The value of the silver could be recovered, but a good man's life was lost forever.

He accepted the loss of his rifle as only a minor irritation, telling himself that at least he didn't have to carry its weight while running. With some luck and a lot of caution, he should be able to avoid any Indian confrontations and wouldn't need it. If he got to St. Augustine in one piece, he could get new weapons, then possibly track the Indians, and maybe even recover the treasure.

He continued his steady pace along the beach.

Burnham sat in the still canoe, facing a solid wall of mangroves spreading from mainland to barrier island. Damn! This just couldn't be. He'd been so sure the river ran all the way to St. Augustine. Dummett had all but said that. But now, from what he could see, it apparently didn't. Then he remembered.

There was a haulover somewhere. Dummett had told him about the many places along the lagoons where the waterways didn't connect. Long ago, the Indians found the narrowest strips of land, over which they cleared paths to haul their canoes and boats from one body of water to the other. In some cases they found natural ditches that filled with water at high tides, capable of floating shallow-draft vessels. At other places they relied on brute strength, often using rollers made from logs to drag their boats across the dry land. Maybe he could do the same—if he could only find the right place.

He turned the little craft, slowly following the shoreline, staring intently into the heavy growth of mangrove, trying to force the appearance of a haulover site by the power of wishful imagination alone. But none appeared.

He reached the western shore, seeing only the mouth of Smith Creek and remembering Dummett's warning that it was a trap. Depressed, he sat a long time gathering his thoughts and swatting at the whining mosquitoes darting around his face. It didn't seem fair that he should survive the fusillade of lead in the attack, and escape that savage on horseback, only to sit here in agony until the searching Indians found and killed him.

But where did he get the idea that life was fair? Life was for the taking—and keeping. He owed his life to Mary and the children. It was theirs, in trust for the responsibility he bore as their husband and father. He slowly willed his optimism to return. Lifting his eyes toward the river and grinding his teeth in determination, he turned the canoe and sailed back out to the center of the basin.

Then he saw it. No more than fifty yards from where he began his search, a slight break appeared in the foliage, the indentation wavering in and out of focus. Now he could understand why he'd missed it at first; the mangroves were so undefined they blended as one. Pulling abreast of the opening, he saw a narrow slough curving sharply to the east, behind the wall of mangroves. He paddled the canoe into the slight mouth of the creek, noticing a worn trail running along the bank. It was the only sign he might be on the right track. The sail, drooping in the still air, blocked his forward view so he lowered it, unstepped the small mast, and pulled out the centerboard.

The waterway narrowed until he could touch either bank with his paddle. He continued to thrust the paddle into the murky water. Then, with a jolting thump, he ran aground. He blew a breath of exasperation through pursed lips and stepped resolutely into the water.

The sun was now a white hot brilliance pouring down to heat the dead air trapped by the slough. Realizing he had taken no food or water since early that morning, he filled his cupped hand and lifted it to his mouth. He spat the first brackish mouthful, but chided himself for his weakness and again drank. Once past the first swallow he realized the water was only a little salty and was able to hold it down.

He grabbed the prow of the vessel and strained to slide it over the grassy bottom. It lifted appreciably when freed of his weight, but still scraped across the high humps of shell-covered sand. He began to question his stamina. Would he have the strength and endurance necessary for the pull at the haulover?

He fell back into the canoe and took up his paddle. Maybe this slough was the haulover. If it was, he would soon be in a proper lagoon and be able to sail. Even as this thought raced through his mind, he saw the slough narrow sharply—and end.

He drifted toward the curtain of mangroves, his mind going numb. All this time and effort, his energy so desperately needed for survival, wasted on a dead end.

Then he saw the trail on the bank continue through a break in the foliage. "This is it," he shouted involuntarily. "The haulover!"

The bank was eroded from the many hulls dragged over it, but a short growth of weeds blanketed it, indication that it hadn't been used much recently.

A few minutes later he stepped ashore, tied the boat's painter to a tree, then followed the trail inland to convince himself this actually was the haulover. After several hundred yards he knew it was and, resigning himself to the task ahead, he returned to the boat.

He sat on the spidery roots of an old cabbage palm and rested. The bullet wounds were bleeding from the strain of paddling. Removing the bandages, he cleaned the purplish holes with brackish creek water, wincing at the sharp stab of pain from the salt. He gritted his teeth and tightly retied the bandages.

He considered leaving the canoe, then quickly dismissed the idea, knowing he would need the boat when he reached the river on the other side. Yet, the idea of pulling it across dry land filled him with dread. And then there was the chest. Should he bury it or try to take it with him? Damn it all! The fortune inside that chest was the reason for this trip, the reason for his wounds. He'd abandon it only when convinced he couldn't continue. He owed that much to Dummett, but not at the cost of his life.

Grabbing the bow of the canoe with both hands, he struggled to lift it until a groan burst from deep within his throat. He rested a moment then again strained upward, but stopped again when a blood-smeared flash of light blurred his eyes. The vessel was only partly onto the bank. Exhaustion forced him to quit and seek a better solution. A short search in the underbrush resulted in finding three small logs that could be used as rollers. He wrestled the chest over the gunwale, allowing it to thump to the damp earth, lightening the canoe. He then strained against its bow once more until it rose enough for him to nudge a log beneath it with his foot.

In a surprisingly short time the canoe rolled ashore. His spirits soared. To celebrate, he gave himself a well-earned rest, then pushed to his feet and struggled to replace the chest safely into the canoe. Blowing on his hands, he began his journey.

Inky shadows blurred the details of Burnham's path as the sun settled into dusk. Overhanging mangrove and myrtle limbs slowly turned from gray to black as they traced their swishing arcs across his neck and ears.

He estimated he had dragged the load at least three miles—aching muscles and over-labored lungs made it feel more like ten. Rivulets of sweat burned his eyes, then dripped from his nose, chin and arms. The air was dead, weighted with the oppressive heat. Head-high canes, stunted scrub-oak, tall reedy grasses—all wove a barrier to block whatever breezes might be trying to get to him.

Then the trail degenerated into black, sticky muck. The pulling was easier in these low slicks, but the stink released by the dragging canoe cloyed at his breath. Like tiny unseen demons, whirling clouds of gnats and salt-marsh mosquitoes rose from puddles of stagnant water to swirl around his head. Some crawled into his nostrils while others hit the cuts on his neck and arms like little shafts of lightning. Burnham was certain he had swallowed hundreds of them.

Darkness finally came. Shortly after, the full moon lifted over the horizon. Suddenly the slashing of the limbs ceased as he broke into a clearing. A blessed, soft wind bathed his face and carried away the gnats and mosquitoes.

He released his grip on the canoe and slowly raised himself to his full height for the first time in hours. He stretched his arms above his head, wincing at the stab of agony in his shoulder. Sitting gingerly on the gunwale of the canoe, he rested and considered his situation.

His wounds hadn't bled for some time so he wasn't worried about loss of blood weakening him further. But his back and legs cramped and burned with an agony he'd not felt since working on his father's Vermont farm. Pain still lingered in the wounds, but the misery was now no more than a numbness that he accepted as tolerable if he favored the arm. In truth, the thorn lacerations and mosquito bites were a damn sight more irritating than the wounds.

He decided to move on. The full moon would light his way along the poorly defined trail and the night's coolness would help fight his exhaustion. Tomorrow he'd get plenty of rest while sailing.

He rose, steeling his mind to the torturous task, grabbed the bow and began to pull.

Sometime in the blackest hours before dawn, he stumbled over a root and felt himself toppling backwards out of control. As his head struck the ground, a white light exploded in his mind. For a confused moment, he lay moaning, aware only of the blinding throb behind his eyes. Good Lord, how easy it would be to just lie here, to sleep and not worry about awakening. No, that's foolish talk, he told himself. You're being a fool. Get up, fool. Get up. He rolled over onto his knees and raised himself slowly to his feet, holding his head in his hands.

He staggered once, lost his footing and lurched backwards off the bank to fall into the Matanzas River.

Golden cloudbanks formed a backdrop for St. Augustine as the little canoe glided swiftly past Anastasia Island. Burnham lay against the stern, numbly holding the paddle into the water, aiming toward the blunt walls and massive ramparts of Fort Marion.

He rose slightly to grasp the mainsheet with a swollen hand and jibed the sail, feeling a stinging jolt when the craft came over to the starboard tack. Lying back, he concentrated on steering steadily toward the city's waterfront. Squinting his eyes against the glare of the descending sun, he turned toward a wharf thrusting from the seawall of a large, porticoed building. He was dreamily aware of a blur of people moving on the wharf. His senseless fingers fumbled and loosened the mainsheet knot, allowing the canoe to grind gently to a stop against a barnacle encrusted piling.

Two men immediately stepped down into the water beside the small boat and gently took him by the arms, easing him to his feet. He swayed momentarily, then felt himself lifted onto the rough, wet slabs of the wharf.

Through the pounding of blood in his ears he heard a familiar voice behind him. "You were spotted coming up the river. Lordy, I'm glad to see you." He turned to the voice, feeling his face twist into a painful smile while relief flooded his mind. Powerful arms grasped and lifted him in a bear hug.

"Dummett," he cried. He heard his voice cracking with emotion as he stared down at Dummett's smiling face. "I saw...I saw them shoot you in the back and...and you went down like a rock."

"They shot a little late." Dummett laughed softly. "I went down so they *couldn't* shoot me." He released Burnham and held him at arm's length, his damp eyes staring at his friend's bloody shirt. "You look like you got in the way of a few."

Two soldiers rushed up carrying a stretcher, gently eased Burnham back onto it. Followed by the crowd of people, they moved slowly toward the large building looming against the last rays of the setting sun. Burnham lay stiffly on the canvas litter, holding back the groans that threatened to burst from his lips with each jolting step.

"They hit me on the first volley," he told Dummett. "Remember how you told me what good shots they were? Well, the one chasing me fired four times. Didn't even come close." He forced a smile, then continued. "Every damn shot went into the sail."

Dummett laughed. "Hell, son, that's exactly what he was shooting at: the sail. They believe the sail is filled with air like a balloon and if they punch holes in it the air'll leak out and stop the boat. Looks like a lot of ignorance saved your life." He turned toward the people crowding behind them. "We'll get Burnham fixed up and take him to the Colonel's house later."

The litter bearers crossed the old Spanish seawall and up to the porch of the large building.

"The St. Francis Barracks," Dummett said, sweeping his arm toward the imposing wooden building. "Garrison for the 4th Artillery Regiment. Old Doc Holbrook'll have you in good shape in no time at all."

Inside, the men helped Burnham onto a table in a clean, well-lighted room. After a thorough examination, the elderly doctor gave him a small dose of laudanum. Gently probing the hole in Burnham's shoulder with thin, silver forceps, Doc Holbrook finally grasped the lead ball. Burnham felt his muscles tighten to the breaking point as the doctor worked the ball free from the hole.

"There, now," Holbrook said, holding the ball up where Burnham could see it. "That didn't hurt a bit. I didn't feel a thing." He laughed and threw the ball into a trash bucket. After smearing the wound with a yellow salve, he began to bandage the shoulder. Dummett and Burnham exchanged the stories of their experiences after they separated.

Dummett had arrived in St. Augustine only that morning, convinced that his friend was dead and the retrieved treasure was lost. He planned to leave early the next morning to attempt tracking the small band of Micco-sukees and take his revenge for Burnham's death. And to recover the chest, if possible. A sentry posted high on Fort Marion's ramparts spotted the small canoe and Dummett immediately got the word. He suspected at once that it was Burnham.

"It was like seeing you return from the grave," he told Burnham, a slight quiver in his voice.

Doctor Holbrook finished dressing the wounds. "Get some rest, son, and no more sailing for awhile."

Dummett motioned for the litter bearers, but Burnham waved them off. "If I can pull that damned canoe halfway up the Florida peninsula, I guess I can walk through the town."

They thanked Holbrook and left the building. Burnham paused on the riverfront street for a moment. A sign nailed to the corner of a building said it was Marine Street. He gazed south over the river and the desolate, scrubby savanna surrounding it.

"A once-in-a-lifetime experience," Burnham said. "I hope." He spat the last two words as if they were sour to his tongue. They laughed, then walked slowly west on St. Francis Street.

When they reached the Street of the Old Church, St. George Street, they turned the corner and stepped through a wrought-iron gate into the court-yard of a large house, an old stuccoed coquina residence with a large porch running its length under a second-floor balcony. Light flickered from several whale-oil lanterns, dancing soft shadows onto the wall of the small garden enclosure.

Near a small grape arbor, an emaciated man sat wrapped in a shawl. "My father, Colonel Thomas Dummett," Dummett said as they approached him. Burnham took the man's paper-thin hand in his, feeling the fragility of the bones beneath his palm.

"Saved the gold my Douglas lost," the colonel mumbled with a crackling voice. "Much obliged to you. Can't run things on lost promises." He looked from Burnham to Dummett with eyes that were cold and damp, yet tinged with a feverish glow.

"Please excuse us, Papa," Dummett said. "Lieutenant Burnham needs some rest and I want to get him settled in. You need to move inside, also." He turned and led Burnham into the old house.

Inside, Burnham felt a momentary vertigo until he realized the walls of the room were not square. A narrow staircase rose to his right, its treads lying at charming but crazy angles. They passed through an arched doorway, crossed a small hall and entered the next room. Two young women dressed in similar gowns leaned over a cherrywood table, rubbing emery rouge on the silver service and buffing them to a high sheen.

A plump, turbaned, colored woman entered carrying a cast-iron pot of bubbling stew. The aroma started juices flowing in Burnham's mouth. He couldn't remember anything ever smelling so wonderful. Dummett stepped up behind the servant and draped his arms over her shoulders.

"My favorite lady, Maum Molly," he said glancing at Burnham, but turning back quickly when she raised a spoonful of stew for him to taste. "She's been feeding me like a hog since I was old enough to chew."

"And this lovely, young lady," said Dummett, taking the hand of the plain-faced girl sitting nearest the door, "is my baby sister, Miss Anna Dummett." She rose slightly and half-curtsied, murmuring an almost audible greeting.

"My other sisters live out in town," Dummett continued. "Their husbands are in the Army and Navy, off fighting the savage redskin, to save Florida and the way of life the colonel has grown to love."

The contempt in his voice was unmistakable. Dummett sat at the table, looking intently at the other young lady, a girl of about twenty.

He reached over and took the buffing cloth from her hand. "Ladies, I present Captain Mills Burnham, the friend I feared I'd lost. Burnham, this is Leandra Fernandez, who I've told many times before that she shouldn't do manual household tasks," he scolded.

The young woman turned to stare directly at Burnham. He found himself looking into startling eyes of deep jade framed by light, coppertoned skin. She nodded in a slight bow, then turned sharply to Dummett.

"Am I so fragile that I can't do my share?" she asked, her voice a deep contralto tinged with a subtle trace of Spanish accent. "I *am* your father's servant, you know." A dimple appeared in her cheek, lifting the corner of her mouth into either a sneer or a smile. Burnham couldn't decide which. She turned her attention again to the silver.

Anna Dummett coughed slightly. "Well, Captain Burnham," she said, her voice soft and shy. "How does it feel for your resurrection from the dead to be so well received?"

"To begin with," Burnham said, "I'm only a lieutenant."

"Oh, the Army'll promote you right away when I make my report," Dummett stated, his eyes fixed on the slave girl. "You'll probably get some sort of award, maybe a medal or something—if I embellish it enough."

"Of which you are most capable," Leandra said, smiling.

Certainly Burnham had seen women with a beauty to rival Leandra's, but for the moment he could not remember when. Looking at the high, exotic cheekbones, the generously curved lips, the smooth, coppery skin, it was difficult for him to imagine her as a slave. Anna Dummett had a regal bearing for one so young and so plain, but Leandra wore her confident composure like a crown. He found himself comparing the disparity of her ancestry. The light coloration, the emerald brilliance of her eyes, the soft Spanish accent and the pert attitude she seemed to hold in check—all were traits in contradiction to his experience with Negroes.

"Excuse us, ladies," Dummett said. "We have decisions to make." He led Burnham into a large sitting room. Thomas Dummett had moved into a large, overstuffed chair before a roaring fireplace, arranging golden doubloons into neat stacks on a small table before him. Beckoning with a quaking finger, he motioned for Burnham to draw up a chair, and carefully eased three tall stacks of doubloons toward him.

"It may be presumptuous on my part to make this overture," the old man said. "I know the military offers few opportunities for acquiring wealth. My son has proven that. He also has told me of your desire to bring your young family to Florida and settle here." He pointed to the three stacks. "These coins will pave the way..." He held a palm up at Burnham's startled look. "This is hardly charity," he stated, "nor should you see it as a reward. It is simply yours by right of earning. You placed your life in jeopardy. It would have been more than easy to abandon the burdensome chest. You have earned your share."

The narcosis from the laudanum was wearing off. Burnham pressed his hands against his temples, struggling to ease the throb beginning to pound his eyes from behind. "Sir, I want—more than anything, I want to make a place for myself, for my family. But—"

"Take the damn money," Dummett growled. "It's yours."

Thomas Dummett looked at Dummett with rheumy eyes, the quivering fingers of one hand gripped tightly in the other. "We are pleased you have allowed us this time from your valuable lessons to the household ladies, and to offer your advice on this matter." He slowly lowered his head, saying, "However, in this instance you are certainly correct and your sagacity is appreciated."

Dummett seemed unaffected by his father's words. Burnham looked from father to son in bewilderment. Then he shook his head and addressed the issue. "No, I can't accept the gift. I *could* use a loan until I find a situation of some sort. Then I would certainly repay it." His heart seemed to flood to near bursting when he realized that the chance known only in his dreams might be at hand. Soon he might have Mary and Frances with him. "Can you make me a paper?"

"All right, a loan then," said Dummett, pouring the coins into one of the leather bags and handing it to him. "But we don't need a paper. Now, Papa, what can be done about finding this man some honest work? The army'll discharge him now that he's wounded. At least his enlistment will run out long before he recovers from the holes in his hide."

"Let me discuss the matter with my friend, Dr. Seth Peck, and see what we can come up with." The old man returned to his golden stacks.

Burnham hefted the weight of the sack in his hands as his thoughts ranged over the two thousand miles to Vermont, a distance that earlier had seemed unconquerable. The sack of gold shrunk the distance to only an irritating step separating him from Mary. He now had the means to bring Mary and baby Frances to Florida, but the vision that flooded his mind was of the screaming Indian on horseback slashing through the shallow water toward the boat. And he saw that the boat held not himself, but Mary and Frances.

A cold shiver passed through his body and he looked again at the sack of coins.

BOOK TWO

1839 — 1844

BOOK TWO

1820 – 1861

Chapter 5

J acksonville's waterfront shivered itself slowly awake in these early morning hours. In the sandy ruts of Bay Street, two draft horses leaned into their collars, dragging a creaking dray through the fog. Burnham trudged in its wake of swirling moisture, turning north on Pine to skirt the river marsh. At Forsyth, the heavy wagon rumbled across the wooden bridge and turned back toward Bay.

Burnham scrunched his neck lower into the collar of the wool mackinaw jacket against the chilled air drifting in from the St. Johns River. He nodded to sailors sitting on planked saloon porches in squares of dim light, cradling steaming coffee mugs in their worn hands. Most of them would sit where they were for hours during the coming day, some awaiting the lading of their ships, while others, on the beach in a land foreign to them, hoped to pick up rumors of shorthanded ships. Their evenings were spent relating tales of life at sea, sharing the only semblance of brotherhood and family known to them. Only on rare occasions did their gathering erupt into violence, resulting in a few broken heads and cut faces.

At the corner of Market Street, Burnham argued with himself for a moment over whether to check out the Liberty Street Ferry or get coffee. The hot coffee won. He swung open the door to Hart's Inn and entered.

In the empty dining room, he waited a moment for the missing waitress, then stepped to the coffee urn and filled a china mug. The hot coffee sloshed over the brim onto his hand as he eased to a window table overlooking the river.

Hanging his hat and jacket from a clothes tree in the corner, he slid his braces over his shoulders, adjusted the buckles, then let them dangle loosely from his waistband. Relieved of their tension, he slumped into a cane-bottom chair, sipped the coffee and watched the diffused ball of the sun rise beyond the translucent curtain of fog. He stared along the riverbank at masts thrust above the low-lying mist. His thoughts rambled like the spider-web tracery of the rigging disappearing down into the fog's soupy wetness.

"And how's our good deputy this fine morning?"

Startled, Burnham jerked his head around. Isaiah Hart, trim and dandy in a peach-colored suit, stopped before an ornate wall mirror to admire himself. Satisfied with his image, he poured a cup of coffee, signaled the waitress who had just come in from the kitchen, and marched to Burnham's table. "Want some eggs?" he asked in a voice touched at the edge with a dainty, Anglican accent.

Burnham leaned back in his chair. "No, thanks. Mary will have things up and going at home. I'll eat with her and the kids before I go back to the office."

"You look tuckered. Any problems with the job?"

Burnham smiled and sipped his coffee. "None I can't handle."

Hart laughed. "Not too peaceful here for you, is it? This place is certainly calmer than most seaports."

"Oh, it's not that. I'm right happy with the peacefulness. Lord knows I've had all the violence any one man needs. It's just...I don't know...I guess I'm the only one in this town not getting rich. Everyone's busy making more money. No one causes any trouble except an occasional sailor—or McGirt." He sipped his coffee, frowning as he set the cup back on the table. "But, me? I'm just walking around, watching. I'm not building anything for the future."

"I felt the same way at your age. Course, it was another place, another time. Didn't have the opportunities this new territory offers."

"If I could build like you've done, I'd be satisfied. Hotels, steamer line, freight..."

"It didn't happen by accident. I did it the hard way, saving every cent until I got a foothold in business." Hart looked up as the girl handed him a platter of ham and eggs. He pricked the yolks with his fork and smeared the yellow around. Dicing his ham into small chunks, he hashed them into the eggs.

"How does Mistress Mary like it down here?" he asked.

"Loves it, but hates my job," Burnham replied, turning to stare out the window. "She expects every morning that someone'll haul my lifeless body home on a plank." He looked at Hart and grinned. "It might happen today."

"So you're going to McGirt's Creek then? Are you taking another deputy? You'll need some help, won't you?"

"No, I'm just going to feel out the place—unless, of course, you'd like to come along. We could carry along a couple of ass jawbones like Samson did and clean out the place." Burnham smiled at the incredulous look on Hart's slim face.

"If I wanted to commit suicide, I'd have taken the deputy job myself instead of hiring a poor, ignorant Yankee." Hart shoveled the rest of his breakfast into his mouth and stood. "You should take help, though. Old McGirt's not in control anymore and it's not a Sunday school out there. His nephew, Ratch, is probably behind the mess."

"Well, I'm going on your complaint," Burnham said. "And you're right. If it's like what I hear, the place needs to be shut down." He slurped the rest of his coffee and walked with Hart to the door. "I can handle it though." He paused and looked into Hart's eyes. "If they're halfway civilized—which I doubt."

Leandra Fernandez pulled the crocheted mantilla tighter around her shoulders against the chill of the morning breeze. Aromatic steam rose from her cup of hot coffee to blend into the misty fog swirling around the second floor balcony on the south side of the house. She slowly cut the edge of her hand through the moisture on the varnished rail, rolling the beads of water ahead until they touched and merged into a small pool that she knifed over the rail's edge. She set the cup down and peered through the mist lying across the roofs of St. Augustine.

To the southeast, far beyond Anastasia Island, the arc of the sun burst above the sharp line of the ocean's horizon, driving golden lances into the soft underbelly of a purplish cloudbank. As the glow fanned across the city, pigeons cooed in the eaves of the house across the narrow street, slapping their wings while nervously shifting their perching positions.

The best part of the day, she thought. Clean and unsullied.

When she heard the quiet snick of the outer door below, she stepped back against the stucco wall. After a moment she eased back to the balustrade and looked down onto the stooped shoulders of Douglas Dummett. Her heart seemed to stutter as he ran his fingers through his black hair.

He eased a broad-brimmed felt hat onto his head, then looked in both directions along St. Francis Street. After standing for an indecisive moment, he shrugged his shoulders and trudged through the misty fog along the sandy path toward the bay.

He seems so subdued, she thought, like a wild stallion tamed and halter broken. Oh, how she wished she could do something...anything...to brighten the spark in those dear eyes.

He had been an essential part of her life from her earliest memory, and yet a fissure now seemed to lie between them. Was it her fault or his? When she first became aware of him as a man rather than as a brother, she had erected defenses to guard her emotions. But this didn't mean she wanted him shut out of her life.

Of course, he still accompanied her and Anna on their afternoon trips to market or to the savanna near the river to pick blackberries, but the banter was gone. In its place stood a barrier. She recalled the thrill of earlier years when he'd scoop her from the ground and swing her in breathtaking sweeps. They had a closeness then, a nearness that was precious. She resented the loss. Now he avoided any contact with her. Was it because she was a slave? Because she was a Negro?

The unforgettable memory of discovering she was a slave glimmered at the edge of her consciousness, then sprang full-blown into her mind. She had been fourteen when it happened.

A new field hand had raised his splayed fingers to her breast as she passed him near the Carickfergus sugarmill. She froze for a moment in shock before slapping his hand away.

"I don't want you to get whipped, so you'd better keep your place." The heat in her voice reflected the flush she felt in her face. "I'll tell my father if you ever try anything like that again."

The man smirked, the grin splitting thick purple lips beneath a broad nose. "Gal, that old white man ain't your father. I done hear all about you from the other niggers. How you ain't white. You a nigger just like all us other niggers, only we's dark and shows it. We don't juju like we's something we ain't." His laughter rang in her ears as she ran.

The memory still burned intensely, as it had then. She recalled running to Maum Molly, sobbing into her shoulder and recounted the event.

"There, there, child. Things ain't never bad as we sees them. The Colonel now, even iffen he ain't yo' real father, he be the best you got."

In shocked confusion, she had listened to Thomas Dummett later while he told of buying her as a baby from her real father, a Minorcan named Fernandez. Her name. Not Dummett—Fernandez. Yes, her mother was a Negro, the Minorcan's slave. "But you became my little girl then, just like you were my own child."

Since that day their relationship was no longer real to her. She became aware of her status, realizing why she had to pick up after Anna when they were little, why she got Anna's old dresses when Anna got new ones.

Leandra never again saw the young slave who had harassed her; he just disappeared. Nothing was ever said again about her status until she and Anna were leaving for school in Savannah. "Leandra, you take care of Anna," Thomas Dummett had said. And those words clearly defined her position. She was Anna's maid.

Yet she still felt she belonged, that she was in some way part of the family. Relationships formed while young often live beyond reality. Anna remained her sister, Douglas her older brother. Until recently, that is.

Now Douglas treated her almost as a stranger. And deep within her, she knew it was a reality that would never change. He was white and she was black. He was the master and she was the slave. But she also knew that she loved him with a love that could never be realized.

"He's at loose-ends," said a low voice from behind her. Anna stepped through the door onto the balcony, watching Douglas disappear into the fog. "He's so strong it's difficult for me to imagine he might have problems," she said turning back to Leandra.

Leandra sipped her coffee, hoping her face wouldn't reflect the thoughts she had been harboring. "He's just winding down, I guess, to the slower pace of civilian life."

"You're concerned over him as I am." Anna's tone put the truth to the accusation. "I've long suspected it's even more. Is it?"

Leandra turned to look into the wide-set black eyes studying her, wondering how much Anna might know or have guessed. Then she returned her gaze to where Douglas had vanished into the mist.

"Yes," she replied. "It's more." Then softly, "God help me, it's more."

"Oh, Leandra. I am so sorry. I only suspected..." Anna's pause was more eloquent than anything further she might have said.

Leandra continued to stare into the fog. "What will be, will be. And I suppose what can't be, won't."

Anna stepped close and placed a timorous hand on Leandra's shoulder. "I—more than anyone—can understand and grieve with you. Only an ugly woman can truly know how painful unanswered love can be."

"You aren't ugly."

Anna smiled. "Plain, then. Beauty is a badge that only a plain woman can see. The sadness here is for a beautiful woman like you to not have your love returned."

Leandra felt the hot sting of tears.

Anna stepped to the door. "Don't fret. There's always the chance—"

"Anna, I'm colored!" Leandra sniffled and clenched her fists. "I'm not going to wake up one morning and be white."

"You're as white as anyone," Anna said, her voice soft, yet full of compassion. She handed the girl a handkerchief. "Now, fix yourself and let's go get our breakfast.

Burnham turned into the yard of the small, county-owned bungalow. A giggle of delight was his only warning before a laughing bundle of gingham dropped onto his shoulders from the limbs of a maple tree. "Daddy," Frances cried, hugging his neck from behind with soft, plump arms.

He swung her around, then pulled her tightly against him. "You're too big a girl to be climbing around in trees," he teased. She laughed and squirmed free. Grasping one of his fingers in her hand, she led him into the house.

In the kitchen, he eased up behind the small woman fussing over a pot of grits bubbling on the stove. He slid his arms around her, cupping the soft fullness of her breasts beneath the apron.

"And you can unhand me now, you maniac. Aren't two like her more than enough for you?" She flashed a puckish smile and turned in his arms to kiss him.

Mary's auburn hair was pulled up into a bun with soft tendrils straggling down into the moisture beading on her forehead. He lightly pecked her upturned nose, then released her to walk to the corner where his son lay on a blanket pallet. He scooped the boy high toward the ceiling, smiling at the sharp gasp and squeal he always emitted when handled this way.

"I don't suppose I'll ever get the hang of these strange foods," Mary said, turning back to the steaming grits. "I'll have your meal in a jiffy."

Burnham pulled a cane-backed chair back from the table and sat. He studied her while bouncing the boy on his knee, this beautiful woman who had never questioned their emigration to Florida. Her relief over his safe return to New York had turned to wonder over his tales of the paradise in the territory below the States. Her wonder had turned to disquiet over his tales of death and suffering from the savages inhabiting paradise—and from paradise itself.

Yet she had quickly set aside her fears when he told her he wanted to move to Florida. "I live by the creed of the biblical Ruth," she had said, looking into his eyes and smiling impishly. "Entreat me not to leave thee, for I be tired of sleeping alone."

This small house in Jacksonville was a sore disappointment for Burnham, but Mary's eagerness in arranging their meager furnishings was infectious, causing him to relax and accept the house. His pay was too low for private lodgings and his pride too high to allow him to touch the remaining Dummett doubloons.

What was it Douglas had said on that island? *The land'll take care of you, boy. It can make you wealthy.* Sure. Here he was, surrounded by the wealth of land and sea, but owning none of it, and with little prospect of ever owning any.

By the time Burnham's enlistment ended, Colonel Dummett had visited Doctor Seth Peck. Together they had mulled over various situations, finally agreeing to call in a debt of honor from their old friend, the Honorable Isaiah David Hart, founding father of Jacksonville.

Their combined influence resulted in getting Burnham appointed deputy to the DuVal County sheriff. The position was to be filled upon the impending retirement of the current deputy. Within a week of his acceptance, Burnham had embarked on the long sea journey to New York.

His reunion with Mary was made even more tender with his introduction to a new son, Mills Olcott Burnham, Jr., a name he wouldn't have chosen, but one he accepted with pride.

In New York, he found temporary work as a gunsmith, but the low salary forced him to dip into Colonel Dummett's gold. He wanted to keep that hoard of coins intact to lower the debt he felt honor-bound to repay. The enforced wait made the year seem even longer, creeping into 1839 on the dragging heels of bleak wintry days.

Then, in July, he received word from Hart of his official appointment as deputy. Burnham booked passage on the brig *Ajax*, bound for the Bahamas in August, with layovers in Bermuda and Jacksonville.

Their arrival in Florida was an enchantment to Mary. Her finger pointed at each new sight as they entered the broad mouth of the St. Johns—the rampant colors spanning the spectrum, the foliage plants growing like she could never have imagined, the sea life darting below the water's surface all around them. After reminding her that he had seen and experienced each sight, he felt a twinge of guilt when she turned to share her rapture with Frances.

Now, Mary interrupted his reverie by setting his breakfast on the checkered oilcloth. "And are you going to McGirt's Creek tonight?"

"You know I have to," he answered. This was the toughest part of his job, having to look into her pleading eyes when she began her campaign. As she had done on every day since he took the office, Mary McCuen Burnham was going to beg him to give up the job and look for something less threatening.

"Do you wish this lad to grow up without a father, without discipline?" she asked, taking the year-old baby from Burnham.

"I imagine he'd get plenty of discipline if I weren't here. He'd get his share and the full ration you'd normally give me."

She swatted her towel at him. "And how do you suppose I'm to raise the three of them alone in this land of heathens?" She put the boy back on his blankets.

"Three?"

"Course. You think all that playing at night the way you do is free? If you plan to dance, you must pay the piper." She laughed at him, and turned back to the stove.

He sat for a drawn moment savoring the realization of what she was telling, feeling his face light up.

He cocked an eye at her. "Another baby?" he asked, slowly allowing his lips to curl into a grin.

She nodded.

With a little whoop, he sprang to his feet and grabbed her to begin a little jig around the kitchen. When Frances began clapping her hands and singing a merry ditty, he stepped back to take a short hop into the air, clicking the heels of his boots, landing lightly, and taking Mary again into his arms.

While they danced, he looked at his daughter through a shimmer of moisture and said to her, "With you singing, I'll dance with your mama for the rest of our lives."

"At least now you'll be carrying a pistol as you go to dance with the hooligans at McGirt's Creek?" Mary asked, pushing his hands from her.

"Mary, Mary," he sighed. "I've told you this before. Wearing guns is a sure way to get killed. I'm not good enough to fight with guns. I don't *want* to fight with guns—ever again. There's been no situation here I couldn't handle without a pistol. If it comes to trouble, I'll back off and arm myself. But until then, no."

Later, he watched Frances playing with the baby while Mary poured water from a tin bucket into the dish basin. He remembered the year of separation from them and wondered how he had endured. His trials during that year had been survival, but moments like these were the essence of life.

McGirt's Creek! A cold shiver rippled the length of his legs. Would he be able to overcome the fear lurking along the dark edges of his mind?

Dummett stubbed his cold, chewed cigar into the ceramic pot. He stood for a moment, unsure of why he stood, but certain that it was better than squirming in the chair. Wandering around was better than doing nothing. He wasn't even sure why he'd come into the Burns Boarding House public room. Shaking his head, he pushed open the etched glass door and left the building.

On Aviles Street, he watched a mule strolling aimlessly through the sugar sand. If you have nothing better to do, he told himself, following a mule couldn't hurt. So he followed.

It wasn't so much that he had nothing important to do. As the Collector of Customs for the Port of New Smyrna, he had political obligations to meet and contacts to make, both in New Smyrna and St. Augustine. He found himself here in St. Augustine about every other week. Making contacts. At least that was what he told himself. But he also found himself making excuses to be around Leandra, something he'd never done before. Nothing much had changed, he guessed, but there was no denying the rush of blood to his face when he found himself in her presence.

She had developed into a fine looking woman. Fine looking, hell! She was beautiful. But she was still only a little girl, nine years younger than he was. Much too young for him.

What in hell was wrong with him, carrying on like this? Why should he be thinking of their age difference, when the real difference was more important? She was a servant—a nigger.

The mule led him to the waterfront. When it stopped to spew a golden stream into the sand, he was reminded of rum. He left the mule to its business and walked down Marine Street until he reached St. Francis. After walking west a block, he stepped into Tovar's Tavern.

For over an hour he sat alone, drinking dark, Jamaican rum, trying to tunnel his concentration away from Leandra and to block the buzz of conversation from a group of Minorcans bellied to the bar.

"Hey, Dummett. What you doin'?"

Dummett glanced up at the burly man.

"Does that high yaller bitch still be living in your old man's house?" The man snickered and turned back to the bar, tossing down his drink and signaling the bartender for a refill. "She's table-grade. I'd take a little touch of that if I thought no one would hear of it." He paused, looking back at Dummett. Then he slurred, "You tapped that keg yet, Dummett?"

Dummett sighed and pushed himself to his feet. He walked over to the man, stepping into a thick cloud of onion breath hanging in front of the man. Biting off the words, he asked: "What was it you said?"

The man smirked at him.

"Never mind," Dummett said, shaking his head. "Look at this." He held a knotted fist about six inches to the side of the man's face.

At the instant the man turned his face to look, the fist caught him flush on the point of his whiskered chin. He crumpled like a sow hit with a sledgehammer.

Dummett stared at the man's limp form for a moment then raised his eyes to the other men. "Anybody else want in on this conversation?" They hastily concentrated on their drinks.

Dummett retrieved his hat from the table and left.

Burnham guided the buggy down the sandy road from Jacksonville, winding through pine flats, passing small farms in various degrees of development. While most of the homes were nothing more than wattle shacks, some were well built.

The community at McGirt's Creek was like many scattered across the panhandle of the Florida Territory. A small general store fronted the road near a high sand dune. Behind the store, a rickety warehouse teetered on the bank, threatening to fall into the creek.

A sign on a double post announced McGirt's Saloon long before the curve of the road allowed him to see it. The saloon, a weathered plank building overlooking the creek, had a rear porch supported by pilings driven into the creek itself. Out front, a half dozen nondescript horses stood hipshot with heads drooping at a hitching post.

He drove his buggy into a small field and dropped the brick rein-anchor. Standing for a moment in the waning light, he slapped dust from his pants, taking the time to review what he knew of the place and its legendary proprietor.

Old James McGirt was a veteran of the war of revolution, this dating him at least into his eighties. Some said he was a hero of that war, but most believed he had been only a drummer boy with the continental army, too young to do any of the awesome feats of his reputation. His older brother, Daniel McGirt, had served under George Rogers Clark in the Battle of Vincennes in 1779, and probably James had been there too.

Whatever the truth, he had made his mark on this region, settling here with Daniel and bending to the winds of the time, living first in harmony with the Spanish by assuming Spanish citizenship, then switching to the English when they bought Florida, and back again to the Spanish. Now he had gone full circle and was again an American citizen. He and his brother had made a fortune running British blockades during the 1812 war and, now that Daniel was dead, James owned the property on McGirt's Creek.

Burnham had heard of McGirt's extensive holdings of forestland up on the St. Marys River, where he cut and shipped oak north for the shipbuilding industry. These were admirable enterprises, unlike the cause for Burnham's trip today.

Was the old man a common highwayman, or was he again bending with the winds of time? Travelers had made complaints of robbery and assault by thugs at the creek. Reports had come in of mysterious disappearances, people leaving villages like Newnansville and never making it to Jacksonville. Of course these disappearances could have happened anywhere, and it was still possible that they could have been victims of Indians, although the Seminoles had been driven deep within the Everglades of south Florida.

Burnham walked unhurried to the screened door, pausing to check the interior through an open window. A card game was in progress at a table near a corner, the players shouting above the tinny clatter of music from an automated piano across the room.

Behind the bar, two men in deep conversation glanced up as Burnham walked into the saloon. The older man wore a mane of thick, white hair, his body small and trim, his erect stature belying the years mapped by his wrinkled face. The other man was young and large, redheaded, with a forehead that sloped back from a purple-veined nose.

Burnham stepped around warped tables to the bar, leaned on it and spoke to the older man. "Are you Mr. James McGirt?"

"I be," answered the man, his voice firm and friendly.

"What you be wantin' with him?" The young lout leaned over the bar, glaring at Burnham.

"Get out of the way and I'll tell him." Burnham snapped out the cold words. His stare locked onto the old man, avoiding the red-rimmed eyes of the young brute.

"I'll call for you if need be, Ratch," said James McGirt, stepping around him to face Burnham. "What be yore business with me, Deputy?" he asked.

"Well, if you know who I am, you probably have some idea of why I'm here," Burnham answered. He turned slightly, keeping Ratch in view as the young man moved to the end of the bar.

"I seen you in Jax," James said. "It don't make no nevermind. I don't know much anymore 'bout what's happenin' in my world."

"Do you know of the robbing and killing that folks say is happening in your world?" Burnham asked, unsure of the way the play was going. "Some folks in the county want your world closed down."

"You can't come in here runnin' no bluff like that," Ratch yelled. "We don't need no law buttin' into our business."

He began moving down the bar toward Burnham. The old man looked bewildered by his nephew's outburst.

"I only came to see what the situation was," Burnham said evenly. "I came unarmed to show my peaceful intent."

"Don't need no weapons to put yore head up yore ass," Ratch said, reaching forward to tap Burnham on the chest with a forefinger. Then, without warning, he snatched a handful of Burnham's shirt, jerking him forward into a bone crushing bear hug. Burnham gasped as the air was driven from his lungs. The man's knee began to hammer at Burnham's groin. This was not what he expected. Amazement crowded his mind. This lout was trying to crush his balls—he could damn sure get hurt.

He squeezed his legs together in defense and struggled to free his arms. Reaching into the man's armpit, he gouged his fingers deep into the soft muscles. The man's elbow lifted slightly from his side and Burnham wiggled his arm free. He drove a stiffened thumb hard into the indentation below Ratch's ear, behind the jawbone. Ratch howled and stepped back, holding his hand tightly to his neck.

Burnham leaned to his left, then slammed his balled fist into Ratch's belly just below the breastbone. Ratch bent forward holding his stomach as a fetid cloud of air whooshed from his mouth. Burnham grabbed the scraggly beard with both hands, drew back his leg and drove his knee up with all the leverage he could get into the blow. The knee caught Ratch flush on the nose. Burnham felt the cartilage give way with a satisfying crunch. Switching his grip to the greasy hair, he smashed the blood-splattered head forward against the oak planks of the bar. Again. And again. And again. Ratch crumpled unconscious to the floor.

Burnham whirled to face the card players. They sat frozen in their seats, expecting, he guessed, that Ratch would make quick work of him. After staring at him for a moment, one of the men turned back to the table and threw down the deck of cards. "Whose deal?"

Burnham turned back to the limp bulk, pulled Ratch's belt loose and looped it around his throat. Then, crossing the wrists behind the beefy neck, he strapped them together, snagging the leather against the man's Adam's apple. As he rolled Ratch to his back, a Derringer pistol fell from his waistband to the floor. Burnham scooped it up and turned back to James McGirt, who stood leaning against the shelves of bottles behind the bar, a sardonic grin on his withered face.

"I've watched that boy bust heads in here since he was fourteen. Yore the first what beat him," the old man cackled. "He's had the Indian sign on me since I don't know when, doing what he pleased, like he damn well owned the place. I didn't have the balls to face up to him, but you tell him for me, if he comes back here, I'll kill him on sight. You ain't gonna have no more trouble out here."

"I'll have to come get you if you kill him," Burnham said.

"And do what? Put me in jail? Hell, son, I'm ninety-three or there-abouts, and on a downhill drag. Time don't scare me no more."

"And see, the cut on your face is but a sign that you have no business delving into other people's troubles." Mary snuggled close to Burnham in the darkness, pulling the light sheet over her head.

"You know, I wasn't scared during any of the fight, neither before or afterward." He lay in comfort, his long legs stretched over the end of their small bed. "Before, I always felt a panic after the trouble, wondering if I was a whole man."

"The bit of life stirring in me loins is proof enough you're a whole man," she said, nuzzling into the thatch of hair on his chest.

"That's not what I mean. Dummett can kill in combat and not stir a feather over it. My guts quivered like aspic when I got away from the Indians on the river, but not today," he said.

"Takes a brave one to have the need to prove himself over again. Any fool can go do it when he's got no fear. Go to sleep then, me brave lad, and worry your mind no more about it."

He lay in the moonlit room and pondered the day's events. Sure, he could have been killed by the insanity of Ratch McGirt, but he had acted with aggression and strength, an assured strength. He felt pride swell his chest, lifting Mary's head with its expansion. Would his strength always be with him? He didn't know, and he surely hoped he would never have to test it again.

When he drove into Jacksonville with Ratch hanging out of the buggy's boot, small clusters of townsfolk cheered him. At first exhilarated by the excitement, he quickly remembered the danger and violence that had led to it. No, he didn't need that kind of excitement. He was content to lie here with his wee Irish woman. Maybe, with Mary's luck in his pocket, things would settle back into the boredom he now relished.

He tilted his head down to her ear. "I got the price of a piper. Wanna dance?" he whispered.

Chapter 6

A shiver of apprehension rippled through Douglas Dummett as he neared the courtyard gate to his father's house. An unseasonably cool, August wind swirled loose papers and sand around his legs on the darkened St. Francis Street. He paused for a moment to gather his thoughts and to consider his argument, knowing that his father would reject the proposition if he saw Douglas' real intent.

In truth, Douglas himself was not sure of his real intent. He only knew he had reached the point where he could no longer contain himself around Leandra. Her lithe body offered more temptation than he could control.

Early in the year, he had left St. Augustine for Mount Pleasant to remove himself from her presence. With the help of two of his father's slaves, he had built a one-room shack near the site of the old house burned by the Seminoles.

He settled into a monotonous existence that soon drove his loneliness to the surface. At times such as these, he would leave the shack and roam the woods, accompanied by a couple of hounds, searching for a coon, a possum, or a fox. But his thoughts always returned to Leandra.

When he allowed his thoughts to wander, they drifted through erotic scenes with Leandra. Cursing to himself, he would banish these dreams the instant they formed. He tried to tell himself that what he felt was nothing more than physical desire brought on by enforced celibacy, that it was the solitude of the silent shack that made his life no more than a mere endurance without her.

Other men bedded their slaves, sneaking out to the quarters at night, hiding their sexual activities from wives who were probably aware of them and often relieved to be freed from the chore. But Douglas admitted to himself that his desire for Leandra went deeper than just bedding her. If that was all it meant, he could do it and get it out of his mind. But was that all it meant?

Each time the thought of bringing Leandra to Mount Pleasant edged into his consciousness, he immediately shoved it into the background. The plantation did need hands to rebuild it, and the Colonel's slaves in St. Augustine were in danger of contracting the yellowjack. But house servants? He didn't really need house servants. Yes, by God, he did. His political positions called for the necessity of hosting social activities-and he would need a hostess to lend an air of social propriety to the gatherings. Leandra would be perfect for this. Near white, she would not be as objectionable to the wives of his friends as some black mammy might.

Now he stood outside the gate to the Colonel's house, questioning his motives one last time, but still aware he would soon face his father to fight for his desires, employing all the skills he possessed.

Inside the house, he went directly to the sitting room and stood by the fireplace, waiting with a feeling of childish anticipation while two white-haired servants helped the old man into his chair. They wrapped a shawl around the Colonel's shoulders and lifted his feet to a stool. After placing a light wool blanket across his legs, the two slaves left the room.

Colonel Dummett stared at Douglas for a long moment, then cleared his throat with a hacking grunt. "You have something you want of me?" he asked. "You certainly haven't been around lately for any other reason." His voice had the raspy sound of a file on metal. He eased his body to a more comfortable position.

"I'd like to take all the hands back to Mount Pleasant to work the place," Douglas began. His voice sounded as if it came from beyond his body. "It needs to be put back on a profitable basis. Also, I'll need the men to rebuild the house there. You can't afford to continue supporting them. You're going to lose them if they don't begin to earn their keep. It'll pay us to have them at the plantation. I'll leave enough here to maintain this home and to meet your needs." He caught himself twisting his hat between his hands and dropped it onto a table as if it were a banner proclaiming the lie to his intentions.

"And which of my house servants do you wish to take with you?"

"Well, I'll need Maum Molly to run the house," he answered.

"And?" The Colonel's eyes were becoming inflamed, seeming to burn with a passion he was fighting to contain. "Who else would you need?"

Intuitively Douglas knew the old man was aware of the reason for his visit. This knowledge deflated his hopes.

He coughed into a closed fist. "I would think Leandra might serve well as my hostess. My political positions require certain entertainments, dinners and such." By now he wanted nothing more than to drop the whole thing, but he would not, could not, waver before his father's sarcasm.

"And of course Leandra would be there to appease your lust." The old man's voice rose, quavering in time with the trembling of his hands. "Don't look so surprised. Everyone here knows of it. Your stares speak more truthfully than your tongue."

Douglas turned and walked to the fireplace. He kept his back toward his father while scuffing his boot through the thin layer of cold ash.

"You're right," he said finally. "And maybe they speak more truthfully than my heart." Turning to look into his father's eyes, he spread his hands in supplication. "I have needs that must be met. Father, I can't...I won't expose myself again to the ridicule I received from the hands of a white woman. I figured—"

"I know what you figured," the Colonel interrupted, his red-rimmed eyes beginning to bulge. "By God, man, I'll sell her first. I have loved her like a daughter, but I'll not have my family tainted with the blood of Ham. You're no better than that whoremonger, Zephaniah Kingsley, wanting to take a nigger to wife."

Douglas clapped his hands over his ears, trying to still the loud pulse drumming into his brain. "I have no desire to take her to wife," he said bluntly, staring at the old man. "I only want to take her."

At that, the Colonel gasped for air through pursed lips, his eyes straining widely, a flush mottling his cheeks to a purplish hue. He gripped the arms of his chair and struggled to his feet. Douglas reached for him. Halfway up, the old man began to strangle, clawing at his chest with both hands. Then he lurched forward, crumpling to the floor.

"Oh, God, no!" Douglas cried. He rolled him over and lifted his shoulders. The Colonel's eyes fixed for a second on Douglas in painful accusation, and then the air eased from his lungs and the eyes began to glaze over, their luster gone forever.

Douglas sat holding his father's frail shoulders as Anna appeared in the doorway and began to whimper.

Douglas leaned on the rail of the small steamer as it made its way into Mosquito Inlet. He stared at the wall of mangroves lining the waterway as if looking into his father's accusing eyes.

The day after they buried the Colonel in the old Huguenot cemetery, his will was read and executed. Douglas' mother, Mary, received the St. Francis Street house and all of the income from the old man's investments. Douglas was given what he knew he wouldn't have if his father had lived: the slaves, and the shared ownership of Mount Pleasant with his sisters. He now owned Leandra Fernandez.

But the price was prohibitive.

For several days he had walked around town, alone, thinking, weighing options, finally deciding he would take the men to Mount Pleasant. Their families would remain in St. Augustine until the time came when he had homes built for them-and a home for himself.

He would leave Leandra in St. Augustine with Anna.

He had not spoken to Leandra since that horrible night of his father's death. On every occasion of their meeting, he had turned and walked away from her. When the time came to take his men to Mount Pleasant, leaving Leandra was one of the hardest tasks he'd ever performed. Yet, he had set the course to be followed and what was done could not be undone. If a great emptiness accompanied him on the trip, the fault was his alone.

Dummett and his men departed the steamer at the old pier at Mount Pleasant. By nightfall of the next day, they had cut saplings and palmetto thatching, building rude lean-to shelters for the men while the plantation was being rebuilt.

Day after day, into the blistering summer heat of 1840, the little plantation struggled through the agonies of rebirth. The men cleared over two hundred acres of palmettos and pine that had reclaimed the old fields. At first, he tried to save the sugar cane that grew volunteer in the fields, but he soon realized that cutting the saplings and grubbing out palmetto roots destroyed the cane roots anyway. Finally, he ordered the men to strip the fields.

They cut a stand of cypress near the old house site, shipping the logs to the Pacetti mill up on Moultrie Creek to be sawed into planks. In the early months of 1841, they constructed a house from these cypress planks.

Three bedrooms branched from a large, sitting room. To protect the main house from fire, the separate kitchen stood away from the main house, connected to it by a roofed breezeway. A dormitory building for the single women stood on one side of the kitchen and a barracks for the men on the other. Farther out back, cabins for the married families were erected from pine logs.

By March, the men had planted forty acres in vegetables to supplement the fresh game provided by the hunters. During the remainder of the year, more fields were cleared and planted in sugarcane.

Immediately after the planting, they built a barn, with stalls for the small herd of milk cows and bins for storing the root vegetables. Dummett thought it was a fine barn. The men now had a renewed sense of pride in their abilities.

Everything was completed to his satisfaction by early December. Dummett could find nothing more to do. He announced to the men that he was taking them to visit their families for the holidays. They had returned to St. Augustine only once—Christmas, the year before. Dummett found himself caught up in their excitement over the coming trip. Last year, he had forced himself to cover the feelings that clutched his soul the instant he saw Leandra. Oh, he had been pleasant enough, but at the same time he avoided any private contact with her. Now, a year had passed, and he was anxious to see her.

Their arrival in St. Augustine was a whirlwind of meals and visits. But then the celebrations were followed by the scurry of preparation for the return trip. The women and children would accompany them back to Mount Pleasant. This put Dummett squarely on the horns of a dilemma. Should he take Leandra with him or should he allow her to remain in St. Augustine, continuing the life she had known?

Anna resolved the problem for him. She arranged to accompany him on an early morning walk.

As they strolled through the narrow streets, she waited for him to bring up the subject. When finally they rested on a bench in the Plaza, she broke the silence. "Leandra wants to go back with you."

"With me?" Shock or happiness rushed through Dummett. He didn't know which.

Anna arched her eyebrows and smiled. "Well, maybe she just wants to be with Maum Molly and help get the plantation settled."

Dummett felt his body sag. But apparently Anna sensed his sudden disappointment. "Of course," she added, smiling, "Maybe, just maybe, she wants to be with you."

Dummett stood and looked across the river at the sun rising over Anastasia Island. "Impossible. She knows the circumstances. Our...differences."

"Do you think that matters to the heart? Her knowledge and her intellect can't control her love."

"You know nothing about this."

"Love? Or the circumstances? I know of both, and I know..." She let her voice fade and sat in silence. Dummett felt she had stopped short of telling him something, and he discovered he was not sure he wanted to know what it was.

Upon their return to the house, Leandra met them at the door. After a dizzy rush of blood to his face, he asked Anna to stay with him for a moment and, for the first time in almost two years, he spoke directly to Leandra.

"I need you at Mount Pleasant to be my hostess. However, I'll not force you to go. You may stay here if you wish. You make the decision." He waited for her answer.

She glanced at Anna, then smiled and said, "I will go."

Two weeks later, Dummett helped the families move into the new cabins at Mount Pleasant and saw to the settling of the unattached men in the barracks. Later, he met with Old Cudjoe, his overseer, and they worked out a division of duties for the men.

Maum Molly helped Leandra with the establishment of the house staff, assigning sleeping quarters to the single women in the small dormitory. Leandra took one of the small bedrooms in the main house. Dummett stayed away from the house, entering only after sundown.

Maum Molly supervised the serving of their first meal at the long, oak dining table, Dummett at one end and Leandra at the other. Cicely carried dishes of food from the kitchen, placing them on a side table where Maum Molly served the plates.

As he swirled the food around on his plate, Dummett kept his head lowered, resisting the desire to look at Leandra, and feeling shame for having that desire. Finally, when he did glance up, he was surprised to find her staring at him. She had not touched her meal.

"I'd think you'd be hungry," he said. "You worked so hard today." She smiled at him, her face blooming into an even lovelier image than he thought possible. "I thought there must be something wrong with the food." she said. "You were only picking at yours."

"No, it's fine. I'm just a little tired today. It's really very good. Look." He forked a slice of ham and aimed it toward his mouth. Halfway there it fell to the table and bounced toward his lap. He caught it in his left hand and stuffed it into his mouth in one motion.

As she burst into laughter, he put a surprised look on his face, saying, "I always eat ham on the first hop."

He leaned back in his chair and smiled at her. "I'm glad you decided to come. You can see I needed the help."

The rest of the evening passed in small talk, mostly about his plans for the plantation. She listened, speaking only when he asked a direct question. He talked as if he were afraid to let silence come between them again.

He was surprised when Maum Molly served a small blackberry cobbler in fresh cream. "How did you pick—"

"Oh, we has our ways, Cap'n Dummett." ." She cut her eyes toward Leandra. "Miss Leandra gets a lot of good out of everyone."

Dummett savored each bite of the cobbler, wondering why he had punished himself for two years without the company of women.

After the meal, he sat for a while, smoking a cigar and watching Leandra help Cicely clean the table. Then he excused himself before she finished and retired to his bedroom, reading by candlelight until past time for him to feel sleepy. Deciding some rum might make him drowsy, he walked into the sitting room, crossing the darkness to the liquor cabinet.

He took the small decanter of rum and turned to go back to his bedroom. Leandra stood near the doorway, wearing only a thin sleeping shift.

Staring into the depths of her green eyes, he felt a sense of vertigo wash over him. With an effort he broke the trance and walked slowly back into his bedroom and removed his robe. Raising the mosquito net, he sat on the edge of the bed. He sensed her presence in the room before he saw her.

"Why?" she asked, stepping from darkness into the faint sphere of candlelight. "Why do you resist my love? You know it's there. Is your shame so strong it overpowers your heart?"

He felt his skin flush as his eyes wavered before her steady, defiant gaze.

Her voice dropped to a whisper. "I am yours now, and I am happy to be. Do you want me to leave?" she asked.

"No," he answered. His throat constricted around the word.

She stepped toward him, letting her shift float to the floor. For a long moment, she stood before him. The flickering candlelight cast an olive sheen to the swell of her dark breasts and lay shadows into the mysterious valleys of her body. Fixing her eyes on his, she entered his bed.

With a strangled cry of anguish, he took her into his arms and pulled the warmth of her long body to his. He seemed paralyzed by contradictions boiling within him, the passion of power and conquest held in check by a tender sense of shielding. As she pressed the mound of her loins against his turgid body, the moisture of her mouth soothed the dryness of his lips. A musky fragrance permeated the tendrils of her hair caressing his face.

Their arms intertwined like the clinging grasp of ivy. The broad muscles of her back rippled beneath his gripping fingers. Taking his hand, she pressed its palm against the taut nipple of her breast. For a moment they lay straining, each against the other, until her exploring hand pressed between them and her fingers found him.

Surrendering to the insistent pressure of her hips, he felt her hand guide him beyond the moist momentary resistance. Then the primal rhythm slowly enveloped him, growing in tempo with the hammering beat of his heart.

The cold light of morning did little to disperse the thin haze of fog from the surface of the river. Dummett sat on an outcropping of coquina rock overlooking the riverbank, sipping a mug of steaming coffee. His favorite bluetick hound lay at his feet.

Leandra was asleep when he rose from the bed, the damp sheet twisted around her long legs, its whiteness stark across her bronze back, except for the vermilion stain of her virginity. Her raven hair spread fanlike across her cheek and pillow. Somehow, her lush body wasn't as provocative as it had been last night, but rather seemed to have a childlike vulnerability as she slept.

Dummett had resisted the urge to return to bed. Instead, he gathered his clothes and left the room.

Now, relaxed on the rock, his mind agitated by the turbulence of his feelings, he relived the passion of their lovemaking. He felt the pall of guilt as he thought of her race and her status as a slave.

He forcibly tried to blank his mind by looking at the river, hoping to submerge his fears in the peaceful scene before him.

Then, he saw a black skimmer flying above the placid surface of the smoky water. Suddenly it stopped the beat of its wings and glided close to the surface. Its orange beak dipped into the water and trailed a widening vee-wake. The beak lifted and Dummett saw the fish it grasped. A few powerful wingbeats lifted the bird in a curving arc toward the mud flats to the south.

The graceful male bird stretched for a landing on the shell nest mounded beyond the grassline. The female moved aside as he settled to regurgitate the fish into the mouths of the nestlings. Mates, Dummett thought. Even the birds mate with like species. He had heard it before: birds of a feather flock together. An old saw—Poor Richard or somebody. He couldn't remember. But did it apply to his relation with Leandra? Were they birds of a feather or were their feathers different? She didn't feel different last night.

He stood, stretched his arms, and then threw the dregs of the coffee into the river. He strolled along the bank toward the mud flats, the hound nuzzling his hand as they walked. The mud flats were covered with the mounded nests of the skimmer colony, each containing eager nestlings, and most guarded by females. He stopped, wondering about his female.

Would she build a nest and would their nestlings be of his species? He remembered his father once describing a particularly intelligent slave. "Almost human," he had said of the slave. Dummett closed his mind to this, refusing to visualize Leandra as not being human. Her body was human, her desires were human, the same as his. The question remained; ignoring society's fiats, was there any wrong in taking her as his mate?

"Hell, no!" he boomed his decision. The hound bolted around into a stiff-legged stance and growled at him. Several of the nearby skimmers looked at him in nervous agitation. He turned and trotted to the house.

As he entered, he yelled, "Leandra."

She stepped to the bedroom doorway, rubbing her eyes.

"Collect your things," he said. "You're moving into my bedroom."

She stared at him for a moment as if stunned. When the realization hit her, she squealed and ran across the room to him. He scooped her into his arms, squeezed her, then set her down. Turning her, he slapped her on the fanny. She stood there as he left the house, wondering what was missing. After a moment she realized that she was waiting in vain for some mention of the word love.

Chapter 7

Dummett left the cane field and headed for the barn. As he walked, he outlined in his mind the work for the rest of the day and his plans for tomorrow, thinking of the many things he must do to tie up the loose ends before grinding the sugarcane.

A haze of smoke drifted in the air, its pungent tang a nagging memory of earlier years when these same fields produced sugar. Yesterday's burn had sent black, oily smoke boiling angrily into the sky. Buzzards and red-shouldered hawks sliced through the swirling, heated air, scooping up rats and rabbits fleeing the line of fire.

Now the rows of cane stood free of scrub and underbrush, denuded of shucks and ready for the cutter's blade. Several small fires still burned, but were being doused with sand. By morning, the fields would be cool and ready for the cutters.

The yellowish orange light filtering through the haze reminded Dummett of the eerie moments before a hurricane. As the stillness preceding a storm promises violence, this light seemed to warn of danger still lurking in the fields. The burn had disturbed snakes. Ants still lived in their hills, ready to spill out onto the cutters like lava from a volcano. Broken cane stalks thrust upward at waist level like rows of spears, capable of piercing the eyes of any man careless in stooping as he cut.

But the long knives were the most threatening. Dummett knew that many of the men would sustain wounds. Most would be minor, but all were subject to infection.

A year's work had culminated in this burn. By March 1842, he had planted four hundred acres in sugar cane, the crop he decided would be the quickest to convert into money. And now, in the humidity of this August, they would begin the harvest.

This first crop was important to Dummett. While he didn't really need the money—and there would be little from a crop so small—the success would be proof that he could manage a working plantation. It seemed to him that he would always be trying to compete against his father's successes.

To this end, Dummett had worked vigorously in the fields, side by side with his lowest field hands.

He snapped out of his musing as he stepped into the clearing where the house stood. Dummett was proud of the way Leandra had asserted herself as mistress of Mount Pleasant. Beset with complaints from the married women over supplies, she found little time to herself. She handled each problem with a wisdom that allowed the women to maintain a sense of pride. When Cicely whined that Old Dorothy, the seamstress, had taken a better bolt of cloth for her own use, Leandra assigned Cicely's daughter, Jenny, as apprentice to Dorothy. When Philips accused Hannah, the cook, of getting more food for her family than the rest of them, Leandra assigned Philips' elderly mother, Delia, the job of accounting for, and distributing, the supplies to the quarters.

As other spiteful jealousies rose to the top of the social unit like scum on a pond, Dummett knew she dealt with them instantly, yet with justice, solidifying her position as mistress in the eyes of the servants.

Leandra now had the household whipped into shape, with all areas meshing like well-oiled cogs. Dummett was pleased—no, he was relieved—that Leandra could contend with those problems leaving him free to concentrate on the plantation. With women living together this close, he knew Leandra wasted a doubloon's worth of energy in solving every two-bit problem.

Going to the lot behind the barn, he checked the little mill one last time, a Fairbanks he had retrieved from the ruins of Dunn-Lawton. His men had dismantled it and scoured all the rust from the three cast iron rollers and their gears. The machinery had been greased and could now be turned by hand. Mounted on a massive tripod of thick cypress trunks, it was to be driven by the men. As one crew walked an endless circle turning the long radius beam connected to the gears, another crew would feed the cane into the rollers to be crushed. The juice would then run down the sluice into pails to be carried to the kettles.

Grabbing the radius beam, Dummett walked a quarter circle, smiling in satisfaction at its smooth operation. He could do no more to prepare for the grinding. Releasing the beam, he turned and walked to the house.

Leandra saw him coming and ran to the kitchen, telling Hannah to cut some ham and spread ground mustard sauce over it while she sliced a loaf of fresh bread. Checking her appearance, she pulled off her apron, then rushed back into the sitting room where she was casually dusting a table when Dummett entered.

"I'm hungry enough to eat a cow," he said, throwing his hat on the table. Leandra picked it up and hung it on its peg by the door.

"Maybe we can find some scraps for you in an hour or so." She smiled as Hannah brought in a pewter tray of ham slices and a glass of fresh buttermilk.

Waiting until Hannah left the room, he wrapped his arms around Leandra and squeezed. Holding her breath for a moment with her eyes closed, she rubbed her cheek against his bearded face, then pulled gently away to hold back a chair for him. "Captain Dummett, what will people say? It's the middle of the day."

"What they don't see they can't talk about." He sat and forked up a mouthful of ham. "We need to host a dinner party," he said. He glanced up, enjoying her look of surprise. "You have this place running as well as any in New Smyrna. Might as well show it off." He stuffed the rest of the slice of ham into his mouth.

"That would be nice. When would you—"

"Soon as the sugar's made," he said, rising and striding to the door. "Nice lunch." He jammed his hat on his head and was out the door before she could respond.

Burnham pulled steadily on the oars, feeling the strain on muscles unused to labor in recent years. Glancing across his shoulder at the pall of smoke rising above Mount Pleasant, he sculled an oar to swing the skiff's bow more in line with the dock. Almost there, he felt he was running out of time. He had been planning his argument since leaving Jacksonville two days earlier, but the time approached when he would have to present it.

Early in 1841 the Federal Congress had passed the Armed Occupation Act, unlocking the door of opportunity to any that had the guts to push it open.

Colonel Samuel Peck, Seth's brother, had approached Burnham with his scheme the day the news of the act reached Jacksonville.

"Basically, anyone can file on a quarter section anywhere south of Pilatka," he explained to Burnham. "All we have to do is defend it, with force if necessary, for seven years. But one man alone hasn't got a chance." Peck proposed a selective colony—many families banding together into a community of mutual support. Burnham's imagination soared, aroused by the simple idea.

"It's not a novel concept," Peck said with modesty. "Oglethorpe planned the Georgian colony of Federica on St. Simons Island in the same manner."

Within a year, the two men had enlisted commitments from men offering a cross-section of talents in the craft of community survival. A hunter, carpenters, sailors, a cobbler, a physician—all were seduced by the heady glow of opportunity.

Others, with less to offer, saw the primitive existence as a possible restorative to lost health or simply as an adventure. Forty men answered the call, committing themselves and their families to the experiment, pledging their strengths and assets to its success.

The volunteers levied an initial tax on themselves to buy basic tools to be warehoused against the day of departure. Axes, hoes, adzes, hemp rope, shovels—these were bought in bulk and stored with sacks of vegetable seed, bolts of cloth, paraffin, lead and powder.

Each colonist filed his homestead petition through Peck on land lying along the Indian River, from the Sebastian River south to the narrows above the ocean inlet at Fort Jupiter. Land allocations were planned to provide mutual protection. Burnham was surprised at Peck's organizational skills and equally surprised when everything worked out as the man had predicted.

He and Colonel Peck discussed Dummett for over an hour one gloomy afternoon in St. Augustine.

"He'll be the one man we can depend on if any problems arise with the Indians," Burnham told Peck. "He knows more than anyone about handling men in times of defense. By far, he's the most powerful ally we could find."

Burnham left Jacksonville the next morning on a steamer bound for New Smyrna. Upon his arrival, he rented a skiff and now found himself approaching the plantation lying beneath a cloak of smoke.

As he tied the skiff to the dock at Mount Pleasant, he was surprised to see a new home standing on the same Indian mound where he and Dummett had retrieved the silver cache four years earlier.

He walked up the sloping lawn and knocked on the door. After a few minutes with no answer, he walked around the house in time to see Dummett leaving the barn carrying an ax.

"Ho, Dummett," he yelled.

Dummett dropped the head of the ax to the ground and leaned on the handle, staring at Burnham for a long moment. Then Dummett recognized him, yelled and sprinted toward him. He grabbed Burnham in a bear hug and lifted him from the ground.

"By Jupiter, it's good to see you," he said, setting the tall man down.

Dummett's appearance surprised Burnham. He had expected to see the clean, well-dressed gentleman from St. Augustine of two years ago.

Instead, he faced a grimy field hand. The same black whiskers he wore at their long ago first meeting at Fort Heileman still framed Dummett's grin, although the hairy brush was now speckled with gray.

The two men walked to the well beside the kitchen where Dummett sluiced the dirt from his face and arms.

"Come in the house and let's put your stuff away." Dummett led him through the breezeway into the house.

After taking Burnham's valise into a bedroom, Dummett returned to the sitting room where he jerked a bellpull. In a few moments the door opened and Leandra walked in. Burnham jumped to his feet. "Miss Fernandez, I didn't—" Snatching off his hat, he bowed slightly. "It's good to see you again."

"Thank you, sir," she said. "Please sit down, Captain Burnham. I'll get you some lunch. Please rest."

While she was gone, Dummett told him of rebuilding Mount Pleasant and the movement of the people to the plantation.

"I heard of your father's death," Burnham said.

Dummett frowned as he recounted that last dreadful scene with his father. "I blamed myself so long for his death, but time is a healer. I lost myself in work. Then, when Leandra said she wanted to come here I became the happiest man alive."

"Did Anna and your mother come down?"

"You mean, `Did Leandra come here alone?'"

Burnham felt his face flush. "No, I didn't mean that. But..."

Dummett smiled. "No. Anna and Mother didn't come. And, to get it out in the open, Leandra is sharing my bed and my life."

"You're married?"

"No. No words have been said except between us. Hell, we haven't even jumped over a broom. But it's the same as marriage, although that's no longer a problem. Frances, my wife, got her divorce through a Georgia court and married her army officer—my old buddy." He scratched a match on the sole of his boot and lit the stub of a cigar. "The even flow of my life's been disturbed forever by the treachery of a friend," he said, smiling through the wreath of blue smoke. "And I thank the Lord for it."

Leandra returned, laying out a lunch for Burnham on the table. Then she excused herself and left.

Burnham sat and attacked the ham and potato salad with gusto. As he ate, he outlined his proposition to Dummett.

"You'll get a quarter-section of land free and clear. Our deal is that, within the colony, we'll operate on a barter system, exchanging notes for services rendered, one account canceling the other. As hard money becomes available, outstanding notes will be recouped. We've got some-one who can handle almost any kind of service a family might need, at least until we're all up and operating. Hunters, cobblers, tanners, black-smiths—you name it, we've got someone who can handle it. Except lead-ership. That's why we need you."

"Leadership? Sounds to me like someone's been doing some damn good planning to get this thing rolling."

Burnham nodded his agreement. "Peck's as good as they come. He's a visionary. But, in a crisis, we'll need someone with strength. Someone like you."

"You are someone like me. I think you've got a workable venture out-lined, but it's not for me," Dummett told him. "I have almost everything I could ever hope for—right here. Within the year, this place'll be showing a profit. Hell, I'm not hurting for anything now. Besides, I've got some-thing most of you don't have—my niggers." He laughed.

Burnham felt a pulse begin to pound in his throat and his face felt inflamed. "You're right. I don't own any man, and no man owns me."

"Don't bristle, Burnham. I was laughing more at my situation than any-thing. Leandra's constantly asking for her freedom and wants me to free the whole damn bunch. Wants to be my woman one minute and wants to be free the next." He jumped to his feet. "Eat up. I'll show you my sugar project."

During the next week, Dummett began grinding his cane, but took one night off for a coon hunt with Burnham. Their other evenings were spent playing checkers. While Dummett was no match for him, Leandra sur-prisingly trounced Burnham two games in a row. She then begged off from a third battle, leaving them to wonder if her success was the luck of a beginner or skill.

One morning, as they were watching a crew cutting firewood, Dummett beckoned a young Negro to them.

"Jackson, this is the Captain Burnham I told you about."

Burnham studied the young man. He appeared to be in his early twen-ties, slender, but with muscle weaving across his arms and shoulders like straps.

"Burnham, I'd like for Jackson to go south with you when you make the move, to work for you and help you. It'd certainly help him."

"You know how I feel about that. I couldn't own—"

"Hell fire," Dummett laughed. "You're always jumping to the wrong conclusion. Jackson's a freedman. And so is Martha, his wife."

"Then what—"

"I wants to be your hired man," Jackson said. "I works hard. You gonna be needin' me."

"Why do you want to leave here?" Burnham asked the man.

Dummett interrupted. "Jackson and his wife are prime targets for poachers. Slave traders are moving all up and down between here and Jacksonville. With the Seminoles shipped out, a lot of their niggers who got away are living out in these woods. The poachers are having a field day capturing them and selling them in Georgia."

"Done," Burnham said instantly. He turned to Jackson. "You'll not get rich working for me, but you and your wife will have a place to live and you'll be your own man. I'll send word to you when we move." He offered the young man his hand. Jackson hesitated a moment, looked at Dummett, then grasped the hand.

Burnham left later that morning for home.

By the end of October, Dummett had finished the grinding and cooked the syrup. With only two boiling kettles instead of the usual six, he took his time, slowly ladling the syrup back and forth between the kettles, controlling the heat until it cooked to a thick sludge. Storing it in oak kegs, he let the molasses seep out for several days. Then he cut the damp sugar into cakes and packed them back into the kegs. These were hauled across the river by canoe and shipped from New Smyrna to Savannah. The molasses was poured into clay jars, to be used as sweetener by the servants and to run off an occasional jug of rum in the small still he built in the barn.

The day he received payment for the shipment of sugar, he rushed into the house, called Leandra, and flung three sacks of doubloons onto the table.

"Now you can have your dinner party," he announced.

Chapter 8

Leandra set her grand dinner party plans into motion at once. The good dishes she had brought from St. Augustine were washed and wiped until they gleamed. A menu was planned: seafood courses, a peppery chowder, a beef roasted in the English manner, encased in a batter and slow baked and accompanied by a rich Yorkshire pudding. An orange chiffon cake with crushed wild strawberries would be the meal's culminating dessert.

Dummett acquired a small keg of fine India Brandy. Ebo Thom, one of his most talented and creative hands, was put to work converting the new molasses into dark, golden rum.

Invitations were hand printed, and Dummett delivered them himself to several of New Smyrna's leading families. When the Indian War was at its hottest, most of the planters along the coast had abandoned their property, moving to St. Augustine for safety. However, a stubborn few had returned early: the Sheltons at the hotel and a few others who would rather defend their property than risk losing it. Even Judge Dunham was staying at the hotel in preparation for rebuilding his plantation.

The afternoon of the party, Leandra began her many last minute checks long before sunset. Several lamps burning sweet oil lighted the main room. A new, white linen cloth covered the long table. Cicely, Phillis and Caesar had been drilled for days in the proper mode of serving dishes and drinks.

Old Dorothy had altered one of Dummett's old coats for Caesar and she had sewn new black dresses for Cicely and Phillis. Phillis' dress, with its stiff, white linen apron, enhanced her tall, slender body. The bodice was elegantly touched with lace at the throat and wrists. Cicely's dress, exactly the same, fit her dumpy body as if it were made of flour sacks.

As the hour of the guest's arrival approached, Leandra made one more trip to the looking glass in her bedroom. She found Cicely before the mirror, pressing her hand over her face, caressing it and whispering to its reflection. Cicely smiled at herself as she stroked her arm, seeming to be entranced with the smooth, soft skin. Leandra backed in silence from the room and waited until Cicely came out.

"My, you look lovely in that dress," Leandra said, watching the smile on the girl's homely face grow into a glow that threatened to light the room. When Leandra checked herself in the mirror, she could sympathize with Cicely. She, too, felt lovely in the gown Old Dorothy had made for her. A green silk, as delicate and pale as Spanish moss, its soft sheen enhancing the coppery tones of her skin and balancing the deep emerald of her eyes. Her only jewelry was a gold chain, hanging across her full breasts, shimmering its soft yellow around her slender neck. The bouffant skirt, slashed with darker hues of jade, fit tightly at her slim waist, her pregnancy still a well-kept secret, a secret she would gladly share with Dummett after the party.

"Folks a'coming," Cicely squealed.

Leandra hoisted her skirt above her ankles and ran into the main room, joining Dummett at the window to watch their guests arrive. Big Will and Ebo Pompey, both sporting new livery outfits, were helping three people from a sailboat to the dock.

A few minutes later, Ebo Pompey opened the door and announced Mr. and Mrs. John Shelton, and Judge Dunham. Dummett greeted them, shaking hands with the men.

"And I'd like to present my Hostess, Leandra—"

"Mrs. Dummett. Your servant, Ma'am." John Shelton bowed low from the waist and took her hand. Leandra felt her face flush as she waited for Dummett to correct the mistake. He didn't. Instead he held out his arm to Mrs. Shelton and escorted her to the long couch by the window. Leandra struggled to regain her composure.

Soon, the room filled with people. The last to arrive were Mr. and Mrs. Thomas Williams, a planter from the Spruce Creek region. His elderly, widowed aunt, Mrs. Augustus Roney, and her maid accompanied him. After Mrs. Roney settled onto the couch, Leandra directed the maid to the kitchen.

The men stood near the fireplace, sipping small glasses of the heady blackstrap rum while exchanging small talk of planting matters. Dummett's plum-colored linen suit hugged his form like a kid glove, exacting admiring side-glances from all the women in attendance. Leandra felt deep satisfaction in the knowledge that she belonged to him.

Still experiencing a mild state of euphoria, Leandra watched with pride as Cicely and Phillis served tea to the ladies with practiced ease. And Caesar, so elegant in his black coat, hovering near the men, unobtrusively refilling any glass that came close to being empty.

"My dear Mrs. Dummett, your home is marvelous. And those girls— my, they are so efficient, so...well trained."

Realizing that Mrs. Williams was speaking to her, Leandra was slowly pulled from her reverie. "Excuse me?" Then realizing what the lady had said, she answered, "Oh, yes. They're just perfect."

"I wish I could train my Sukie as well," Mrs. Williams continued. "She's a breed, you know—half Seminole, half nigra. She can't learn anything. Washing and cleaning, that's about all. Oh, sometimes I send her to market but..."

"They're all so slow to learn," another gushed. Cicely, pouring tea into Leandra's cup, glanced up at Leandra as if expecting something. She frowned after the moment passed and moved away toward the door leading out to the kitchen.

In a few minutes, Maum Molly opened the door slightly and caught Caesar's eye. He walked gravely to a side table, rang a small brass bell and announced; "Dinnah is served."

The gentlemen sat their glasses on the side table and crossed the room to assist their ladies. Leandra was moving toward Mrs. Roney to help her when the woman's maid entered the room. Leandra moved back a pace when the maid leaned close to Mrs. Roney and whispered something. The widow's face blanched, and she stared at Leandra with widened eyes.

"Excuse me," she said in a quivering voice. She turned to Mrs. Williams and spoke quietly. Leandra saw a look of shock cloud Mrs. Williams' eyes.

Leandra looked around the room for Dummett, but he was still over by the fireplace. She threaded her way through the men toward him. By the time she reached his side, all of the guests were grouped at the other end of the room, standing quiet and unmoving. Dummett looked up and saw them.

"Come now, Ladies...Gentlemen. Everyone to your places. Dinner might get..."

"I'm sorry, Dummett, but I've been called back home unexpectedly." Thomas Williams' fierce eyes glowed in the bright room. Leandra moved back into the shadows in the corner.

"There hasn't been anyone come in..." Realization darkened Dummett's face as he saw everyone gathering up belongings and edging toward the door. "Williams, you're lying. What's the deal here, man?" He stalked across the room.

"Now, there's no need for a scene," Williams said, his statement supported by a low murmur from the other men.

"The hell there's not. What's going on?" he yelled, startling the man back closer to the others.

"If you're so insensitive that you pretend you don't know, then I'm sure telling you will serve no end." By now most of the guests had left the room and Williams turned to leave. Dummett grabbed him by the shoulder and spun him around. "Dammit, you're in my home. You're going to tell—"

"As you wish, sir, but out of your home," Williams said, backing through the door. Outside, he walked over to where the other men were clustered. Leandra stepped through the door behind Dummett, but stayed close by the house. Williams turned to Dummett.

"You invited us to a social function and, under false pretenses, foisted a slave upon us as your wife."

"Dammit man, I never told you she was my wife." Leandra could hear the rage in Dummett's voice.

"But sir," Williams continued through gritted teeth, "you never told us she wasn't. We thought she was white. The biggest insult was to our wives. White women do not have social intercourse with a nigra concubine."

Dummett screamed and lunged for Williams' throat with both hands.

As he struggled to get a better hold, several of the men grasped him, shoving him away from Williams.

He stood then, facing the men, his fists clenching and unclenching. "By Jupiter, if I've insulted you, then call me out, you bastard. Let's have at it," he yelled.

Williams was loosening his cravat from his throat. "No," he said. "I'll not fight because of a nigra wench."

"Then I'll call you out, you coward. Any of you." He pointed his finger at Williams. "And I'll kill you on sight if you don't fight."

Judge Dunham stepped forward. "Dummett, you'll probably see this better when your head has cooled." He paused and shook his head. "I've known you and liked you for many years, but be warned. If you kill anyone, I'll hang you."

With that, the group turned and walked to the dock.

Dummett stalked back to the house on stiff legs. He stopped when he saw Leandra. "It's not your fault," he said through gritted teeth. "It's mine, for thinking I could have you and keep my friends." As she held out a hand to him, he brushed past her and stormed into the house. Moments later, she heard the dinner table crash to the floor.

She walked to the dock and stood in the deep shadows, listening to the voices from the sailboats across the dark water. After an hour, all was still and quiet. She returned to the house and lay on the couch. Sobbing, she huddled with knees drawn to her chest until sleep deadened the pain.

She was the whitest person living in the land of white people, until her face began to turn black, then blacker until the people were following her everywhere, pointing and jeering, shoving and laughing, until...

Dummett nuzzled her cheek, waking her and holding her as she jerked herself up from the couch into the light of a new day.

"Relax. Everything's all right." He held her in his arms. Feeling the tension flow from her body, she nestled her head into his shoulder.

They sat entwined for awhile, each feeding on the emotional contact with the other. Finally, Dummett rose and lifted her to her feet. Maum Molly entered the room carrying a pot of coffee and two cups.

Dummett poured their coffee as Leandra sat. "What in hell happened last night?"

Silence quivered before Leandra's eyes while her thoughts raced back over the evening's events. Dummett watched her as if he were reading those thoughts.

"You know, don't you," he said.

"Yes." She scraped a spoonful from the sugar cone and stirred it into her coffee. Finally, with resignation in her voice, she said, "I guess someone in the kitchen took offense at something I said...or didn't say. In the kitchen they say what they feel. Apparently one of them said something and Mrs. Roney's maid learned I was colored. I saw her whisper something to the old woman just before it all broke loose."

"Then it had to be Cicely or Phillis. They're the only ones who could have—" He jerked to his feet, overturning his chair. "Damn it to hell, I'll sell every nigger in that kitchen."

"No! Please, no." She looked up at him as tears overflowed her eyes. Remembering how Colonel Dummett had sold the young slave for telling her she was a Negro, Leandra felt a cold fear in her stomach.

She inhaled deeply and held it as she spoke, knowing she was again violating the cardinal rule of being a colored woman; never speak of freedom to the master. "They're family. If anything, you should free them, not sell them."

"Family be damned. They're slaves and they've crossed my path with trouble."

"Would you sell your son?" she asked, letting her breath ease from her burning lungs.

"I don't have a son who's a slave," he retorted. Almost instantly she could see awareness cross his face. He stared at her for an interminable time, the question unasked, but hanging in the air between them like an incubus. What should have been a moment of joy was turning into a continuation of her nightmare.

Gathering her resolution within herself, she stared deep into his eyes. "He *will* be your slave if you don't do something about it," she said. "I am with child."

His brow furrowed as the statement sank into his mind. He turned from her and walked across the room to stare out the window. When he turned back toward her, a sense of relief flooded over her. He was smiling.

"How do you know it's to be a son?" he asked walking back to his chair.

"It wouldn't dare be anything else," she answered in a quivering voice. He reached toward her and stroked her hair. She leaned her face into his hand. "Promise me," she begged, "not to be angry toward the women. Let me handle the problem."

He sat and poured some coffee into his saucer. Lifting it to his lips, he winced at its heat, then smiled. "Suits me," he said. "Hell, with you being pregnant, getting fat and lazy, I guess we're going to need all the help we can get around here."

That afternoon Leandra rang the bell and Cicely came in from the kitchen.

"Walk with me along the river," Leandra said while tying the strings of her bonnet.

Cicely walked quietly behind Leandra beneath the pines. Leandra waited to speak until they reached the rocks overlooking the mud flats. She sat and patted the rock beside her. "Sit here and let's talk," she said.

Cicely turned her eyes to the skimmer nests on the mud flats. She sat on the rounded edge of the coquina rock.

"Was it the woman saying colored women are slow to learn that made you so angry?" Leandra asked softly.

"No'm." Cicely continued to stare into space.

Sure of herself now, Leandra rested her hand on Cicely's shoulder. "I am so sorry," she said. "I didn't have the nerve to dispute the woman. I was lost in myself, in the glory of the moment, of being Mrs. Dummett. I should have—"

Cicely began to cry, huge sobs wringing from her soul as if she were losing it. "Miss Leandra, I—I called you a nigger—that gal was in there, in the kitchen—I knew soon's I said it she—they didn't know..." Wrapping her arms around her head, she bent at the waist and buried her face in her knees.

Leandra lifted Cicely's head and wiped the sobbing woman's damp face with her handkerchief. Then she eased her arms around Cicely's shoulders and hugged her tightly. "Shush, now. It's all right. It's over and nobody was really hurt. Captain Dummett lost his temper, but he needs that now and then." She chuckled. "And you and I both learned a lesson. It's over."

Looking up, Cicely tried to smile through eyes awash with tears. "Missy, you is the best. Ain't nobody ever gonna to call you nigger again and live if I knows about it."

Leandra touched the girl's cheek, tracing her finger along the jaw line. "Shush now," she said again. "I just want you to be the same Cicely I've always loved."

As the new year of 1844 began, Leandra finally felt secure in her position as mistress of Mount Pleasant. Apparently, Cicely had become her knight-errant and the entire entourage of servants had been won to her. She had never been treated with more respect and deference than now. Ironically, it was almost as if they belonged to her rather than to Dummett.

On a balmy February day, she and Cicely crossed the river in the *Flying Fish*, the new cypress canoe Dummett had built. Marsh, a young Negro whose arms were the size of most men's legs, was in charge of a crew of five other young giants whose main duties were to power the vessel faster than any other on the river.

Upon reaching New Smyrna, Leandra and Cicely walked to the outdoor market, a series of stalls where merchants and farmers sold their goods.

Leandra held the basket close to her swelling stomach as she studied vegetables in a stall. Cicely stood beside her, balancing and weighing yams in her hands, her leathery face clouded with a look of indecision.

"Well, you done got one cookin' in de oven, ain'cha, honey?"

Leandra knew without looking that it was Sukie, the half-Seminole slave from the Williams plantation. Leandra had seen the girl at the market on two occasions months earlier. Sukie had never shown open contempt for Leandra in their past meetings, but Leandra always felt a hatred lying in the girl's heart, just below the surface. She pulled the basket closer to her stomach, stood more erect, and moved down the walkway toward Cicely without answering.

"Is de little bastard goin' to be white lak his daddy?" Sukie followed along behind Leandra, giggling as she reached forward and gave Leandra a slight nudge.

"Here now, girl. You stop dat," Cicely shouted. "You got no call to mess wif Miss Leandra."

"Hooty tooty, now. Miss Leandra. Lordy, Lordy, she done turnt com-shittin'-pletely white now." Sukie howled with laughter and poked Leandra again.

Leandra turned, her face tightening with the anger commencing to simmer within her. "Don't touch me again or you'll pay for it."

"How you gonna make me pay? Maybe you gets yore master to have me beat. Or sold. Maybe you gets him to buy me. Maybe he'd lak to make a baby in my belly better'n he done yores." She laughed as two other colored women came over to watch the fun.

"Bad 'nuff when house niggers think dey better'n field hands." Sukie curled her lip. "Bitch lak you dat lay fo' de white master, you ain't worth livin'." She raised her voice for her audience. "Means you crazy in de head. Next thang, you think you is de wife, married and white yoself. You ain't nothin' but a punk, a ho', selling yoself for nothin'."

Leandra stood silent, eyes burning as she stared at her tormentor for a long moment.

"White men sneaks into de quarters late at night," the girl continued, "and slinks out befo' daylight, but de women don't hump and live in de master's bed. You does, and with dat crazy, bastard, injun killer of all..."

Cicely's fist slammed into Sukie's eye, snapping her head sideways. She lost her balance and fell backwards into a stall of onions.

Tears welled, then spilled from Leandra's eyes, running down cheeks no longer taut as resignation replaced her anger. Without a word, she turned and left the market with Cicely scurrying after her. At the shell road, they walked south, toward the dock at the old fort.

"Bitch," she heard Sukie screaming behind her. "All de white folks, de white women lak Miz Williams, ain't none of 'em wants nothin' to do with dat nigger-humpin' Dummett. I done heard 'em talkin'. You de nothin' ho' of a nothin'."

Leandra walked at almost a trot, her legs feeling stiff and awkward. She heard Cicely running to keep up, but, like a blessing, she could no longer hear the strident taunts of Sukie. It seemed an eternity before she reached the dock where Marsh helped her into the canoe. Cicely sat wordless, clenching and opening her fists, all the way home.

All the next week, Leandra stayed in the house. Maum Molly took over the duty of shopping at the market in New Smyrna, but when she returned from her first trip her old head was bowed to her dried chest.

"Dey done it agin, chile," she said. "But it warn't just Sukie. It was all of 'em dis time. Dey cut you up lak fatback."

"We can't mention it to Captain Dummett," Leandra told her.

The following Thursday, Dummett crossed to New Smyrna to attend court. He returned by mid-afternoon. Even though she caught only a glimpse of him as he stomped past the house on his way to the slave quarters, Leandra saw rage clouding his features like a storm. She slipped out the back door where she could hear.

"Cudjoe!" he shouted. "Cudjoe, get out here!" When the overseer came running out, Dummett slammed his hat into the dirt.

"I want everyone packed and ready to leave by morning. I want all the tools boxed. I want all the household goods, the furniture—everything—loaded into the wagons and ready to move by daybreak." He kicked his hat, then stomped to a nearby tree and drove his foot against its trunk. He spun back around.

"The women'll travel in the canoes. Assign two men to each canoe to paddle. The rest of us, men and wagons, will go on the barge. We'll come back later for the stock."

"Where is we goin'?" Cudjoe asked. "And why?"

"I'm selling my share of the damned place to my brother-in-law. I'm not living around people who think they can talk to me any way they want without a killing happening." Spotting Leandra, he paused. "We're going to live at Dummett Cove on Merritt's Island." He stepped toward her.

Much of the rage was gone from his voice, replaced with resignation as he took her into his arms. "And to hell with them all."

BOOK THREE

1844 — 1853

BOOK THREE

Chapter 9

Beyond the bar at the Indian River Inlet, the schooner *William Washington* lay dead in the water, her canvas up but slatting uselessly in the still, morning air. The sun was high enough above the horizon to glint shards of metallic reflections from the rolling surge of the ocean.

Several families clustered on the foredeck to catch these first views of their new home. Frances and Junior stood hand-in-hand at the rail while Burnham held the three-year-old George on his shoulder, the boy enthralled at the prospect of sailing through the shallow inlet into the Indian River. Beside him, Mary cradled the baby, Katherine, to her bare breast, taking advantage of the stability of the ship as Captain Pinkham waited for the land breeze and the change of tidal current through the inlet.

Burnham looked astern where three other large schooners lay at the ready. The cargo holds of all four vessels were stacked flush to the decks with building materials, home furnishings, and tools—all the necessary goods for subsistence in this new venture.

Burnham felt the first caress against his cheek of an offshore breeze building from the east. He walked back to the stern, stood George on the deck between his legs, and leaned against the taffrail.

"Won't be long now," he said to the lounging captain. "Do you figure on the bar giving us enough draft?"

"Oh, we'll get across with no trouble," replied Captain Pinkham. "The bar shifts over the years but the soundings I made yesterday evening were nigh the same as at Matanzas Inlet."

Colonel Samuel Peck and Ossian Hart, son of Isaiah, walked around the cabin to the stern.

"Captain, Mr. Hart is concerned as to whether the Indian River is deep enough for navigation," Peck said. "Can you explain it to him?" Peck, the head of the Indian River Colony, took the arm of the delicate appearing young man and pushed him slightly forward.

Pinkham chuckled, looked from Burnham to Hart, and said, "Ain't you men got nothin' better to do than to worry about my job? I been in here twice, to Fort Capron right across from the inlet, and on down to Fort Pierce, about four miles. In the river, the channels between the islands are narrow, but the tide flow sucks water through the slots like a millrace, scouring them deep. The river *is* shallow everywhere else, but we'll off-load your goods to shallowdraft boats. Won't pose no problem."

Burnham sat on a box, shifting George to his knee. Leaning back against the transom, he relaxed, willing his muscles free of the tension built from the days at sea. He looked at the men, Peck and Hart, then let his gaze shift forward to others at the bow—his new neighbors and partners in this brave endeavor.

Brave? He didn't see any bravery on his part. This colony was his chance to slip the bonds of poverty. Others were in much the same straits. But for men of wealth like Peck and Hart to abandon the comforts of home and business, to uproot their families to homestead a wilderness, seemed to be a reckless temptation of fate.

Burnham shifted his position on the box and studied Peck as he stood looking down the beach to the south. Samuel was the brother of Dr. Seth Peck and Captain Fenn Peck of the *Essayons*. Burnham had not seen Fenn since his first day at Fort Heileman, but had heard of the sinking of the valiant little steamer. Though brothers, Samuel and Fenn were as different as a dust devil and a hurricane. Samuel was small and erect, and he didn't walk like other men—he marched. Burnham considered him to be the closest to a military martinet he had ever known. Most of the people aboard were dressed in wrinkled, frumpy clothes after the many days on the ship. Peck wore his immaculate clothes as if dressed in a military uniform. The cane he carried as a swagger stick accentuated the illusion.

While sure of Peck's organizational skills, Burnham had dire reservations about the man's ability to lead such a diverse, headstrong group through times of hardship. The men of the colony were each in their own way uniquely self-motivated. That was probably their strength, and yet it might well prove to be the weakness of the group. Peck had a military background and Burnham knew the man had wanderlust, having moved his family many times in the last several years. Would he stay here and see the homestead process through?

As he thought of the other men, Burnham realized that none had the powerful personality needed to mold the colony into a capable unit. Without a strong leader, the colony would never conquer the Florida wilderness. If they lost Peck?

Captain Pinkham jumped to his feet as the schooner lurched sideways in the grip of the rising tide. In only a few moments more, the sails filled with the fresh offshore breeze. Orders flew across the deck and men leaped to their stations, getting the vessel under way.

The *Flying Fish*, skimmed swiftly over the dark water of the Indian River, driven by the powerful oar thrusts of six Negroes. From his position in the stern of the cypress canoe, Dummett watched the rhythmic dipping of the oars and thought of a water beetle scurrying across the surface. The bright, morning sun reflected mahogany sheen from the bare backs of his men.

The work had gone well this morning. The trees they had grafted were just beginning their sap flow, and he knew the grafts would take nicely. During the past month he had transplanted several hundred trees purchased from Hibernia Plantation. By his latest count he had over four thousand bearing trees. After another good week, he would be able to rest and the men could catch up on their gardens and domestic chores.

More than forty grown men now worked the place. The women and children brought the population to well over a hundred, causing logistics problems in their care. Leandra, however, was efficiently handling most of these problems as she had done at Mount Pleasant. The profit from last season's orange crop had enabled her to buy new osnaburg cloth for the women to sew into work pants and shirts for the men. The trees he had grafted should begin to bear mature fruit next season, doubling his income from the groves. The quality of life at Dummett Cove would soon match that of Mount Pleasant.

Dummett lay the tiller over, aiming the canoe toward the dock in Dummett Cove.

The men shipped their oars as the canoe glided to the tee-shaped dock. Dummett sprang out and hurried to the storage shed. "Get these seedling pots loaded," he yelled to Cudjoe. "I'll be back in a jiffy."

He strode up the shell path to the house, following the smell of oak burning in the fireplace. At the door the odor changed to the mouth-watering scent of bread baking in the Dutch oven.

In the months since their arrival at Dummett Cove, Leandra had turned the old house into a home. The walls and floor were made from the heartwood of Merritt's Island pine, so hard he called it Merritt's Island mahogany. The floors had been scrubbed until they gleamed with a clean, yellow hue. New curtains had been sewn and hung. A rug, woven from rags, now covered the trapdoor that led to the fresh-water cachement below the house.

Dummett slipped through the door and tiptoed toward Leandra's pregnant form stooping to swing the Dutch oven from the coals.

She spoke without looking around. "You smell bad. Even if I hadn't heard you, I would have known you were here from the stench of sulfur. What have you been doing?"

Dummett changed directions and slid into a chair at the table. He reached for a loaf of fresh bread cooling on a rack. "I stumbled into that artesian well at the new grove."

She stood and pressed her hands into the small of her back while she leaned back, stretching. Glancing over her shoulder, she saw him holding the loaf and squealed, slapping at his hand. "You must eat yesterday's first."

He grinned. "That's all right. I'm hungry as a bear."

Leandra took the fresh loaf to the breadbox and removed yesterday's half-loaf. At the table, she sliced through the golden crust with a wide, butcher knife.

"Not a bear," she said. "A panther."

Dummett stuffed the first slice whole into his mouth, poking at the edges until it all went in. "What?" he mumbled, scattering crumbs across the table?

"A panther," she said. Easing down into a chair, she took his hand in hers, rubbing her fingers across the calluses on his palms. A bright smile fired the jade of her eyes. "I have found your totem," she said. "In you lives the heart of the swamp cat."

He searched her face, waiting for the joke. When he realized she was serious, he shook his head. "Nigger talk," he said, wishing he hadn't when she winced at the words.

"I'm sorry," he said. "All right. I'm a panther. So, what are you?"

She was silent for a moment, then smiled her forgiveness. "I am controlled by the rhythms of the hawk."

He grabbed another slice of the bread. "At least you can fly when you're tired. Us panthers get hungry running around on four legs."

He abruptly stood and glanced at the bed, then back at Leandra. He grinned and shook his head. "No time," he argued with himself. "Gotta get back to work."

As he left the house, he heard the silvery tinkle of her laughter.

Burnham stared at the stump as if concentration alone would move it. For over an hour, he and the young Negro, Jackson, had pried and chopped and pried some more before the stump released its grip on the earth and popped out like an over-ripe tooth.

"If we both have to drag it out of the way, we'll be wasting time." Burnham looked up at the dirt-streaked man. "One of us should get rid of the stumps while the other starts digging on the next one."

"But Cap'n, it gonna take both of us to drag that chunk through the sand. It must weigh over a hundred pounds."

"Dragging it through the sand will make it seem more like three hundred." Burnham grabbed the stump and turned it around, breathing heavily from the exertion. "There's got to be a better way. Maybe lifting it is best."

"No way you gonna lift that," Jackson said, shaking and brushing sand from his hair.

All his life Burnham had been stronger than most men, but now he wondered how any man, or any two men, could lift this stump.

He spat on his hands and rubbed them together. Squatting before the stump, he found two opposing roots that he grasped. Pausing for a moment, he drew in a deep breath. Then, shoving against the ground with his legs while jerking upward with his arms, he snatched the stump from the ground, ducked under it and again thrust with his legs and arms. Then he was fully erect, with the stump at the end of his upstretched arms, and it seemed to be only a slight burden.

Keeping his balance, he staggered to the edge of the field and let it slam down into a cleared area, the beginning of a pile. Trying to rub the soreness from his arms, he walked back to help Jackson attack the next stump.

They labored until they could no longer see, finally quitting when Burnham realized one of them might be injured in the waning light. He walked over to the pile and counted—eighteen stumps, eighteen hundred pounds. Old Captain Fenn Peck had nailed it right to the church door— *"Welcome to Floridy, Lieutenant. You is now a mule."* Burnham chuckled. Peck would fill his drawers if he could see him now.

Jackson was grinning at him. In the dusk, his white teeth glowed like piano ivories. "We done good, Cap'n," he said.

The two men slumped their way toward the camp under the yellow lantern of the rising full moon.

Dummett sat outside on the porch, his face bathed by the unseasonably cool air of the August night. He leaned forward, trying to look through the oil-papered window but seeing nothing, then lowered his head into his hands. A flurry of noise from within the house caused him to quickly raise his head in expectation. When he realized that no one was coming out to him, he rose and walked out onto the grounds. He wandered aimlessly down to the dock to watch the display of forked lightning against the purple sky.

He wondered what was taking so long. Other colored women had babies with hardly a pause in their work, just stopping for a moment to drop the baby, then continuing with whatever they were doing at the time. Oh, hell, it really wasn't that way. He knew he was stringing his nerves out because it was his child.

And what of it? It wasn't every day that a man had a baby. Well, it was Leandra doing all the work, he admitted. But it was just as hard on him as it had to be on her. Besides, she was built for childbearing and he wasn't. So far, she hadn't yelled or screamed or anything.

And already this morning she seemed to know it would be born tonight. Mumbled something about seeing a hawk nesting—more of that nigger totem stuff. Then, tonight, she had shaken him awake telling him to get Maum Molly, who came in and took over like she owned the place. Ran him out of his bedroom. Hell, she ran him out of his house. And now a thin mist rain drizzled on his head and he was miserable.

A cry echoed through the darkness, causing him to step jerkily off the bank into the shallow water. *A limpkin*—the bird's hoarse, lonesome cry, sounding so much like a baby's wail, had fooled him once earlier tonight. And a panther's scream from across the cove about an hour ago had almost caused his heart to stop, thinking it was Leandra.

He stepped back onto the bank, pulled off his moccasins and squeezed the water from them. He stared in the darkness at the soggy leather. Now I've got wet feet, he thought. And if I stand here in the rain, I'll have a wet ass. Why should becoming a father cause such misery?

Leandra twisted the towel tightly, rolling the knots into tighter knots. Concentrating her thoughts, she steadied her breathing, pulling long draughts deep into her lungs, forcing herself to relax while she awaited the onset of the next wave of excruciating pain. The anticipation was almost as bad as the pain itself. Her body stiffened each time the rhythmic contractions swept over her and built to a peak of almost unbearable intensity. Grunting deep in her throat, she pushed with every ounce of her strength until she felt the last shred of energy leave her body. Gratefully, she felt the pain ebb, leaving her limp and drenched with sweat.

She lay back against her pillow, feeling that her insides were being pushed out, but her main concern was that she might slip past the barrier of her resolve and scream. She was determined that Dummett would have a wife who could stand up to her duty.

The thought of Dummett at this time was a vexation to her soul. After the months of growing love in her body, she had thought that the child would be her only clear goal on this night. She wanted to think only of the child, to marvel on the miracle itself.

But Dummett was there—in her mind.

Again, the pain began its assault. As she felt the thrust within her, she twisted the towel and gathered her strength for the push.

Then a gush burst from her, spraying her thighs with warmth...Relief flooded over her. The pressure was gone. Maum Molly was holding the baby upside down, cutting the cord with a sharp knife as the child made its first whimper followed by a lusty cry.

"A boy," Maum Molly said, turning him over and cleaning him with a towel. Leandra's eyes followed her every move. "A fine son. Ugly, as I expected." She smiled at Leandra. Quickly wrapping him in a soft blanket, she lay the boy on Leandra's bare breasts.

Leandra eased the blanket away from the baby's face. "Oh, you're beautiful," she cooed. The baby stopped crying, his brow knitted into a frown, his eyes moving as if searching for the source of the sound. Though startled by the deep green eyes inches from her own, she felt instinctively that he recognized her voice. Even as the baby grasped her finger in a strong fist, she knew he was cast in her image. His skin was much lighter than hers, having the slight hue of a hazelnut. She touched the baby's cheek to her nipple and watched in wonder as he turned and sucked the nipple into his mouth. Chill bumps spread warmly over her body as she felt the child struggling to pull sustenance from the nipple.

"You'll be my life when I have no other," she said quietly. She looked up at Maum Molly. "His name is Charles. He's *white*, you know." She looked down at him, caressing the soft cheek pressed against her breast. "And I'll be your life when you have no other," she told him.

Beneath the umbrella of a large oak, Dummett tried to light a cigar, dry for the moment but threatened by the growing storm. The cry of the baby, punctuated by a streak of lightning above the treeline, seemed to him as loud as the following thunder crash. He stopped the match halfway up and stood transfixed for a moment, listening to the bellowing from the house.

Then, awareness hit him as the flame touched his fingers. He cursed as he shook the match loose. He turned to run through the downpour to the house, bounced from a tree and ran headlong into the cove.

"Dadblame it, Frances, this hat's too little even for George." The plaited, palmetto hat perched like an inverted bowl atop Burnham's head.

"Then I guess I get the first one," she said with glee, stretching for the hat he now held just out of her reach.

"Father, you'd best not be teasing the lass," Mary said from the door of the tent, "or you'll never get a hat to fit you." She stepped into the sunshine, shielding her eyes from the brilliant glare.

Burnham took her hand and walked with her to the framework of the new house. He had trimmed pine saplings and tied them together with sisal twine to form a twenty-foot square birdcage. He waved his hand at the structure and smiled. "I call it 'The Mansion'."

"A tad small for such a fancy title, don't you think?" Mary asked.

Burnham stepped back, looking at her swollen belly and laughed. "If you keep shucking kids out like orange pips, I'll be adding rooms to the house every year."

"Then, mayhap we have the need to build separate quarters." She took Frances' hand and they walked down the newly cut path to the bluff overlooking the river. "We'll go to fetch some more palmetto fronds," she said holding up her large butcher knife. "I'm thinking we can weave them tight enough to hold water. They'll make good bowls. Keep an ear out for the babes napping in the tent."

Burnham watched them walk along the bluff toward the forest, thinking that they should be gathering fronds for house thatching, not bowls. Dummett had once told him that palmetto was nature's best roofing material. He certainly had no choice. That's all he had available.

A cough from behind startled Burnham. Dropping the bundle of fronds, he drew the knife from its scabbard beneath his armpit, spun on a heel and crouched in a squared-off stance. At the edge of the clearing stood an Indian, his arms raised shoulder high, his palms facing outward.

Chapter 10

T he Indian spoke in clear English. "I am Holatter Micco. I am chief
of the Miccosukee Tribe, and I come in peace."

Surprise held Burnham speechless for a moment as he gauged
the distance to the rifle leaning against his tent. His eyes quickly scanned
the woods behind the Indian for others when the realization burned into
his mind that Mary and Frances were out there and that Jackson was
working alone in the field, unarmed.

The Indian seemed to read his mind. "You show concern for
your women and your slave. That is good. Rest assured, they are
safe. I am alone, here only to speak with you."

Burnham thought for a long moment, then relaxed. "You're welcome to my home." He began to smile as he waved his arm at the
patch of canvas tent and the birdcage framework of The Mansion.
"Such as it is," he laughed.

"It will be an adequate home," Billy Bowlegs said. "A man like you
will build well when time allows." He walked into the clearing and followed Burnham to canvas stools near a cooking pit dug in the shade of a
large water oak. He sat and arranged his shirt across his bare knees.

The man's head was wrapped in a red shawl held in place by a silver
band, the turban adorned with white egret plumes. Sunlight glinted from
silver crescents suspended from a necklace ending in some sort of silver
medallion. Strands of blue beads covered the sleeves of his brightly deco-
rated shirt. Burnham stepped to his wooden trunk and extracted a pouch
of tobacco, two briar pipes, and a clay jug of rum. "You're the one
my people call Billy Bowlegs?"

"Wyomey," the Indian said, lifting the jug to his lips. "Good,"
he pronounced, a smile flitting across his square face. He handed
the jug back to Burnham and accepted a pipe of tobacco.

"Yes. I am Billy Bowlegs. We have watched since you arrived.
You are leader of your people," the Indian stated.

"No," Burnham replied, shaking his head. "Our leader is Colonel Peck. He lives up the river to the north."

"I have seen this man. His work is all done by slaves. He watches,
doing nothing for himself. Our leaders also have slaves, but we work with
them, as I watched you do. I have seen others of your people who have
only built their huts and now sit back to watch life."

"You've been watching us?"

"Yes. I watch you work in the field beside your slave. I watch you show great strength. One night after you stopped work, I tried to lift one of the stumps. My back felt pain for three days."

"Jackson's not my slave. He's my friend."

Standing, Billy Bowlegs pointed his arm across the clearing. "You first cleared and planted a garden for the immediate needs of your family. After that you build your home. It is wise to do needed things first. You will be leader of your people. So I speak to you now." He sat back on the stool.

"What do you want?"

"Trade. And peace. Your army destroyed our fields across the land. Our pumpkins, beans, peas, rice, and tobacco are gone. We are pressed into the Pah-hay-okee, the big water by the swamp. We are few, but we make a place for us. The land again gives most of what is needed but our women desire things as do all women. Our children need things, as do all children. The white man has what my people desire and need. In return we have much to offer you."

"A trading post is being established by a man named Barker, upriver, on a bluff near the river we call San Sebastian."

"We know of it. My people wish to come, to trade in peace. I ask you now to be my *sense bearer*, to speak to the trader with assurance that we mean no harm to your people and want no harm to our people."

"It is done," Burnham said. "I deem it an honor to speak for the leader of the Miccosukee."

Billy Bowlegs rose and walked to the rifle leaning against the tent. "It is new," he said, looking at it.

Burnham took the rifle and checked its loads. "It's one of them new Colt's revolving rifles." They walked to the edge of the bluff where Burnham fired six shots into the water as fast as he could thumb the hammer and pull the trigger.

Billy Bowlegs stood enveloped in white smoke, awe clouding his face more than the smoke. "Bad gun," he said sadly. "Kill many Indians with it."

"I hope not. I pray those days are forever gone." He looked toward the woods. "My wife will be worried over the shots. She should be here any moment. Will you take a meal with me?"

"I must go. My journey home is long. We will return." He walked to the edge of the clearing, where he faced Burnham for a long moment, holding up his empty hand. Burnham turned when he heard Mary and Frances running into the clearing. When he looked back, Billy Bowlegs had vanished.

"Hold on, men," Samuel Peck yelled above the clamor of voices. "Let's have some order here or we'll never get anything decided." As the din settled he nodded to Burnham.

"I believe the man," Burnham said, looking at the faces of his neighbors. "When a chief comes all the way from the Everglades to prepare the way for trade and peace, I'm willing to give him a chance. He could have sent some men over to test which way the wind blows and scared the hell out of us, maybe got them killed or some of us, maybe even started the war up again. I think it was a pretty smart thing for him to do, and pretty damn brave too."

Burnham sat back on his bench and again everyone began speaking at once. He studied the faces of the men in the group. Some showed anxiety while others seemed clouded with fear and anger.

After Billy Bowlegs had left, Burnham had gone immediately to Peck's place. Together they decided to call the men in to Fort Pierce for this meeting. Most had arrived when the meeting began, with only the Barker group absent. Their trip from Barker's Bluff near the Sebastian River was the longest anyone had to make.

Major William Russell stood on his bench and waved his hands for silence. "Men, I'm as leery as the next man about taking snakes to my bosom. But you know there's not many of them. Colonel Worth of the Army was by here not long ago and told me that the nest of snakes has been defanged. Chekaika and Tiger Tail are dead. Wildcat has been captured and sent to the Arkansas. Old Sam Jones, he's senile. Worth says they can't have more than a hundred or so warriors and most of them are hardly more than children. The old leaders—Halleck, Alligator—they're gone. The war's over. They're harmless."

"Let me throw in my penny's worth," boomed a voice from the rear. Burnham turned and saw Barker pushing his way to the front. Ratch McGirt crowded in behind him.

Barker stood before the men and held up a soft, deerskin robe.

"I got this here from a Seminole just this mornin'. He come in just before we left and my new partner here, Mr. McGirt, traded him a sack of seed corn fer it. Now, they got thangs like this that ain't valuable to them but is to us, and we got thangs that ain't so valuable to us. Ain't that what trade's all about? I'm fer it, and I ain't skeered of 'em. Let 'em come, I says."

Several men crowded around him, fingering the robe and all talking at once. Peck stood on his bench and again yelled for order. The men slowly took their seats.

Dan Bowen stood and began talking so quietly Burnham had to strain to hear him. "I seen 'em out in the woods when I was ahuntin'," he said. "They're down to mostly arrers. They don't have no powder nor lead. I been in their camps and talked with 'em. Their women is farmin' the 'glades and it's all the men can do to keep 'em in meat with them stick weapons." His voice rose a little in volume. "But if we was to help 'em a little with some powder and lead, they can take keer of their own and also trade us fresh meat. I'm the only hunter here and I can't supply the whole damn colony. And they got pelts and vegetables what would help us till we get more set up on our own. I thank you for listenin'." He hurriedly sat down when another man yelled, "I ain't for givin' them savages no powder and lead." Only a few raucous cheers answered this.

Burnham stood on his bench, held out his hands palms down as if he was pushing their volume down. "They still have their old flint muskets," he said. "One of those can kill you just as dead as a new Colt. But they're not about to take on the army again. They don't have the men or the weapons for it. If we're going to live here, we're going to have to live with them, not against them." As he stood there, most of the men nodded in agreement.

With that the meeting ended, the men breaking up into small groups, men from one end of the colony taking advantage of the opportunity to visit with their friends from the other end.

When Burnham wandered over to speak to Ossian Hart, Ratch McGirt stepped in front of him. McGirt sported a new scar running from his crooked nose to his chin.

"So, you've joined our adventure," Burnham said, looking steadily into the piggish little eyes.

McGirt returned the stare for a moment, then grinned insolently and walked off. Burnham shuddered as he watched the lout disappear into the crowd.

Mary was preparing a squirrel stew over the cooking pit when Burnham returned from the meeting. "And did anyone have a plan for handling the savages?" she asked, spooning stew into a woven palmetto bowl.

"The Indians won't cause any trouble," he replied, sitting at the rough table beneath the oak tree. "I just wanted everyone to know they were around so some fool won't start banging away when he sees one." He paused to sip some of the steaming broth, then looked into her eyes. "Ratch McGirt's down here, and he looks meaner than ever. We've probably got more to fear from him than all the Seminoles in Florida."

"I have no use for any of them, McGirts or Seminoles. I'm fearful of them all."

Within the week he finished the house and began work on one for Jackson and Martha. The one room shack had no flooring, but Mary, Frances and Martha wove several palmetto mats that could be taken out and shaken while the sand floor was being raked. The room had one window, screened with a trapdoor mat of palmetto that could be opened during the day and closed against the mosquitoes at night.

For furniture, Burnham built two bunks from wood scrapped from Sam Peck's new house. Peck's house had been framed in Savannah and shipped down on his schooner, the *Josephine*. It was by far the most elegant structure on the Indian River. All of the other families were living in leanto shacks even smaller and rougher than Burnham's.

The day after they finished Jackson's house, the two men went to the five-acre field they were clearing. They had been grubbing out palmetto roots for an hour when Burnham heard a shout of greeting from the edge of the woods. Two young Seminoles stood in the shadows. Burnham judged them to be in their late teens. Their out-stretched hands were empty, but two shovels and an axe leaned against a tree.

"Welcome," Burnham said, walking toward them.

"You are Burnham. I am Tommy Jumper," one of them said. "My friend is Dan Osceola. We are here to see to your farm." The two boys were dressed almost identically. Brightly colored shirts, belted at the waist, hung to their knees. The one named Tommy Jumper wore a necklace braided from strands of golden-colored wool. The two Indians picked up their tools and walked into the field.

"I don't understand," Burnham said, falling in beside them as they walked. Dan Osceola stooped and lifted a handful of the dark, sandy loam soil. He smelled it, then tasted it. "Good," he said and smiled at Burnham. "This will do you fine. What have you in mind to plant here?"

"I don't know yet." Burnham was becoming more confused as Tommy Jumper began to pace across the field. He quickly caught up with the lean, young Indian and said, "What are you doing?"

Jumper stopped and looked at Burnham. "We are part of a gift from our people—from Chief Billy Bowlegs, to Burnham, leader of the white clan."

"I told him, I'm not the leader of this group."

"We heard of the meeting of your clan and know of your part in making peace between our people. You make our lives richer. Billy Bowlegs will now make Burnham's life richer." He continued his pacing across the field.

"It's a hundred paces across," Burnham said.

Jumper stopped. "Then we must make it three hundred. Will pineapples make money in the white man's market?"

"Yes," Burnham answered, his mind slowly beginning to grasp the picture. "Shipped to St. Augustine and from there up north...yes, they would demand a dear price. Can they grow here?" he asked in wonder. Jumper laughed at this.

"You set them out and only have to weed them occasionally. My father had a field many years ago and took them to the old city. Your people bought all he could bring."

"I imagine so. They aren't raised in the states. Only in the islands of the Caribbean. Look here, I can't allow you to do this."

"How long would it take you to clear and plant the land?"

"I've been at this for three months."

"There is nothing more to say. We return tomorrow with more men." The two youngsters each shook Burnham's hand in turn, then walked to the woods and vanished as quickly as they appeared.

Burnham stood staring at the trees for a minute, then looked at the pitted field, the reward of his months of labor. In resignation he slowly walked home where he related the events of the morning to Mary.

"God bless them," she said gleefully. Then she frowned. "But I'm still fearful of them."

Twenty Indians arrived the next day and attacked the palms and pines. A brace of oxen was brought in to snake the trunks to a growing pile. When the field was naked of trees, the oxen ripped the stumps and roots from the ground, leaving the field cratered with potholes. Within two weeks, the field had increased to fifteen acres. A black column of smoke boiled upward from the pile of wrecked tree trunks and roots.

Then the Indians scattered over the field like locusts and, in one morning, the holes were filled, the soil was tilled and ready for the pineapple slips. That afternoon, six thousand were mounded in and mulched with bunchgrass.

As Burnham walked down the rows of plants trying to thank the Indians, each in turn smiled, took his hand and pumped it up and down. Then they picked up their tools and melted into the woods at the edge of the large field.

In moments, Burnham stood alone with Tommy Jumper. With tears in his eyes, he grabbed the boy's hand and shook it.

"I don't know how to thank you...your people." He tried to keep his voice from cracking with emotion and failed.

"You and I have one more chore," Tommy Jumper said. "You must meet me at the abandoned fort on the mound in the dark hour before sunrise tomorrow." He turned and left. As Burnham walked home in the fading twilight, he wondered why the Indian would want to meet at Fort Pierce. Then he stopped and took a last, lingering look at his good fortune.

Dozens of mullet jumped and splashed the stillness of the moonlit river. Burnham moved down to the shallow bank from the old Indian mound marked with the ruins of Fort Pierce. The water slapping against the coquina rocks at the river's edge set his mind at peace. Squatting on his heels, he breathed the briny air.

The movement of something in the corner of his vision startled him, causing him to lurch and stumble into the water. He stood sheepishly as he saw Tommy Jumper at the helm of a small sailboat moving slowly toward him across the shallow water.

The boat was about twelve feet long, and overhung with a broad, canvas mainsail, and its boom extending well beyond the stern.

Tommy Jumper dropped his lines and turned the boat into the bank. "We must hurry," he said to Burnham. "We have little wind and it will take time to cross the river. The tide is almost right to take us through the cut into the ocean."

Burnham stepped into the boat near the mast and sat on a thwart. Pushing the boat into motion with a small paddle, Tommy Jumper pulled the mainsheet taut. The boat heeled slightly, then righted and began to ghost across the river. As they moved into deeper water, the Indian lowered the centerboard. The boat took on a livelier heel and a sharper increase in speed, gliding past the large island at the mouth of the inlet. Burnham fought an impulse to ask the intent of this journey.

They soon passed through the inlet, moving out to sea on gentle swells of slick, green water. Burnham remembered how motionless the schooners had been in this same soft breeze just caressing his cheek with its presence, but that now sent the small sailboat skimming swiftly along.

The boat was about a mile offshore when the rising sun peeked above the horizon, brushing the stars from the sky in its spreading glow. One bright star hanging inches from the sun resisted its luminescence. Burnham pointed at it. "The morning star," he informed the boy.

Tommy Jumper nodded his head as if in awe. "It is not as the others. It is one of the wanderers...the stars that move."

"Well, to be correct, those are planets. That one is named Venus."

"Our name for it is Oo-wah-chic Shee-mah-lee-fah Coo-chay: the bashful star. It shows itself for a moment but stays close to the sun, then hides in the sun's brightness during day. It is like our people. I may roam, but I must be near the protection of my tribe, hidden and protected in its power."

So much for educating the ignorant savage, Burnham thought, smiling with tightly shut lips.

"We must be alert now," Tommy Jumper said. "Turtles are all around us if we can find them."

"What are we—" Burnham grabbed the mast with both hands to balance himself as the Seminole cut the boat sharply to the right and pointed ahead.

Burnham looked across the bow at a large shell floating on the surface ahead of them. Burnham glanced at the sun. The bashful star had vanished. It was time to go to work.

"Take him by his back flippers and pull him in," the boy directed. "Be careful of the barnacles!" Burnham moved to the bow, waiting. As the boat neared him, the loggerhead turtle was startled and began swimming violently. Burnham reached forward and grabbed both rear flippers. Pulling his knees under him, he heaved upward. The turtle slid across the gunwale and fell heavily onto its back in the bilge of the boat. It pulled itself into its armor in resignation as if, tired of the game, it would rest and wait its moment of liberation in complete security.

"Now Burnham will never go hungry." The Seminole beamed proudly at Burnham. "In the three hottest moons, the she-turtle nests on the beach to lay her eggs. There she is easy to capture by turning her over. Rest of the year, she is captured from boat, like this."

The wind picked up as the morning grew older, and by noon they had taken two more turtles, the huge bodies filling the center of the boat.

As they neared the inlet again, Burnham saw the first of the bars pass beneath the boat. Tommy Jumper saw him looking overboard. "Reef. Many languousta—crayfish—live in rocks below. My people further south catch them in traps. The sea is good to man."

Back in the Indian River, they sailed south toward Burnham's home. He leaned back against the gunwale and considered what he had learned. If he could find a way to keep the turtles alive until he had a large number, there might be a ready market in shipping them to the states and to Europe.

Tommy Jumper guided the boat to the bank below the bluff at Burnham's homestead and tied its bowline tightly to a stunted mangrove. Lifting one of the turtles from the boat, they flipped him upside down in the edge of the river. Tommy Jumper showed Burnham how to dress it out, packing the meat in its own shell. Then he scurried around the shallows, gathering a large number of the soft coquina blocks. Stacking them higher than the surface, he built a small enclosure tilting inward, leaving small openings for fish to pass through. They released the other turtle into the pen.

"Turtle kraal," Tommy Jumper said. "Fish come in, the turtle eats. When you are in need, you eat turtle."

They carried the shell of meat to the top of the bluff, where the Indian looked deeply into Burnham's eyes. He then solemnly shook his hand, saying, "May peace live in us, Brother." He turned to go.

"Your boat!" Burnham shouted. "You forgot your boat."

"Your boat," said the boy.

Chapter 11

The winter passed almost without notice. The climate remained mild, right into the new year and the pineapples thrust their green spikes upward. Tommy Jumper's prediction of the small amount of care required by the pineapples proved true, and by March the field looked more like a parade ground of rifle bayonets than a self-sufficient money crop.

Freed from the chores of farming, Burnham spent the days learning to handle the little sailboat. In exchange for most of the meat from one of his turtles, he obtained a jib from James Price, an English sailor.

After a month of exploring the near region of the Indian River, Burnham ferreted out the location of several places where a shrimp-baited hook was guaranteed to deliver a twenty-pound whiting or an even larger redfish. He built several wire shrimp traps and dropped them into the deep water below the bluff.

George accompanied him on his explorations, showing surprising adeptness at the helm of the *Jumper*, the name Burnham had given the boat. He was disappointed that Junior, two years older than George, showed no interest in the boat. Junior had dug and planted a small garden at the edge of the clearing and spent his days caring for it. At first Burnham resented the child's solitary isolation, but Mary soon set him straight.

"Leave him alone and he'll be all right. He's sensitive to life. He wants to nurture it, to watch things grow."

Burnham accepted the situation but determined to bring the boy more into family projects. Maybe I can get him into the pineapple field, he thought. At least that would put us working together.

On his first trip into the ocean, Burnham took George with him, giving him the tiller as they sneaked up on a turtle. Burnham missed the first one, but their efforts meshed on the next and Burnham pulled in a forty-pound loggerhead that he traded to John Hutchinson in return for a load of cypress planks John found on the ocean beach.

By late summer, Burnham had visited most of the settlers from Jupiter Inlet to Barker's Bluff near the San Sebastian River. He was surprised, and disappointed, to find that many of the original settlers had given up their homesteads and left. Those who remained had made headway against the Florida wilderness, showing a toughness that the quitters didn't have.

His visit to the trading post at Barker's Bluff proved uneventful. McGirt was reasonably civil to him under the eye of Barker, their only conflict coming when Burnham wanted to barter turtle meat for gunpowder. Ratch rested a heavy thumb on the scales when he weighed the powder, but reweighed it when Burnham complained to Barker. Burnham wondered how long the men of the colony would stand for one in their midst cheating them. He vowed to himself to stay out of it, that he'd had enough of McGirt's trouble. He'd let others handle the problems next time. And he knew in his heart that there would be a next time. A man like McGirt would cause violence no matter where he went or what he did.

Burnham sat in the small, tin tub near the artesian well, leaning forward to let Mary scrub his back with a rough sponge. He hugged his knees, shivering, as waves of warmth spread through his body from her massage. The April evening was balmy, with a slight breeze keeping the mosquitoes away. She finished with a quick rinse of his broad back, slapped the sponge across his shoulder and stood upright to stretch her arms.

"Well," he said, scooping water up over his chest with cupped palms, "it was good while it lasted."

"And would you be tellin' me again of this great journey you're plannin'?"

"It's no great journey, just a little exploring on the river to the north."

"All the way to its head? And you've no idea how far or how long it'd be takin' you?"

"Shouldn't take more'n a couple of weeks or so. If we can map its depth, we might be able to use the Indian River's inside route to St. Augustine for transporting our produce. I know it'll be slower, but it might be safer than going outside in bad weather. When Peck took our first crop north, the wind was against the Gulfstream. Chopped the water up something awful and damaged his schooner. Someday, this waterway could be open all the way from St. Augustine to Fort Dallas on the Mayaima River. Why, it'd be like a highroad, an artery of transportation for settlers down from the north."

He paused to stand, then grinned, reaching for the towel she offered. "And besides, I can stop by to visit Dummett. It's been a while since he and I chatted."

"I hate it when you go off like this," Mary said. "The Indians put a fright in me coming around all the time. Makes me fear for the young'uns. And the noises at night—the bears and panthers. When you're gone I can't sleep at night without riding off on a nightmare."

"You know I need to go," he said. He studied her dear face carefully in the flickering lantern light. He saw concern, but not fear. "I'll speak to the Indians, tell them to stay away from the house while I'm gone. They won't bother you."

In the two years they had lived in the palmetto shack, Mary had never complained of loneliness or fear. In fact, he had often marveled that she had never complained of any form of privation, although Burnham knew she did much with what little they had. If she needed spices for cooking, she and Frances were creative in gathering herbs from the woods. They dried them, crushed them, and tried them in small amounts in the food until they hit upon just the right combination. And while the food was meager, it was wholesome. Burnham was gaining weight. He estimated his six-foot two-inch frame now carried well over two hundred pounds.

He knew her fears of the Indians were somewhat tempered by the occasional haunch of venison she found left by them in front of her door. This provided a welcome change from the beans and greens that were their usual fare. The children were thriving on the life, never whimpering or complaining. They had never known any better. And Mary found it hard to complain about anything that benefited her children.

Lying in bed that night, he snuggled up to Mary's back, slipping his hand around to feel the swell of her belly. Pregnant, and with four kids already, she might have been less understanding of his plan, yet she had given her blessing to his trip, saying as she fell asleep, "We'll be all right. We always are."

Two days later he loaded the *Jumper* with bedding, some camp gear, food and water. As he got under way, George began to cry into his mother's apron, begging to go. Burnham looked back and realized that, while a six-year-old might act like a little man most of the time, he's really just a little kid. He's earned it, he thought. Why not take him? He would be good company. Burnham smiled and swung the boat around.

A screaming wind drove the whitecaps on the river into spindrift. Burnham strained to see through the opaque curtain of rain, barely able to even make out the bow of the little boat. George lay huddled by the mast, a shivering, sodden mass of boy and clothes. Burnham's concern over the boy's safety overpowered any concern over his discomfort. He squinted into the wall of water to his right, unable to make out the trees he knew were there. The sailboat was in a cocoon of swirling, hammering water, isolated from the rest of the universe.

"We've got to get to leeward of the east shore," Burnham yelled to his son above the howling din. "I'll point us into the wind tight as possible. I don't think this old mains'l will hold if we're too much abeam." He leaned forward, shouting louder. "Stay low in the bilge. You hear?"

He pushed the tiller hard to port and the little boat turned tightly into the wind. Then, as the bow threatened to cut across the wind, he eased back. Immediately, they picked up speed, to the point where Burnham was afraid he was overrunning his vision, knowing he might drive full speed into the riverbank. But he could not back off. He had to get them off the river. Now!

Suddenly their speed abruptly slackened and through the grayness he could see the bank ahead. The trees were cutting them off from the wind's fury; however, enough still reached them to maintain steerage. He let the boat fall off to the left, then angled it toward the bank.

A small cove opened up about fifty yards to his left and he slacked off even further to clear a small point of land. He held off until he was well into the cove, then drove the boat onto the bank. They struck so hard George tumbled forward into the bow.

"You all right, son?"

George pushed himself up into a sitting position, looked around, and then nodded.

"You stay right there. Don't move until I get us secured."

Burnham grabbed the bowline and went over the side. He sloshed through thigh-deep water to the bank and climbed, sliding in the muck near the top. He saw a pine, ran to it and threw the bowline around the solid trunk, then around his waist. Leaning into the line, he struggled to lever the nose of the sailboat up onto the bank.

"Think you can get the sails down," he yelled to George.

The boy nodded. "Yes...I think so..."

"Try it then. But son, be careful."

George crawled back to the mast and slowly pulled himself erect. Burnham watched, his muscles bunched and hardened, realizing he'd asked a six-year-old to perform an adult's chore, but the boy, bracing his small body, began to hank down the jib and mainsail. A few moments later, the sails were down.

"Now sit down!" Burnham yelled.

When George was huddled in the bottom of the boat, Burnham pulled and tugged until the hull cleared the water at the centerboard trunk. Hurriedly, he tied the line to the tree.

"All right." He lifted George into his arms, hugging him to his chest. "I'm proud of you, boy. You're a real little man, you know that?"

Hunkering over to shield his son from the driving pellets of rain, he half ran, half stumbled inland until they came to the shelter of a large oak. Breathing a silent prayer of thanks, he lay between two protruding roots and snuggled the boy against his side.

Dawn fought its way through a haze of fog, the dim sunlight sparking a myriad of dancing reflections from tiny droplets of water clinging to blades of grass. The air carried a slight chill, reminding Burnham of early autumn mornings in Maine. He went into the woods and returned with several fat-pine sticks that he arranged on the ground in a star pattern. Soon a small fire was drying their clothes and easing cramped soreness from their muscles.

He crawled down into the boat to retrieve his skillet and a slab of white bacon. He sat there for a long while, looking out over the placid surface of the river and studying the cove that opened to the north. It was about a hundred yards across at the mouth, but he could see no land at its back. Very deep, he thought. With that knowledge, he hurried back to the fire to prepare their simple breakfast. By the time they finished eating, the sun had burned the fog from the water and he could see that the cove cut sharply to the north, becoming a wide creek between high banks.

They bailed the boat dry and repacked it. Burnham pushed the *Jumper* from the bank and raised the sail in the still air. As he began to paddle, he decided to check out the creek. He could recall no mention of it by any of the men he had talked to about the river. He continued to paddle the boat along center of the creek. Suddenly George squealed and pointed to a hill rising high above the eastern bank.

"Indian mound," Burnham told him. "This was probably a village site, maybe for a hundred years or more."

The boy watched it with intent interest as they glided past. By standing, Burnham discovered he could see across the western bank through gaps in the trees. The land here was quite narrow, and the Indian River was visible beyond it. Then, a little over a mile from their campsite, the creek suddenly widened. The eastern bank curved sharply away, and Burnham found himself looking across a two-mile sweep of water.

"George, this isn't a creek." His voice was taut with amazement. "It's a dadblamed lagoon, ever bit as big as the Indian River."

A gentle breeze filled the sails, pushing the boat onto the open expanse. Ahead, to the north, the lagoon extended over the horizon, beckoning Burnham with that curiosity of exploration which is timeless in man. The bottom sped by, quite visible, and much shallower than the Indian River, not more than six feet deep.

A couple of hours later, George rose impulsively, pointing and yelling. "Daddy, look! Islands!"

Burnham pushed the tiller, laying the boat off on a reach. Looking around the jib he could see the smudge of two small islands in the middle of the river ahead.

Within minutes they closed on the islands and he could see a third land mass, very large, lying behind the first two. The second island appeared to be covered with snow and he realized it was a snowy egret rookery.

"We'll just have to name the first island after you," he grinned at his son. "George's Island. Has a nice ring to it, don't you think? Now you'll be famous forever." He laughed at the animation on the boy's face.

"Are we allowed to do that?" George asked. "Can we name an island?"

"Of course. Discoverers always get to name their findings," Burnham replied. He pointed to the island covered with egrets. "How about Bird Island for that one?"

"And look, Daddy!" The boy jumped up and down in his excitement. A deer stood on a point of the large land behind the two islands.

"Sit down and quit rocking the boat. I guess we'll have to name that one..." He thought for a moment, then asked, "How's Buck Point sound?" George nodded vigorously in agreement.

They were now moving to the left of George's Island and the water shoaled to less than three feet. Burnham saw that the third land was much larger than the others; it extended for miles to the north. He steered the boat into a mile-wide slot between this new landmass and the western bank separating them from the Indian River.

An hour later, the waterway narrowed and several small islands blocked their path. After threading their way between them, they entered a creek that narrowed drastically within a mile. In spite of himself, Burnham again experienced the almost forgotten fear he'd known six years earlier after the attack by the Seminoles, when the Halifax had done the same thing. Reluctantly, he brought the boat around and headed back the way they had come.

"I'm naming this Newfound Harbor," he told George as they sailed south back toward the islands.

Upon reaching the lagoon, they turned back to the north. Late in the afternoon, Burnham steered the *Jumper* toward the Eastern Shore where they could hear the crash of surf on the ocean beach.

"We must be somewhere near Cape Canaveral," he told George as they skimmed along a hundred yards from the bank.

Within the hour, he saw a large hook of land point out into the lagoon. He aimed for the cove he saw opening from it. When the boat entered the cove, thousands of ducks rose in startled indignation, blackening the late afternoon sky with their numbers and deafening the ear with their cries and the slap of wingbeats.

In moments they were alone in an almost landlocked little harbor with schools of mullet darting frantically from their path. Burnham steered toward the high riverbank and the pine and oak hammock towering above them.

After landing the boat and securing it to a scrub of buttonwood, they off-loaded their equipment. Several yards inland they entered a clearing, dominated by the largest Indian mound Burnham had ever seen. Around the clearing's edge, huge oaks spread their thick limbs like a protective canopy.

While setting up their canvas tent, Burnham marveled at the serene beauty of the area. In particular, he noted the absence of mosquitoes and gnats in the stiff, cool breeze. This would be a wonderful place for someone to live out his life, he thought. It has everything. Fish and fowl and, from the looks of those trails through the thin underbrush, game animals must be plentiful.

He listened intently, trying to hear the ocean, but heard only the overture of the crickets' evening symphony. The river line had continued straight, so he concluded the land had pushed the ocean away from him. This meant they were probably somewhere on Cape Canaveral. A prickly, warm shiver crawled down his skin when he realized he was standing on land first seen hundreds of years earlier by the Spanish explorer, Juan Ponce.

"Daddy, come see! What kind of tree is this? It ain't a palm." George's excitement brought Burnham's thoughts back to focus on the present. He walked to where the child stood looking at a tree with broad fronds arching gracefully toward the ground.

"Don't say ain't, George," he corrected quietly as he looked at the yellow fruit hanging from the tree. Pulling his knife from its scabbard, he reached up and cut a stalk free.

"Bananas." He peeled one of the stubby crescents and handed it to George. After peeling another, he bit into it and closed his eyes as its creamy softness filled his mouth with flavor. "Son, if this ain't the Garden of Eden, it doesn't exist."

"Don't say ain't, Daddy," George giggled through jaws bulging with the fruit.

"Well, son, we just found the best name for our new lagoon."

"Let me say it, Daddy. I want to name it. The Banana River. That's a *good* name, ain't...isn't it?" The boy stuffed another banana into his mouth.

"A real good name, son. A real good name. It's not really a river, but then neither is the Indian River."

The next morning, they continued north into the seemingly endless Banana River. Yet, in only a short time, they saw a faint, bluish line spread across the horizon. Within minutes the line resolved itself into palm covered land. This time, however, he could see a broad creek cutting into the land and curving away into the distance.

They entered the creek, instantly losing the drive of the wind. Burnham dropped the sails and they took up paddles, moving slowly along the winding waterway. By the time the sun reached its noontime high, they had passed through a maze of countless islands and found themselves passing from the creek into a large lagoon.

The lagoon was about three miles wide here and the water was again ten-foot deep. A large point of land stood out from the far, western shore.

"Sand Point, I bet," he said, squinting at the distant land. "Son, I believe we're back on the Indian River." He steered the *Jumper* north along the Eastern Shore toward the bulbous curve of land where he could see the lagoon falling away to the right.

Later, he saw the familiar blue line of pines and palms smeared completely across the lagoon and realized he was near the river's head. He turned to the east, where he could see the gray ruins of a fort's stockade outlined against the backdrop of pines.

"That's Fort Ann," Burnham said. "Abandoned. We'll camp there tonight and figure how to get through tomorrow. There's supposed to be an old Indian haulover to Mosquito Lagoon beside it."

They were passing across the opening to a wide cove in the shoreline to the right when a thin column of blue smoke in the distance caught his eye. He tacked the boat and headed toward the smoke. Just inside the cove, the small boat ground to a halt over a sand bottom only inches below the surface. He immediately pulled out the centerboard and the boat floated free.

Across the cove, he could make out shacks on the shore of a creek running out the back. Burnham paddled slowly toward the buildings and soon the *Jumper* drifted up to a pier reaching across the ankle-deep water. A dugout cypress canoe bobbed near the pier's end. On the pier stood a black-bearded man and a small boy, surrounded by baying dogs. The man took their line, tying it fast to a cleat.

The man was Douglas Dummett.

"It seems we do most of our meeting with me helping you onto a dock." Dummett said, leading Burnham and George through the growing dusk up a shell path. The small boy from the dock ran ahead toward the house.

Dummett's house was a neat looking double-penned log building, the two pens united by a covered breezeway. Single doors led into two rooms from a porch screened with mosquito netting.

The room they entered was unplastered, but clean and in perfect order. The end opposite the door was taken up by a huge fireplace built of coquina rock, over which was a shelf filled with books, with an old rifle hanging above them. Furnishings were limited to two bunks with mosquito netting, a rude table, a few cowhide-bottomed chairs and some stools. Leandra Fernandez stood near the fireplace, her dark beauty reflected in the features of the boy standing behind her grasping the folds of her gingham dress.

"Captain Burnham, it's a pleasure to have you in our home." She curtseyed slightly and smiled at him. She eased the boy from behind her, and pushed him forward. "And this is our son, Charles Dummett."

Burnham thought she had put a slight emphasis on the last name, but wasn't sure after the moment passed. He had forgotten how disconcerting her startling green eyes and her rich, contralto voice could be.

Soon, Leandra set steaming dishes of greens and ham hock, corn and okra on the long, plank table in the middle of the room. A rich aroma filled Burnham's nostrils, setting the juices of hunger flowing in his mouth.

"I'm hungry, Daddy," George said, running to the table.

"Then let's wrap ourselves around some fried chicken and cornbread." Dummett chuckled and lifted the boy into a chair. "Leandra, get the rest of the food on the table."

After the meal, Leandra took the boys into the other room for sleeping and the men moved to the porch. "Always a good breeze here," Dummett said as he poured a glass of rum for Burnham. "Keeps the skeeters away, but a good screening is still a safe assurance. Get enough skeeters in one spot and they can kill you."

They relaxed, smoking their pipes in the darkness and sipping the rum.

Dummett coughed self-consciously and leaned forward in his chair. "How's the idea of statehood strike the folks down at your place?"

"Nobody really took note of it. It doesn't affect us much."

"Statehood took a long time coming—committees meeting in Tallahassee for years, arguing over first one damn thing then another. Wasting time. Hell, they had a constitution and framework for a state government by '39."

"I know," Burnham said. "There was talk of splitting the territory in two when I came in '37, that maybe Georgia and Alabama would annex the two parts."

"That never would've worked. The Federal Congress wouldn't take even one Florida Territory until a free state wanted in, which happened as soon as Iowa Territory qualified last year."

Burnham sighed. "I guess it's a sign of modern times that even our national politics are governed by the slavery issue."

"Hell, it's going to get worse before it gets any better. But enough of that. What's happening at your place?"

Burnham brought him up to date on the Indian River Colony, relating his good fortune in gaining the friendship of the Indians and all they had done for him.

"I couldn't have made this trip if the Indians hadn't helped me clear my land."

"That's their nature. They'll do almost anything for somebody they respect. You need to keep their friendship."

"That's strange advice coming from an old Indian killer."

"Hell, that was war. I never made any bones about my feelings for them then. They were killing white folks. They were in the way of progress. Where they are now they don't bother nobody." Dummett paused to pour more rum. "But that was a long time ago. Hell, I already get a pension from that war. I see the Indian through different eyes now, probably because of the situation here."

"Leandra?"

"Yeah. With her, I'm on both ends of a forked stick. I need her. She makes me feel—" Dummett stopped, looked toward the room at the other end of the porch, then relaxed into his chair. "It's all right," he said. "She can't hear us."

"But you love her."

After a long pause, Dummett answered quietly. "Yes...I do, but she's a nigger...a slave. My not facing that is what killed my father."

"How much of that's her fault? Or yours, for that matter." Burnham looked sharply at Dummett. "I lost a good friend, John Metcalf, back at

Fort Heileman, over a conversation just about like this. Should we continue?"

"There's nothing you could say that I haven't said myself," Dummett said.

Burnham spoke in quiet tones, telling him of the argument with John Metcalf. As he slowly formed the words, he attempted to convey the shock of finding the hatred Metcalf had built into his nature. But when he began to tell of Metcalf's death, the memory of losing a friend already lost through mindless bigotry caused his thoughts to tumble. After a moment, he sat silent, sipping his rum and staring into the darkness.

Dummett refilled their glasses and broke the silence with a self-conscious laugh. "What do you think of my fine little two-year-old?" Then, as if he felt a need to explain, he said, "He's three-fourths white."

"I think he's a fine, handsome little boy." Burnham hesitated, then blurted out, "Dammit man, you just did it again. Who cares what part of what color he is? What's your problem?"

Dummett lurched to his feet and slammed his palm against the wall. "It's not the boy. It's Leandra...it's me. To me, she's...she's my wife. We didn't stand in front of a parson. Hell, we didn't even jump over a broom. But to the rest of the world, she's just a nigger, and I was losing my friends in New Smyrna. Their women treated her like scum when she went to market there. Then an old friend threatened to call me out if she even looked at his wife on the street. Hell, I couldn't live with that. So I left and came here."

Burnham digested this for a moment, then said, "You really should listen to what you say. In one breath you call her a nigger and in the next you complain about your friends doing it."

"And that's why I'm all tore up over it. I've tried not to show her disrespect, but there have been times..." Dummett walked back to his chair. "I'll just have to live with it. I guess that's about all I can do. I sure as hell can't live without her."

"Sounds like love to me," Burnham smiled.

They finished their rum and Dummett showed Burnham to one of the beds inside. "Leandra will sleep in the other building with the boys," he said.

Later, as Burnham lay thinking, it occurred to him that his friend's strength was the cause of his agitation. The problem wouldn't bother a lesser man.

The next day, Dummett took Burnham on a tour of the homestead. The well near the house was about twenty feet deep and equipped with a sweep. To the south, a storehouse stood elevated upon posts. "The stilts keep the bears and panthers out of my provisions," Dummett answered Burnham's questioning gaze.

The two boys followed the men everywhere, but while George was sticking his head between his father's legs to see better, Charles would lag behind, staying completely away from his father.

Burnham was impressed with all he saw. The original trees planted in 1828 were large and productive, the brilliance of the abundant oranges stark against the black-green foliage.

"I lost only a few trees to the freeze we had in thirty-five," Dummett told him. "Groves up around Pilatka were wiped out. These survived because the lagoons on both sides of us hold heat. It's a rare winter that makes us dress warm here."

He told Burnham of growers coming down to him during the past year for stock to rebuild their devastated groves.

"I'm trying something new," he said proudly, pointing to a field of young trees that had not yet begun to yield. "I budded these higher on the trunk, above any possible frost line. I think the stock would survive even the most severe freeze."

He guided Burnham through eight large fields that stretched all the way from the Indian River to Mosquito Lagoon. In answer to Burnham's unspoken question, Dummett said, "There's fifteen thousand trees on the place."

"And here I was, proud of my little fifteen acres of pineapple," Burnham said dryly.

"Six slaves with the right tools can clear land lots better than any bunch of lazy Seminoles," Dummett replied. "But you're right to be proud. Your fifteen acres of pineapples will earn more than thirty acres of oranges, just not as often. Takes seven years for a tree to start yielding but from then on it does it every year. Pineapples take two years to make fruit."

On the Mosquito Lagoon side of the peninsula, at what Dummett referred to as the Lower Grove, a small house stood on piles in the lagoon a short distance from shore. About six feet above the water, the little platform building contained four built-in bunks. "My summer house," Dummett said jokingly. "I use it for duck hunting and drinking."

That afternoon, they took the boys up to the haulover in a dugout canoe. The canal opened into the cove beside the decaying ruins of old Fort Ann. They drifted up to the cut in the bank, a shallow depression running across the strip of land to Mosquito Lagoon. It was dry.

"We'll probably be heading back home tomorrow. I haven't lost anything north of here and I don't care to drag the *Jumper* across this dry ditch."

"It fills when the tide rises on the Mosquito Lagoon side," Dummett explained. "If you was to go this way, you'd have to wait for it to fill."

As Dummett said this, Charles reached overboard, scooped a handful of water and threw it on George. Dummett slapped the child so quickly it startled Burnham. The boy immediately burst into tears. Dummett sat still for a moment, a look of stricken agony etched deeply across his face. Then he took the little boy into his arms and hugged him until the sobs diminished.

The trip back to Dummett Cove was marked by an awkward silence. As soon as they landed, Charles fled down the dock, with George following in confusion.

Later, when the men were sitting on the porch, Dummett drank off a half-pint jar of rum in one long swallow. "I don't know why I did it," he said avoiding Burnham's eyes. "All I saw in that instant was a nigger boy abusing a white child."

"It didn't hurt George. How can you see Charles as a nigger? Dammit man, he's your son."

"I know, and I love him. It's just...you wouldn't understand how I've thought on this since he was born. Your boy is white."

"So is Charles." Through the heat filling his ears, Burnham could feel the unheard sobs in the man's voice, and had a momentary urge to take the older man in his arms and console him as Dummett had done Charles earlier.

Dummett poured more rum into his jar and lowered his head. "You gotta believe this is the first time I ever hit..."

They sat drinking in the dusk until Burnham realized he was feeling the rum. Aware of the chance he might say something stronger than he had already, he excused himself and went to bed.

They left for home early the next morning.

Chapter 12

I n the corral at Mount Pleasant, Douglas moved in toward the year-ling bull, slowly swinging the loop of a catch rope around his head. This bull was to be the answer to the problem of power for his small sugarmill. As soon as they gentled the young animal, they would take it back to his new sugar fields at Dummett Cove. His brother-in-law had graciously sold him the bull for a highly inflated price. Knowing the bull would allow him to find more productive work for his field hands, Dummett figured he had a bargain.

The yearling bull lowered its head between hunched shoulders, but Dummett could see its red eyes staring up at the swinging catch rope as he began to circle the beast. The bull scratched a spray of sand back with a forefoot, then broke sharply to the side, away from Dummett.

"You hammerhead," he yelled, throwing the loop over the bull's horns. Jerking the rope tight, he ran to the snubbing post. "If I could train a pig to turn that press, I'd shoot you." He threw a quick half hitch around the post, then scrambled out of the bull's reach.

"Cap'n, iffen you snub his nose up against the post, I'll snag his hind leg with a rope. Then us can get the ring in." Old Cudjoe stood well away from the bull. He turned to the field hands sitting on the corral fence rails and grinned widely. "Us gets the ring in his nose and he be as easy to lead as all you married folks."

"Dammit, Cudjoe, I told you I'm not married." Dummett glanced from the corner of his eye at three-year-old Charles sitting on the top fence rail by Old Pumpery. Seeing a dark look cloud the boy's face brought an instant regret. My mouth's done it again, Dummett thought.

He breathed heavily, then walked over to Cudjoe. Slapping the old man lightly on the shoulder, he smiled at the cloud of dust he raised. "You're not too old to get your ass whipped, you know."

"Yassuh, like all them other beatings I ain't never done got." Moving in behind the feisty bull, Cudjoe tossed a loop at the animal's rear foot, missed it and hauled in the rope. On his fourth try, the loop slid under the foot. He snapped the rope, flipping the loop up the leg. Bracing his feet, he swung the rope around his butt and leaned back into the bight, jerking the bull's leg off the ground.

Dummett ran to the snubbed line and began to haul it in. Soon, the bull's nose was against the post. Ebo Thom, the blacksmith, sidled up to the post, his eyes widening as he neared the bull. "Do it," Dummett yelled, his hands burning from the hemp slipping through them. "He's helpless."

Ebo Thom snapped the shiny brass c-shaped ring into the pliers, inserted it into the soft muzzle and squeezed the long handles together. The bull bellowed his wild-eyed pain for an instant then lunged to the right, falling on his side. Dummett snapped a swivel with a short piece of line into the ring, then yelled, "Stand clear."

Cudjoe flipped his line loose from the leg, then scooted across the corral behind Ebo Thom as the young bull scrambled to its feet. Dummett grasped the ring-line and loosened his catch rope from the horns. Dropping it, he turned and jerked gently on the ring-line.

"You're not going to learn to work any younger," he told the bull as he began to walk slowly around the corral. Surprisingly, the bull settled into a skittish walk behind him. Once, the bull swung his horns downward as if to gather himself for a hook, but Dummett again snapped the line gently and the animal settled down.

After a few turns around the corral, he motioned for relief and Cudjoe pushed Old Pumpery toward him. "Come on," Dummett said to the hesitant, mossy-haired old man. "He's really gentle. He just had to find out who's boss. Tug easy at the line if he causes any trouble and don't take your eyes off him." Handing the line to the old man, he walked to the gate, where he turned to watch for a moment.

Old Pumpery walked gingerly ahead of the bull, keeping the line taut and alert for any threatening motion from the animal. The heckles and laughter from the watching men soon loosened him up and he began a jaunty strut.

"Don't get too cocky," Dummett yelled at the old man. He turned to the others. "Now all you men get back in those cane fields and douse whatever fires you can find. And don't anybody get his ass burnt."

The men shouted as they slipped down from the rails and loped from the corral.

At the instant Dummett reached for the gate, Old Pumpery screamed. Spinning around, Dummett was horrified to see the old Negro impaled on one of the bull's horns. The bull was humping his head upward, driving the horn solidly into the man's back.

Dummett sprinted forward and slammed his shoulder into the bull's neck, causing it to stagger off-balanced to the side. He wrapped his left arm around the straining neck from above and began punching the bull in the throat while swinging his legs upward in an attempt to pry the old man off the horn.

Finally his thrusts pushed the body free, flinging it like a broken doll onto the ground.

Dummett gathered his feet under him. Reaching forward with his free hand, he grasped the ring and jerked downward with all his strength. The bull dropped to his fore-knees.

Recovering his footing, Dummett dragged the stumbling bull to the snubbing post and threw a double half hitch around it with the line. He ran back to the circle of men now surrounding Old Pumpery.

"Move back," he shouted. "Dammit, let me through."

He pushed his way through the knot of men. Cudjoe, sitting on the ground, held Old Pumpery's head and shoulders in his lap. Charles knelt in the sand beside them, crying softly.

The old man's lined face was relaxed and Dummett could see that the eyes were clear, but a froth of blood bubbling from both nostrils confirmed the certainty of a punctured lung.

"It sho' does hurt, Cap'n." Old Pumprey's voice gurgled. A cough expelled a misty spray of crimson onto Dummett's shirt.

"You'll be all right," Dummett told him. "Just hold on till we can fix you up."

The old man's eyes darted back and forth, looking at the blood on Dummett's shirt. "I sorry, Cap'n. I think I just shit..." The eyes stopped moving, staring fixedly through Dummett.

When the old man's body didn't move for a moment, Charles lay his small hand on Old Pumpery's shoulder, called to him and shook him. He looked up at Dummett through eyes filled with tears. "Papa, Old Pumpery's not moving...not answering me. What's wrong with him?"

Dummett got to his feet and stared down at the body for a long moment, then said, "He's dead, Son. Get up from there."

"But Papa, I loved Old Pumpery. Didn't you love Old Pumpery? How can he be dead?" The boy's voice quivered with his pain.

"He just is," Dummett said, lifting the boy from the ground and handing him to Ebo Thom. "Yes, I loved Old Pumpery," he told the boy.

He then shoved through the crowd of men and strode stiff-legged from the corral to the barn. Grabbing two shovels and a twelve-pound maul, he returned to the corral.

"Cudjoe, have two men bury him down by the river where he'll have a good view." He dropped the shovels and walked over to the snubbing post. Swinging the maul high over his head, he smashed it down on the bull's forehead, killing it instantly.

Charles' scream tore through his mind like the sudden screech of a hawk in flight. He turned to step toward the boy. When Charles saw him coming he screamed again, stretching his arms around Ebo Thom's neck, trying to crawl over his shoulders. Through the wailing, Dummett could hear his son's anguished cry, "Please don't hurt me, Papa."

The sails ran up their masts and ballooned in the stiff wind. As the large schooner *Josephine* slid backward through the water for a moment, Burnham spun the helm to starboard and the bow swung off-wind to port. The ship's timbers groaned as she heeled sharply and slowly leaned into a smooth, forward motion. Her lee rail dipped toward the frothy water, slamming across the waves, building speed. Burnham held her on this tack until he felt she had reached her best pace, then eased off a couple of points.

On the foredeck, his crew flaked lines and winched halyards tight. His chest swelled with the pride of ownership as it always had when he considered his good fortune.

Three years earlier, Colonel Peck's wife died, leaving him alone with six children. The man's grief and hardship soon led to disillusionment with his homestead. Through his neglect, most of his slaves slipped away in the night and were never found. With no laborers, his sugarcane fields lay fallow after only one crop.

Peck had approached Burnham with a proposal.

"The *Josephine* is not large enough to pay me to put her into my ocean-going fleet, but she's ideal for coastal transportation. If I take her with me, your harvest of pineapple will cost you dearly when you ship them to market in St. Augustine. I have an investment of love in this colony and want all of you to have a good life. So, let's trade, your next crop for my schooner."

Burnham knew he would be without hard money for another two years if he didn't convert his crop into cash. But during the last two years, he had learned to live well from the offerings of land and sea. Mary had never complained about the nearly uncivilized life. In fact, she had taken his provisions and made a comfortable life for them in the palmetto shack that had grown one room larger after the birth of another daughter, Louisa.

But, as Peck spoke, Burnham was probing an even greater idea. He knew Peck had written his own crop off and was trying to salvage something from the situation.

"If the pineapple market continues getting better up north," he said. "My crop will be worth a lot more than that schooner." He paused to let that sink in, then asked, "What arrangements have you made for your homestead and your house?"

"None as of yet. I was thinking that maybe several of you might want to pool your money to buy my land."

"No one here has that kind of money. How about this? Your fields have not been cared for and your pineapples lie neglected in the field. I'll work both places, clean up your fields, and give you both crops if you throw in the house and land with the ship." Burnham's heart seemed to rise to his throat. He could hear Dummett's voice, echoing over time: *The land'll take care of you, boy. It can make you wealthy.*

To his surprise Peck accepted on the spot. A few papers were drawn and the deal was made.

When they moved into the large house, Mary ran through the spacious rooms, then said, "Lordy, I've died and gone to heaven."

Many members of the colony had fallen on hard times, often due to their laziness. Most lacked the will to live with the land or do the work necessary to gain from it. Others were unfit by reason of their backgrounds. It was from these that he was able to build a crew capable of handling the *Josephine*.

Burnham had gone throughout the colony from Jupiter inlet to Barker's Bluff, checking with all the men, offering a small share of the profits and the chance to use old skills in new ways. The Englishman, James Price, was the first to sign on, followed quickly by the old man everyone called Crazy Ned, a Swedish sailor who had once fallen from a ship's topmast to the deck, suffering some brain damage. James Middleton, a Georgian, took on the duty of ship's carpenter. Young Phil Herman signed on as able seaman, filling out the crew and giving Burnham a man capable of working in the rigging of the sixty-foot schooner.

Now, Burnham was making his second trip in the *Josephine* to Charleston, but it was the first carrying a crop that was all his. On his previous trip, he took turtles for shipment to Europe, but they had been roughly handled and had arrived in England in poor condition, with many dying during the crossing. The little profit allowed him to buy a few of the staples that Mary had done without over the years.

With this shipment, he was trying something new; he had carved little wooden pillows to place under the turtle's heads and he planned to sponge their eyes frequently with saltwater. He believed that, if they were cared for properly, the turtles should survive the passage.

Two weeks ago, Burnham sailed the *Jumper* to the trading post at Barker's Bluff where he purchased some supplies for the *Josephine*. On his return trip home, he was surprised by the young Seminole, Tommy

Jumper, hailing him from an island in the river narrows south of Barker's Bluff.

The young man took the line while Burnham beached the boat. They spoke for nearly an hour concerning the trading post.

"The fat one, McGirt, cheats the Miccosukee on every trade," Tommy Jumper complained. "His knives will not hold an edge, his cornmeal has white worms, and his wyomey makes our people ill."

"Whiskey does that to people."

"This is not good wyomey. It is white man's rotgut."

"Barker tries to keep Ratch McGirt straight," Burnham said.

"Barker is bad too. Like the fat McGirt, he cheats the Indian. Much trouble soon if they do not stop."

Later, as Burnham sailed toward home, he realized the young Seminole was angrier than he had ever seen him, and an angry Seminole was often a dangerous one.

Now, an overnight sail in the Gulfstream brought them into Matanzas Inlet south of St. Augustine, where the pineapples were off loaded onto one of Peck's barges. On the tide, Burnham took the *Josephine* across the Matanzas bar and back into the Gulfstream for the long journey to Charleston.

By late afternoon they were abreast of the St. Simons Light where he decided to move into the harbor and give the men a much needed shore rest. Within the hour, the schooner swung from the hook in the placid bay and the men went ashore to the village by the lighthouse.

In a small saloon, Burnham ordered two bottles of rum for his men and one for himself. While the men sat at a table, Burnham took his glass and walked to the door, looking up at the octagon shaped tower of the nearby lighthouse. This was the closest he had ever been to one. The light was inactive this early in the afternoon, but with dusk approaching, Burnham knew the lamp would soon be lighted.

"Are you the captain of that schooner out there?" asked a voice behind him.

Burnham turned and saw the grizzled features of a short, stubby man dressed in a blue coat with brass buttons.

"I am. Captain Burnham, at your service sir," he said.

"I'm Captain Robert Bloxham. I see you admire my light."

"You're the keeper? Must be a strange life, sleeping all day and staying awake all night."

Bloxham laughed. "Well, I don't get to sleep all day."

Burnham held up the bottle of rum and raised an inquisitive eyebrow. Bloxham nodded acceptance and held out his glass. "And I rarely have to stay awake all night," he added.

He led Burnham outside and they sat on a porch bench, sipping their rum in the last glow of sunlight. Bloxham explained the life of a light-house keeper.

"We have few needs that aren't cared for by the government," he said. "We're better supplied than most army units."

Burnham listened, absorbed in stories of a different lifestyle than he could imagine. The old man was garrulous and inclined to tell of every adventure he could to the new listener. "I don't talk much to my assistants. We're usually on different schedules. Besides, we've lived together so long, we treat each other like old shoes—use them and throw them under the bed when we don't need them."

As the mantle of darkness descended, Burnham was startled when the cupola of the tower sparked into life, and he could see three long fingers of light—one red, one white, and one blue-radiating to the horizon.

"Why three beams of light, and why are they colored?" he asked.

"The color's the legacy of the light's builder and first keeper, Mr. James Gould. He put colored glass over each lens in a patriotic gesture to represent America. The three beams are the timing for the identification signal. The lens turns once a minute. A ship sees the red flash, then ten seconds later the white, then twenty seconds to the blue. This is followed by a gap of thirty seconds and the sequence begins anew."

Burnham pulled out his turnip watch and timed the flashes. They were exactly as Bloxham said. He gave the timepiece stem two turns before he replaced it.

"Amazingly simple," he said.

The remainder of the trip to Charleston was uneventful, marked only by a minor squall that the *Josephine* took well in stride. Burnham entered the harbor with the two-storied Fort Sumter to his starboard and drove straight for the church spire that served local traffic as a secondary light-house.

After arriving in port, Burnham saw to the arrangements for shipping the turtles to England, personally instructing the freighter captain in the care of the turtles, especially the sponging of their eyes. Giving his crew only one day of shore leave in the port city, Burnham departed before dawn the next morning for St. Augustine under clear skies.

Mary dipped a ladle of steaming water from the reservoir of the wood-burning cookstove and carefully poured it into the bowl of cornstarch. Through the open window, she could see Frances in the back yard, leaning over a steaming tub, sloshing indigo bluing through a load of fresh-washed clothes.

Household chores were a blessing to Mary. Without them, and without the company of the children, she felt she would perish from loneliness. Burnham had been gone a week. She estimated he should be in Charleston by now, but she knew the gulfstream would quicken the journey there. The time of the return trip was dependent on fair winds. A southerly wind could beat the stream's countercurrent into high waves and make for a slow passage home.

Mary paused in stirring the cornstarch, setting the bowl down. She pulled her damp blouse away from her shoulders and turned her face to the soft breeze from the open window. Brushing a straggle of hair from her face, she glanced at George playing in the corner of the room with his two lead soldiers. That boy, she thought. So much like his father—so fascinated by anything military and so nearly grown up. She sometimes thought his childhood would be over before he had a chance to be a child.

He was now nine years old, and proving to be an irritant to his older brother with his imaginative tales. She turned her attention to Junior lying on the floor, absorbed in *Murray's English Reader* that Burnham had bought for him in Savannah. The boy's fingers twisted a strand of hair as he intently read the pages. This was her scholar, a throwback to her father with all his studious endeavors, and gentler than a boy of eleven years had any reason to be.

"Mama, Mama, look! I see an Indian!" George had dropped his soldiers and was leaning out the window.

"Now, George," she said. "You know there's no..."

"He's lying, Mama," Junior said, rising to push George away from the window. "He does that all..." Junior paused as he pulled the curtain back from the window. "He's right, Mama! That Dan Osceola Indian is standing out by the barn." George ran toward the door.

"You stay right where you be," Mary shouted. "I'll get Frances." She opened the back door, trying to keep her voice calm as she called to the girl.

"Frances, come in the house."

"I'm not finished," Frances answered. "I have to take these clothes out and..."

"Frances Augusta, you come in this house—right now!" She struggled to control the hysteria building in her as she saw the Indian walking toward the back yard.

Frances dropped the stick and began walking toward the house. Then she saw the Indian and started to run. Dan Osceola stopped by the large shade tree and held up both hands in the sign of peace.

"Mrs. Burnham. I must speak," he said.

Mary ushered Frances into the house, then stepped out, closing the door behind her. She walked to the boiling pot, picked up her oak stick and began lifting the clothes from the water to lay in the basket. She knew in her heart this young Indian presented no danger, yet she had to battle within herself to remain calm.

"Captain Burnham asked you people to stay away from our home when he leaves. You have always done so. Why are you here now?"

"There might be trouble. Trader Barker, with his man McGirt, cheats our people with his trade goods. His tools, his whiskey—bad. Our people had council. We stop trading with him. But four of the younger men argued to punish him. They left the council in anger." After a short pause, he lowered his head and continued, softly, "My friend, Tommy Jumper, leads the young men. Our chief has fears of what they might do."

"What has that to do with us?"

"Our chief sends me to ask when Captain Burnham will return. We are trying to find the young men—hold off trouble until the Captain returns. Holatter Micco wishes to council with him—stop Barker cheating."

"It might be several weeks before he gets back," Mary admitted.

Dan Osceola thought for a moment before speaking. "I will report this to my chief. If trouble comes, stay inside. You will be safe. No Miccosukee would harm the family of Burnham." He turned and trotted into the woods.

Mary continued to lift the clothes from the tub, trying to make the scene appear normal to the children. When she was certain he was gone she called Frances out to help her begin the starch rinse. By midmorning their chores were finished and she decided to take the children down to the river to swim and lie in the cool breeze.

They had reached the edge of the bluff when she heard the drumming hooves of a galloping horse.

Major Russell burst from the woods and drew his lathered horse to a sliding halt beside her. Swinging down from the saddle, he stumbled but checked his fall by jerking on the reins of the wild-eyed horse.

"You must leave...hurry, they can't be too far behind." Strands of thinning hair were windblown across his hatless head. Then Mary saw that the sleeve of his white shirt was soaked with blood. A chill shivered its way through her body in spite of the heat in this shadeless spot.

"Who are behind you?"

"They killed my brother-in-law, Barker. My wife...how will I ever tell her?" He grasped the pommel of his saddle and ground his forehead into his arm.

"Please," she said, knowing the answer as she asked. "Who killed him?"

"The savages," he groaned. "About dusk last evening. They chased us... and we ran and I was hit...but I got away." He paused as he struggled to catch his breath. "I caught my horse and got away. Barker went down from a gunshot and I saw McGirt jump into the river. I don't know if McGirt is alive, but I heard Barker's screams as I ran. They must have been scalping him while he still lived." He stopped, again gasping for breath as he looked at her, his eyes staring as if he was seeing her for the first time.

"I've ridden all night to get here."

"Did you warn the other settlers along the way?" Mary asked.

"I yelled to them as I passed that they were to come now to the fort." He grasped the saddle and swung up. "I must hurry and send word on to everyone. Captain Pinkham's gone but we'll take his schooner. We leave as quickly as we can make preparations. Get to Fort Capron when you're ready. And hurry." He gouged his heels into the horse's flanks and galloped off.

"Mama. What'll we do?" Frances asked. She looked calm, too calm, Mary thought, for a fourteen-year-old girl. "You said Dan Osceola told you—"

"I know, child. He said to stay in the house." Mary gathered the children together and ushered them back toward the house. But her mind was a torrent of confusion. Could she trust the Indians to honor their pledge of safety? What if everyone left? They would be here alone, without protection.

By the time they reached the house, she had made her decision. "Frances, we must pack whatever bags we can with clothes. We'll go on the boat."

Sending Junior to help Jackson and Martha get ready, Mary set the rest of the children to the task of selecting a minimal amount of clothing to pack.

Within the hour, they had loaded two small bags onto the *Jumper*. As she seated the children in the sailboat she tried to calm them. "We'll be back. The schooner will probably just go offshore and wait till things settle." When Junior arrived with Jackson and Martha, she glanced once at her home, then took her place in the boat.

George took the helm and they set off for Fort Capron. They arrived amidst a bustle of agitated humanity. Many families were there already, most with only the clothes they wore. Only a few had managed to salvage any household goods.

Major Russell was frantically directing the loading of people onto small rowboats for transport to the large schooner lying in the middle of the river. "No, No! You can take only what you can carry," he was yelling at a man who was trying to load a bedstead into the boat. Russell grabbed the bedstead and slammed it to the ground. He then herded the man's family into the boat along with others that sat dumbly waiting.

As George read the scene, he turned the *Jumper* and steered directly to the schooner, where he helped Mary and the children aboard. Then he sailed the boat ashore. Running it onto the bank, he pulled it into a dense growth of underbrush and covered it with palmetto fronds.

"Hurry," Russell yelled to a lanky farmer who had just ridden into the clearing with his wife and baby on a mule. "Let the animal go and get into the rowboat. We're just gonna make the tide as it is."

George scrambled aboard as the overloaded rowboat got underway for the schooner.

In what seemed much too long to Mary, the schooner eventually cleared the bar at the inlet and drove away from the beach.

Rumors flew wildly around the deck as the people stood in shocked groups under the burning sun. Every time the size of the Indian band was mentioned, the numbers grew.

It soon became apparent that Major Russell was sailing the boat north, leaving the area. Angry voices were raised in protest. "How about the people what ain't here yet?"

"They'll have to get out as best as they can," yelled a livid Russell.

"Iffen it weren't for the thieving scum at the Bluff this woun't have happened," one man screamed at Russell. Others yelled agreement, their faces clouded with anger. Finally, Russell mumbled something about needing some salve for his wounded arm. He turned the helm over to one of his crewmen and went below.

The torrid sun beat down with intense heat. Mary rummaged through the bags, searching for head coverings for the children. Finding some aprons, she tore them into shawls. George, watching her wrap one around Junior's head, waved her off as she turned toward him. "I'll get on top of the cabin in the shade of the sail," he said. "Use it on the babies." He scrambled to the cabin roof and stood leaning in the breeze against the mainmast, holding tightly to the halyards.

Mary had just settled the other children against the cabin wall in the small pocket of shade it afforded when the door to the cabin burst open and Major Russell staggered out onto the deck. He had poured a black substance over his tightly bandaged arm. Before he went below, she wouldn't have believed his appearance could become wilder, but now his red-rimmed eyes glowed with a strange light and she caught a whiff of brandy as he passed her. Mary stepped around the cabin to watch as he lurched back to the helm, jerked the wheel from the crewman, spinning it viciously in an arc. The vessel careened from its course.

Moments later Mary heard Frances scream. "Mama! Come quick! George is hurt."

The anguish in Frances' voice froze Mary in place for an instant. Then she forced her way through a crowd of people to the foredeck. As they parted, she saw George lying on the deck, his head drenched in blood.

A crewman kneeling beside George looked up at her, his face etched with distress. "It weren't my fault, Ma'am," he said. "He was standing on the cabin roof right by me. When the ship jerked around, the boom swung across the wind and hit him. I yelled but he looked over at me 'stead of ducking."

Mary sat on the deck and pulled George's head into her lap, unmindful of the blood soaking her dress. His eyes were closed, but he was drawing shallow breaths through his pursed lips.

Someone sat a bucket of water beside her. She dipped the hem of her dress into it and washed the blood from his cheek. Probing gingerly at the back of his head, she found the split in the scalp. She could feel the wide crack in the bone beneath the skin.

"There, there, lad. It's going to be fine soon," she cooed softly to him as she began to gently rock. She felt him stiffen in her arms for a moment then his body went limp. She began to cry as she saw the last breath softly part his blue lips.

"You stupid son of a bitch," Burnham screamed as he lunged across the small apothecary for Major Russell's throat. Several men jammed into the small room grabbed him, pulling him back.

"You ain't got no call to speak to me that way." Russell wiped a lather of spittle from his lips, then winced from the alcohol Doctor Seth Peck poured into the hole in his arm. "I did what I had to do. What did I get from it? Gangrene. Look how black my arm is. I'm going to lose it. But I saved your family."

"Saved my family? The hell you did. My son is dead! You killed him. My family wasn't in any danger. Now we've got nothing, right back where we were six years ago. All our property, everything...gone." Burnham shook loose from the arms holding him. "I'm all right," he told the men. "I won't hurt him. He's not worth the effort."

"No one made anybody leave," Russell yelled at the group. "Everybody was pretty quick to get on my boat." He looked directly at Burnham, a look of sorrow erasing the anger on his face. "And your boy's death was an accident. God knows I'm sorry about that."

Burnham stepped back by the door of the room, struggling to keep a check on his flaring emotions.

Big Phil Hermann shook his fist at Russell. "You financed Barker and McGirt," he shouted. "And you knew they were cheating those Indians. Hell, for that matter, they were cheating us, your neighbors, and you knew it! But you let it go on." This brought shouts of agreement and the tightly packed mass of men surged forward threateningly.

"Men! Let's hold up now," Burnham said. "I guess we all knew about the cheating." He paused and looked into the faces of the men who had been his neighbors. "If we had been more concerned, I guess we could have stopped it. But maybe we were all too busy trying to get ahead to take notice. And I guess Russell is right about the panic driving everyone to his boat. Maybe we ought to back off till we cool down. There's nothing we can do about it now."

He turned and walked from the doctor's office. Shoving his hands into his pockets, he walked slowly down Bay Street, thinking of the recent events. He had been in St. Augustine for three days repairing a shroud on his mast when the schooner arrived with the refugees from the Indian River. He recognized it immediately as Pinkham's.

As he watched the ship dock, his thoughts raced madly through possible reasons for its presence in St. Augustine. Then, when the refugees began to stumble down the gangplank, he saw a body carried on a litter, followed by Mary, Frances, and his other children. He could see Mary's face, clouded with grief. She looked at him and, after a moment of confusion at his presence here, she burst into tears. Frances ran to him, tears streaming down her face, and nestled into his protective arms. He quickly searched the faces of his other children. Then, the horrible realization struck him. George was not among them!

He took his family to Anna Dummett's home. After hearing the news, she and her mother agreed to put them up for as long as it would take Burnham to decide what he was going to do.

He made arrangements for George to be buried the next morning in the Public Burial Grounds. Even now, as he stood at the seawall overlooking the slate-gray waters, the women of his family were washing his son's body and dressing him in his best clothes.

He shook off the painful image and began to sort out possibilities for the immediate future. He knew in his heart that most of the families of the colony would not return to their homes at Fort Pierce and, without them, neither could he. The Indians would be no problem and would, in fact, probably help him. But could he survive with only their help?

The problem plagued him. *The land'll take care of you, boy. It can make you wealthy.* Dummett's admonition was always with him. But now he'd lost the land. If he couldn't return to his homestead, what could he do? Return to Jacksonville and law enforcement? Rejoin the army? Had his loss stripped him of the confidence he once had? No! There was a way. There had to be. His only possessions were his family—what was left of it—and the *Josephine*.

He felt a need for Dummett. If he had ever learned anything, it was that he could get help from his friends. He felt an overpowering urge to find someone who would just listen.

Two men stood in front of a cigar shop, deep in conversation. One looked up as he approached, nodded in his direction and said something to his companion. The other man turned and walked vigorously toward Burnham.

"Captain Burnham, I'm Colonel John Marshall. Could I buy you a drink and talk to you. I have a proposition that you might find appealing."

They walked back down Bay Street to Mickler's tavern. Minorcans. Burnham's thoughts were jolted as his memory flashed to another failed colony: the Turnbull Plantation at New Smyrna. He recalled Dummett telling him about Doctor Andrew Turnbull bringing Minorcans eager to live on, and work, the plantation. The venture failed when Turnbull's promises degenerated into near slavery for the colonists. Their bloody rebellion had resulted in St. Augustine becoming a center for refugees. And now the Indian River Colony had joined those ranks.

As he poured rum into Burnham's glass, Marshall offered condolences for the loss of his son. "It's a fierce land we live in and I suppose tragedy is a part of living here that we can all expect sooner or later." He paused for a moment until Burnham glanced up at him. "If it's any consolation to you, I heard that Major Russell got real nasty and insisted that Dr. Peck amputate his arm. After the surgery, the doctor determined that the black stain was ink. Russell had poured it on himself while he was drunk thinking it was salve. Some said Peck knew about it before he sawed the man's arm off."

Burnham shook his head and looked down at his rum. "The Lord moves in mysterious ways," he said quietly. "It doesn't matter."

Marshal cleared his throat and began to swirl wet circles on the table with his glass. "Let me state my proposal in simple terms. We can work out the details later. I'm rebuilding the sugarmill at Dunn-Lawton."

Burnham looked up sharply and said, "I thought the buildings were all burned."

"They were, but they weren't destroyed. They're built from Coquina blocks—all structurally sound. I'm in the process now of rebuilding. We'll be finished in about a month, ready to begin operations."

Burnham listened as the Colonel outlined his plans for buying cane from nearby plantations and processing the sugar and molasses. "We'll be the only operational mill on the East Coast," he said as excitement widened his eyes. "I need an engineer and manager to take charge of the operation. Dr. Peck tells me you probably won't be returning south and he says you have the prime requirements for my project—a feeling for machinery and the intelligence to learn quickly."

Burnham put his head between his hands, his mind a turmoil. Flashes of George's still form drifted before his eyes, and the anguish of Mary's cries penetrated his consciousness.

Marshall continued softly. "I can offer you a home for your family and you may choose either a straight salary or a percentage of the business. I'd prefer you to accept the percentage. As a partner you'd certainly stand to make more money. You'd be completely in charge of the mill and I'll oversee the development of the cane fields on the property."

"I'd give you all the effort I have, no matter the arrangement," Burnham said. "Do you mind if I discuss this with my wife after my son's funeral and let you know, say, tomorrow evening?"

Marshall nodded. Burnham excused himself and left, returning to the seawall, where he sat for the rest of the daylight hours.

Chapter 13

Burnham stood in the purgery, one of the two sugar curing rooms in the large sugarmill. The Cuban, Raphael Olivaros, ran his finger through the molasses seeping from a hogshead sugar cask into large troughs on the floor, then stuck it in his mouth. He looked up at Burnham, shifted the huge cigar to the other corner of his mouth and said, "Salty and grainy."

Burnham nodded. "I know. We'll ship it to Jamaica for rum."

The two rooms held over a hundred of the hogsheads. He estimated the rate of flow as the molasses dripped into the wooden troughs, then left the purgery.

Even though they were winding down the last stages of sugar production, the bustle of activity around the mill was raucous. Burnham stood for a moment in the shade of a massive liveoak, its limbs thicker than many of the neighboring trunks. He looked at the sugarmill, admiring its lines and the soft pastel hues of its coquina blocks. With its high, arched windows, it reminded him of an old Spanish mission. A blue haze drifted from one of the two chimneys thrusting above the two-story building.

During October and November of 1852, wagonloads of cane had been sent up the conveyors to the second floor, where a steam driven press crushed and squeezed the sweet juice from the stalks to drip down into the holding troughs.

The mechanical process had been simple for Burnham to develop. The nearby ruins of the Bulow and Dummett sugarmill had given him several ideas that he quickly incorporated into the rebuilding of Dunn-Lawton. The process of making sugar, however, was totally beyond him. Olivaros had been in Dummett's old militia company, the Mosquito Roarers, settling back in St. Augustine when the Indian wars of the thirties ended. Burnham found him there and the Cuban was proving to be the best asset he had. The old man had grown up on plantations in Cuba and knew instinctively when each stage of the sugar was finished.

Thirty feet east of the sugarmill, the spinning blade of a sawmill was chinging its way through a long, pine trunk, slicing a yellow plank from its side like a knife cutting through a slab of bacon. At least twenty other logs were stacked near the saw. Thick globs of resin bled from the scars of lost limbs, permeating the air with the rich odor of raw turpentine.

The straight-grained planks cut from the hearts of the pines were to be used for the flooring and interior walls of his new home. The building would begin when the sawing was finished. Marshall had approved the plans Mary had sketched, and Burnham was anxious to begin the construction. Mary had been patient in her acceptance of living once more in a palmetto shack, but he knew she would never lose her disappointment in the abandonment of the fine home on the Indian River. Burnham felt lucky in having Mrs. Marshall and her two children so close to give Mary and the children the companionship they so desperately needed to help ease the pain of isolation.

The site of their new home had been selected and cleared, a cool, shady area a hundred yards north of the mill. The mill was surrounded by a glen of large oaks, maples, and magnolia. Marshall's men were doing an outstanding job of keeping the undergrowth—palmettos and Spanish bayonet—grubbed out. He chuckled to himself, remembering Marshall's tactic that first year.

The colonel had taken his men on a walk through the underbrush, and within minutes had uncovered several pygmy rattlers, a five-foot diamondback rattler, and a pretty but deadly, red, yellow, and black banded coral snake. As he led the men through the underbrush, Marshall occasionally ducked, allowing his followers to blunder into the sweeping web of a banana spider. The homesteader of this sticky insect trap, painted in vibrantly lustrous yellows and reds and sometimes as large as a man's palm, would abandon his disintegrating barrier and move to the nearest island of refuge—usually the face of the man enmeshed in the net. Upon leaving the tropical growth, he had the men check each other for the tiny deer tick that hitches a ride on any animal brushing against the palmetto leaves. They found an average of twenty per man.

Marshall never had to give the order to clear the area of brush, and never again worried about its maintenance. The men were religious in this duty.

"Captain Burnham, I would talk."

Burnham snapped out of his reverie, turning toward the voice. He recoiled when he saw the Indian standing in the dense shadow of the trees across the road. Then he recognized him.

Dan Osceola was no longer a boy. Standing almost six feet tall, he had filled out to over two hundred pounds. A multi-colored shirt belted at the waist hung to his knees over buckskin leggings. His only other adornments were a turban crowned with three egret plumes and a braided necklace of golden wool. He wore the grace of his manhood proudly like a medal.

"Dan. Welcome." Burnham held up his hand as he walked across the road to the Indian.

"I could not be sure of welcome," Dan said, returning the salute. "The killings three years ago...we heard of your son's death. I was sorry. George would have been a fine man."

"Thank you," Burnham said. "I appreciate your sympathy." The Indian's buckskin leggings were caked with dried muck, indicating to Burnham that he had journeyed a long way, through areas not fit for travel, avoiding the well-used roadways through the state. He stood beside the Indian now, wondering, but unsure of the reason for the meeting.

"I wanted you to know," Dan said, "Chitto Hadjo captured the four young men who killed the white trader, Barker. They were tried in our council and court during Green Corn Dance. One tried to escape and was killed. Holatter Micco delivered the other three to General Twiggs at Fort Brooke." He paused for a long moment and gazed blankly into the shadows of the forest. Then he seemed to gather himself back to reality and said, "My heart is empty without the friendship of Tommy Jumper."

Burnham felt a dread boiling in his stomach. "What do you mean? What happened to Tommy?"

"You did not know? Tommy led the attacks on the whites."

"But those three young men given to the military authorities for trial for murder. I heard about it only recently. They were found hanged in the fort's jail—suicide."

Dan Osceola smiled through tight lips. "We were told by the soldiers that Tommy and the others braided the ropes themselves from their blankets. The only braiding Tommy ever did was this necklace that I now wear to honor my friend."

Burnham remembered the outrage following the killing at Barker's Bluff three years earlier. The same four young Indians raided a trading post on the West Coast a few days later, killing two white men. By the time the rumors got around it was believed that more than a hundred Indians were on the rampage, and the Army transferred fourteen hundred men into the state to do battle. Governor Moseley of Florida mobilized two hundred volunteers and personally borrowed twenty thousand dollars to finance the effort.

The actions of four young, misguided Indians had resulted in the waste of all that manpower and money over fear of a people who, at the time, numbered less than four hundred men, women and children.

Had his son not been killed and his home and property lost, Burnham might have seen the irony in the situation. As it was, he saw only the tragedy.

Burnham laid his hand on the young man's shoulder. "I lost as much as most because of the panic," he said slowly. "I hold no grudge against your people. They were pushed into anger; there's no doubt about that. But there should never have been enough anger to kill Barker and McGirt. Or anyone for that matter, especially Tommy and those boys."

Dan Osceola looked quizzically at him. "McGirt is not dead. After your people left, he was seen going into empty shacks and houses along the river, taking goods, loading a large skiff."

"That bastard. There's your real thief," Burnham said. "A scavenger. He lives on the misery of others."

Dan Osceola grunted assent. "All peoples have men like him." He paused, looking away from Burnham as if working himself up to saying something. Burnham waited politely until Dan finally asked, "Are our people welcome and safe in the white villages over here?"

Burnham had anticipated the question. "I'm really not sure." He thought for a moment, choosing his words carefully. "Why would you want to go to the white villages? The whites will surely mistreat your people"

"I know. We have some contact with whites near Fort Brooke. But can it get worse than now? They have set aside a reservation for us in the worst land. It is against your law for us to cross its boundaries. And they want to send those of us who remain to the Arkansas country, to live among our enemies, the Creeks. Even the great Coacoochee, Wild Cat, has gone.

"But those of us who remain, we will never leave. This is our land—all of it. My body is made of its sands. The Great Spirit gave me legs to walk over it, eyes to see its ponds and rivers, its forests and game. Why can we not live here in peace? I can live in peace with the whites although they steal our cattle and horses, cheat us, and take our lands. They may chain our hands and feet, but our hearts will always be free. Only by leaving the reservation will we be really free. But we must know what to expect."

Burnham knew that, as a nation, the Indians had acted honorably, demonstrating their desire to cooperate in justice over the matter. Parleys had been held between the military and the Seminole chieftains. As a result, over a hundred of the Indians voluntarily left Florida. And yet those remaining, knowing the duplicity of the white government, feared to venture amongst its people.

And now, Burnham faced a longtime friend, who bravely came into what he knew might have been danger, but who was also afraid to range at will over his own homeland. Servitude and slavery sometimes took the form of freedom. It was hard to tell the difference.

"For sure you will want to stay off the north end of Merritt's Island. That's where Dummett lives."

The young Seminole's face took on a look of shock. "But Dummett is an honorable man."

"Dummett is an Indian killer."

"No. That was war. White men killed my people. My father killed white men. But the war ended. Now Dummett is the brother of the Seminole. Some whites had taken Tommy's father, the great chief Jumper, killer of Major Dade, and were about to hang him. Dummett saved him. Long after Jumper died, my people carry respect for Dummett, as they now respect you. When Tommy was born, Dummett gave his mother a blanket of golden wool. When the blanket aged and tattered, Tommy's mother cut strips of it to braid into the necklace he always wore with pride. This is the third she has made—and the last." His hands reverently held the woolen loop.

Burnham shook his head in wonder. "I'll be damned. Dummett—the man has depths. I'll talk to people around here, tell them of your honorable intentions, and see how they feel. When will I see you again?"

"Soon." The Indian turned to leave.

"Good luck then, and peace be with you."

A moment later Burnham was alone, his mind a turmoil of memories. He had been unable to quench the hatred he felt toward Barker and McGirt. Their deaths had left him with no one to strike out against. His anger had erupted only against Major Russell. Even though he knew Russell was only indirectly to blame for George's death, he still carried a grudge he couldn't shake. He thought time had dulled his grief. He was wrong.

Now, with the news that McGirt was still alive, hatred sprang full-blown into his mind.

George was not his only tragedy. His family had suffered through the loss of their home and whatever future it held. Poverty might have become theirs for life. Landing the job at Dunn-Lawton had been pure chance, based on an accident of timing. He might have been forced into St. Augustine by the panic before Marshall needed him, or worse, after Marshall had already found an engineer. Either way, Burnham wondered what he might be doing now if he hadn't found this job. He shuddered at the thought.

The deal Colonel Marshall gave him was probably the best he could have done anywhere—twenty percent of the profit on the mill as salary. Marshall withheld some of Burnham's money as savings, "In case some day I decide to take on a partner, you'll be able to afford it." That idea became a goal to Burnham. He learned something new everyday. The work was certainly hard but it also fascinated him.

The mill had earned enough the first two years to give him sufficient hard money to provide his family a comfortable life, if living in a palmetto shack could be considered comfortable. At least they were well fed. Now, at the end of the third year, they would have a nice, new home overlooking the river, and all aspects of their lives should improve.

"Señor," Olivaros interrupted his musings, yelling from the second floor engine room. "Colonel Marshall. He is coming along the road." Burnham quickly climbed the stairs to watch Marshall approach on horseback down the King's Road.

Burnham didn't like what he saw. Marshall had left with his family three weeks earlier on a steamboat for Charleston, combining a business trip with a family vacation. While there, he was hammering out contracts for the sale of the sugar and molasses. Burnham realized that Marshall was now alone, riding with his head lowered. The horse walked with a swaying gait, as horses will when tired from a long journey. Why was Marshall returning on horseback? And where was his family?

Marshall's horse stopped at the turn of the road leading through the sugarmill. The man just sat there, leaning on arms crossed over the pommel of the saddle, with his chin slumped to his chest as if he didn't know where he was.

Burnham ran down the stairs and around to the horse. "Marshall, welcome back," he said, reaching for the reins. Marshall slowly raised his head and stared vacantly at Burnham.

Burnham led the horse around the building to the well. Something's sure as hell wrong, Burnham thought as he helped the Colonel dismount. Holding the man's quaking arm, he guided him to a bench and fetched a dipper of water. Marshall drank deeply. His eyes sought Burnham's in a look of beseeching pain. "They're dead," he said flatly.

"Who? Who're dead?" Then, he saw the dull depth of pain in Marshall's eyes and knew before the man could speak.

"Merriam...and my boy, Samuel. We were on the Richmond...the boilers blew up. Off of Fernandina...on the way home. I don't know why I wasn't killed...or Robert. He was standing right beside his mother. But we weren't even hurt. God, I wish I had been."

"I'm so sorry, John. When—"

"The bastards were racing. We had come up beside another boat." Marshall's eyes took on a fierce set for a moment, then subsided back into glazed resignation.

Burnham sat quietly by Marshall, draping an arm across his shoulders. When he did, Marshall leaned slowly in, lay his head on Burnham's chest and began to softly cry.

"What'll I do, now? What'll I do?" He repeated the phrase over and over through heavier sobs tearing from his throat. Burnham held him gently for long minutes until he felt the man begin to relax.

Finally, Marshall shook his head as if to clear it. He rose, slowly, with the effort of an old man.

"I'm sorry," he said. "I thought I was over that." He stretched his arms to his side like a man awakening, then dropped them limply to his side. "I couldn't even bury them. Nothing to bury. They were never found. I left Robert in St. Augustine with Dena Dummett until I can return for him. She's already raising three sets of orphaned children."

"Dena Dummett? Who—"

"Miss Anna Dummett. They call her Dena—Grandmother. The woman's an angel. I bought that horse...hoping that taking time to return would..."

"Nothing will ever quite do that," Burnham said, thinking of George. He led the man down the lane toward his house, reflecting once again on the violent nature of life in paradise.

A month later, Colonel Marshall and Burnham stood on the new dock at Dunn-Lawton, looking over the quiet water as they awaited the appearance of the mailboat. Boxes containing all of Marshall's possessions were stacked neatly on the planks. Mary had helped him pack after he told them he was leaving for good. When he came across an item that had belonged to his wife, he held it a moment, then handed it to Mary, for her to keep. As she took it, he held on a little longer as if he couldn't bear to let it go. Then he released it with a sigh of finality and reached for the next item.

Now, with the remnants of his former life neatly boxed behind him, Marshall waited to begin the existence of the rest of his life. In the month since his return, Burnham tried to help Marshall push his grief below the surface, as he himself had done when George died. Dammit, life should go on. But he knew now that Marshall would only go through the motions of life for the sake of his surviving son.

Burnham had been shocked when Marshall told him of his decision to sell the sugarmill.

"So I'm looking for a buyer to take it off my hands," Marshall had told him. "I've thought it through. Robert and I can live comfortably back in Baltimore on what I'm asking for the sugarmill. I want you to have the first option to buy it."

Burnham felt his hopes soar when he heard these last words. To own the mill—he could think of no better goal in life. Then Marshall told him the figures.

"It's worth much more, but I'm only asking eight thousand."

The words kept echoing in Burnham's brain. Eight thousand. He might as well have asked for the Moon. Even if he could sell the *Josephine*, and he doubted he could, it would only be a drop trying to fill a bottle. He had the money in savings that Marshall had been withholding but it certainly wasn't enough. He doubted he could ever find enough money to finance the purchase without taking on a partner. He wished now that Marshall had never mentioned it.

The only possibility left to him was to approach Dummett to see if a partnership of some sort could be worked out. While he was certain Dummett had the money, he was not at all sure Dummett would be interested in the sugar business. In fact, Dummett no longer raised sugarcane, having grubbed out even the fifteen acres of cane at Merritt's Island, setting orange trees in their place. Oranges didn't need the care to grow that sugar did, and the harvest required less work. Having a family dependent on you made security more important.

Dummett's family had increased with the birth of Louisa two years ago. The last letter Burnham had from him bore the news of Leandra's latest pregnancy, the baby due about now. There was little chance Dummett would give up the groves at Merritt's Island. But he might want to invest in the mill, set up a partnership. This was Burnham's only hope. And this was what he told Marshall.

That was how they had left it, with Marshall agreeing to wait two weeks before approaching any other prospects in St. Augustine, giving Burnham time to visit Dummett.

"Even if you can't buy it, and I'm sure you can," Marshall told Burnham, "you will have no problem staying on as engineer. No buyer in his right mind would cut you loose."

Burnham thought that was poor consolation. To have the turnip offered but get only the greens made for a dismal meal.

A full moon hung below a dusty field of stars, illuminating the ocean beach with a cold light. Burnham hunkered down tighter into the depression in the dune, trying to elude the spray blowing from the exploding surf. Salty air cut into his lungs like knives. He felt miserable, yet exhilarated. Beside him, Douglas Dummett folded an extra wrap of a blanket around his shotgun barrel.

"Can you kill an insane bear with that cannon?" Burnham asked.

"This old ten-gauge'll stop them in their tracks. What do you mean insane?"

"The sane bears are home with their wives." Burnham turned his face away from Dummett, away from the wind. The moonglow did little to brighten his view of the beach that at this time was barren of bears.

"Like I said, best time to get bear on the beach is during turtle season. The bastards love those fresh eggs. But we'll probably get one. And this is another reason I can't go in with you on the sugarmill. How could any man give up such a pleasure as this?" He turned up the collar of his coat, and scrunched his neck down into its protection.

Burnham squirmed deeper into the loose sand, trying to duck under the harsh wind. "I guess being damn near broke is reason enough to not go into the sugarmill with me," he said.

"Well, I'm not exactly broke, but there's no spare money, at least not that kind. Not anymore. About ten years ago I was pretty flush...before I threw away Mount Pleasant to come down here. Starting over siphoned off any surplus."

Burnham smiled through chilled lips. Threw it all away. How can a man who has it all make that choice? Of course he knew the trauma Dummett had gone through, but it took more imagination than Burnham possessed to understand throwing it all away and starting over.

"At least you had it when you needed it. That was a blessing," he said.

"If I'd been broke then, I'd have done it anyway. Nothing's worth living a lie. It would have taken me longer to get going, but I'd have made it. And so will you. You've got the right idea in wanting to own the place, but it's probably best you don't get it. You'll never make it buying someone else's dream. You've got to live your own dream. You could stay for awhile with whoever buys the mill, salt your money away, then do what I did—get a homestead. Make your own dream."

Burnham chuckled. *"The land'll take care of you, boy. It can make you wealthy."*

"What's that?"

"Oh, just some advice a friend gave me fifteen years ago."

"At least you're willing to work and that makes you better off than those two fools down there at the Cape."

"Who?"

"Cousins of mine—Carpenter and Scobie. The lightkeepers, about fifteen miles south of here. A dollar a night to climb that tower in whatever weather, just to nurse that lantern. But that's not why they're fools. The government would allow them to homestead a hundred sixty acres each, but they say they're too old to mess with it. Too damn lazy if you ask me. They'd get out from under that lightkeeping job too if they could find someone fool enough to take it. They got pensions coming."

Dummett raised his head sharply, and began unwrapping his shotgun. "Get ready," he whispered into the moaning wind. "We have a visitor."

Burnham looked down the beach to the south. At first he could see nothing. Then he saw the black bear loping slowly along above the tide-line. Swinging its shaggy head from side to side, it snuffled for food thrown up by the surf. When it got to the line of fish Dummett had laid as bait, it stopped, picked up a large trout and snapped it in half with one toothy bite.

The bear moved up the slope of the beach to the next fish as Dummett cocked both hammers on the ten-gauge. Dummett stood and took aim. The bear saw him and reared to its hind legs with a challenging roar.

Dummett fired his first barrel into the bear's chest from fifteen feet.

The charge of lead knocked the bear backwards, tumbling it down the slope. It struggled to its feet as Dummett reached it and fired the second load into its face. The bear screamed, shook a bloody froth into the wind, and lunged toward Dummett.

Dummett instantly dropped his shotgun, lowered his shoulder and slammed into the bear below its knees. The bear seemed to turn through the air like an acrobat, landing on its back with a whumph. Dummett scrambled to his feet at the edge of the surf and edged around the bear, up toward the dunes. The bear jerked a couple of times, then rolled once down the slope, coming to rest in the surf.

Dummett darted forward, scooped up his shotgun, then backed away to the dunes, watching the bear closely as he began reloading.

"Is he dead?" Burnham yelled above the whine of the wind.

"I don't know. Why don't you run down there and poke him to find out?" The bear lay face down in the water, washing back and forth with his legs anchoring him to the sand.

"Wait long enough and he'll drown," Burnham offered.

"Damn right. I can wait."

"How did you retrieve the others you killed this way?"

"Never done this before. Always wanted to, but couldn't get anyone to go with me." Dummett laughed at Burnham's startled look.

"That stunt was the stupidest, luckiest thing I ever saw anyone do," Burnham said. "Why didn't you run when he charged?"

"I'd be mauled by now, probably dead. Even a dying bear can hurt you if he grabs you. It wasn't stupid and it wasn't luck. I'd thought it through before."

"You thought through what you'd do if a bear charged you?" Burnham laughed. "You're also the lyingest—"

"Well, not a bear." Dummett's grin seemed to light the darkness. "But I have thought about what I'd do if a mule raised his hind legs to kick at me. If you move away, his legs get full thrust and he'll kick the shit out of you. By jumping at his ass, he only gets a short haul with his legs and it's sort of a push. He can't hurt you so much. So, when the bear charged—"

"You're really serious."

"Damn right I am. A bear's not much different from a man. I've pulled the same stunt on a dozen Indians, diving at their legs. In the war, when I was about to go into a fight, I'd think through every possible thing that could happen to me, so when something did happen I could react without thinking." He paused, winked and grinned again. "Kept my hair on that way."

They waited until they were sure the bear was dead before dragging the carcass into the dunes. Sharp knives made quick work of skinning and quartering the animal. Dummett wrapped the meat in the bearskin and lashed it to a litter. A short hike through the dunes was followed by a long canoe trip across Mosquito Lagoon. Passing through the Haulover Canal, they had to step out into the chilly water several times to drag the canoe across large rocks lying just below the surface.

"The canal's caving in bad now," Dummett said, pointing at the crumbling banks. "If this keeps up we'll have a tough time getting through here in another year."

The sun was rising above the horizon when the two men glided up to the dock in Dummett Creek and tied the canoe beside Burnham's sailboat.

Now a dull throb was setting in just behind Burnham's eyes from lack of sleep. He knew it would be a while longer before he could rest. Dummett always had a few minor chores to take care of, almost as if the man feared relaxing.

Beyond the boathouse, in a large cleared area, a fire burned under a black cast-iron pot, lighting a small portion of the land still hidden from the early sun. Leandra was cutting soap chips from a yellow bar into the steaming water. When she saw them, she wiped her hands on the apron stretched tightly across her large belly. She yelled something to the house as she waddled down the path toward the dock. Before she could get there, the old Negro, Ebo Thom, ran past, rubbing his fists into sleep-laden eyes, to begin unloading the canoe.

By the time Dummett and Burnham showed the man what to pull from the canoe, Leandra had walked to the end of the dock and rested her back against the rail. Dummett walked over and exaggerated his leaning around her bulk to kiss her. "We got us a bear," he told her as he patted her belly. Then looking back to the pot steaming over the fire, he said, "I thought I told you to let one of the servants do the washing."

"And I told you I would do my share," she answered, staring evenly at his face.

Dummett winked at Burnham and raised his hands in mock despair. Nine-year-old Charles carefully stepped onto the dock balancing a pot of hot coffee. The bundled-up toddler, Louisa, carrying two tin cups, followed him. Stepping past the boy, Dummett scooped the little girl to his shoulders. Casting a look of disapproval at Dummett, Leandra took Charles by the shoulder, moved him to her side, and hugged him. Taking the cups from the little girl's hands, she filled them with coffee.

"This is my baby," said Dummett. "Little Miss Muffett."

"Name Louisa, not Mup-phet," the girl said solemnly.

Burnham thanked Leandra as she handed him a steaming cup. Her beauty once again struck him. Her pregnancy and the frowsy housedress did little to detract from it. "This coffee will sure go good this morning," he said to her. "If I was up north, I'd say it was going to snow."

Dummett drank off half his cup with the first gulp. "I told you about Christmas day of '35. Started out with a chill just like this. By noon the whole damn territory was a sheet of ice. Killed every young orange tree we had at Mount Pleasant. I didn't lose a tree down here."

Leandra herded the children off the docks and toward the house. "Breakfast will be ready when you get in," she said over her shoulder to the men.

"Fine woman. Fine day," Dummett said as they watched Ebo Thom unload the canoe in the gray light. "Hell, it's a shame you don't have the lighthouse job. You could go bear hunting with me all the time."

"I'm not tough enough to go bear hunting with you," Burnham said.

"If you had that job you'd be tough enough in no time."

Burnham wondered if he would ever be tough enough for anything by Dummett's standards. For sure, he doubted he would ever reach the state of planning and forethought Dummett had. However, as they walked to the house he was already thinking ahead to other finance options. Who could he find to invest in the sugarmill?

It was almost noon by the time Burnham finally curled up on the cot in the kitchen. He slept through the bustle of dinner preparation. Dummett woke him at dusk to the wonderful aroma of frying onions. A quick wash in the bowl on the porch and they sat down to a meal of broiled bear steak and fried potatoes.

Burnham watched as Dummett patiently helped Louisa handle her little fork. The man was a mass of contradictions: so subject to instant violence and yet so gentle. Burnham also wondered about Louisa's temperament. She had maintained a sober, almost placid, appearance since he met her. It was a rare two year-old who never giggled. Charles also seemed subdued, but with a fire that seemed to lie just below the surface. Burnham's daughter, Frances, would be trying to monopolize the table conversation. Charles was intently cutting his meat yet soberly watching the men, listening to their talk.

Suddenly, Leandra gasped, and leaned back stiffly in her chair. Then, after a moment, she stood and lay her napkin beside her plate.

"Captain Dummett, sir. You are about to become a father again. Please take the children and Captain Burnham to the porch to finish their meals and send for Cicely." She walked to the bed in the corner of the room and pulled its covers back.

Within minutes, Burnham and the children had moved to a table on the large, screened verandah, while Dummett was fetching Cicely from her cabin.

"The baby is coming," Charles told Burnham.

"Yes, I know, Charles. What do you want it to be?"

"I need a brother to play with, but I guess he'd be too young to do me much good."

"Oh, but you could help him learn all you know—fishing and stuff."

"No," the boy said soberly. "Mama needs girls to help her now that some of the servants are gone. It should be a girl."

A drizzling rain set in as Dummett ran through the darkness with Cicely.

"I thought Maum Molly was your midwife," Burnham said as Dummett caught his breath.

"Oh, she died. Couple of years ago. Didn't you see her grave over at the edge of the clearing?"

"How many died? Did you have an epidemic of something?"

"No," Dummett said, pulling a chair up to the table. "Just Maum Molly."

Burnham looked at the boy, then back to Dummett.

"But Charles said a lot of your servants were gone."

"Yeah. I had to sell eight of them. I needed the money to buy seedlings."

"You sold them?" Burnham heard the disappointment in his own voice.

"I didn't break up any families," Dummett said defensively. "And I'm paying the price for it now in many ways. You saw the business with Leandra this morning? She was madder than hell when I sold them. And now that I need them, my labor force is cut. Makes more work for everyone. Leandra wants me to free them all anyway—gouges me about it every chance she gets. But what would they do? They'd starve to death on their own, or go out and get caught and be sold again. Or stay right here and I'd have to support them anyway. Same thing. There's no such thing as freedom for them."

"Jackson has his freedom," Burnham said. "And he's certainly supporting himself."

"Jackson's different. He's got skills, and he's got guts."

"So do most of your people. Jackson had one thing going for him they don't—he was free when he met you. That gave him your support and mine."

Dummett stared at Burnham through a heavy silence that was punctuated by a crash of thunder. Just as he opened his mouth to answer, a baby cried from the house, and Dummett curled his lips into a smile.

Almost at the same instant, the rain softened then trickled to a stop. Dummett rose and walked to the screen.

"The clouds are blowing away and the moon's coming out," he said almost reverently. "This one's going to be my peacemaker."

"What's that?"

"The baby. The night Charles was born, a storm blew up and got worse when he arrived. Louisa's night was humid and boring. But this baby stops storms—a peacemaker." He thought a moment, then chuckled. "Listen to me rant. I'm beginning to sound as superstitious as the nig— the servants."

Cicely came to the door. "A baby girl," she announced proudly. "Miss Leandra say her name be Kate."

Burnham left Merritt's Island before dawn, with Dummett accompanying him as far as the haulover. The rising sun glinted from small ripples on Mosquito Lagoon as his sailboat skimmed north to the Hillsboro.

The beauty of the river did little to dispel the depression that set upon Burnham once he was alone. He knew he would approach Isaiah Hart and the Pecks for financing, but he also felt in his heart that they would turn him down. Dummett wasn't the only one whose fortunes were being affected by the economic depression. All he could hope for was to strike some sort of deal with whoever bought the sugarmill, similar to the deal he had made with Marshall.

As he passed Mount Pleasant later in the afternoon, his memories of that adventuresome trip with Dummett crowded his mind. Had fifteen years rushed by that quickly? He was thirty-five and the father of four children, and had no more prospects than he had that day long ago. Was he destined to labor for others the rest of his life? You marry a woman, he thought, drag her into the wilderness of a new state and can't care for her any better than this. What kind of man treats his woman this way?

The days passed slowly, time itself seeming to bog down to a flow like the molasses seeping from the hogsheads. Burnham worked into the new year, cutting the sugar into cakes and packing them for shipping. By February all was ready and he accompanied the shipment to Jacksonville. While there, he dropped in to visit with Isaiah Hart at the hotel.

It was as he suspected. Hart's cash flow had slowed to a trickle. However, Hart wasn't interested from another standpoint. "I don't speculate in an enterprise that I don't know well enough to control."

Burnham returned home, arriving at dusk. Mary was sitting on the dock bench as he tied his boat to a cleat. He tossed his valise to the dock and climbed from the boat. Mary stood to kiss him, then handed him a letter. It was from Marshall.

Without a word, Burnham took Mary's hand and they walked slowly to the bench. They sat for a while, watching gulls swoop across the darkening surface of the water. The silence was broken only by an occasional shrill cry from a gull. Finally, Burnham sighed, opened the letter and began reading aloud.

Dear Burnham,

I know you will be disappointed to hear that I've sold the sugarmill. I apologize for not getting back to you before this, but I have been under the weather and have not attended to business as I should.

Major William Russell is the new owner of the mill. I could not refuse his offer, as it was extremely higher than my asking price.

The money I am holding for you is deposited with the State Bank of Jacksonville in your name, with interest at six percent accruing from the date of first placement with me.

I am sorry we could not have made a deal, but I am tired of the mess and glad it is over.

There was more, but Mary chose that moment to reach over and touch Burnham's cheek.

He carefully folded the letter, then leaned back against the bench and put his arm around her shoulders. "I could never work with Russell. This ends us here."

He shook his head sadly, then looked at her in resignation. "So! We start over again. One more `again' added to all the rest."

"We'll make do," she said.

"You're not disappointed?"

She turned her head toward the cleared site where her new house would have been built. "Of course, but the milk be spilled and there's no need to cry." She brushed his lips with her fingertips. "You're destined for better things. We have enough set aside to see us through for a while, and you will find better." She rose and pulled him to his feet. Throwing her arms around his waist, she squeezed him once and stepped back. "We'll be having our supper now. You can begin your search tomorrow."

A torch flared in the encroaching darkness as a slave hurried about some duty using the light to guide his way. Burnham stared at its glare for a moment. A thought nibbled at the perimeter of his consciousness, then flared as full-blown as the torch.

"I think," he said slowly, "destiny has already selected for me."

Burnham left Dunn-Lawton at sunup the next morning sailing under an overcast sky. The grumble of thunder did little to dispel the depression that enveloped him since reading Marshall's letter. The chill in the damp air above the river had a sharpness that penetrated into his bones and seemed to slash to the core of his mind. The inactivity of sailing gave him no release from his doubts and fears. Was the job of lighthouse keeper the best he could find?

He had tossed in bed all last night, wrestling with the problem, knowing there was no other viable option short of selling himself cheaply and to no advantage to his family. His job of deputy sheriff had taught him the dead-end futility of working for governmental agencies. Although taking the lighthouse job was in the same category, at least he would be able to file on land. It seemed to him that trying to make a success of a homestead was his only chance.

As a drizzling rain began, he huddled back in the stern to continue his two-day trip and his lonely argument.

Burnham straddled a chair in Dummett's kitchen. A pulse throbbed behind his ear predicting the onset of a headache.

"I think the job pays four hundred dollars a year," Dummett said. "And that's not so bad. Hell, my military pension's only a hundred and twenty a year."

A baby's cry from the next room seemed to echo into Burnham's tired brain. He propped his elbows on the table and rested his chin in the palms of his hands. He had long since lost the argument with himself and wished he was back home, trying to find a better option.

Dummett leaned over and gripped Burnham's shoulder. "You'll have the security of the government salary behind you while you establish the homestead."

"I thought of all this, and it sounds all right from that point of view. But it's so isolated down here. Do I want to cut my wife and children off from everything? Make them live again in a palmetto shack?"

"Granted the cape's isolated, plus the work's hard and boring. But you won't be living in a palmetto shack. There's houses for the keepers." He slammed his fist into his other palm. "And you'll be free, beholding to no man but yourself."

"If I can get the position."

"Hell, man, getting the position's no problem. No one else wants it, for the reasons you just named. But the potential advantages are so great." He paused and smiled. "And you can go bear hunting with me."

"At least it's hard money, and I guess it's more'n enough to keep the wolf from the door until I can prove up on the homestead." Burnham could hear the fear hiding under the resignation in his own voice. He wondered if Dummett could sense it.

"Sure it'll be enough," Dummett said. "And Scobie's garden is already planted. Mary will like that."

"You're sure Scobie and Carpenter want to quit?"

"No doubt about it. They've even put out dodgers in St. Augustine begging for a replacement."

"Well, I want to visit them and hear them say they're ready to quit. I don't want to take any man's job from him."

The next morning, the two men set out in the *Flying Fish* with its six Negroes sending the canoe skimming around Black Point. They passed through the creek Burnham and George had discovered eight years earlier and finally into the Banana River. In a short time they passed Duck Pond and ran the canoe up on a spit of sand on the eastern bank. From there, a three-mile walk along a narrow path took them to the ocean beach.

They approached the lighthouse tower through a broad canefield. An old man sat on the steps of a house north of the lighthouse, so intent on the ivory carving in his hands that he didn't see the two men until Dummett called out to him.

"Scobie, go stir old Carpenter's stumps. Your lives just took a turn for the better."

The wizened little man stood and stared for a moment, then turned to scamper up the short flight of steps onto the porch and into the house, yelling "Carp! Carp! Wake up. Company's come."

Moments later, he returned, followed by another scrawny man who could have passed for his twin. Both men had full beards hanging past the top buttons of their red long johns. The second man was busy pulling the straps of his braces over his thin shoulders.

"What say you, Cousin?" The old man, Scobie, shouted even though they were now at the foot of the stairs.

Dummett introduced the men to Burnham, each solemnly shaking his hand in turn. When Dummett announced that Burnham was interested in taking the lighthouse job, the two men faced each other, then stomped their feet and, with shouts of joy, began to dance erratic circles around each other, looking like a couple of bantam roosters facing off over a particularly lush hen.

"You're sure covering your disappointment well," Dummett grinned.

"Course and all, we ain't got no rose covered cottage waitin for us," Scobie panted. "But anything will be rosy after this." Then to Burnham: "Not trying to talk you out of it, of course."

"Not much chance of that," Burnham said. "This job's about all that's left for me. I just wanted to make sure I wasn't stepping on anyone's toes before I went after it."

The men showed Burnham around the compound. The house had two apartments of four rooms each and was a story-and-a-half high. A wide porch extended around the north, east, and south sides.

Dummett looked at the wall separating the apartments. "We can cut a door through here and make it one big house."

"You boys ready to go up?" Scobie asked, laughing and jerking his thumb upward. "Course and all, you gonna get a touch of Lighthouse Leg. Yore thighs'll be so damn stiff tomorrow you won't be able to swing them outta the bed. But you'll have plenty of time to get over that after you're the Wickie."

"The what?" A frown furrowed Burnham's brow.

"Wickie," Scobie grinned. "The head string lighter." Then more solemnly, "The keeper of the Canaveral Light."

"This was built in 1848," Dummett told Burnham as they climbed the circular stairway around the inside of the tower. "It's wooden, right at sixty feet tall, but to tell the truth I never believed it was high enough. Ships have to come in too close to see it. Come on outside and look."

They stepped onto the flooring of the lantern room, then through a door to the gallery. The view made Burnham suck in a deep breath; he could see for miles. Off to the north, the spray-drenched beach stretched until it eventually vanished into misty infinity. Below them, the Cape thrust out into the Atlantic like a proud breast, then curved back sharply into a bight making the beach to the south seem to arc for miles into the haze.

"Look out there," Dummett shouted above the whine of the wind. He pointed out across the ocean, beyond the surf line. At first Burnham saw nothing unusual. Then, way out toward the horizon, he could see spray crashing upward.

"The Bulls," Dummett said. "Those are rocks, about five miles out, and below the surface most of the time. It's low tide now so you can see them.

"When the tide is higher, those rocks are deadly to a ship. The Gulf-stream flows north about twenty miles offshore and it's pulling water in from its sides. That builds up a strong southerly countercurrent along the shore."

He stopped and with a forefinger drew a diagram in the salt coating the window of the lantern room.

"That current intensifies as it sweeps around the cape here. Believe me, an unwary ship caught in it has a hell of a time getting loose, especially if she's a sailing vessel. When she turns to pull away from the cape, devils await her. The wind is usually slapping her in the face and the Bulls are waiting with their horns up to gouge out her bottom."

Burnham had a mental picture of a ship struggling for its existence in the rushing waters. "How far is the light visible?" he asked.

"On a clear night, I think a ship can see it about eight miles out. But if she's that close, the offshore winds and the countercurrent can put her smackdab inside reach of the Bulls."

"What about a taller tower?"

"There's been talk by the Lighthouse Board, but nothing more. This trouble over the slavery issue has kept congress too busy to worry over some little obscure light down in the wilderness."

Burnham took another long, dreamy look at the ocean and misted beaches, then shook his head to pull himself back to reality. "I guess I want the job. Now all I need to do is locate a good place for my home-stead?"

Dummett led him around to the western side, where Burnham could look across the thin ribbon of the Banana River to Merritt's Island, its pines seen as a cool blue strip from this distance.

"Where we landed is probably the best land on the Cape. It's high, shell marl land, the richest in the area. You'd have access to the river for trans-port, it's protected from the wind by the bulk of the cape, and it's close enough to the lighthouse to work your grove."

"Yes, you're right. George and I camped near there in '46." His jaw tightened with the memory. "I liked it then." He stared across toward the green, expanse of hammock, visions filling his mind as well as his eyes. "How do I get the job?"

"Paul Arnau is the Collector of the Port of St. Augustine. He and I share local control over the light. The Lighthouse Board was formed a couple of years ago—naval officers, engineers. They'd have no reason to not approve your appointment."

Four days later, Burnham sat with Dummett in the St. Augustine office of Paul Arnau, waiting his appearance.

"He's got a little more to do here than I do in New Smyrna," Dummett commented dryly as they looked at the desk buried in paper.

As he spoke, the door opened and a slightly built man entered, his arms crushing a stack of papers against a stained shirt. His thinning hair wisped in random geometrical figures across a shiny scalp.

"Gentlemen, I'm sorry I'm late," he muttered breathlessly as he dumped the stack of papers on the desk. "I had to gather up these records...spilled coffee on...Dummett, you're looking fit."

"Paul, if you didn't take that work home with you, you wouldn't have to drag it back."

"Well, I don't suppose that's ever a problem with you." He smiled pleas-antly, then held out his hand to Burnham. "Captain Burnham, I'm pleased to finally meet you. We've handled many shipments from you and Colonel Marshall." A frown wrinkled his large forehead. "Damn shame about his family. I was truly shocked to hear about it. But, please, Gentlemen, be comfortable," he said, pointing to two upholstered chairs.

"If you know of Burnham's reputation," Dummett said as he leaned back in his chair, "then I'm sure you'll agree with me that we can quit worrying about the Cape lighthouse."

"There's no doubt in my mind, none at all. When I read the note you sent around to me last evening, Dummett, I was overjoyed to hear of his decision to take the position. My only reservation is whether the captain will like the work enough to be permanent." He cocked a brow at Burnham.

Burnham placed his large palms on his knees and leaned toward the man. "Mr. Arnau, my major responsibility is my family. This position will give me the opportunity to develop a homestead and provide us with the security we need. And frankly, I believe the lighthouse work'll be a source of pride for me."

"Yes, I should think so. There's fine land on the Cape available for homesteading adjacent to the federal reservation. And, of course, you'll not have to do all the work at the lighthouse yourself. You'll be authorized to employ two assistants of your choosing...if you can find them."

"I have two assistants in mind," Burnham informed him, "at least on a temporary basis."

"Fine, fine. Then we can draw up the contract, have you sign it and forward it to the Lighthouse Board for their approval. That's merely a formality."

"What's happened to the proposal for a new light? And the new canal?" Dummett asked.

"The bids will be let soon, I'm sure, on the canal, but I'm not at all certain about the time frame for the new lighthouse."

Within the hour, the details of the contract were worked out and the papers drawn. After Burnham signed the contract, Arnau rose and shook his hand, then shuffled the papers together.

"I'll forward this to the Board and await their decision. As soon as the contract is countersigned I'll contact you."

Later, as Burnham and Dummett walked to Louisa Fatio's boarding house on Hospital Street to take rooms for the night, they passed the Alvarez Tavern. Dummett opened the door and ushered Burnham inside. "My turn to buy rum for the new Wickie," he said.

BOOK FOUR

1853 — 1861

Chapter 14

Burnham held Frances' hand as they walked from the house to the tower. At its base they paused as Burnham jiggled through a ring of keys.

"How many steps are there, Papa?" Frances asked. While Burnham pushed a key into the brass door lock, she put her hands on her hips and tilted her head back, looking up the length of the tower.

"Fifty-two."

"And we have to carry that oil all the way to the top?" She looked down to stare at the five-gallon can with the wire bail.

"I'm afraid we do, honey. But we're going to engineer a better way." He was already envisioning a block and tackle lift for not only the oil but all the cleaning equipment as well. Thousands of improvements could be made in this place. He knew the next several days would be as full of work as the nights. "When we get up there, you just stay back out of the way and watch. And learn. Anything we might pick up from those old-timers will save us a lot of trial and error later on. And we can't afford any error."

Frances nodded her head solemnly, then walked over and sat on the oil-can. A calico blouse covered the bib of her overalls. Burnham realized with surprise that the male outfit in no way made the seventeen-year-old girl look boyish.

Knowing he would need help after the old men left, Burnham had asked Junior to take on the job of assistant. Junior's response, a vigorous shake of his head, spoke louder than his whispered "I need to spend my time working in our new groves." After his initial disappointment, Burnham easily gave in to Frances' pleas for the job.

"Why shouldn't I make the money?" she asked, knowing the position paid two hundred dollars a year. "We can use it, and I'm already here. I can do the job as good as any man you could hire."

Burnham had no argument with that, but insisted that she be there when they went up this first night. She would have to pull her weight if they were to be successful. Jackson would handle the job of second assistant, taking his instruction from Burnham after the two old men had gone.

The family's arrival that morning by schooner had bordered on disaster. With the schooner anchored just beyond the surf line in the bight of the Cape, the family was rowed ashore in a lighter. The instant the boat touched the beach, a following sea shipped aboard, sinking the rear of the craft. A sailor leaped ashore with a line and secured it to a palm tree in the dunes. By the time the men finally dragged the boat free of the surf's clutch and onto dry land, Mary and the children were drenched but safe.

Scobie and Carpenter, scheduled to leave the following morning on the schooner, had moved the crates containing their belongings from the house to the storage shed, making room for the trunks and boxes of clothes transported from the schooner. Once the old men were out of the house, Mary and Frances spent the day scrubbing its interior and airing it, while Burnham and Junior set up the beds and other furniture.

Although Burnham was sure he had absorbed the procedure for operating the light, he accepted the offer from Scobie and Carpenter for one last "hands-on" demonstration. Now, about two hours before sundown, Burnham saw the two old-timers walking across from the storage shed toward the tower.

When they arrived, each man solemnly shook hands with Burnham, then grinned at each other as if they had just found a treasure.

Scobie patted Frances on the shoulder. "Ya'll prob'ly tired from all that work you done today. Me and old Carp, we'll get ya started, then we'll sleep till midnight and take the second shift. Course and all," he said, looking at Carpenter, "hit'll be strange for us. We rarely never been able to do a shift together."

They began the long climb, with Burnham carrying the night's supply of lard oil.

At the top, Scobie suggested that Burnham and Frances just watch as they prepared the lamp. "Let us do it one last time. It'll remind us again why we're leaving."

First the men went outside to the gallery and scraped the salt from the windows, cleaning them to let the light through. Then they carefully wiped and polished the glass lens prisms with spirits of wine. After trimming the wick, they cranked the windlass, tightening the coil spring that turned the lens pedestal. Engaging the pawl that drove the ratchet gear, they used a pocket watch to time the turning rate of the lens, adjusting it to an accuracy of within one second. The fixed beams would now sweep the horizon in an exact time sequence. Any ship's captain seeing the flashes would know he was seeing the Cape Canaveral lighthouse and no other.

The work was finished a half-hour before sundown, when they would fire up the lantern. As the shadows of dusk lengthened across the land below, they all stepped into the fresh breeze on the balcony to watch the sun sink in the west.

Frances walked around the tower twice. Each time she passed her father, she shouted shrilly above the wind, pointing to something that had caught her eye and imagination.

"Wound up tighter'n the lantern spring, ain't she?" Scobie yelled in his usual manner.

"No more than me," Burnham said, laughing at his daughter's excitement. Then he swept his arm across the horizon. "Dummett tells me the light can't be seen from too far at sea."

"On a clear night, from a deck ten feet above water, the light's seeable a hair over eight miles. About where the Bull is, the shoals offshore. We've seed our share of shipwrecks since we been here."

Scobie walked over to Carpenter and yelled something into his ear. The old man nodded and left the gallery.

"I sent him on down to get some early sleep. He's getting a might-bit old and I got to take keer of him."

Scobie went on to explain the watch system. "Say it's the keeper's night to sleep in. The first assistant has got first watch in the tower till midnight. He calls the second assistant to take over till sunrise. Then, next night, you rotates everbody one notch. Course and all, that don't mean nothin if you ain't got two assistants. Me and old Carp, we just swapped first and second watches ever night."

As Burnham stood awaiting sundown, his thoughts were intent on the techniques of keeping the light operating. "What kind of visibility do we have on foggy nights?" he asked.

"None to speak of," Scobie answered. "Course and all, the fogbank seems to explode with light when the beam passes through it, prob'ly cause the light bounces offen the drops of water. But if a ship was close enough to see it, she'd be already aground. And there ain't a damn thing we can do about it."

"What about a foghorn?"

"No good. The shallows are futher out than the sound could go against the offshore wind." The old man walked to the door to the lantern room. "We got to get crackin'. By the time we get that lamp fired up, it'll be stone-dark."

The days stretched into work-filled months. Burnham hung a pulley from an eye-bolt under the floor of the lantern room and rigged lines for hauling the heavy oil buckets to the top. Jackson took on the task of dismantling the storage shed and re-erecting it beside the tower, and by January of 1854 he had finished the move. Burnham then started him building a similar shed on the homestead, near the plot he had selected as his first grove.

To make the chore of starting the lantern's rotating mechanism easier for Frances, Burnham replaced the windlass with a geared wheel. He bolted weights to each end of a flat, thirty-foot gear chain, and threaded the chain across the cogs of the gear. Then he lowered the weighted ends through a hole in the floor. Now she simply pulled the chain to wind the spring. This winding would turn the light for at least two hours.

As he worked, he felt a growing confidence. No, it was more a realization of maturity, as if he had been destined for this position in life all along. His decisions came easily and he knew in his heart they were right.

His enchantment with the Cape grew deeper from daily seeing the natural spectacles of this strange land. From his vantage high on the tower, his eyes were blessed by sunrises saturated with the unimaginable hues from the palette of a mad painter.

Burnham's only concern in this paradise was the violence of the weather. Mountainous clouds of black, boiling fury would build over the ocean in the afternoons, slashing the purplish backdrop with nails of forked lightning, hanging out there for hours before moving in on the Cape and dumping their torrents, abruptly quitting as if a valve had been closed. Within minutes the sun again baked steam from the earth.

Offshore breezes constantly bathed the canefields surrounding their home, but inland, near the river and woods, the air was saturated with a heavy humidity. The tiniest physical act, walking, or even breathing, would pop a soaking sweat from his pores. But this too was a blessing, for the zephyrs that did find their way through the trees evaporated the sweat, cooling his body as if he'd been bathed in snow.

In early February, Dummett arrived with six of his men in a large sailing canoe. They unloaded two barrels of thick-skinned lemons, three hundred seedlings, and a variety of tools. Directing his men with the intensity of a military campaign, he soon had them at work in the field Burnham had selected for his grove. Within two weeks, using block and tackle, they cleared fifteen acres and had the ground ready for planting. Impressed with their efficiency, Burnham remembered the back-breaking work the Seminoles had done for him at Fort Pierce.

The day after the field was ready, Dummett set the men to digging long straight furrows in five acres of the field, about eight inches deep in the loamy soil. Laying a board across a stump, he clamped on a meat grinder.

"Took me a while to figger out this trick," he told Burnham. "I used to cut open the fruit and strip the seeds out by hand. That was stupid. Now I just grind them up coarse and plant the slurry. In a few weeks, the seeds'll germinate and sprout. They'll come up too close together so you'll have to thin them."

By early afternoon, the men had planted the seedlings in the other ten acres. Dummett waved his hand at the line of thin sticks that were the basis of Burnham's new grove. "These'll be ready for budding next year, but don't worry, I'll show you how. Nothing to it."

"I couldn't have done any of this alone. Without your men to help—"

"This is probably the last heavy work I can do for you," Dummett interjected. "I've sold these men. Deliver them in two months. In the meantime, I'm renting them out to the government. They start the digging on the new Haulover Canal next week. About time."

"Are you having money problems again? I can—"

"Nah, nothing I can't handle. My last crop was delayed in shipment, in Jacksonville, and the whole mess turned mushy. I didn't get much for them, at least not what I expected."

He whistled shrilly through his fingers and waved his arms to get his men's attention.

"Good job, men. Let's clean up and loaf."

The men grinned and broke for the woods and the river beyond.

Burnham straightened from his task of shoveling muck from the irrigation channels between the rows of young trees and mopped his face with a sweat soaked bandana. He almost missed the faint shout.

"Halloo. Anybody about?"

The voice seemed to be coming from the river side of the grove. Dropping the shovel, he picked up his rifle and moved cautiously toward the sound, now more than one voice.

As he rounded the end of the row of trees, he saw three soldiers standing by a flat-bottomed rowboat loaded with gear. One of the men was yelling again when Burnham responded.

"Hold it down. What can I do for you?"

The young man doing most of the yelling, a stocky redhead, shoved his campaign cap back on his head and snapped to attention. The other two followed suit.

"Are you Captain Burnham, Sir?" The "Sir" came out almost as loud as the earlier shouts.

"Son, you better relax a little," Burnham laughed. "You stiffen up like that in this heat and we'll be picking you up off the ground. Yes, I'm Burnham."

The young man held his position. "Sergeant Henry Wilson and detail, Sir."

Burnham smiled, realizing he would have to play the game before this bantam rooster hurt himself. "At ease men. Do you have orders?"

The two privates immediately relaxed, but the sergeant handed Burnham an oilcloth packet and snapped to parade rest.

Burnham opened the packet and removed the detail's orders. After reading them, he looked up at the sergeant. "I gather you men are here to guard the lighthouse, but none of these papers tell me why."

"Sir, ain't you heard?" Wilson looked at the others, as if verifying something. "I know this place is at the end of nowhere, but I'da thought somehow you'd—"

"Get on with it, Sergeant. And stop 'sirring' me with every breath. I'm not in the army."

"Sir—excuse me for that, sir," Wilson dug his heel into the dirt. "Dammit sir, you're a Federal officer and it's hard not to—"

"Wilson. Why—are—you—here?"

"The Indian War. Old Billy Bowlegs done started another one."

"Hell, son, I knew about that. That's not a war. Last year some government crew was surveying down by the edge of the Everglades. The idiots got into Holatter Micco's garden—Billy Bowlegs—tore it all to hell and gone. His pumpkin vines grew up into the trees and they shot down his pumpkins. Hacked down his banana trees, then laughed at him when he complained about it. I've known Billy Bowlegs for years. He's as predictable as rain in a thunderstorm. He attacked that crew the next morning. A few surveyors got wounded, but that ended it. Now, that flare-up's being treated like a full-scale war."

"Those Seminoles attacked the Cape Florida Lighthouse and killed some of the keepers." Wilson looked at his companions for confirmation, which he immediately got.

Burnham snorted and shook his head. "That's the Army for you—can't ever get the straight of it. That lighthouse attack happened years ago, back in the forties. Well, your orders say you're to stay here and that's that. Get your stuff and follow me."

An hour later, Burnham watched the three young soldiers struggle to erect their heavy canvas tent in the dunes east of the tower. He had suggested they set up a mile inland, in the shade of a breezy pine flat, but Wilson had quickly vetoed that idea.

"Our orders are to protect the lighthouse twenty-four hours a day. We can't do that if we're sleeping way to hell over yonder." Burnham could hear the brass in the redhead's voice as he snapped the statement.

The tent had rollup sides and mosquito netting, so he supposed they would survive the elements. The letter had informed Burnham that he would have to provide rations for them, but a schooner would call within the week with extra supplies.

From the edge of his vision, Burnham saw Frances step onto the front porch. "How old are you boys?" he asked.

"I'm twenty-five and Studdard here's twenty. Haisten's only eighteen."

And Frances is twenty, Burnham thought, right in the middle of this bunch of stallions.

"I guess we better get the drill straight," Burnham said. "You'll draw your rations from Mrs. Burnham, but you do your own cooking and cleaning. She's got more'n enough mouths to stuff. You'll have to police your area, but no other work's required. If you jump in and do something needing done, I'll not complain." He paused for a moment as Frances approached, then said quietly, "My daughter's friendly and I got nothing against friendship, but I don't suppose I got to say much in the way of a rule. You boys don't seem to be suicidal." The soldiers had already spotted Frances walking toward them and they grinned widely at Burnham's comment.

That evening, after supper, Burnham walked out to the tent, dragging a large, green mangrove branch and carrying a pie that Mary had baked. The soldiers had placed logs around a firepit in the sand and were sitting on them, smoking quietly and swatting mosquitoes. Their faces lit up like the campfire when they saw the pie.

"Don't expect it too often," Burnham told them.

He broke off several twigs of the green mangrove and pitched them into the flames. In moments a thin, smoky haze swirled about the area, driving the mosquitoes away. He sat with them as they demolished the pie, and listened while they told him about themselves.

"I been in the Army longer than these children," Wilson said, pointing at the others. "Couldn't get along with my step-papa," he said. "Told the Army I was eighteen and they took me in. I was sixteen. Went to Mexico under General Zachary Taylor, then back to Floridy at Fort Dallas on the Mayami River. Studdard and me herded two hundred head of mules across to Fort Brooke on Tampa Bay. Took us six weeks."

Studdard threw a branch on the fire and said, "We both transferred to Fort Pierce in 1850. We was in the Navy for a while." He grinned. "The Swamp Navy. We hounded them Injuns all over the glades, in boats that we dragged more'n we rode in." He paused, then said, "Didn't do much good. Never really saw them. Haisten joined up with us in Key West last month."

"So you see, Captain," Wilson said sternly. "You got no fears about the Seminole torching this tower. We're good soldiers and we know what we're doing."

"I've no doubt about it," Burnham agreed. "But, we're going to get this straight, Sergeant. I've got friends among the Seminoles. They come by here often to visit, and I have no fear of them burning the tower. I have no fear of them at all." He paused to let this sink in.

"If they should come while you're here, I don't want you buckos shooting my friends. You got that?"

"But Captain, we got our orders."

"Your orders are to protect the lighthouse, not to shoot my friends. You just follow my lead if they show up and we'll be all right."

Burnham and Jackson spent the next several days working in the grove, shoveling muck from the irrigation ditches and cutting a connecting trench from the artesian well at the north end of the property.

During his early mornings in the tower, Burnham watched with growing interest as the young soldiers scurried over to the house to help Frances with her outdoor work. In their exuberance they piled so much wood under the wash pot it was encased in a circular wall of flame for over an hour. They continued throwing wood on the fire until Frances finally ordered them to stop; she couldn't get to the pot and the water was boiling out.

Their next project was to attack the weeds in the flowerbeds she had planted in front of the house. As he watched from above, Burnham was soon laughing so hard he thought his ribs would crack. The boys couldn't tell the difference between a flower and a weed. With each boy trying to outdo the others, the beds soon resembled a war zone. The object of all this energy walked around the house in time to see her last begonia fall to an industrious hoe. Burnham could hear her scream as she attacked the boys with a broom. In poor military fashion they retreated in a frantic scramble for their lives.

Within a week, Frances had organized the young men's attentions into an informal schedule of sorts. In the mornings she walked along the beach with the redheaded sergeant in search of rare seashells, and in the afternoons she and Studdard walked the mile inland to sit and talk in the swing Burnham had hung from a shady liveoak.

Burnham spoke to her only once concerning the situation, telling her that she was to feel free and comfortable around the young men, but she was not allowed to go anywhere with them out of sight of the tower.

"You've got yourself a lot of attention you never had before and you should enjoy it. It's part of life, but you're my daughter and I'll have to worry about you long after they're gone. And they will leave, you know. I just don't want to see you hurt." Then, as an afterthought, he laughed and said, "And I don't want you to hurt them. You got a lot of power here you don't realize."

Then, only two days later, Wilson invited himself along when she and Studdard went to the swing.

At supper that night she was furious. "He doesn't know his place," she stormed. "He's pushy and insensitive to privacy...just another damn Yankee. Mama, I swear they were about to fight, right there with me watching."

"Don't swear," her mother said. "You'd best be settling on one, and let the others be."

"Others? Haisten's so bashful he won't even speak to me, and Studdard lets Wilson boss him around something terrible. It's all that Wilson's fault."

Burnham laid his fork down and wiped his mouth on a napkin. "You won't have the problem much longer. I've written to the Lighthouse Board asking that the boys be recalled. I'll tell them about it today. So just let it ride and, if things get too warm, back off."

Frances looked at her mother, a sadness in her eyes. "Then I'll be alone again."

"Alone?" Burnham boomed, laughing. "Girl, your family's not leaving—only the soldiers."

"That's what I mean," she said.

Henry Wilson looked through the tent's mosquito netting toward the beach at dunes bathed in a bright yellow glow from the moon. Sweat pasted his long-johns to his body and soaked his cot. Frances' face seemed to be etched into every dune he could see in the moonlight.

Giving up on sleep, he eased quietly to his feet, and crept from the tent. Standing erect, he arched his back then stretched his arms above his head.

A luminous stretch of stars coated the sky as usual but everything else seemed wrong. The air was still and oppressive, seeming to have a thickness and weight. He swatted furiously at the mosquitoes swarming around his head and shoulders as he gathered fresh mangrove limbs from the brush pile and heaped them on the fire-pit coals. In a few moments, thick smoke rose and drifted aimlessly around the area. The mosquitoes vanished as quickly as they came.

Henry looked at the beach. Only a thin line of froth along the sand marked what was usually surging surf. The ocean was flat and oily looking, with only occasional swells heaving slightly as if some leviathan lay beneath the surface, breathing heavily. The sea oats in the dunes stood motionless with no breeze to move them.

He sat on a log and began filling his pipe. He hadn't seen anything like this on the ocean beach since coming to Florida. A stiff breeze always blew in from the sea, but this stillness made him shiver. He remembered it had been like this inland, down by the big lake near the Everglades, the heat sucking the sweat from a man until the skeeters and no-see-ums stuck to the skin.

He lit his pipe with a burning twig, and rested his elbows on his knees.

An eerie moan sounded above him, like wind blowing through the attic of an abandoned house, yet no wind stirred. He raised his eyes to the tower looming over him. Must be some wind up there, he thought, but immediately discarded the idea. There was no wind anywhere.

The beams from the lantern circled the tower smoothly, the fingers pointing first at the calm sea then swinging around to the land. He began to feel slightly giddy from watching them, or was it from knowing that Frances was up there, working her lonely shift in the light's glow?

He couldn't understand the way she was behaving lately. What had turned her away from him? Her refusal to walk along the beach that morning was a surprise. Her explanation that she needed rest made some sense, but she had gone with him on other days when she was due to work the night shift.

Maybe it had something to do with Captain Burnham requesting the detail be recalled to St. Augustine. Henry knew they would have to leave sooner or later and he guessed the sooner they left the better it would be for him. This girl was unlike any other he had ever known and she was burning herself into his soul.

He had known others, Sutler's daughters and such, but he never really *knew* them. He had spoken to them, or had a twirl with them at barn dances, but he hadn't really talked to them. He hadn't ever gotten to know their families. And this girl's family was beginning to grow on him.

His life at home with a father and mother was only a dim memory. His papa had died and Mama had remarried while he was still a tad. Then came the army, much too soon, ending his childhood. Now, the Burnhams were beginning to remind him of all he had missed. In his view, Captain Burnham had all that was good in life: healthy, loving youngsters and a good woman. Course the boy, Junior, was a little strange, always so quiet and spending all his time in the garden or the grove.

There! He heard it again, a moaning that reminded him of a wounded soldier's cry of surrender to pain. Then, with a start, he realized it was coming from the tower. He took a timorous step forward, then threw down his pipe and sprinted for the tower door.

Inside he took the steps two at a time, again feeling a cloud of mosquitoes swarming around his head. Ignoring them, he pulled hand over hand on the circular banister, running upward until he reached the lantern room.

The light was rotating smoothly. The only sound above the moan was the snick of the ratchet as the weight pulled the chain through the gears.

But the room was empty.

"Miss Burnham?" Nothing.

"Frances," he shouted, looking wildly around the room. The moaning now seemed to surround him. He pushed on the door to the balcony, brushing his arms across his face to clear the mosquitoes. The door seemed stuck but the latch was loose. He pushed harder, opening it a few inches, then stepped back flailing at the thousands of mosquitoes pouring through the narrow opening. He felt the stinging burn of tiny branding irons on his wrists and neck. Closing his eyes and holding his breath, he leaned his weight against the door. It didn't move. Something was blocking it from the outside.

Reaching through the narrow opening at the bottom of the door, he felt a body lying on the balcony floor—Frances. Grabbing her shoulder, he pushed her away as far as he could, then stood and shoved hard against the door until he could squeeze through.

The mosquitoes swarmed thickly over his face, into his eyes and ears, his nostrils and mouth. A metallic taste threatened to lock his jaws as his throat filled with the insects. He coughed and spit as he fought a gagging panic. Covering his nose and mouth with one arm, he reached down blindly with his free hand. His fingers touched, then grasped the bib of her overalls through her blouse and pulled her up to him. God give me strength, he prayed. She was so limp. He wrapped his arm around her upper body, pulling her face tightly against his chest, feeling his heart thumping against her cheek. Then he staggered through the open door into the lantern room and jerked it shut behind him.

Keeping her face against his chest and his arm protecting his, he started down the stairs, her feet dragging and bumping the risers behind them as they descended.

At the bottom, he kicked the door open and pulled her limp body over to the fire pit with its screening smoke. Laying her on the ground, he began wiping mosquitoes from her face. She was struggling to pull air through her open mouth when he realized her mouth and nostrils were caked with the insects. He scraped his fingers through her mouth, under her tongue and behind her lips, then tried to get his stubby fingers into her tiny nostrils. Giving that up quickly, he pressed his palm over her mouth, then covered her nose with his mouth and sucked the insects from her nose, pausing only to spit them out and take deep breaths.

After what seemed like an eternity but could only have been a minute or so, she began to pull whistling air through her nose. He turned her head toward the fire and thrust his fingers deep into her throat until she began to heave. And then she vomited, the fluid cleansing her nose and throat as it gushed forth. He rolled her onto her side, then ran to the tent line to snatch a towel, yelling, "Help! Wake up! Help me!"

By the time he got back to her, Studdard and Haisten had burst from the tent. The yellow flare of a lantern bobbed erratically down the path from the house. He began cleaning her face but Studdard took the cloth and eased him aside.

"Relax," he said. "I got her."

"Skeeters," Henry gasped as Burnham ran into the circle of light. "Thousands. On the tower—everywhere. Have to get her inside..."

Burnham dropped his lantern, lifted her into his arms and ran toward the house, yelling back over his shoulder, "Bring Wilson—all of you—get in the house."

He carried Frances to her room, yelling for Mary to get some water. The other children stood wide-eyed in the doorway until Mary shooed them back to their rooms. She began bathing the girl's face. When Burnham saw the swelling and welts from the hundreds of bites on her neck and face, he felt a coldness run through his body. My baby, he thought, and I let this happen to her. He shuddered, then went to the kitchen for a bucket of lard.

As Burnham walked through the parlor, the soldiers were settling Wilson down onto the floor.

"Put him on the settee and one of you come with me to fetch water to bathe him."

Henry struggled as the men lifted him. "Captain, I'm in my long-johns and..."

"Dammit, man, you just lay still and don't worry about that. Everyone here knows what long-johns look like and yours sure don't look any different."

By the time Mary had undressed Frances and coated her with grease, the men were finished cleaning Wilson. The parlor was filled with the mosquitoes they had scraped from him, and Haisten was chasing around the room swatting them.

"He musta had a jillion skeeters on him and in him," Studdard told Burnham as he took the lard bucket from him. "Cap'n, she'd a died iffen he hadn't gone up there."

"I know," Burnham said, quietly gazing down at the man who had delivered his girl as surely as a midwife.

Donning a hooded jacket, he left the house to waken Jackson to man the light for the remainder of the night. "Carry a smudge-pot up there with you," he told him. "And stay in the lantern room."

A soft breeze fanned Burnham's cheek the next morning as he stepped from the porch followed by Studdard and Haisten and walked over to the soldiers' tent. He had checked Wilson as he passed through the parlor. The man's face, neck and shoulders were swollen and covered with nasty welts. Burnham imagined Frances would be much worse this morning.

"I guess we've got some new rules to live by," he said as Jackson walked over from the tower."

"The skeeters weren't so bad as long as I stayed inside," Jackson said. "I guess they don't cotton to the smoke from the smudge pot."

"I never heard of mosquitoes swarming that bad," said Burnham. "That little rain night before last..."

"Injuns!"

Burnham snapped his head toward Haisten, then looked in the direction of his pointing finger. Two Seminoles were walking toward them through the canefield. He turned back to Haisten and was horrified to see him raising a rifle and cocking the hammer.

Burnham screamed, "No!" and lunged for Haisten, striking the barrel with his forearm as the gun fired, the blast exploding in his eardrums. Scrambling to his feet, he snatched the rifle from Haisten's grasp, yelling above the ringing in his ears, "Dammit—I told you. They're harmless."

He turned in time to see the Indians rising from the canes where they had dived when the gun fired. He waved, and the Indians walked cautiously toward him with their right arms raised.

"Captain Burnham," Dan Osceola said in greeting.

Burnham tossed the rifle aside and stepped forward to meet them. Dan Osceola swung a deerhide-wrapped, haunch of venison from his shoulders and took Burnham's hand. Burnham didn't recognize the second man, a youngster of about eighteen, but Dan introduced him, grinning. "My baby brother, Charlie, who thinks he's a mighty hunter for killing this deer with only two shots and a club with which he finally beat the vicious beast to death. It is our gift to Mrs. Burnham."

The men were dressed in colored shirts that reached to their knees, with brown tanned buckskin leggings and large turbans made from red and black checked shawls folded and wound around their heads. Dan Osceola wore the golden wool necklace, his heritage from Tommy Jumper, which now bore a silver gorget.

"Is this new?" Burnham asked, pointing at the medallion.

"My people have honored me by making me a subchief. Holatter Micco gave me this after our battle against the—maybe I shouldn't say this."

Burnham weighed his thoughts and looked at Studdard and Haisten as he spoke. "Old friend, I know of your cause and I sympathize. Were you in danger on your journey here?"

"Patrols were everywhere. We traveled the Chukochatty trail across from Tampa Bay and left it when needed, but we were fearful. The soldiers..." He paused again, looking at Studdard and Haisten.

"You have no problem here," Burnham said quickly.

"We visit the trading posts to find if fear has driven away our welcome."

Burnham led them to the porch where they lowered their totes and sat in the cane-bottomed chairs he pulled forward for them. Studdard and Haisten wandered over to their tent as Burnham began the story of last night's near tragedy. When he heard of the mosquito bites, Charlie Osceola left them and walked to the dunes. Burnham watched curiously as the young man wandered around searching, then stooped to pull something from the ground.

He returned, holding out a plant that resembled cactus.

"The Spanish call this aloe. For burns...the bites of mosquitoes."

Charlie Osceola cut the pale green, succulent flesh of the plant, showing Burnham the ooze of creamy lotion and directed him to rub it onto the skin.

"Great healer," Dan Osceola said, nodding sagely.

Burnham hurried into the house and gave the plant to Mary, instructing her to treat Frances and Wilson.

When he returned, the Indians had stepped from the porch and were swinging their totes to their shoulders. Dan Osceola extended his hand to Burnham. "We must hurry. We will stop at Dummett Cove to visit, and we want to be near New Smyrna by nightfall." He shifted his tote to a more comfortable position and smiled. "It's best we pass that place in the dark."

"May you have peace," Burnham said, grasping the man's hand.

Henry sat on the porch beside Frances, pretending to gaze across the field. From the edge of his vision he watched her intently stitching a hem along the edge of a pillowcase. She hadn't spoken to him since they came out.

He coughed once and she looked up sharply at him.

"Are you all right?" she asked.

"Just a tickle in my throat...pollen or something."

They had been together like this for two days now, sitting silently as she rocked and sewed. The swelling had almost immediately left their faces with the application of the aloe, but Mary had insisted they rest and "let the poison get out of your systems."

Studdard and Haisten had wandered over a couple of times to visit with Wilson. Studdard was now respectful in his attitude toward the sergeant but Haisten was almost reverential. Studdard had greeted Frances quietly, then left her to her sewing, reminding Wilson of General Taylor's words: "Leaving the field of battle to the victors."

"My heels are still sore." Her voice cut sharply through his thoughts.

"Beg pardon?" he asked, turning his head to look at her. Damn! The skin on his neck felt tight as dried deerhide.

"Couldn't you have been more gentle? You banged my heels on every step down the tower." Her jaw flexed as if she was grinding her teeth together.

"Now just a minute, Ma'am. I surely didn't have time..."

"A gentleman would have lifted my feet, not dragged me down like some caveman hauling a woman to his den."

"If you hadn't gone up to work the light like some man, the skeeters wouldn't of et you and I'd be out fishing right now."

"Are you saying I'm no lady? I'm more lady than any you've ever known," she retorted.

He squirmed his chair around slightly toward her.

"I never said..."

"Sir, I'm busy right now. Please go argue with someone else."

He squirmed his chair around away from her.

Dammit! The word came to his tongue but was stopped by his tightly clamped lips. What'd I do? he asked himself, shouting the thought inside his head. Women!

The next morning Burnham looked down the beach from the tower and saw Dummett, accompanied by a pack of hounds, approaching slowly just north of the cape. He quickly descended and ran to the house to have Mary begin preparing a breakfast of coffee, biscuits and grits. A quick peck on her cheek and he hurried back to the porch.

With only a grunt of greeting instead of his usual "Gonna be a fine day", Dummett opened his tote and removed a folded blanket, laying it out on the floor.

It contained two Seminole medicine bags and the golden wool necklace, broken where the silver gorget had been torn from it.

"Found the boys buried under a large oak on the bank of the Hillsboro," Dummett said. "Over near Live Oak Hill. Foxes were digging them up. That's how I spotted them. They'd been dead about a day, I guess— scalped alive and then beat to death."

Burnham felt the heat of blood rush up his cheeks to his temples as the words burned into his mind. "I guess I same as killed them," he said. "I should have never let them go north from here. But why would soldiers kill them, then bury them?"

"Weren't soldiers. I made out it was three men afoot—one pair of boots with holes in the soles, two with shoes. And it wasn't your fault any more'n it was mine. Hell, I could've tried to stop them at my place, but they weren't children. They knew the dangers."

Dummett pushed the necklace slightly with the toe of his boot.

"I gave Jumper the blanket that was made from."

"I know," Burnham said. "Tommy wore it proudly in respect for you. And now Dan."

"Buried them where I found them...deep. Said some Indian words over them. Never had to bury an Indian before."

Dummett folded the blanket back over the medicine bags.

"I hate like the dickens to tell Mary about this," Burnham said.

"Don't tell her, then."

"Guess I have to. She'd want to know."

"Well, it can't be helped. I'll send their belongings to Billy Bowlegs," Dummett said as he stuffed the blanket back in his tote. "Oh, I almost forgot. I brought you some mail. Looks like a government letter."

The soldiers left two days later. The family walked with them to the river, except for Frances, who stayed behind, standing on the porch. About a hundred yards away, Wilson stopped and looked back for a long moment. She raised a timorous hand as he lowered his head, turned and walked away.

In the three weeks following the soldiers' departure, Frances was despondent, dragging through the motions of her household chores, head down like a whipped puppy. Burnham was unbending in his decision to not allow Frances up the tower. With no replacement for her duties, he and Jackson began a series of alternating all-night shifts. He had considered having Junior take the duty, but the boy was so involved with the grove, and so useful to the family welfare that Burnham quickly discarded the idea.

He suspected the unspoken cause of Frances' pain, but avoided discussing it with her, knowing it would be unwelcome. Then, one night as they lay in bed, Mary brought up the subject to him.

"We must find something to give her hope for a future."

"Maybe so," he answered. "She's sure a bucket of pain to herself and everyone else."

"She hurts and I'm sure she doesn't even know why, or at least won't admit it even to herself."

"Well, she'll just have to get over it."

"Women don't just `get over' something like this. We must find something—she needs something to look forward to."

He lay quiet for a moment, then slid his arm beneath her shoulder. "Maybe we could find a way to send her north to school." He felt the dampness of tears on his arm.

"Oh, could we? It would do so much for her, let her meet other people, see how they live. I want so much for her to be happy."

As he drifted into sleep, he could still feel an occasional shiver from her as she lay in the dark, in pain for her baby.

The next morning at breakfast, he was thinking of some way to pose the idea to Frances when they heard a faint shout from outside. Frances jumped up and ran laughing from the kitchen.

By the time he got to the porch, she was running down the path toward Henry Wilson and, moments later, into his arms. Burnham turned to Mary as she stepped from the house.

"Guess the problem's been solved," he said, putting his arm around her waist. "And I guess we can forget about sending her to school."

Burnham sat in his place at the head of the dinner table with Mary and Frances beside him. Henry sat alone at the other end, his face flushed. The younger girls had crowded noisily around the table but Mary shooed them out.

After a long moment of silence, Henry coughed slightly and said, "I know this probably seems arrogant, but I just had to come back. By the time we got to St. Augustine I had my mind made up."

Burnham tilted his chair back on two legs. "Did you get permission or did you just leave?"

The young man's face reddened even more than Burnham thought possible. "No, sir! I resigned. My hitch was up anyway at the end of this month. I talked to the chaplain there and he arranged for an early discharge."

He paused, glanced at Frances, then turned back to Burnham. "Sir... Ma'am, would you mind...could I talk to Frances alone for a bit?"

Burnham hesitated while Mary laid her hand on his arm, looking at Frances. When the girl nodded, Mary said, "Of course, you may."

Frances stood and walked to the door. Henry sat rooted to his chair. "Are you coming?" she asked. He blushed again and jumped to his feet, opening the door for her.

After they left, Burnham walked to the fireplace mantle and began stuffing tobacco into his pipe.

"What do you think?" he asked Mary.

"Let's wait and see," she said. As she stood, Burnham saw that she had twisted the hem of her apron into a knot.

The young couple was outside over an hour. When they returned, Henry again sat at the end of the table, but this time Frances sat beside him. He was silent until she nudged him with an elbow.

"Uh, sir...I would like to have your..."

"He wants to marry me, Papa," Frances interrupted. "And I said 'yes'."

"Well, now," Burnham said, sucking noisily on his dead pipe for a moment. "I think...I'd like to hear him say it."

Henry jumped to his feet, almost to military attention and snapped, "Sir, I would like to marry your daughter."

Burnham also stood, facing him across the long table. "I think..." and he paused until he felt he had milked the silence for all the suspense he could, then smiled and said, "You do my daughter an honor, sir, and you have my blessing...and her mama's."

Frances' shout of glee as she ran around the table into Mary's arms brought the children crowding back into the room.

One week later, on March 30, 1856, Henry and Frances stood before the altar in St. Augustine's Trinity Episcopal Church and exchanged their vows.

As they did, Burnham nudged Mary and whispered, "Our family's growing again."

"Yes," she said, smiling. "And this time it's a lot easier on me."

Before leaving St. Augustine, Burnham helped Henry file homestead papers on the quarter-section adjacent to his. Within the week they had returned to the Cape. Henry was soon indoctrinated into the position of assistant lighthouse keeper.

On their free days, Burnham and Henry roamed the beach as far as ten miles in both directions, gathering driftwood lumber and hauling it back to the compound and stacking it behind the storage shed. Soon the pile had grown sizably and by the first week in June they began building a house near the Indian mound on Duck Cove.

Two months after beginning the house they had finished two rooms and, with Jackson's help, had built a sturdy oak bed, a table and four chairs.

"We'll build more rooms as our family grows," Henry promised Frances the day they moved in.

The days settled into a routine, with each much like the last. Burnham was pleased to see Henry develop a close friendship with Junior, who seemed to sparkle under the older man's attention and apparent need to learn the nature of growing things.

Burnham had bought block and tackle gear from a Ships Chandler in St. Augustine. Daily, the four men attacked the landscape, the winch attached to one tree until all the nearby palmetto roots had been ripped from the ground. Then, axing that tree down, they attacked its roots from another. In this manner they hopscotched over a forty acre patch that lay across both homesteads.

Burnham saved the trunks of two large cypress trees and, by working on them a little each day, had soon fashioned two broad-beamed dugout canoes. One was rigged as a sailer and the smaller was propelled by a large pole in the Seminole fashion. He named the sailing canoe the *Osceola*, and the other the *Frances*.

On a bright morning in early fall, Henry and Junior thinned out yearling trees from Burnham's field and carried them to the new field.

At mid-afternoon, Henry wiped his face with a bandanna as he watched Junior digging yet another hole in the black earth and setting a yearling in it dead center. "You keep takin' so much care in settin' those trees," he said to the boy, "and you'll have us here long after the folks have et all the cornbread and buttermilk."

Junior turned his face toward the older man and smiled radiantly at him. "The straighter they grow, I figger the easier they'll be to care for and to pick."

"Work hard now and work easier later, huh? I guess that's a good way to look at it. I never had to plan my work before, just took whatever orders was threw at me and had at it." Henry stepped on his shovel and lifted a clump of dirt. Then, dropping to his knees, he set a tree and carefully plumbed it with his eyes before scooping the dirt back in with his hands. "Seems like a good way."

Junior grinned at him, acknowledging his approval. "I guess it's sort of like Mama making me eat my greens to grow up straight and tall," he said. "You treat any little plants right and soon they'll be fine, big ones."

They worked steadily then without speaking, but Henry watched the boy from the corner of his eye and realized that, even with the care he took, Junior was planting three for every two Henry got into the ground.

His earlier feeling that Junior was a little strange was soon replaced with a respect for the boy's natural ability with plant life and for his willingness to work hard. His admiration had grown with every day they worked together. Although it seemed Junior talked only when necessary, maybe out of shyness, what he did say was backed by the sure knowledge of his experience.

By the time the sun dropped below the western trees they were finished. An easterly breeze cooled them and brought with it the mixed odors of turned earth and salt air. Junior sighted down one of Henry's somewhat crooked lines of trees, then down one of his own straight rows. "Ain't bad," he proclaimed, the shy grin again lighting his face. "You'll get better at it as you get older."

Henry chuckled. "I think it's cornbread and buttermilk time at your place. Let's go."

As the two walked slowly along the path toward the lighthouse compound, Junior placed a hand on Henry's shoulder. "We done good today," he said.

The simple gesture brought sudden tears to Henry's eyes, forcing him to turn his face away as he searched for the cause. Fulfillment. That's what it was. Through a providence he couldn't account for, he had been given a wife, a home, a brother and sisters, parents, and a future. He smiled, and increased his pace. He didn't feel near as tired as he thought he should.

Chapter 15

"**Y**ou are going and that's the end of it."

Dummett scraped the rest of the fried potatoes onto his plate and looked at Charles from the corner of his eye.

"Papa, I ain't got no use for going up there."

Leandra stood and tugged the bellpull to the kitchen. "Listen to you. 'I ain't got no'—the fact that you still speak that way after the schooling we've given you is a good reason for you to go." She handed the empty serving plate to Cicely as she entered the room. "Yale College will be good for you."

"That's not the main reason though," Dummett said. "You're fifteen, almost sixteen. Hell, son, It's by damn 1859. I'm not getting any younger and you're going to have to do more around here in years to come. It's time you learned how the world works, meet other people, learn something that'll help us in business. You'll be more valuable to me with an education than you are now."

Leandra's eyes sparked like an axe on a grindstone as she sat firmly in her chair. "You could have chosen a better way to say that," she snapped. "He's not a servant you know."

Dummett shook his head. "And you know what I meant. Let's not..."

"No, let's keep it buried. That's your way; like it'll go away if you don't face up to it."

"I can see it'll never go away and it's sure as hell not buried; you dig it up more and more lately. Let's not bring it up in front of the children."

Charles looked at the girls sitting quietly eating, then back at his parents. "Bring what up?"

"Never mind," Dummett said. "I've made all the arrangements and you *are* leaving next week. I went to Yale College and it's a fine school. Your Mama and I can't teach you no more."

"Anymore," Charles retorted as he stormed from the room.

Dummett stared at the door for a moment.

"You know," he said to Leandra, "this must be God's way of showing me how hard it is to be God."

By 1860, Sand Point was growing into a thriving community. Two stores, a hotel, a church and a post office served the fifty white inhabitants of the outlying area.

The Martin Hotel stood on a corner lot overlooking the river point, surrounded by a glaring, white road of crushed shell. As they walked from the store toward the hotel, Burnham and Dummett could see the crusty old man sitting in an overstuffed chair on the porch. A shotgun lay across his knees and a pair of crutches leaned against the wall behind him.

"Gentlemen, you're walking a mite too fast," he said as they stepped onto the porch. "Gotta be careful. You might work up a sweat and I'd have to fine you."

"Colonel Martin," Burnham greeted the man, swinging the croker sack of supplies from his shoulder to the floor. "A good sweat puts the mouth in better tune for a touch of rum. Care to join us?"

The old man removed his hands from the shotgun and grasped his right wrist with his left, twisting it slightly. "Twisted my arm, you did," he said, struggling to his feet. Pitching the shotgun to Burnham, he reached for his crutches.

"What's the gun for Harvey?" Dummett asked.

Harvey Martin hobbled through the door Burnham held open, shouting over his shoulder, "Gonna kill me any nigger..." He stopped and squinted an eye toward Dummett. "No offense intended toward you nor your'n," he said.

"None taken," Dummett assured him.

"Anyways, any nigger comes 'round here looking to get his freedom by force is gonna get both barrels—and so's any abolitionists what come here and open they mouths."

"I'll hold Burnham for you then, and you can get a clean shot at him," Dummett said as they entered the hotel's public room.

Harvey Martin settled his boney frame into the twin of the porch chair and let out a snicker that sounded like pants ripping.

"He don't count. He ain't got no niggers to abolite or whatever they calls it."

Dummett laughed and fetched three glasses from the kitchen, setting them down on the table in front of Burnham, who took the rum bottle from his duffle-bag and poured.

"He'll sure as hell try to talk you into freeing yours," Dummett said.

"Long's he don't talk to the niggers, he's harmless. Nobody notices when a roach farts," Martin said smacking his lips noisily as he sipped the rum.

"What's got you so riled?" Burnham asked.

"Where you boys been? Locked up?" Martin's voice dropped to a growl. "God tossed a stone into the black pool of slavery, a stone by the name of John Brown. Made a hell of a splash."

"John Brown? Never heard of him."

"Abolitionist what used to be out in Kansas. Way I got it, he raided the Harper's Ferry Arsenal up in Virginny a month ago, he did. Way I got it, he planned on buildin' him a army of niggers in Virginny and takin' over the whole south. Some army colonel named Robert Lee busted his raid and hung him, but hell's broke loose everwhere. They's carryin' guns and Bowie knives in the United States Congress, northern senators on one side of the hall and southerners on the other, yellin' and cussin' and spittin' and challengin'. They could be havin' nostril-to-nostril duels ever mornin' for breakfast if they was a mind to."

Martin paused to lubricate his throat with rum as Burnham and Dummett exchanged solemn glances.

"Think he's all right?" Burnham asked.

Dummett shook his head. "Damn, I hope so." Then to Martin, "My boy's up in Connecticut at Yale College. Do you think there's going to be trouble?"

"Hell fire, yes. Already is. Way I got it, most of the south didn't really give a big shit 'bout slaves, most folks bein' pore and not ownin' any, but when the slaves rise up in arms like that Nat Turner thing a few years back, ever body gets scared and bands together. A nigger army—Lord, that's scary. Way I got it, lottsa folks wants to pull the southern states out-ten the union."

"That's war talk," Burnham said. "Enough of that could make it hot on any southerner up north."

"Especially Charles. He could get it both ways." Dummett poured another glass of rum and downed half of it. "Well, we'll have to see which way the slop pours, but if I find it's really bad I'm sending for him."

"You boys stayin' the night?" Martin took a bell from his vest pocket.

"You still charging me six-fifty a month to hold that room?" Burnham asked. "I bet you rent it when I'm not here."

"Hell, the six-fifty says I'll kick whoever's in it out if you need it; it don't say I got to keep it empty." Martin rang the bell, and a colored servant eased so quickly into the room from the hallway that Burnham wondered if he had been out there listening.

"Clear that old coot outten Captain Burnham's room," Martin told the servant. He held his glass out to Burnham for a refill. "See? It's done."

His crooked grin did little to dispel the chill that lay in Burnham atop the heat of the rum.

Dummett held his hand level, spreading fingers that were as stiff as stovebolts. The hand trembled like an unbalanced ashpan as he clenched the fingers into a fist then straightened them, willing them to relax. They didn't.

Stretching his arms above his head, he tried to loosen the knots that ached through his neck, renewing the memory of his old gunshot wound. He poured a cup of coffee and left the kitchen. After walking across to the porch of the main house, he set his cup on the table beside the empty jug. A viscid scum coating the inside of his mouth magnified the dehydration from last night's rum.

He stepped into the yard and twisted an orange from the nearest tree. The long blade of his knife curled the skin from the blossom end. Biting the fruit in half, he savored the juice spurting into his parched mouth. He spat out the pulp and tossed the other half toward the hog pen.

He knew yesterday's confrontation was not over, but merely suspended by Charles' fatigue. The boy had been sullen when he arrived from New Haven. Dummett met him in New Smyrna on April 22, waiting an extra day because of the delay in the ship's arrival. From the instant he saw Charles walk down the gangplank, he could tell by the set of his jaw that the boy was angry over something. No, not angry—enraged!

Charles sat stiffly in the bow of the boat as they returned home, his back turned defiantly to his father. A drizzling rain set in on the river, seeming to drain the energy of the boy's anger. He said nothing until they arrived at Dummett Cove.

Then, in the kitchen, he dumped his load of frustrations on Dummett and Leandra, at first a dejected declaration, then the anger unleashing a torrent of accusation.

"You should have told me."

"Told you what? Now look, Son. Don't come in here—"

"I'm a Negro." Then his voice growled, "A nigger."

Leandra placed a hand on his arm. He pulled back, sharply jerking his arm free.

"I'm so sorry," she whispered softly, her eyes filling with tears.

"Charles, you've known all your life you were part colored," Dummett said.

"Not colored. Nigger. I didn't know what that meant. All my life, six-teen years I've spent on this place, and I didn't know what nigger really meant." His voice rose in pitch and intensity as he spoke.

"What happened?" Dummett stepped toward the boy, but again Charles backed away.

"They treated me like slime—the other students—like I'm not even human. A nigger. They hated me." He began to cry, the words splashing out sharply, expelled by his sobs. "Some of them...a few decent...some of them were horrified, asking me if I was a slave. I felt degraded. A slave!" He looked coldly into Dummett's eyes. "Am I your slave, Papa?"

"Well, legally..."

Charles stamped his foot. "Legal be damned! I'm either your son or I'm a slave. Which is it? Whose world do I live in?" His green eyes seemed like icy jade as he stared at Dummett, waiting for an answer.

Then, after a moment of deadly silence, he stalked from the room. Dummett turned to Leandra, feeling the impact of their eyes clashing, her eyes filled with the unspoken accusation of old. Then she verbalized it, and it hung in the air between them. "You should have freed him when he was birthed. Why didn't you?"

He stalked from the kitchen to the porch and, in the empty hours of the stormy night, drained the rum jug before staggering off to bed.

Now he stood by the orange tree, looking at the freshness that always followed an all-night drizzle. The early-morning sun struck glints from the drops of moisture lying along the dark green veins of the leaves. A morning like this always infused within him a sense of hope, a sense of the renewal of life. But now, as he looked at the damp, matted humus beneath the tree and a patch of mold along the gnarled limb, a shiver of apprehension rippled through his being.

Someone was moving in the house. The squeak of dry hinges and the rattle of cups carried across the lawn in the early morning stillness. Then he heard Leandra scream.

"Douglas! I can't find—where is Charles?"

Dummett ran to the house, jerking open the screen door as Leandra ran onto the porch.

"His bed—he's not in his room. His bed hasn't been slept in. Is he out..."

"I haven't seen him," Dummett said, turning and running back out to the kitchen.

After an hour of searching the outbuildings and the groves, he gave up. Charles was nowhere to be found

Charles stumbled on a protrusion in the sand, awareness slowly creeping into his mind. He stared for a moment at the rock while his last memory rushed into his consciousness.

He recalled standing in his room in the loft, staring at the door, crying, clenching his jaw until he felt his teeth must surely shatter under the pressure. Then a blinding light—a blinding light—flooded his mind, bringing with it a sound like the squeak in his ears when the pressure fell before a storm. The squeak began quietly, then increased in volume and pitch until he jammed his fists tightly against his ears.

Then nothing, until he stumbled over the rock.

He stood on the ocean beach, now wearing only his small clothes. They were damp, but already stiffening with salt as they dried in the warmth of the early morning sunlight.

He had no idea where he was. He could see the prints of his bare feet trailing away in the distance behind him, placing the dunes to his left as he had walked. North! He had been walking north. But to where? Definitely away from Dummett Cove. Seeing the ocean told him he had somehow crossed Mosquito Lagoon during the night.

Papa's ten-gauge shotgun lay cradled in his arms.

He began to walk slowly—north. No sense going home. Yes, North...to Mount Pleasant? Apparently he was trying to walk to New Smyrna, putting miles between him and Papa. Why? Because he knew Papa was to blame for his being colored. Papa, not Mama! Mama was colored, but Papa married her, didn't he? Married? Were they? The question had never occurred to him before. Was Mama a slave, owned by Douglas Dummett, like he owned Cicely?

Then, a memory—more a picture—of these same thoughts from last night just before the blinding light. He struggled to focus on the image. Papa had passed the curse of Ham on to him. Had that awareness triggered a hatred so strong he had lost touch with reality? Is that why he had the shotgun? To kill Papa?

No!

He loved Papa. Papa was everything. Maybe that was it—he had left home to keep from killing Papa!

But why couldn't he remember?

He trudged onward, his steps carrying him farther north.

Sometime after the sun reached its peak and started its downhill rush to the horizon, he saw Turtle Mound peeking above the dunes to his left. Three hours later he knew he had arrived at Mount Pleasant. He still didn't know why he was there but he felt relieved that he was no longer at Dummett Cove. He felt safe, because now Papa was safe.

He tried to remember who owned Mount Pleasant, but knew it wasn't family. Lathrop—that was it, the man's name. Not family. Maybe he should keep walking, go to St. Augustine and Aunt Dena.

Dropping to the sand at the base of a bluff, he laid the shotgun by his side. He closed his eyes, but after a time he gave up the struggle to sleep.

Again, pictures moved through his mind: his roommate at Yale, wordlessly packing his belongings and leaving; himself sitting at table, alone, while young men who had been his friends sat at other tables, nodding their heads in his direction and whispering, cutting their eyes away as he stared back at them.

Then came the final humiliation, a physical attack by two boys more destined to be mine workers than scholars. The shouts of "Nigger, go home!" and "You can't pass for white up here!" The taunts continued for the two days following the beating, until he sent a telegraph message to Florida and left for Dummett Cove.

He realized he would be a nigger the rest of his life, and the label was a brand on his soul, a mark of shame. It was now obvious to him that Papa was ashamed of his family, imposing an exile on them, secreting them away in the wilderness of Dummett Cove while he continued to move in the society of men, under the sanctity of his whiteness.

As these tormenting thoughts and pictures engulfed him again, his anger grew until he could no longer sit. He rose, stalked to the surf's edge and began throwing shells into the water, merely with anger at first, then gripped by a fury beyond his control.

The blinding light returned, burning more deeply into his brain than before, and carrying more pain than he could stand.

As Charles' mind moved from the depths of darkness, he seemed to be in a dream world, a world of emptiness, a world where he was embracing an obelisk as if he were worshiping it.

He awoke with a start, to find himself in some sort of field, his legs and arms wrapped around a post. His fear froze him in that position as he looked around, trying to orient himself. How did he get here? Above him, he could see a canopy of stars. Moving his eyes slowly downward across the darkness, they focused on a dimly seen treeline surrounding the field and, farther down, he recognized a corral fence—the old corral in back of the plantation at Mount Pleasant. Where Old Pumpery died. A dying place.

The post to which he clung so tightly was—the snubbing post. Where Papa killed the bull. A killing place.

He began to whimper. "What's wrong with me?" he cried, the pain of fear digging deeply into his inner being. "Sick, I'm sick...a nigger—forever. God...help me." The high-pitched squeak returned, threatening to split his head open.

Holding the post tightly with his left arm, he scrubbed his right hand into the sand surrounding him until his groping fingers found what they were searching for. Dragging the shotgun around alongside his body, he reached for the trigger with the toes of his bare foot.

The blinding light returned for an instant.

Charles Lathrop carried the tragic news from Mount Pleasant to Dummett Cove. He sat now, hat twisted in his hands, not knowing the words of comfort to offer this strange family. He coughed slightly and looked at the three girls crying near the wall, stared at their light, coppertoned arms embracing each other. He turned back to Dummett.

"Remembered him right off from the last time you brought him to town," Lathrop told him. "Found him in that old field back of the house. Looked like he'd tripped and the gun went off."

The black-bearded man, Dummett, sat on the edge of the couch in the parlor, his arm across the shoulder of the woman, her remarkably beautiful face distorted with grief. Her anguished cries had finally subsided to a mournful whimper, reminding Lathrop the way his hounds acted after a beating.

Lathrop glanced again at the girls, comparing their skin color to the woman's, the woman who was so notorious in New Smyrna for her color. Yes, he could see they were definitely not white. If he hadn't known that already, he'd have picked them as white for sure. He shook his head and clucked his tongue.

"Mr. Dummett, I didn't know if you wanted him here or in New Smyrna. We cleaned him up and laid him out in my bed. I didn't know..." His voice trailed off as Dummett sighed and stood.

"I'd like to bury him at Mount Pleasant, if you don't object," Dummett told him. "It was my home for so long, and he..." Dummett bent forward, wiped his hands across his face, then straightened. "We'll come up tomorrow. I need to get word to my sister in St. Augustine."

"We got us a telegraph wire in New Smyrna, now," Lathrop said. "If you'd like, I could..."

"I'd be much obliged."

Lathrop stood and walked to the door. Dummett looked back at his wife, then followed the man from the house.

In spite of the afternoon's warmth, Leandra shivered as she leaned against Louisa's shoulder and held tight to Mary's hand. Beyond the freshly dug grave, Kate stood by her Papa, her tiny hand lost in his. Kate was the only one not crying. The eight-year-old reached up with her free hand and stroked Dummett's arm, humming soothingly and quietly as everyone stood in silence. Like the whisper of rain, the rustling of dried leaves played a soft counterpoint to Kate's voice.

Leandra was grateful that Dena and the Burnhams had met them in New Smyrna. While they crossed the river to Mount Pleasant, Dena attempted to console both Dummett and Leandra, but when they approached the open grave, she had moved behind Leandra, leaving her to share her grief with her daughters.

When Leandra saw Dummett's head snap up, she turned slightly to see the Negroes approach with the casket, with Charles. Behind them, in the corner of the field, the charred remains of the fence and snubbing post still smoldered where Dummett had burned them. The grave was on the spot where Charles' body had been found—where the snubbing post had stood.

The Negroes, the men of her son's life, tears glistening on their cheeks, carefully centered the wooden casket over the hole and tenderly lowered it into the ground, then walked a respectful distance away, their heads bowed.

Kate stopped her humming and the mournful silence shrouded Leandra with its weight. She wanted to scream, to break its hold on her...to awaken the boy lying in the hole at her feet.

She felt Dummett's eyes watching her, but she resisted the impulse to look into their burning depths.

She felt other eyes. Her eyes searched the woods near the smoldering fire until she saw it. A large, red-shouldered hawk perched on a high limb of a slash pine, clutching a dead rabbit in its talons, ripping the flesh with its sharp beak. It paused to stare directly into her eyes, seeming to probe into her soul.

A sound forced its way past her mind. Mills Burnham had stepped to the end of the grave and was speaking, his soft voice a bare murmur in her ears. "This boy, a child of love, born in a time..." He coughed to clear his throat, then continued.

The words, droning into the mist of her memories, were in eulogy to her son, but she blocked them out, hearing instead, within her mind, her own voice from long ago. *"His name is Charles. He's white, you know."* And then, *"You'll be my life when I have no other, and I'll be yours when you have no other."*

As they entered their house after the funeral, Dummett reached out to Leandra. "No! Don't touch me. You killed my son," she screamed, feeling hysteria rush through her.

"Me? How did I..."

"We both did. We should have known."

She pulled the bonnet from her head and walked to the caneback chair, sitting sideways on its edge. She slumped forward and covered her face with her hands. Tears filled her eyes and spilled from between her fingers. She felt his hand on her shoulder and jerked away as if she had been stung.

"No!" she screamed again. She felt his hand go away.

"But...we didn't..." he stammered. "How did we kill him? He must have been insane."

She raised her eyes and looked at him through the blur of tears. She began to rock, back and forth, and his face wavered in and out of focus.

"He wasn't insane. And what if he was?" She bit the words off short, as if they tasted bitter. "He should never have been born in the first place. You should have known how it would be. Look how they treated us... even though you were white. Could we have expected any better treatment for him?"

Dummett sat on the floor before her, twisting the black felt of his hat between his hands.

"We had him...our love made him. We couldn't help that, could we?" He reached out his hand toward her face. "I love you."

She pulled back sharply. "You finally picked a memorable moment to tell me." Then, for a moment she felt a warm wave of tenderness sweep through her. "I've waited all my life to hear you say that, but now..." A shiver cleared her mind.

"No, we couldn't help that," she said. "He was born. But Maum Molly warned me. I should have never entered your bed without the freedom papers for my children, signed and under my pillow."

"You know I always intended to do that. I just never got around to it, never thought it was that important."

"You were never a nigger."

"No, dammit, that's not my fault either."

"What about the girls? Will you write their papers now?"

"I'll write the papers. Things the way they are in Washington, probably won't be any Federal Court to give them to." He stood and walked toward the bedroom, loosening his shirt.

"No, you bastard!" She rose in fury from the chair. "You will never... enter my bed again...until my girls...are freed."

He turned, staring at her for a long moment, then stalked from the house, slamming the door behind him.

That night he slept in the boathouse and early the next morning began building a sleeping shack about two hundred feet south of the house. While working on the shack, he attached a long shelf to the side wall of the main house and ordered Cicely to serve his meals there.

Kate occasionally came out to sit with him at his lonely meals, but Leandra stayed indoors the week of the building and he never saw her. The other girls sometimes, in their play, came over to watch him work, but stayed off to the side, away from Dummett.

The morning after the shack was completed, he entered the house for his belongings. Leandra, sitting in a rocker, watched him as he stripped his books from the shelves to stack them in a wheelbarrow.

"You don't have to do this, you know," she said.

"I know what you said." He continued to stack his books.

After a long silence, Leandra said, "You are the master here. You can stay if you want. It's your right."

"Couldn't prove it by me." He snapped the words off sarcastically and turned to face her. "Apparently I gave up being the master when I took you as wife."

"Douglas, you don't have to..."

"You shouldn't have said what you did. Those were your true feelings, I know, but you shouldn't have said them." He lifted the handles of the wheelbarrow and left without looking back.

Chapter 16

The furor over the states-rights issue escalated throughout Congress, but news filtered to the Cape with the slowness of blackstrap seeping from a hogshead. When news did arrive, usually brought by some traveler passing through Sand Point carrying an outdated newspaper, it was already old news, crowded out by more recent events or rumors. By the time Burnham heard of Lincoln's election, South Carolina had already seceded from the Union.

In early March, 1861, Dummett brought over a special issue of the St. Augustine *Examiner*, telling them of the formation of the Confederate States of America. Burnham had been unaware of Florida's secession from the Union.

"There's sure to be war," Burnham said to the men sitting at the kitchen table. Henry had his elbows propped on the table, his red-stubbled chin nestled into the palms of his hands. Junior sat rigidly upright, silent as the discussion of the older men boiled around him. Frances, her pregnancy a presence in itself and nearly full-term, was quietly helping Mary prepare dinner in the background. Burnham knew that each woman was listening intently to the conversation. Katherine had taken the younger girls to the garden.

"It's not my war," Dummett said. "I don't own any niggers now and—"

"You never told me. When did this happen?" Burnham was again struck by the man's reluctance to discuss his business until after the fact.

"I sold the last of them right after Charles..." Dummett stared into his cup as he sipped his coffee. "After Charles died," he finished. "Cicely asked to go to my sister, Dena, so I sent her papers along and Dena freed her. Old Cudjoe's still with me. Gave him the choice of being sold to someone who could care for him better'n me, but he didn't want it."

Henry leaned back in his chair and looked at each of the others in turn. "I don't know what to do. I got feelings for the Union, my army service and all. But Florida's my home. Has been for years. How can I fight against people I'll live amongst for the rest of my life? How can I fight at all with a child on the way?" He shook his head slightly as Frances turned to him. A momentary shadow of anguish passed over her face, but she quickly regained her composure and resumed peeling onions.

"Papa, what about me?" Junior asked. His face was ashen and his eyes, usually so serene, were staring fixedly at his father.

"Son, twenty-three years of life gives you the right to choose who you face death with." Burnham swallowed hard as he said this, fighting the dreadful fear building within him, knowing the dangers confronting this gentle boy. "One side or the other's bound to get you. Like Henry, I have feelings for the North, but I've lived here all my adult life. And Florida's the only home you've ever known. You each have to weigh your beliefs, and then live by them.

"But the way I see it—for me mind you, not necessarily for you—there's more to it than getting along with my neighbor. There's truth, truth as I see it and no one else."

"Papa, I feel the same way you do about Negroes and their freedom."

Burnham thought for a moment, then stood and walked over by the window. "I'm not talking about Negro freedom," he said. "Or even states rights. I'm talking about people rights. I'm talking about choice, what I just said to you—the right to choose who you might die with, where you'll live, and how you'll be governed. All that boils down to is choice. Sure, the Negroes should be free, but I'm talking about my freedom."

He paused, turning to look at the men. He saw nothing in their faces that told him they understood. "My grampa lived in England and watched the colonists in this land stage a revolution against their country. Those men believed they should have the freedom to choose a way of life different from what England told them. So they fought. If they'd lost, they would've been branded traitors, and many would've been hung for treason. But they won, and were honored as patriots."

Both women had stopped their chores and were leaning against the countertop, wiping their hands on their aprons, listening.

"That lesson," Burnham continued, "freedom won at great risk, impressed Grampa so much that he pulled up his roots and emigrated to America. I heard him say it a dozen times, `I moved here because I could'."

He looked at Mary's silver-streaked auburn hair, then grinned at Junior. "Your Grandpa McCuen left Ireland for the same reason, bringing your mama with him, thus ensuring my slavery."

Mary wadded her towel and threw it at him.

Burnham walked to her and wrapped his arms around her for a moment, then turned back to the boys. "I think the people up north will fight to free the Negro. I think some of the southerners will fight to keep them enslaved. But I think most of the South merely wants to preserve the right of states to control their destinies. The Union was born of secession from England, and I see nothing any different in the Confederacy being born the same way."

"There might be another option for Henry," Dummett said. "Heard about it over at Sand Point. If you should choose to join the Confederate Army, there's a new company formed over in Gainesville, called the Home Guard. It's sorta like the militia I was in. Being a new papa and all, you might be able to get some kind of guarantee from them to keep you in Florida."

"I'll think on it, and hope I can work it out," Henry said. "Let's just pray it don't come to that."

Burnham sat down at the table and listened to the men talk. His mind wandered to his own situation; what would he do if the Confederates pushed him one way and the Federals pushed him another? Either way, he must preserve his position. At all costs.

The land'll take care of you, boy. It can make you wealthy.

The old words haunted him and he knew whoever won, this lighthouse would still be here and his land would still be here. But would he? He would have to see to it. He could only wait and pray, as Henry said, that it wouldn't come to that.

But by April it had come to exactly that. The Confederate forces had attacked Fort Sumter at Charleston, South Carolina.

War was declared.

After long discussions with each other and Burnham, Henry and Junior decided to enlist in the Confederate Army.

On a bright morning in the first week of May, they prepared to leave. Burnham would take them to St. Augustine where they could find transportation to Gainesville.

Frances lay her head on Henry's shoulder as they walked slowly toward the river dock and the *Osceola*. Behind them, Mary grasped her son's hand in both of hers. Burnham and the four younger girls trailed the group. Both women were struggling to restrain themselves, neither wanting to send the men away with memories of tears.

But as the sailboat heeled away from the landing, Burnham knew the tears were there.

8 July, 1861

My Dearest wife,
I hope this finds all well at home, the folks and you and the new baby,
whatever it is. Me and Burnham—he dropped the Junior soon as we got
here, said it made him sound like a child—we are both well. It didn't take
me much to get back into the rut of army life, but Burnham is being slow
to take to it.
Our clothes are holding up fine for the most part, but we rub holes in
our socks most every day and sew on them most every night. As they say
in the army, the food ain't bad—it's awful.
I got my guarantee not to leave Florida, but it looks like we will both be
leaving soon anyhow. Right now we're up by Tallahassee somewhere. We
got sent here two weeks ago, and this company is headed out. We don't
know where yet, but the war is mostly in Virginia, and war is what we was
sent to do. Some men here says the war will be over in ninety days, but
that was sixty days ago. Maybe we will be home in another thirty.
Kiss my baby, whatever it is. I hope you remembered to name it Alfred if
it was a boy and you pick it if it was a girl.

Your loving husband,
Henry

BOOK FIVE

1862 — 1873

BOOK FIVE

1865 — 1871

Chapter 17

Burnham left the tower before dawn, too tired to bother with extinguishing the lantern. When allowed to burn out its supply of oil, the wick always blackened the prisms heavily. Jackson had been plowing a field by the river preparing to plant a new crop of corn so Burnham had taken over all the tower duties. This was his third straight all night shift.

He stepped into the kitchen and slumped into a chair at the table. When Mary sat a mug of steaming coffee before him, he leaned forward and propped his elbows on the table and cupped his chin in his hands.

"There be no more salt," Mary said as she served him a plate of grits and eggs. "I had to scrape the cone to the core for the supper last night." Watching her walk back to the stove with a slight bend to her back, Burnham felt a flush of anger that she should have to be so upset.

The supply ship had not delivered to the Cape for more than a year, and the family was faced with a dire shortage of everything. Burnham had sailed to New Smyrna late in 1861 to telegraph the Lighthouse Board, but the wire service had been taken over by the Confederacy, and they weren't about to allow U. S. messages of any kind be sent.

After his breakfast, Burnham took Mary's hand and led her to the supply shed to take stock of their staples.

"Coffee's near gone, we're low on sugar, and the last of the wheat flour be crawling with weevils," Mary said. She stared at the two nearly empty oil drums, then looked up at him. "We can make do on what we got, but how can you burn the lantern without fuel?"

"Can't," he said quietly and guided her out the door. "I might have to render down some gator fat. I guess things could be worse. We've always got the land. We're not about to go hungry." He hugged her and gave her a little pat on the fanny, sending her off to the house.

The land'll take care of you, boy. It can make you wealthy. Maybe it wouldn't make them wealthy now, but the land would have to take care of them. It was all they had. He shrugged off his fatigue and began his morning work, walking numbly through the chores of feeding corn to the cattle and turning the six long-haired West Indian sheep into the pasture to graze. He bought the sheep right after Henry and Junior left. They were the last purchase he was able to make with United States currency. Now that the Confederacy was printing money, some of it was drifting down to Sand Point and no one would touch Federal money.

He watched the sheep nuzzling out the roots of the short-cropped grass and wondered if they would survive even long enough to breed. As he looked, he was seeing mutton on the hoof more than the growing herd he had envisioned when he bought them.

A voice broke his reverie. "Gonna be a fine day. What's got you so solemn?"

Burnham looked up to see Dummett and his daughter, Kate, walking along the river path toward him. They smiled as if sharing some secret joke, Kate skipping to keep up with her father's swift stride. She stopped and curtseyed to Burnham.

"Mornin', Captain Burnham," she said and broke into a run to catch up to her father. "Can I tell him, Papa? Please?"

Dummett stopped and looked at her thoughtfully. "Well, it is news of importance to the world, so go ahead, then find the other children." He tousled her hair as she hugged his waist. She turned to Burnham with the hint of a smile replacing the solemn look.

"We got us three new litters of pigs, all at the same time," she blurted. Her dark face flushed brightly with pleasure when Burnham grinned and hopped into the air, clicking his heels smartly together. She giggled and ran toward the house.

"She's special," Burnham said, watching the girl run up the steps to the house.

Dummett beamed with pride. "Frances is your oldest and she watches over the little ones, right? Well, my Kate watches over her older sister as well as the younger one. Like a little mother. Takes a big load off of Leandra." He laughed. "She's a grownup in a tiny body."

"So you got new pigs, huh?" Burnham asked.

"They all farrowed the same night," Dummett said. "Soon's they're weaned, I'll have Cudjoe bring one of the litters over here. You got anything to trade?"

Burnham shook his head slowly. "I'll find something. The pigs'll be a blessing when they're grown, but our problem is right now. Things are going to be tight here for a while. I don't know—"

"That's a crock of sour milk, man. We've got the best of this war. Which reminds me, I bring news of a different nature." He gestured for Burnham to follow and turned to walk toward the ocean beach.

"Our friend, Paul Arnau, got a letter from Mr. Stephen Mallory of Pensacola. He's the new Secretary of the Confederate Navy. Your light's got to be shut down."

Burnham stopped abruptly. "They can't do that. This light is Federal property..." He stopped, realizing the humor in the statement he was making.

"Guess that don't cut no ice with the Rebs, does it?" Dummett grinned, then continued the stroll toward the beach. "It seems Arnau is a dyed-in-the-wool Confederate. He's formed a group—call themselves the Coast Guard. They're going to see to it that the lights are shut down everywhere in Florida. Arnau took down the St. Augustine lens himself."

"But the light's vital to shipping," Burnham said. "What about all the ships that run these waters?"

They walked down the dunes onto the beach and sat on its down-slope.

Dummett tossed a shell into the surf, then leaned back on his elbows and crossed his legs in front of him. "The Yankees took Fernandina last week so I guess they're in Jacksonville by now, maybe even St. Augustine. They control the entire eastern seaboard except for Charleston, and they have her blocked off tight enough nobody can get in or out. So they are the major shipping in these waters. The Rebs want to make it hard on them."

"What'll the Southern ships do for navigation?"

"Hell, they figure they know these waters and the Yankees don't. You got to do it, Burnham. When the St. Simons keeper wouldn't douse his light, they packed it full of black powder—blew it to kingdom come."

Burnham winced. "Damn! That was the most beautiful light tower in the country." He bit off the words bitterly. "A work of art, if anything made by man ever is."

"I heard Arnau's Coast Guard is headed this way. Either way—his or yours—this light's got to go."

They sat quietly for a while, each lost in his own thoughts, when Burnham remembered Dummett's earlier remark. "What did you mean, 'we've got the best of this war'?"

"Well, to start with, you don't have the chore of that damn light anymore, at least for now. We're sitting here alone and have only our families to worry over. Between us, we can raise everything we could possibly need. If we use our heads, we can survive in good stead."

Burnham digested the thought for a while, then stood and walked to the surf line. After a moment he shook his head and turned back to Dummett. "If ships can't get in or out, how will we get our oranges and pineapples to market?"

"We won't even try. We'll only raise what we need. The days of shipping forty thousand boxes of oranges a year are over for a while. About all they're good for now is animal feed and fertilizer."

Dummett rose and scuffed his moccasins in the sand, drawing the outline of Florida. "We were the third state to pull out of the Union. We've contributed men and material to the war until we're short ourselves. Now there ain't nothing we got that the Confederacy needs or the Yankees want. Florida has no factories, no natural resources such as iron ore, and now there's damn few men left for farming or defense. We're sticking out down here like a sore thumb, and must care for ourselves as best we can. That means us—you and me."

Burnham nodded agreement and the two men began to walk along the beach. For the rest of the morning, they discussed options and finally came to an agreement for a division of labor.

Burnham would raise corn with the help of his daughters and Jackson's family. In return for his share of the corn, Dummett would provide both families with sugar and molasses, and his rifle would furnish them meat, from venison and bear to rabbit and squirrel.

Fish could be taken in abundance from the rivers with little effort. Burnham had often put a lantern in the bottom of an anchored boat, and it would fill by dawn with mullet that had jumped at the light. Ducks and other waterfowl covered the rivers more than six months out of the year.

Each family would maintain a truck patch for vegetables that could be grown at various seasons throughout the year and would keep for some time after their harvest.

When Dummett reminded him of the forge in the lighthouse shed that they could use to make needed repairs to equipment, Burnham laughingly suggested that they build a still to process rum.

"Hell, yes," Dummett agreed, smacking his lips. "We got to have staples. A little taste would go good right now," he said, pulling his clay jug from his tote.

As they walked back to the lighthouse, they made plans for a trip the following week to nearby villages and cities to search for other staples, such as wheat flour, salt, and gunpowder.

The next morning, Burnham and Jackson climbed the tower and dismantled the lantern. After the prisms and clock mechanism were lowered to the ground, they were thoroughly cleaned, coated with the last of the grease and packed into wooden boxes. By mid-afternoon they had carried the boxes to Burnham's orange grove and buried them.

A week later, Burnham set out in the *Osceola*, stopping by Dummett Cove to pick up Dummett.

The narrow Hillsboro River teemed with life as they drifted slowly along with a mild breeze. Lazing back in the boat, they relaxed, enjoying the peaceful sounds of nature, banishing all thoughts of the war from their minds.

Approaching Ross Hammock near the little community of Live Oak Hill, they heard the thunk of axes biting into trees. Spicy wood smoke drifted over the face of the river. Within minutes they came upon a crew pouring buckets of river water into large wooden casks mounted on mule-drawn wagons.

"Salt works," Dummett said. "I'd heard they were going to start up."

Burnham angled the boat toward the wagons. They beached it and walked inland to a spacious clearing where ten immense sugar kettles appeared to be floating in roaring flames. Brine boiled clear and rapid in some, while a white froth coated the surface of others. In one half-empty vat, large bubbles skittered and popped on a layer of dirty scum. The clearing was filled with men bustling at chores: stirring the cauldrons like witches over their brew, hauling water, or chopping wood.

Burnham walked over to watch four men scooping what looked like wet sand from the bottom of two vats, spreading it on smooth oak planks to dry in the bright sunlight.

Dummett pointed at burlap sacks of salt stacked in an open leanto. "We'll fetch a couple each when we get back. The brown stuff's only fit for salting beef and pickling pork, or maybe as licks for the stock, but those clear white crystals is table grade."

They continued up the river to Live Oak Hill, where they left the boat and set out walking cross-country on a wagon lane that led through prairies and alligator-infested swamps. The path occasionally cut through pine forests where squirrels barked angrily at them and the walking was easier.

They camped that night in an oak hammock and by noon the next day they reached the shores of Lake Monroe. In the hazy distance south across the water, the ruins of old Fort Mellon caused fragmented memories of the Indian war to rush through Burnham's mind. He stared at the broken palisades for a long moment, then turned and walked toward the spires of smoke curling above the trees to the north. Shortly, they entered the town of Enterprise, passing the Brock House, a large hotel overlooking the lake.

The town appeared to be part of the landscape, seeming to grow from the scrub palmetto, the old brick of the buildings blending into the murky shadows of pines and liveoaks.

They entered the dark coolness of the general merchandise store, enveloped by the richness of the odors of leather and spice. The odors belied the mystery, however, of empty shelves. There was no leather, no spice.

"Howdy, gents. Nice to have company." The voice drifted disembodied down the vacant aisles and echoed from the rows of bare shelves.

Burnham answered, "Halloo. Where are you?"

"Behind the counter. Come on back."

They walked to the rear of the room and saw a portly man wearing a dirty apron, leaning back in a cane-bottomed chair, swatting lazily at droning flies with a rolled newspaper.

"Nice day," he said, not bothering to rise. "What can I do for you?"

"We're from over by the Cape, looking for supplies." Burnham looked around the empty room. "You gone to keeping your goods somewhere else?"

"Ain't none," remarked the man. "Ain't been none for most of the year, except some trade goods I get now and again from settlers hereabouts."

Dummett rolled an empty pickle barrel around the counter and sat on it. "We need flour, coffee, spices, tobacco—stuff like that," he said. "Don't suppose you'd know where we could get any?"

"Mister, if I knowed where you could get any, I'd get some myself."

Burnham laughed at this logic and raised a hip and one leg onto the counter. "If you're out of everything, why do you stay open?"

"A man's gotta do somethin' with his time, don't he? Besides, I got some thangs. I got benzene mothballs, old newspapers, clothes hangers—thangs like that. All the essentials." He laughed bitterly. "Men, I was cleaned outta most everthang right after Sumter was fired on. The stuff you needs ain't to be had, nowhere." He stood slowly and hesitated for a moment. "I do have some sheets of lead from an old newspaper plant linin' my meat shelves. Could you use that?"

"Damn right," Dummett said.

"I also got several bolts of bedtickin'. How about that?"

"Damn right," Burnham said.

He pointed to the paper in the man's hand. "And maybe some of those newspapers if they got news we haven't heard," he said.

"I can tell you a lot of the news," said the man, pulling the bottoms from the counter shelves and sliding squares of lead onto the floor.

"I 'spect you want to know of the war. Well, you heard about Fort Sumter?" He paused and cocked an eyebrow at them.

Dummett nodded and the man resumed.

"The first battle we heard of was last July at a place right outta Washington City, Manassas Junction, a little creek called Bull Run. We whipped the Yankee's ass good there. Then we won one in late summer at Wilson's Creek in Missouri. But the Yankees hurt us bad nearly a month or so ago in Tennessee—couple of forts, Henry and Donelson, on the

Cumberland." He paused and reached into his pocket for a corncob pipe that he stuck between his teeth. "Don't suppose you men got no tobaccy?"

Burnham handed him his pouch. "Will you take Spanish gold for the lead and cloth?" he asked.

Dummett snapped his head around. "You still got some of that? Man, you hang on to it better'n my papa did."

The store keeper squinched his face and looked up from stuffing tobacco into the crusty, cob pipe. "Well, Cuban coins was de-legalized back in '50. I don't know. Money ain't much good to me now. What I need is goods what can be swapped with the settlers hereabouts for other thangs."

"The gold's as good to you as that lead is," Burnham said. "Besides, what money is any good? U. S. money's no good here, and our new government hasn't seen fit to send much of theirs our way. Gold will always be gold, no matter who's money wins the war."

"That's a fact," the man said. He looked at the five sheets of lead. "I figure you got fifty pounds of lead there, and six bolts of cloth. How's five dollars sound? I'll throw in a old rucksack to carry the lead."

The bargain made, Burnham and Dummett prepared to leave the store, but the storekeeper seemed reluctant to let them go. "Are yore womenfolk safe?" he asked. "Been a lot of talk of scavengers around the countryside, some killin' and rapin' going on." Seeing he had their attention, he continued. "Ain't Yankees neither. Rebs. Not soldiers, but men what lives in Floridy, too cowardly to fight in the war—stealin' and killin' from they own people."

"I don't expect they'd want to travel into our wilderness," Dummett said. "First place, they wouldn't know anybody was living there."

They thanked the man, lifted their sacks and left the store, walking toward the Brock House.

Two days later they were in New Smyrna, where they found the same situation in the shops and general merchandise stores, but no supplies of any sort.

"We'll eat cornbread. It tastes better and it's better for you," Dummett said.

"I like it." Burnham agreed with a smile that crinkled the stiff hairs of the new beard he was growing.

The men walked to the city docks on the Hillsboro.

"I need to see to Charles' grave before we leave here," Dummett said. "I hired Mr. Lathrop to build a crypt and I'd like to tell Leandra about it."

Borrowing Mr. Sheldon's skiff, they rowed across to Mt. Pleasant. They visited Lathrop for a while, then walked to the field where Charles was buried.

The sarcophagus was about two feet tall, its coquina walls already taking on an aged and weathered grayness beneath the timeless marble slab covering the crypt.

"Sacred to the memory of Charles Dummett..." Dummett's voice quivered, then broke when he read the dates of the boy's birth and death etched into the marble.

They stayed in silence for several minutes, then Dummett turned on his heel and trudged back across the field to the river. After returning Sheldon's boat they began the long walk along to Live Oak Hill.

Hours later, when they reached the *Osceola*, they dumped their goods aboard and set out on the river. A south wind kicked up small whitecaps as the little boat labored into its force. Within minutes black, roiling clouds spread across the sky to a sharply defined blue edge near the horizon.

When the soft drizzle began, the river took on a smoky haziness, limiting their vision. They continued sailing for a few minutes more until jagged bolts of lightning began ripping the clouds, threatening their safety on the open water. Burnham turned the boat toward shore, toward four heavy skiffs pulled up on the bank. He was about to comment on them when the muffled bark of gunfire echoed from the woods farther up the river.

Chapter 18

When Leandra saw the three rough-looking men approaching through the north grove, she set the basket of damp clothes on the ground and wiped the sweat from her forehead with her sleeve. A momentary twinge of apprehension raced through her but she quickly dismissed it. Many times in recent months travelers had stopped at Dummett Cove, some for directions and others for food and rest. These three were probably no different.

As she stepped forward to greet them, she glanced around the yard, searching for the girls. From the corner of her eye she saw them playing near the tree house by Dummett's sleeping shack.

"Howdy, Ma'am." The speaker was a beefy man with a bushy, red beard splotched with gray. Greasy, red hair sprouted from beneath a floppy black, felt hat. The other two men were skinny and dirty, their scabrous faces and lanky limbs reminding her more of carrion birds than men.

"Welcome," she said cautiously. "Anything I...we can help you with?"

"Wal, that be right friendly of you. We could use us some fresh food. Been livin' on beef jerky for nigh onto a week now." The man's eyes were shifting from side to side, scanning the yard and the outbuildings, seeming to take note of everything.

"Don't see no man around, just an ole nigger down there." He flicked a finger toward the boathouse where Cudjoe was axing and scraping the center of a new dugout canoe. With a hushed grunt, one of the men sauntered down the lane toward the boathouse. The third man eased slightly to Leandra's left. She turned to face him.

Even before the large man moved, she sensed the attack but was unable to avoid the meaty fist that smashed across her cheek, knocking her to the ground. She turned her head and screamed through a red curtain of pain. The girls—she must protect the girls.

"Kate! Girls! Run–hide!"

She struggled to get to her feet, clutching, trying to get a hold on the man's arms, but the redhead shoved her back to the ground. She tried to roll away from him but he slammed a boot into her ribs, leaving her gasping, sucking, trying frantically to pull air into her tortured lungs. She curled her arms across her chest and pulled her knees upward, desperately trying to ward off further blows. God help her, the man was pointing toward the girls. She felt a whimper rise from within her but couldn't make the plea she so desperately needed, to beg him to spare her girls.

"Get 'em," the redhead shouted to the man beside him.

Leandra twisted her head, trying to see if the girls were running, but the redhead grabbed a fistful of her hair and hauled her to her feet. The pain of it sent a spasm through her that sucked air deep into her lungs. Then, across the man's shoulder she could clearly see Cudjoe start up the path and she screamed as she saw the axe smash into his skull from behind. He crumpled into a shapeless heap. The man raised the axe again, smashing it down into Cudjoe's back.

She was jerked forward, stumbling. Her legs crumpled, but the hand in her hair dragged her into the house. With a guttural laugh, the redhead threw her across the room onto the bed.

"Heard about a white-skinned, green-eyed nigger slut bein' here," he chuckled, shoving her back as she fought to rise. "Thought we'd try a piece to change our luck."

One of the other men appeared. "Them little'uns got plumb away." He stood by the bed and began ripping her dress from her in shreds. "Loosen her up, McGirt," he giggled. "I got second humps."

McGirt unknotted the rope holding up his pants. As they fell to the floor, his penis loomed erect and angry above her. She cringed from the sight, then realized that if the men kept their attention on her they might forget about her girls. She leaned back into the mattress and stared directly into the man's eyes.

Inflamed by the look, McGirt dropped to his knees on the bed, grabbed her legs and shoved them high toward her shoulders. Sharp thrusting waves of pain stabbed her as the cracked bones of her ribs grated against one another. One swift grasp tore her underpants from her. The man grunted savagely and rammed himself into her dry, tightened flesh.

As the redhead slammed his hips forward, Leandra felt her soft tissue tear—burning. His penetration drove to the bottom and something inside gave way, breaking with a pain that was almost audible.

"Move, bitch," he screamed, pausing to lift his rocklike fist to his shoulder.

The blow slammed in above her left ear and she felt the bones in her skull give way. Reality wavered in and out for a moment through her glazing eyes. As consciousness fled, she heard, "Hell, I think I kilt the bitch."

"That don't make no nevermind. I still got next humps."

When the shots rang out, Burnham immediately shoved the tiller and the boat heeled sharply across the wind and drove to the shore.

Upon reaching the bank, each man saw to his rifle's load, then Dummett led the way through the trees along the bank, moving silently but swiftly from cover to cover toward ear-bursting blasts of .50-calibre rifles near the salt works. A heavy, blue haze drifted through the trees as if held there by the weight of the rain, carrying with it the acrid odor of burnt gunpowder.

Dummett held out his hand, palm down, and both men crouched in the bushes. Burnham peered through the gray curtain of rain, straining to see more clearly, but as yet could see no movement from the direction of the shouts and gunshots. He waited for what seemed hours but could have been only minutes when Dummett motioned to his left and ahead.

"Yankee soldiers," Dummett whispered above the din of rifle fire.

Burnham moved closer to him and could now barely make out the blue uniform of a man standing behind a pine about thirty yards away. The soldier was standing sideways to the trunk, using it as a shield. He peered around the tree, raised his rifle and snapped off a shot into the clearing, then ducked back to hastily reload.

As his eyes adjusted to the scene, Burnham could see more soldiers, some lying prone behind bushes, some kneeling, but most were crouched behind tree trunks, firing sheets of flame across the clearing. Blue-white gunsmoke belched back at them from the trees beyond. It had to be the salt crew firing, but Burnham couldn't see that far through the rain and gunsmoke.

Someone tapped him on the shoulder and he jerked as if he'd been shot. He sank to the ground in relief when he saw Dummett grinning at him. Dummett motioned for him to follow and began creeping on all fours away from the soldiers.

After crawling about twenty yards, they stopped and leaned against the gnarled trunk of a live oak.

"The Yankees got the upper hand," Dummett said. "We're going to change the odds. Surprise them. Hope they panic. They're not expecting anyone behind them, so we'll fire and reload quick; got to sound like a bunch."

"But we're not soldiers. We're civilians. We shouldn't..." Burnham threw up his hands in frustration as Dummett ignored him and moved away. Crawling again, they quickly circled behind the soldiers. Moving behind a bush, Burnham eased his head around it and saw a blue jacket directly before him, about ten yards away. He raised his rifle, peering with one eye down the barrel at the center of the man's back. His finger tightened on the trigger but seemed to lose the strength to squeeze it. The soldier was young, reminding Burnham of Junior. Junior might be in a battle somewhere at this moment, with someone lining him up in his gunsights. Sweat drenched his forehead and blurred his vision. He lowered his rifle and looked around for Dummett.

Behind him, Dummett instantly stood and fired point-blank into the soldier's back, the concussion of the blast hammering Burnham's ears. The young man spun on one leg and fell, discharging his rifle into the air.

To his left, Burnham saw another soldier turning toward him. He paused until the man's eyes found his. This was different; this man could kill him. Burnham fired, seeing the ball blast a rust-colored spray across the chest of the blue uniform.

Ducking to reload, he heard Dummett fire again. Raising to one knee, he searched for another target, then sighed with relief as he saw the soldiers sprinting low through the brush, away from them.

"They broke," he heard Dummett say. "We've done all we can. Stay put. We don't need to be shot by our own."

They crouched in the bushes. Although Burnham could see no movement in the clearing, he could hear the sounds of men crashing through brush, mingled with the shouts and screams of battle. The crack of rifles now grew faint with distance, less threatening, sounding more like children's popguns than instruments of death.

In minutes, the gunfire became sporadic, then ceased.

Burnham leaned against the trunk of a cabbage palm and wiped the sweat from his forehead with his bandana. His legs quivered and he felt as if cold water flowed through his veins.

They waited for what seemed hours but could have been only minutes when they heard voices, angry excited voices, but unintelligible.

On the far side of the clearing, two men stepped from the woods, crouched low and sprinted to the leanto. Behind it, they dropped to their knees and waited, watching the woods where they had entered the clearing, their rifles at the ready and talking in short, excited bursts. They were dressed in overalls so Burnham knew they were part of the salt crew.

Then, from a point more toward the river, four more crewmen stepped into the clearing, standing upright and making no effort to conceal themselves.

"They're gone," one yelled to the two men behind the leanto.

Soon, other crewmen drifted from the woods in twos and threes until the clearing was filled with men, jabbering and yelling with much arm gesturing and pointing.

Finally, the leader of the salt crew stood on a stump and raised both hands. "Hold the noise, men. Let's get some sorta order here." The others settled down and turned toward him.

Dummett motioned to Burnham to crouch even lower, putting a finger to his lips. Then, cupping his hands around his mouth and raising slightly, he spoke in a clear, calm voice.

"Mister Simmons it's Douglas Dummett." He quickly ducked back down.

The men in the clearing started, rifles rattling as they snapped up into firing position.

"Hold it, men," Simmons yelled. Stepping toward the bushes where Dummett and Burnham crouched, he growled, "If you be Dummett, rise ver-rr-y slow and show your face."

Dummett slowly got to his feet.

"I have Captain Burnham from the Canaveral Light here with me. Ease off on those guns."

Burnham rose and followed Dummett into the clearing.

Simmons turned and spoke to the men. "Some of you men scout around for bodies." Four of them checked their rifles and re-entered the woods.

"What the hell happened here?" Dummett asked.

"Yankees—regular army," Simmons answered. "About a squad, I figger. Damn, we was lucky. Heard 'em coming through the woods in time to take cover."

"We saw their boats back yonder," Burnham said. "Anybody hurt?"

"None of our'n, but I think we kilt a bunch of their'n. I seen bodies as we chased after 'em when they broke and run. I guess you spooked 'em and we thanks you fer it."

"They thought you'd outflanked them," Dummett said. He walked to the water keg and turned a dipperful over his head. Seeing this, Burnham was grasped by a powerful thirst. Taking the dipper, he drank until the cotton was gone from his mouth.

Within an hour, six blue-clad bodies lay in a line at the edge of the clearing.

Burnham walked over to the body of a lieutenant, the only officer. The still face turned up to the falling rain seemed almost that of a child, with soft skin. His long, fair hair was red with the seepage of blood that turned to rivulets in the rain and ran down into the neck of his jacket. Burnham felt his throat tighten as he imagined the features of his son superimposed over those of the dead boy.

He knelt and reached into the breast pocket of the blue uniform, pulling out a leather wallet. Opening it, he extracted some papers. He leaned over them to protect them from the rain and read.

"Letter from his wife," he said looking at the faces peering down at him. "His name was William Budd, twenty-two years old, married only four months ago." He refolded the letter and, lowering his mist-filled eyes, put it back into the wallet.

Simmons directed his crew to begin digging graves.

"The others're long gone, so we're bound to do right by these boys. Enemies they was, but only doin' they duty. They deserves decent burying, and they kinfolk deserves to get they personal effects and find out what happened to them."

Simmons fetched some flour sacks and began tending to each body, removing the contents of their pockets and removing rings from the cold fingers.

The *Osceola* moved from the river into Mosquito Lagoon. Dummett sat silently in the bow, staring fixedly across the steel-gray water. When the rain stopped, Burnham lashed the tiller amidships and moved forward.

"I'm sorry," he said. "I couldn't shoot that boy in the back."

Dummett turned and laid his hand on Burnham's arm. "I understand."

"Did you have the same feeling I had?" Burnham asked softly. "I looked at the dead soldiers and kept seeing Junior."

"Yes." Dummett was quiet for a long minute. "I saw Charles."

Tears spilled onto Burnham's cheeks and ran down into his beard. He turned away, into the spray breaking across the bow, his hands rigidly grasping the gunwales as the heaving boat slammed into the cresting waves.

Burnham started to leave the bow when Dummett spoke again. "At least you have the comfort of knowing you didn't put your boy there. God help me, that's exactly what I did. I put my boy in harm's way."

Burnham reached forward and gripped Dummett's shoulder once, then moved back to his place in the stern. They were silent for the rest of the trip back to Dummett Cove.

As Burnham turned the *Osceola* into the dock, they heard a shrill scream and saw Kate running toward them.

"Come quick, Papa. Mama's been hurt bad."

Dummett sprinted to the house, his mind a turmoil of dread. Halfway up the path, he saw Cudjoe sprawled on the ground with the steel head of an axe buried in his back. He yelled to Burnham, "See to him."

As he ran, the visions of an attack flashed through his mind, knowing that Cudjoe had been killed by a man. Leandra...his pounding heart pumped cold and watery blood through his veins.

Nothing could have prepared him for the horror of the scene that met his eyes when he burst through the door. Leandra lay on the floor, naked, sprawled on her back near the fireplace. The left side of her face was a swollen, purplish mass with two jagged rips slashing her cheek. Blood oozed down across her ear, dripping into a widening pool on the floor. She looked dead, but was she? He couldn't tell.

He shouted her name and dropped to his knees beside her, his hands wavering above her, unsure of what to do, where to touch. The side of her skull bulged outward at the temple. He gently probed the knot with timorous fingers. It was full of fluid. He jerked his hands back to his chest.

Her ribcage was caved in below her breast on the left side. Bruises! Her breasts and stomach were almost a solid mass of bruises. Thickening blood smeared her thighs, seeping from her vagina in time with her labored breathing. She was alive.

Clenching his fists, then flexing them, he reached to lift her, but again pulled back sharply, afraid he might injure her more. God help him! He didn't know what to do. He'd seen human bodies torn up worse than this in the war and had always been able to control his emotions, to act with a cold and detached deliberation. But this was Leandra and he couldn't move.

He felt Burnham's hands on his shoulders.

"She's broken inside too much to move by lifting," Burnham said. "You'll hurt her more."

Burnham looked around the room, then strode to the bed, stripped off the horsehair mattress, and laid it on the floor beside Leandra. He dropped to his knees and gingerly rolled her body slightly onto the right side, pushing the mattress in under her, working carefully until he had pulled it through under her and she was lying fully on it. Rising, he looked at Dummett and shook his head.

"We'd best leave her there," he said. He left the room as Dummett knelt beside the mattress. In moments Burnham returned with a pail of water that he poured into a basin. He sat it on the floor beside Dummett, then gathered a sheet from the bed and tore it into strips.

"You've got to stop that bleeding down there somehow," he said, pointing near her thighs. "Press a cloth in there and maybe it'll stop."

Dummett sat frozen, unmoving, just staring at Leandra. He began wiping his hands on his thighs, palm down, stroking them toward his knees, again and again.

"Dammit, man. Snap out of it." Burnham shoved him aside, knelt and folded a strip of sheet, carefully pressing it against her vagina.

"She's tore up pretty bad down there," he said lifting Dummett to his feet. "Are you all right now?"

Dummett nodded his head. As he stepped back he realized for the first time that Kate was beside him. He turned and lifted her, hugging her, smothering her sobs into his shoulder.

"See to the child," Burnham said. "I'll watch Leandra."

"There, there, Mama's going to be all right," Dummett crooned soothingly into Kate's ear.

"Three of 'em," she sobbed. "Big men, white men, wanted somethin' to eat and one of them grabbed her and she screamed for me to run, to make Louisa and Mary run, and we run to the grove with one of 'em chasing us but we got into the bushes and he couldn't find us, and when he left I made Louisa and Mary climb the treehouse and I sneaked back and peeked through the winderpane and seen one of 'em, a big redheaded man ruttin' Mama like the hog done the sows, hittin' her with his thing, hittin' her with his fists, then another got on her, then another, they cut her face with a beltbuckle..." Kate lifted her head for a moment, sucked in a deep breath and looked directly into Dummett's eyes. "I wanted to stop them, Papa, but I didn't know how. I was scared."

The girl broke into a soft whimper, like a cat mewling, and Dummett carried her to a chair and sat holding her until the sobs faded. Over her shoulder, he saw Louisa and Mary, peeking around the doorway, crying. He held his arm out to them and they rushed to him. They sat like that until Dummett realized Burnham was lighting lamps and that night had fallen.

The girls were calm now, with Mary asleep. He carried her to bed and made Louisa and Kate get in also. Then he walked back to where Burnham was watching over Leandra.

He stood above her, looking at the woman he had loved for so long, trying to feel her pain and hating himself for not being able to. A deep resignation washed over him. "She's not going to make it, is she?"

Burnham looked up at him and got to his feet. "I doubt it," he said finally. "There's nothing we can do for her. If we had a doctor—"

"Well, we don't. The girls are asleep and I'm all right. Why don't you get some rest now. I'll call you if there's any change. I want to be with her..."

Burnham nodded and went to Leandra's bed, tightened the bare ropes and stretched out on them.

Around midnight, Dummett felt Leandra move, then she groaned. He edged the lamp closer and could see she had regained some degree of consciousness. Her eyes were open, but the left one drifted aimlessly around the socket. She fixed her good eye on him and then jerked into full awareness.

"My girls?" Her swollen lips hardly moved and he could feel her pain splitting around him.

"They're all right. Scared but all right."

"I'm...hurt bad...aren't I?" The tip of her tongue flickered across her cracked lips.

"Yes," he answered, leaning over her. "But don't be afraid. You're going to be all right."

"Men...one McCarts...McCarthy...something like..."

"Rest easy. After you're well I'll get them."

"Our lives...we messed them—" She coughed and tried to double over, but he held her in place, not allowing her to twist her crushed body.

"Shush. You're going to be all right," he repeated, caressing her lips gently with his fingertips.

"I've...always loved...you." Her voice was so low he had to lean close to hear her. "Please...free my...girls."

She stiffened for a moment, drew a deep breath, then softly eased it out across her lips. For an instant her eyes focused together. He felt her broken body go limp as her troubled life fled.

He sat for a moment, then touched her eyelids, closing them forever.

Through the haze in his mind he could hear Kate's sobs.

Before sunrise the next morning, Burnham was ready to leave for the Cape. Carrying a lantern, Dummett walked with him down to the dock.

"I hate to leave you now," Burnham said. "Maybe the scavengers went on down to my place. Jackson's there, and I'm sure those damn cowards wouldn't attack with an able-bodied man around, but I'm worried just the same. You think you can handle..."

"We'll make do with the burying," Dummett said.

Burnham nodded and stepped down into the sailboat. He handed three of the sheets of lead up to Dummett who dropped them with a clatter on the dock. Dummett spat into the water beside the boat, looked Burnham in the eye and said, "If it takes forever, I'll get the bastards that done this."

Burnham coiled the bowline, dropped it forward of the mast and untied the main halyard. As he raised the sail, he thought for a moment, then said, "Don't leave those girls here alone if you go after the bastards. Bring them to the Cape. And don't worry if you can't track the sons-of-bitches. Somebody'll get 'em. God'll see to it. Remember, He said, 'Vengeance is mine'."

"Like hell it is," Dummett shouted, planting a foot on the bow and shoving the canoe away from the dock.

By mid-morning, Dummett had fashioned two caskets from scrap lumber. It was a lonely chore, and when he finished, he slowly carried one of them back to the house.

Tenderly, he lifted Leandra to the dining table to begin washing her cold body. Kate moved to his side and silently began helping him. Louisa and Mary stood near the wall, crying and watching.

Tears welled, scalding his eyes as he softly caressed what had been the loveliest person he had ever known. Finally the time came when he was unable to continue, and he motioned for Kate to finish the terrible task. Leaving the house without a word, he went down to the little cemetery.

Hardly aware of what he was doing, he dug the two graves side-by-side, next to that of Maum Molly. No question remained now in his mind about differences between slave and wife. Leandra was his wife, not his slave. She was his family. Cudjoe and Maum Molly were his slaves, but also a part of his family. Were they different from Leandra? Although they were of the same race, their skins were different. But the color made no difference. In death, black and white were no longer colors.

As he continued digging in the sandy soil, he realized that the coloreds had always been his family, the slaves he thought he owned but who in fact had owned him since childhood. They were a part of everything he remembered.

Old Pumprey, Cicely, Delia, Phillis—the names and faces filtered through his awareness, each carrying with it some memory of a happening, something that affected him as he lived.

They continued their march through his mind. Ebo Pompey, Ebo Thom, Lassy and his infant child he raised himself, Old Dorothy, Cudjoe—each a member of his family.

Yet, by society's standards the measure of the worth of each of them was about four hundred dollars.

But did they see him as family? If so, why weren't they here now?

He had sold them.

He cried as he continued to dig. He couldn't help himself.

When he returned to the house, he found that Kate had dressed her mother in the green gown Cicely had made for that long-ago disastrous party. He could do nothing for a long moment but stand staring at Leandra. And as he did, he realized she had not owned a store-bought dress since he'd taken her from St. Augustine those many years ago. Her life after that day had been nothing but one of make do, and not because there hadn't been enough money. They'd had more than enough of that. No, no—he'd just damn well neglected her.

And he didn't know why.

Then, as if he must validate her existence before letting her go, visions of their lives together reeled uncontrollably through his mind, and he realized that what she'd had with him was mere existence. Her only substance of life had been her children. Had that been enough for her?

Now he'd never know. With a choked sigh, he lifted her, placing her carefully and gently into the blanket-lined box. For the last time, he looked at her. He nailed down the lid then turned away to prepare Cudjoe's body. He carried the coffins on a wheel barrow, one at a time, to the shady copse of trees overlooking the cove.

The service was simple. Dummett spoke to Cudjoe as if he were alive, recounting the rich lifetime of memories they'd shared together. When he finished, almost reluctantly he turned to Leandra's grave and asked each of the girls to say goodbye to their mother. Finally he spoke to Leandra, but silently, not willing to share his feelings with even his own flesh. While he groped for the memories, he realized there were few...too few. So much had been left undone. He knew how he had never really been there for her. She had lost a life he had never shared.

He sent the girls back to the house and began filling the graves. As he scooped the first of the yellow sand onto Leandra's casket, a large, abandoned hawk's nest fell from the tree above him, landing on the mound of dirt. He blinked through the tears, saw what it was and pulled it with the tip of his shovel into the grave. The next scoop of sand covered it.

As the canoe glided silently around Home Point and into Duck Cove, Burnham scanned the dock and the woods on either side, looking for any threatening movements that might give away the position of an ambush. The trees were filled with chirping redbirds and a flight of paroquets darted across the clearing near the dock. Nature was giving him an all-clear signal, and he responded instantly. He pulled the mainsheet in tight, shooting the canoe across the water to the dock.

Ashore, he checked the load in his rifle, then ducked low and trotted up the lane toward Frances' house. At the Indian mound he left the trail and circled behind the huge shell pile. He quietly clambered to its top. Lying flat in the grass, he looked down at the house now in full sunlight.

Nothing. No movement anywhere.

He lay there for five minutes, then satisfied there was no danger, he moved down to the house.

Through the open shutters, he could see into the building. Nothing seemed amiss. The furniture stood intact, the beds were neatly made, its coverlets unwrinkled. But where were Frances and the baby? Had she been caught in the yard and dragged into the woods, raped and killed? He ran across the yard to the trail and headed through the orange groves toward the lighthouse compound. Forms expanded in the deep shadows beside the trail, then contracted to nothing as he twisted his head to stare at them. The sweat pouring down his face stung his eyes as he broke from the cover of the grove and sprinted across the canefield toward the tower rising in the distance.

As he neared the buildings, he was startled by movement from the periphery of his vision. Diving into the artesian well runoff to his left, he rolled onto his back, then quickly to his knees. He raised the rifle to his shoulder, swinging it toward its target.

"Cap'n Burnham, welcome back. Is you hurt? Why for you fall like that?"

Jackson stood in the shade of the tower, his hands on his hips and a grin on his face.

Across the quadrangle, the door to the house opened and Mary stepped out onto the porch, carrying baby Alfred.

"Mills, is that you?" she asked in greeting as she sat in the rocker. She began to sing to the baby.

Burnham slowly got to his feet, then felt a foolish flush of embarrassment as he realized he was covered with mud.

The trail led from the house, through the grove, then east to Mosquito Lagoon. The raiders had made no effort to conceal their tracks and Dummett knew the reason when he reached the lagoon. Gouges in the mud marked where the bow of their boat had been dragged onto the bank.

They were traveling by boat and no tracker on earth could follow their trail across water.

Dummett could see where they entered the woods on arrival, their path taking them around the homestead to the east. They had circled the place, scouting it out to determine who was there and if the place presented a threat to the three of them.

Then they had circled almost to the haulover canal before turning back toward the house. He found a spot under a tree where they'd stopped to smoke and probably finalize their plan for the attack.

Dummett went back to the lagoon and sat on a log, staring at the marks in the mud, and across the steely gray water, as if by concentration he might make them appear. He knew any further attempt to track them was fruitless. The only neighbors to the south through the lagoon were the Burnhams. It could be the raiders went into the Indian River and hit Isaiah Hall at his hammock on Merritt's Island, but it was unlikely they even knew about Hall. His homestead was on a hammock closer to the Banana River, a long way inland from the Indian River.

No, they must have headed north, leaving the lagoon entirely, entering the Hillsboro River not long after Dummett and Burnham had left it. They'd probably missed seeing the bastards by less than an hour. He pulled a bottle of rum from his tote and took a long pull. Then he rose and walked back to the house.

As he entered, he spoke to Kate. "Throw some clothes into a bag for you and your sisters. I'm going on a long trip and you're staying with the Burnhams till I get back."

Chapter 19

The news from the outside world dribbled in to the Cape. In late 1862, a shopkeeper in Sand Point gave Burnham a month-old newspaper telling of a battle at a place called Sharpsburg and the massive loss of life there. The article contained a list of the Florida men who had been killed. Frances read and re-read the list until finally the paper began to fall apart. She never found either Henry or Junior listed, but she never shook free of the fear that she had overlooked their names.

That first letter from Henry had been the last. Again and again Burnham tried to explain to Mary and Frances that the war had destroyed the mail service, that the Confederacy didn't have the time or the resources to build a workable system.

"Besides," he told them, "no system is going to get mail to us down here in the wilderness. I'll bet the boys have sent dozens of letters but they've been lost along the way."

Still, that didn't alleviate the women's concern. Not a day passed that Frances didn't wonder whether Henry had been killed.

Burnham's relief at finding his family safe from the raiders didn't relieve the fear of having his loved ones spread out across the reservation and vulnerable to anyone who might drift by. He decided to move his family and Jackson's from the lighthouse reservation to the homestead.

With his family moved in with Frances and the furniture stored in the barn, Burnham and Jackson dismantled the large house, carefully preserving the materials as they worked with pry bars and hammers. As a section came down, the pieces were marked and carried intact by wagon the three miles inland to Burnham's land. By year's end the house was rebuilt, and the men began work on moving the assistant keeper's house for Jackson's family.

Almost on a regular basis, Dummett brought the girls to the Cape to stay while he roamed to some distant community searching for the raiders. Kate pitched in, joining the family in their work, doing more than her share of the chores: gardening, preparing meals, sewing the bolts of bedticking into serviceable clothing. Louisa and Mary Dummett, however, seemed to deliberately avoid the work. At first Frances thought it might be just laziness. When she mentioned it to her mother, Mary laughed, saying, "I heard Louisa tell Kate that she shouldn't do all that work, that it was something servants should do, that we might get the idea they were niggers."

On each occasion of Dummett's return, he detailed his travels to Burnham, telling of scouting out little towns Burnham had never heard of.

"I almost had the bastards over in Kissimmee this time," he told Burnham. "They were there not more'n two weeks ago, but nobody remembered when they left or where they were headed."

As Dummett recounted his unsuccessful searches, Burnham reminded him that Leandra's description of the redheaded attacker fit Ratch McGirt.

"But that sure doesn't prove it was him," Burnham said. "I'm afraid you're going to run into some innocent Irishman and blow his head off with that ten-gauge."

Burnham sensed Dummett's growing frustration and guilt. His failure to find the men added to his grief and seemed to be gnawing at his spirit. Burnham had seen derelict ships in Charleston harbor in better condition. Dummett was constantly dirty. His hair began to thin more rapidly as it grayed, and his clothes were stitched together only in the places necessary to hold them together. Rum was converting Dummett's sharp eyes to bloodshot slits resting on purplish bags.

The dereliction was spreading to all parts of Dummett's life. On one occasion, Burnham accompanied him and the girls to Dummett Cove. The house was a shambles of neglect, with window shutters and doors hanging from broken hinges. The groves were overgrown and choked with weeds. Most of the old slave cabins had collapsed and now lay hidden beneath the repossessive growth of vines and grass.

As if fate balanced the scales, the domestic existence of Burnham's family became a simple and productive routine. Hunger was never a threat. The land gave up its treasures with little work on their part. Fish, game and fowl were plentiful, with Burnham and Jackson hunting daily to take up the slack caused by Dummett's protracted absences. The summer of 1863 was noted for its heat and drought. On rare occasions, Burnham was able to read a newspaper account of some battle. The over-riding common denominator in all the stories was rain. Some said the cannon blasts and musket fire shook the heavens and sent clouds of gunsmoke over the land to cause rain clouds. But little rain reached the Cape. At least the mosquitoes didn't plague them during dry weather.

The Dummett girls were staying home now on the many occasions of Dummett's absence. By 1864, he had located Cicely and Ebo Thom living, and nearly starving, in a shack in Orlando. He brought them back to Dummett Cove, offering them sustenance in exchange for their work in caring for the girls and making repairs to the house.

Louisa Dummett was now thirteen and beginning to take some responsibility for caring for the place. Mary said it was probably a sense of her wanting to be in charge of the servants. Still, most of the physical work fell to Kate. With Ebo Thom's help, the eleven-year-old hammered nails into sagging hinges, made lime whitewash from burned clamshells and soon had the place looking neat.

Dummett would arrive unexpected from a foray and immerse himself into the lives of the girls for a few days, staying sober only long enough to roam the place and admire the many improvements Kate had made. Then he would begin to drink heavily again and within days would vanish for even longer periods of time.

Burnham awoke with a start in the dark bedroom, gripped by an inexplicable panic. Something was wrong—damn wrong. He fought to clear his mind but his sleep-dulled senses refused to respond. Then he heard the noise.

Wind! A lot of wind. At that instant, something slammed into the side of the house. With a little cry, Mary jerked upright beside him.

"What in the world?"

"It's just a storm," he said, touching her cheek gently. "Go back to sleep. I'll see to it."

He eased from the bed and pulled his overalls on over his nightshirt. After lighting the lantern in the kitchen, he kindled the banked coals in the stove into flame and threw in two sticks of wood. The wind rushed around the house as he set a blackened coffee pot on to boil, then walked out to the porch.

Taking a deep breath, he stepped out into the yard. Immediately, the swirl of cold air tugged at him. Looking up, he saw thin, smoky clouds scudding wildly from the northeast. Above them were heavy mounds of boiling turbulence. The gloom shrouding the yard was relieved only by an occasional glow of lightning blooming deep in the high mass of clouds.

Moving to the corner of the house, he was instantly slammed by the brunt of the wind. Leaning forward, he struggled around to the side of the building. The large pine branch that had crashed into the wall lay in the yard. Its jagged tip was caught in the siding, gouging the clapboard as it sprung back against the wind only to be driven harder against the house. Bracing himself, he grabbed a fork in the branch and managed to jerk it free.

As he dragged it around the eastern side, windblown leaves pelted the back of his neck. A palmetto frond skittered against his leg, held there for a moment by the force of the wind before tearing loose and flying off into the darkness. Releasing the branch, he scowled, watching it chase the frond.

Glancing up once again at the clouds, he turned back to the house.

Mary and Katherine were up and preparing breakfast at the stove when he walked in. Both had wrapped bathrobes over their clothes and appeared bulky as they worked side-by-side over the stove. Burnham stretched his palms above the glowing castiron for a moment, then took the hot cup of coffee Mary offered him and sat at the table.

"Papa, it sounds like Mama's banshees wailin' out there," Katherine said. She shivered and pulled her robe tighter against her body.

"Hush, child," Mary said, cracking an egg into a skillet. "The banshees foretell death in a house. 'Tis only the wind ablowin' here."

The door burst open and Anna and Mary Louise rushed into the kitchen to crowd around the stove.

"Why's it so cold?" Mary Louise stared from one to the other of her parents. Mary pushed both girls gently toward the table. "Winter's finally here," she said, "and we're having a bit of a storm."

Anna, still in her nightgown, rubbed her eyes and crawled onto Burnham's lap. He wrapped his arms around her, pulling her head to his chest. "Is it a haricun, Papa?"

"Hurricane," Mary Louise corrected, waggling a finger at Anna. She walked to the stove to get Burnham's plate, sat it in front of him and put her hands on her hips. "Papa, she's ten years old and still talks like a baby." She jerked around sharply when her mother thumped the back of her head with a finger.

"I've told you a thousand times not to be making fun of your sister," Mary scolded. "Be nice now." She hugged the girl, then stepped back to the stove.

Anna stuck her tongue out at Mary Louise, then quickly looked up at Burnham. "Well, Papa. Is it a har-hurry-kane?" A smile set rigidly on her face, reminding him of the way she had smiled through her tears while he was setting her broken arm when she was five.

He squeezed her tightly to his chest for a moment, then lifted her over to the chair beside him and began to hash his grits and eggs with a fork. "I doubt it, darlin'. It's just a bad storm. It'll blow over. They always do." He glanced over at Mary. "Just to be on the safe side, have Katherine take the girls to help Frances and the baby come over here. Martha Jackson and little Andrew are close enough to get in here later if it gets really bad."

Within the hour a steady rain had set in, slanting sharply through the trees and against the house. The wind was still steady from the northeast. Burnham looked out the window and sighed.

"Guess I'll have to go out and secure things." He glanced at the girls huddled together at the table and crossed the room to hug them. "Don't worry, it's just a little storm. We've ridden out worse." He wondered if he really believed it or was saying it merely to console the frightened children.

He pulled an old yellow slicker over a woolen sweater and went out into the storm. Walking across the barn lot, he saw Jackson coming out of the barn. They moved into the lee of the barn, out of the force of the wind.

"You get the equipment and tools from the grove into the shed," Burnham yelled, "and I'll see to the animals."

Jackson nodded, lowered his head and lurched out into the storm.

Burnham's feet slushed through the quagmire of the barn lot, feeling his way to the pen behind the barn. The cow and the Merino sheep stood with heads drooping, huddled together against the rear wall of the building.

Burnham took a rope halter from a peg on the barn and, talking to the cow in quiet tones, stroked her muzzles while he eased the halter over her head. As soon as she felt it, she rolled her eyes wildly and lunged away from him, stepping on his foot in the process. Cursing loudly, he wrapped his free arm around her neck and swung his weight into her, pinning her against the wall. In a moment he had the halter over her head and tied in place. Stepping back, he jerked the rope hard to get her attention, then led her through the rear door of the barn. The sheep darted in around him as he entered, running to a hay pile to again bunch together. Burnham put the cow into a stall and forked in some loose hay. Satisfied that all was secure, he moved back to the door and rested for a moment, watching the rain. Then he lowered his head and stepped again into the fury of the storm.

Rain pelted his back like birdshot as he made his way toward the pigpen by the river. The pigs were lying to the lee of the overturned feeder, hunched down into the muck with their butts toward the wind. Water drained from the lot in rivulets through the mud. He decided they would make out there.

He then walked to the lighthouse.

Stepping from the protection of the grove, he moved into the canefield. He leaned forward, tilting his hat down to block the stinging needles of rain from his face. It took him the better part of an hour to struggle to the tower. He fought against the wind to force the door open. He fell inside, crumpling to the floor. For a long moment he lay there regaining his strength. Finally, he pulled off his slicker and wiped his face on his shirt sleeve. An ache spread across the back of his neck and down into his shoulders, little fingers of pain that reminded him of the work necessary to merely move against the wind.

He forced himself to his feet and checked the tower for loose doors and shutters. After securing them, he put on his slicker and walked to the beach.

Standing in the dunes, looking out over the ocean, he saw it was no longer blue, but muddy colored, an ugly mustard-yellow, like flooded northern rivers he'd seen. Rollers began their final surge at least a mile out, mounting higher and higher as they moved toward him, curling over to finally crash with a roar that seemed to make the ground quake beneath his feet. Air trapped under the tons of water in the combers burst through each breaking wave, blowing columns of spray high into the air to be instantly driven away by the wind.

The clouds were forming differently from any he'd ever seen. Their long striated bands of fury drove linearly, like spears, across the heavens. Yes Anna, he thought, it sure as hell is a *haricun*. And gonna get worse 'fore it gets any better.

The beach was swept clean of driftwood, but fish of every size and color flopped on the sand from one wave, only to be washed away by the next. Shaking his head, he turned and began the long struggle back to the house.

The wind gusted harder, then fell back to the same relentless force. Around him, the ground was littered with small tree branches. Passing the truck patch, he couldn't help but groan at the sight of the destruction. The vine crops were completely gone, ripped from the earth. His melons and pumpkins floated in kneedeep water, the ground having absorbed all it could. He knew the root crops would probably mildew and rot. It looked like a hungry winter ahead. He shook his head sadly as he turned away and continued toward the houses.

When Burnham passed Jackson's house, the man was sitting on his porch out of the wind, his shoulders slumped, seeming to cower before the raging tempest. Deep lines of fear etched his face as he looked up at Burnham.

"I ain't never seen it like this befo'," he mumbled, shaking his head.

"I think you'll be safe here," Burnham yelled above the screech of the wind. "If Martha gets too scared, you bring her and little Andrew over to us. The women'll calm each other."

Jackson stood and grabbed a porch post, shaking it. "I just be scared for the house, Cap'n."

Burnham laughed, wiping water from his face with the back of his hand. "I've always said I'm not afraid of the house blowing down long as the trees stand."

Almost as if cued by his words, a large water oak in the yard crashed to the ground, its roots torn from the earth like a pulled tooth.

Burnham stared for a moment as mud flew like cannon shot from the root crater. Then he smiled and placed a hand gently on Jackson's shoulder and eased the man toward the door. "I 'spect somebody's telling me something. We'd better get inside with our womenfolk."

During the waning afternoon, the wind grew in force, gusts roaring through the trees to slam the eastern side of the house with a continuous clatter. When Burnham thought the house couldn't stand any more, the wind would ease for a minute or so. Then another howling roar would strike the building, just a little harder than the last.

Periodically, he went outside to check the buildings. Lightning lashed vividly through the clouds but the thunder was lost in the nightmarish roar of wind and water. In the rain, he could taste salt torn from the spumes of the sea and blown like smoke the three miles inland.

Finally night arrived, more an envelopment of darkness than a sundown, for the sun had been blotted out all day. About then, Mary noticed water seeping in through the eastern walls of the house. Burnham was forced to go out again.

When he rounded the house into the wind's direct onslaught, he was almost knocked from his feet by rain driven almost horizontal by the violent wind. Turning his face from it, he leaned into its force and groped his way to the side of the house. The wind pressure was so great that the water could not run down the side of the house but was forced instead through the overlap of the siding. Realizing there was nothing he could do about it, he struggled back to the porch and went inside.

Mary and the girls were in the living room. She had brought in four lanterns and built a small fire in the fireplace. Katherine was sitting in a chair by the fire, crocheting something for her hope chest. Mary Louise was teaching Anna a new card game. Trying to keep Alfred's mind from the frightening noise, Frances was on the floor with the boy, playing their *Papa and Uncle Junior* game with some lead soldiers. They all looked up sharply at Burnham as he entered. He smiled at them with what he hoped was a cheery reassurance.

"There's for sure a hurricane offshore", he told them as he shook out of his slicker, "and I'd say pretty close. We'll be all right if it don't come ashore near us. Sleep in your warmest clothes tonight...and try not to worry."

He motioned to Mary to follow him and walked into the kitchen for a cup of coffee. "I'm sure the house'll hold up, shielded like it is by the groves, but if it goes, we need to keep everyone together and get them to the lee side of the Indian mound. It'll block off the wind and rain. If there's a flood, we'll climb to the top of the mound. Either way, if we're careful, nobody's going to get hurt."

He poured coffee into his cup and put his arm around her shoulders. "Just keep everybody busy and act like everything's all right."

As they stepped back into the living room, a violent bang on the door burst it open. Burnham ran quickly to shut it when he realized a man was standing there.

He reached out and pulled the man inside, slamming the door behind him. The man stepped back against the wall. His gray, woolen jacket and loose fitting pants dripped a steady stream of water onto the floor. He stared at the women from red-rimmed eyes sunken into his face above a wooly brush of wild, red beard.

Frances stood and took a step toward him, slowly at first, while peering intently into his gaunt face. Then, suddenly, she let out a cry of joy and threw herself across the room into the man's arms.

"And this is Alfred, your son," Frances said to Henry while smothering his face with kisses. Turning, she held out her hand to the three-year-old who was now hiding behind his grandmother's apron. "Come here, son. This is your Papa we've been waiting for so long." The boy wouldn't move until Mary pushed him forward a step. Then, with a squeal, he ran across the room, where Henry lifted him, crushing him to his chest.

After a moment, Burnham ushered Henry, Frances and the boy into the kitchen to strip off Henry's wet clothes. He went into a bedroom where he took a shirt and pants from Junior's footlocker and handed them through the door to Frances. In a few more minutes, the couple came back into the living room. Burnham insisted the young man sit in his stuffed chair. Frances sat on the floor, her head on Henry's knee, while he held the boy in his lap.

"How in hell did you get here?" Burnham asked.

"By traveling through the length of hell, it seemed," Henry replied. "I'm on furlough. We was in Georgy when they told me I could come home.

Caught me some rides at first, but I walked the whole way from the trestle 'cross the St. Mary's at Fernandina." He stopped to cough.

"Land's sake, child," Mary said jumping to her feet. "You must be starved."

"Yes'um," he said as she went to the kitchen. "The storm hit me during the night, this side of Dummett's old place at New Smyrna. Luck would have it, I had crossed the river there—I'd never got across here in this mess. Walked the whole way from New Smyrna in the dunes mostly. Warn't safe on the beach—ocean's tore it up somethin' ferocious."

Burnham waited until Mary returned with some food before asking the question uppermost in his mind.

"And what of Junior? Know where he's at?"

Henry shook his head. "He got transferred more'n a year ago to General Bragg's Tennessee army."

Frances raised her head from his knee. "Bragg's army fought at that battle of Chickamauga where so many was killed. I searched..."

"And you didn't find their names," Burnham said. "And here's Henry with the proof that they were all right."

After another hour of celebration, Burnham cautioned everyone to get to bed, to save their energies for whatever the morning might bring.

Several times during the night he rose and went to the porch to check the storm's progress. About two o'clock the wind shifted suddenly, now blowing steadily from the southeast. Burnham went back inside and woke Mary.

"It's definitely a hurricane. The eye must be crossing land somewhere south of us."

"How could you be knowin' that?" she asked, her voice slurry with fatigue.

"The winds are like a big whirlpool," he said, illustrating with his hands in the dark, even though he knew she couldn't see them. "When it was blowin' in off the sea, we were ahead and to its right, so the wind swirled in from the northeast. Now that it has passed south of us, we're behind it but still to its right, so the wind's now from the southeast."

"That's all too confusing," she said, lying back and was almost instantly asleep.

The next morning was brighter than the day before, but the rains still fell steadily. The trees around the house were completely stripped of foliage. Palm fronds and small branches cluttered the yard, with many piled high against the house. Several of the cypress roof shingles had blown away, but the house was otherwise intact.

Burnham walked over to Jackson's and found his roof in much better condition. Its location behind the barn had been more sheltered from the winds than Burnham's.

Jackson came out to the porch with two cups of coffee. He handed Burnham one and the two men stood together for minutes, sipping from the cups and staring at nature's violence.

"Funny thing," Jackson said, breaking the silence. "Andrew weren't scairt at all. Kept his mama calm and soothed like he was the grownup and she was the child."

"Well, this land makes a boy into a man pretty quick." Burnham handed him the empty cup and stepped down from the porch. "The wind's a little less vicious now, but we still need to take care."

Burnham leaned against the still forceful winds and trudged back toward his house. As he crossed the barn lot, he was surprised to see Dummett walking swiftly toward him on the trail from the lighthouse. He stepped back to the barn and waited until Dummett arrived. Then they sprinted through the rain to the house.

On the porch, Dummett looked around at the littered yard. "Gonna be a fine day," he said, grinning. "Storm's nearly wore itself out."

"Your place must've come through all right for you to be out and about this early. What in hell you doin' over here, and why are you so happy?"

"Found a wreck just north of False Cape. Surf shoved it right up into the dunes. Schooner. Big one, but we got to go protect it. Come on," he said, stepping off the porch.

"Hold on a bit." Burnham shook his head. "Why would I leave here to save a wrecked schooner and come back to a wrecked home?"

"Cotton, man. The hold's loaded to the brim with cotton bales."

"What about the crew? Any survivors?"

"Nary a soul aboard. That makes it ours if we want it. And I do."

"So? You got a good recipe for cooking cotton? I doubt Miss Mary would care too much for feeding our family with it."

Dummett shook his head in disbelief. "Burnham, you been locked in this wilderness too long. Think, man. The south hasn't been able to ship cotton through the Yankee blockades for years now. The stuff's worth its weight in gold in Europe."

Burnham held up a hand. "Last I heard, those blockades haven't been lifted. Cotton's no good to us if we can't ship it out."

"Got any coffee on hot in there?" Dummett asked, nodding toward the house.

They went in to the kitchen and Burnham poured them each a mug.

Dummett dribbled a puddle of coffee into a saucer and blew on it. He swirled it around for a second. He nodded toward the coffee. "Remember when the war started and we couldn't get this stuff? Then I brought you some, right? Where the hell did you think I got it? Picked it off my orange trees?" He paused as if he were enjoying the moment. "Hell, no. You probably never knew that old Raphael Olivaros who worked for you at Dunn-Lawton was my sergeant during the Indian war. His sons grew up along this coast and been running goods in from the Bahamas right under the Yankee's noses. Those Olivaros boys know these waters better'n their wives' bedrooms."

He grinned happily as he straddled a chair and slurped the coffee from the saucer. "We take the cotton off the ship, dry it out, rebale it. Then we get the Olivaros boys to take it over to the Islands and ship it to England. We'll make a bloody fortune."

The back door opened and Henry stepped in. "Been over checkin' out my house," he said, taking off his slicker and shaking it out the door.

"Well, I'll be goldanged, boy," Dummett shouted, jumping to his feet. "When did you get home?"

Henry turned in surprise. A smile formed slowly on his gaunt face as he held out his hand. "Last night."

Dummett grabbed the hand and pulled Henry into a tight bear hug. "Glad to see you, boy." He released him and glanced at Burnham. "Now I know we can do it. With Henry and Jackson to help my men, it'll be easy as sin." He turned back to Henry. "Junior with you?"

"No," Henry said, pouring a cup of coffee.

"War'll end soon and he'll be home. Drink it fast," Dummett said, pointing to the cup. "Somebody beats us to that ship and it's theirs."

Burnham thought for a moment. He hadn't seen Dummett this spry over anything in a long while. He grinned at him. "All right. Henry and I'll go, but I'm leaving Jackson here for now to care for the womenfolk till this storm runs its course. Sit tight while I tell Mary where we're going." He jerked a thumb at Henry. "Better tell Frances."

After they returned to the kitchen, they loaded tote sacks with beef jerky, powder, lead balls, and percussion caps. Burnham walked to the corner where his rifle stood.

"Leave it," Dummett said. "Pack an extra pistol instead. The rifle will be in the way. You can't climb aboard carrying it."

An hour later they were sloshing through the mud of the trail near the lighthouse, when Burnham saw the tower door ajar.

"Either the storm tore that lock off or someone's in there," he said.

Cautiously, they left the path, slipping through the canefield to approach the tower from the rear. Pulling their pistols, they checked the loads, then eased around to the front. Dummett whispered to them to close their eyes for a moment to accustom them to the darkness. After a bit, he whispered "Ready?" then lunged around the door and into the tower, his pistol leveled before him. Burnham followed quickly behind him, darting to the side as he entered to avoid being outlined in the doorway.

In the murky shadows of the round room, he made out five people huddled on the stairs, one of them a woman dressed only in a suit of sailor's oilskins. The men were nearly naked. The few clothes they had were torn and drenched. One of the men rose slowly to his feet, wiping his eyes with a torn sleeve.

"Gentlemen, I'm Captain Blaine of the schooner *Tyler*, wrecked this morning on these fair shores."

He staggered from the stairs and Burnham stepped to his side to support him, easing him back down onto the bottom step.

Dummett quickly went outside to where he had dropped his tote, returning with his rum bottle.

"Take a nip. Isn't brandy, but it's better for you," he said easing the mouth of the clay bottle to the woman's lips.

After the men had each taken a large drink, Captain Blaine, a tall man in his late forties, distinguished looking in spite of his condition, haltingly told the story of the shipwreck.

"We were all right in the northeast wind, though we had no protection from the rain—every spare nook below is filled with cargo. The current held us offshore a good way. Then, early this morning, the wind shifted hard from another direction and we hit a rock or something. We must've been about five miles out..."

"The Bull," Burnham said. "You're not the first to hit it."

"We rode the ship in till it hit hard on the beach." His voice broke, and he coughed self-consciously, then recovered and continued. "Two of my men jumped into the surf with a line, but were sucked under instantly. We never saw them again. I wouldn't let anyone else try. We stayed aboard till a large swell set the ship up in the dunes. Then we climbed down."

"Where you from?" Dummett asked.

"Darien, Georgia," Captain Blaine replied. "I'll never forgive—I should never have tried this." He looked at the rum bottle. "Do you mind?" Dummett handed him the clay jug.

"We ran through the marshes near St. Simons and slipped out by Sea Island. Didn't see a Yankee anywhere. Thought we'd made it for sure till this storm hit."

Dummett scuffed his toe across the floor. He looked Blaine directly in the eye. "We were on the way to the wreck to take possession for salvage. We could cut you in."

"Not at all," replied Blaine, shaking his head. "I'm through with it. If you've the fortitude to save the cargo, you certainly deserve the rewards."

With that, Burnham directed Henry to guide the people back to the house.

"Dummett and I'll go on to the wreck," he told the young soldier. "Stay till the storm ends. If there's no problem there, then you and Jackson bring my wagon and team to the wreck."

After Henry left with the survivors, Burnham and Dummett walked to the dunes. The surf was crashing high against the sloping sand, nearly to where they stood, then swirling back, the foam mixing and churning in seething whirlpools before being hit by the next comber. The beach was totally submerged in the maelstrom.

"I can't recall ever seeing the tide this high before," Burnham said.

"I have," Dummett said as he led the way north toward False Cape.

When they arrived at the wreck site, Burnham was surprised to see the ship still intact except for the stern. Her bow was thrust high onto the dunes at a steep angle, the keel dug deeply into the sand. The rudder had been ripped off, taking with it part of the stern overhang and the transom. Each wave that crashed into it filled the stern but washed back out through the gap of the missing transom. The mizzenmast was snapped off and lay swirling in the surf, held to the ship by its rigging.

"If nothing else, we'll have enough lumber here to build another barn or two," Burnham said.

"Stout ship," Dummett nodded. "Shame."

They walked to the bow where Burnham could see the anchor chain leading far into the dunes. He cocked an eyebrow at Dummett.

"I set the anchor soon's I found her," Dummett said. He stowed his tote high in the dunes and, grabbing the chain, pulled himself hand-over-hand to the deck. Burnham placed his tote with the other and walked back to the chain, looking up at the steep angle to the deck. He sighed, spat on his hands and followed. In moments he was standing on the slanting foredeck of the ninety-foot schooner.

"We got to stay aboard till the storm's over. Then's time enough to figure how to get the stuff off." Dummett walked down the tilted deck toward the stern. "Lost some bales when the transom busted out," he yelled back to Burnham. "But the rest is holding in place. Gonna be wet though."

They hunkered down in the lee of the doghouse out of the driving rain.

By the sun's glow through the cloud cover, Burnham knew it was around noon. Rumbles from his stomach reminded him he hadn't eaten since before sunup.

"One of us should have brought up a tote with some jerky," he growled.

"Hurry back," Dummett said, grinning.

"Flip you for it," Burnham said, digging in a pocket for a coin.

"Hell, I'll go. I don't want you to hurt yourself. You came up that chain like an old lady."

He stood and shivered for a moment in the cold rain, then clambered to the bow and was over the side in an instant.

Five minutes later, a tote sailed over the rail. Burnham scooted over and pulled it back out of the rain. As he began opening it, the other hit the deck, followed moments later by Dummett, who stooped behind the gunwale, peering intently over it.

"What's the mat..." Burnham stopped as Dummett waved his arm at him without turning. Crawling up beside him, Burnham leaned in close.

"We got company," Dummett said quietly. "I could hear them talking as they came through the...there, over there," he pointed. Burnham raised his head slightly and saw two, no—three, men standing on the rise of a large dune to the north. He pulled his pistol from its holster and cocked the hammer.

As he watched, the men walked toward the wreck. They were dressed miserably for the weather, no slickers, their black felt hats drooped around their heads, dripping water onto thin coats already soaked from the rain.

Dummett stood slowly, keeping a portion of the tilt of the deck between himself and the men.

"Who are you," he yelled, "and what do you want?"

The men fell instantly to their bellies as if shot, then rolled behind the protection of a flattened sea grape tree.

Burnham could hear their excited chatter. Then, after a moment of silence, one of the men, the largest of the three, stepped from behind the tree. He raised his empty hands for a moment, palms out, then wrapped his arms across his chest while tucking his hands beneath his armpits.

"We just wanted to see about salvage, brother," he yelled. "Didn't know anyone was aboard, but see we was wrong. Any chance of hiring on to help you?"

The man's voice was strangely familiar to Burnham. He searched his memory but was unable to recognize it.

As Dummett moved to the rail to speak to the man, a rifle flamed from the tree, the bullet ripping a long splinter from the wood near his hand.

The roar of the shot was carried away by the wind. In the instant it took Burnham to turn toward him, Dummett had dropped flat to the deck.

Hastily, Burnham rested the barrel of his pistol on the rail and fired at the man, who dropped to his knees and scurried back to the tree. The man's hat blew from his head as he crawled, giving Burnham a glimpse of red hair.

Instantly, the tree lit up from the blaze of several shots. Burnham jerked his head down and crawled swiftly around the doghouse.

Climbing onto it, he peered around the main mast in time to see one of the men scramble across to the next dune. He snapped off a shot, knowing that it would be only luck if he scored a hit.

Dummett raised and quickly emptied his pistol into the tree, then rolled to his back to reload. Burnham jumped from the doghouse and crawled up the deck to Dummett.

"I think it's Ratch McGirt," he said as he bit the ends off of paper cartridges and stuffed them into the empty chambers of his colt's revolver. "If it is, we're in for a long battle."

Dummett hand froze for a second in mid-stroke on the plunger of his pistol. He stared at Burnham as the realization penetrated his mind. Then, he seemed galvanized into action. He rammed the plunger down on the lead ball and spun the chamber to the next position.

When he finished loading, he rose to one knee and peeked over the rail, motioning Burnham closer.

As Burnham looked at the face before him, he was struck by the transformation. A new sharpness in Dummett's eyes had replaced the cloudy gaze that had grown on the man in the past year. His nostrils flared and his lips pulled thinly across his teeth in a grim parody of a wolf's grin. The fingers gripping Burnham's arm felt as if they were made of tempered steel. He was again the hunter Burnham had first seen at Fort Heileman years ago.

"Can you keep them busy while I get off this damn boat?" Even his voice was different, clear, spitting the words out as if they were made of bile.

"I guess so," Burnham said. He crawled over to his tote, rummaging through it until he found his other pistol. He quickly loaded the empty chamber under the hammer and moved back to Dummett, crouching against the gunwale.

"What you got in mind?"

"Damned if I know. Just throw enough lead at them to keep their heads down."

Dummett stuffed his pistol into his holster and crabbed his way over to the port side, slipping once on the wet deck. Gathering his feet under him at the rail, he nodded to Burnham and vaulted over the side. Burnham raised, fired two shots into the sea grape tree, then two at the dunes where he last saw the third man. Firing his last two shots back into the tree, he shifted to the other pistol and began shooting it as fast as he could thumb the hammer.

Bullets slammed into the mahogany rail near his head. He dropped to the deck to reload. His wet fingers shook as he pressed the percussion caps over the nipples. Crawling to another spot along the gunwale, he slowly raised to a squat and peeked over the railing. Suddenly, a pistol flashed in the dunes. The man hiding there stood bolt upright, gripping his throat with one hand. He staggered two steps forward, dropped to his knees, then pitched forward onto his face.

Burnham heard Dummett's primal scream even above the wind whistling through the ship's rigging. Dummett sprinted toward the sea grape, zigging and firing as he ran. Forty feet from the tree, he threw himself sideways behind a sand hill and for a moment Burnham lost sight of him.

Moments later, two shots flared behind the tree, punctuated by a scream. Burnham waited, eyes peering into the haze of the rain. If they got Dummett, he knew it would only take the men a short time to finish him. They could come at him easily from two directions and he couldn't hold off both of them.

Then Dummett stepped into the clear, waving his arms.

Relief flooded Burnham's mind as he scrambled over the rail and dropped to the sand. He ran up into the dunes and stopped, looking down into a shallow crater.

One man lay on his back, a large hole in his chest. Bubbles of blood formed on his shirt as he breathed, only to be splattered instantly by the rain. Across the depression, Ratch McGirt sat upright, holding his thigh tightly with both hands, trying to stanch a stream of blood soaking his trouser leg.

"They're both alive," Dummett said, moving to the man shot in the chest. He grabbed a fistful of hair, jerking the man's head from the sand.

"You killed my wife, you bastard."

The man's eyes widened as he saw the raw hatred in the face inches from his own. "I ain't kilt nobody," he whimpered. A stream of frothy blood dribbled from his mouth. "Ever where we ever robbed, Ratch done all the shootin'."

Dummett slammed the head back to the sand in disgust. He looked at Burnham. "This sheep dung doesn't even know who I'm talking about."

He bent forward and, before Burnham could move, placed the muzzle of his pistol against the man's temple, pulling the trigger. The other side of the head bloomed outward, splashing across the sand.

Dummett rose and strode toward McGirt. Burnham stood transfixed for a moment, then stepped in front of Dummett.

"You can't just shoot him," he yelled. "That's murder."

"If that's true, so was the other one. Men who live where there's no law are obliged to make do when they have to. You doubt they're guilty?"

But he stopped. He shifted from one leg to the other in frustration for a moment, then smiled with that feral look he had on the boat.

"But killing him in a fair fight's not murder," he said. Then to McGirt, "Got a knife, rabbit shit?"

McGirt had fallen back before the expected onslaught, but now pulled himself forward to clutch his leg. "I ain't about to fight you, not with this leg shot up," he groaned.

With that, Dummett cocked his pistol and placed the muzzle against his own leg and fired. He twisted and dropped to his knees with his head in the crook of his arm. He stayed there for only a moment, then rose to balance on one leg, letting the other dangle loosely beside it. His upper thigh was now as bloody as Ratch's.

"Draw your knife, rabbit shit. I'm going to kill you." He tossed his pistol to Burnham, drew his knife from the sheath under his armpit and took a limping step toward McGirt.

McGirt scrambled backwards for a few feet, then rose and drew a foot-long knife from a scabbard down the back of his shirt. He scuttled to his right, away from Dummett.

"If I kill you, yore partner there'll shoot me," McGirt screamed, watching warily as Dummett crouched and hobbled toward him again.

"Burnham, if he gets me, let the bastard go. It won't matter none then." He continued stalking the bulky redhead who was taking short, backward hops.

Then Dummett charged, slashing his knife in an upward arc toward the man's belly. McGirt immediately shoved his wounded foot firmly to the ground and shifted smoothly to the side, too quick for Dummett to recover. McGirt's knife whistled down, slicing across Dummett's shoulder as he dove to the ground and rolled.

He scrambled to his feet instantly, his hands empty. He looked around wildly for his knife, then straightened, his eyes locked on McGirt who was now crouched and stalking him.

"So you weren't hurt near bad as I figured," Dummett said, backing away.

McGirt face twisted into a crooked grin. "Nope," he said. "And now I'm going to open you up and see what real rabbit shit looks like inside."

With that, he lunged forward, the knife raised high over his head, grasped in his meaty fist. As McGirt struck downward with a furious grunt, Dummett lowered his shoulder and slammed into him below his knees. McGirt flew into the air, arms flailing as he tried to regain his balance. He turned a slow half twist, then landed on his belly with a whumph. Dummett rolled onto his feet and scrambled around to the center of the depression. He retrieved his knife and crouched, waiting as McGirt got slowly to his feet. The man turned toward Dummett, a look of incredulity etched across his face.

His knife was sticking from his chest, driven halfway to the hilt by the force of his fall. He stared at the knife for a long second, his hands fluttering upward, reaching as if to pull it out, then dropping to his side. He fell into a crumpled heap, then slowly struggled to a sitting position.

Dummett was on him in an instant, grasping a handful of hair and circling his head with the edge of his knife. With a triumphant scream, he wrenched upward, jerking the red scalp from the skull with a loud pop. Then he grasped the handle of McGirt's knife with one hand, slammed the heel of the other against the butt and drove the knife all the way into McGirt's chest.

McGirt fell backward. His legs twitched once and he was still.

Dummett grasped McGirt's shirt, pulled him back to a sitting position, then hauled him up, draping him across his shoulders. He turned and staggered toward the boiling surf beyond the dunes. At its edge, he paused, looked back at Burnham, then shoved the body through the air toward the sea. It hit and was gone in an instant.

He dropped to the sand, breathing heavily.

Burnham walked over to him and sat beside him.

"It's over," Dummett said. "She'll rest easy now."

"Yeah, but we've got to get that leg wound taken care of." He pointed at the dark stain on Dummett pants.

Dummett rolled over to his knees. Dropping his pants, he pointed at a thin furrow in the skin. The groove was still bleeding steadily but it was obvious the shot hadn't touched the muscle.

Dummett winked at him. "You didn't really believe I was going to give that bastard a chance to kill me, did you?"

A wicked grin split his face.

After Dummett dragged the bodies of the other two scavengers into the surf, they crawled back aboard the *Tyler* and settled in to ride out the storm. Burnham found a tarpaulin in the hold and rigged a shelter across the boom of the main mast. During the afternoon, the wind began to haul around until it blew steadily from the south. Then later, the winds and rain lightened, falling more softly by nightfall but showing no signs of stopping. Burnham went below and scrunched down onto a bale of cotton to sleep.

They awoke next morning to a peaceful sunrise, standing to stretch and gaze at a cloudless sky. The ocean was again calm and placid, its gentle rollers caressing a beach swept clean of debris. As far as Burnham could see, only smooth swells undulated the surface of the sea.

By noon, Henry and Jackson arrived driving Burnham's wagon. Later that day, six Negroes led by Ebo Thom arrived from Dummett's groves. All of them were in their sixties, their wiry curls now laced with silvery white, but their bodies still retained the muscle tone of their youth. Clear eyes smiled back at Burnham as he greeted each man. Dummett put two of the men to work setting up a temporary campsite in the dunes.

Meanwhile, Burnham began to plan the unloading of the ship. Captain Blaine had removed the flooring and all furnishings from the interior of the *Tyler* to make room for the cotton. Burnham estimated two hundred bales were packed below deck.

He strung the main halyard from the top of the mast through a roller pulley attached to the end of the mainsail boom. The men winched the bales from below and swung them from the ship to the dunes. They were loaded onto the wagon and hauled the four miles to Burnham's barn for storage. It took them three days to empty the ship. As they left the wreck the last time, Dummett ordered two men to remain and dismantle the ship.

Although Henry had assured him there had been no severe damage to the place, Burnham was relieved to return home to see for himself.

The orange trees had suffered from the pummeling of the wind. The loss of their leaves might retard spring growth, but the majority of the limbs were intact. Fruit layered the ground beneath the trees, but Burnham had planned, before the storm, to let most of it compost in to enrich the soil. The grove should recover nicely.

The truckpatch, however, was gone—pole beans, collards, turnips, potatoes, yams, carrots, onions—all drowned, uprooted or blown away. The loss of the vegetables could be made up from natural growth, such as wild onion, pokeweed, and purslane that Burnham knew would survive nature's devastation and come back in lush profusion. The children wouldn't enjoy the taste as well, but Burnham was partial to salads of the tender pokeweed greens. Yep, they'd make out just fine until he and Henry could get around to replanting the truckpatch.

The men separated the dry cotton bales from the wet. Only a few were damaged by salt water. Burnham tore into one of these bales with his fingers and found the dampness had penetrated only a few inches.

"We'll pull these apart, strip off the wet stuff, dry it the best we can, then rebale it," he said.

By the end of the next week long strips of cotton hung like Spanish moss from twine stretched high near the roof.

Burnham removed and trimmed the end gate of his wagon and spiked it crossways to the end of a thick pole, converting it into a plunger that would slide the length of the inside of the wagon. He strapped a heavy, hemp hawser around the outside of the wagon, then around one of the barn support beams. With the plunger braced against this beam, a triple-pulley system run from the hawser to another beam would pull the wagon tight against the plunger. By stuffing the wagon full of cotton, Burnham figured he could press a load down to a quarter of its volume, tying off the crude bales with twine.

Then Dummett vanished.

Chapter 20

Dummett had gone home twice since the storm, to check on the girls and to see that his groves were being cleaned up by the hired hands. But he had returned to Burnham's barn both times, eager to get on with the salvage.

They planned to go to St. Augustine by mid-December to find the Olivaros brothers and make arrangements for running the cotton to the Bahamas. Dummett returned to Dummett Cove once again, telling Burnham to pick him up three days later on the way north.

When Burnham arrived at Dummett Cove, Kate met him at the dock.

"Papa's gone, Captain," she said, shaking her head. "I took his breakfast out at sunup yesterday. He weren't there. Just gone. No note—no nothing." Her voice was flat, as if she were reading a shopping list. "I'm used to him leaving like this, us never knowing where he'd gone or if he'd come back alive. But I thought it'd ended when he kilt them men. I don't think this time I can sit here and wait. He's not back soon, I'll go myself to find him."

Burnham sailed over to Sand Point but found no sign of Dummett. One man said he thought he'd seen Dummett sailing south on the Indian River but couldn't say for sure. In frustration, Burnham returned to the Cape.

While no news had been heard of Dummett by January of 1865, the cotton had been re-baled and was ready for shipment. In frustration, Burnham decided to abandon the project until Dummett showed up again.

"No sense in trying to move it without him," Burnham told Henry. "I don't know the Olivaros boys and don't have the foggiest idea of how to find them. Besides we got better things to do, like enjoying you here while we got you."

Burnham leaned on the handle of his scoop shovel and rested his chin on his arms. He sniffed the aroma of smoke from the old pecan tree Henry was burning. To him, April had always been a month of rebirth. The pale greens of winter were turning crisp and deep and the air itself carried the bouquets of life.

The man talking to him was skinny to the point of emaciation, reminding Burnham he needed to build a scarecrow for the new truck patch if he expected the birds and rabbits to leave him any vegetables this spring.

Isaiah Hall punctuated his words with a bony forefinger as he talked around a cud of tobacco in his jaw.

"I shouldn't even ha' been in New Smyrna," he said. "Din't really need the junk I'd gone there to fetch. Lordy, can you 'magine bein' there durin' that there storm, not knowin' iffen yore fambly's livin' or dyin'?"

Burnham shook his head in serious agreement, then scooped another load of manure into the wheelbarrow.

"Fact of the matter," Hall continued, "I left in sich a hurry to git home I plumb f'got the plunder I'd gone to fetch—salt and sich. That's why I done had to go back this trip. I'da gone sooner, but I had need of lots of fixin' to do at my place. And, Lordy, the stories I done heard when I got there." The man spit a gob of brown juice into the manure pile. Burnham scooped another forkful and covered it over.

"Feller there told me he'd heard Atlanty was burnt in December, and some Yankee Gen'l name of Sherman done taken his army clear 'crost the whole state of Georgy to the sea, burnin' and killin' as he went." He knit his brow and took the shovel from Burnham. "Missed a patty," he said walking over to a steaming pile the cow had just dropped by the fence. "They captured Savanny. War's over to anybody what has eyes to see. Ol' Gen'l Lee's holed up at some Virginny town, name of Petersburg. Whole damn Yankee army bent on starvin' him out. About the onliest place the Confederacy has left is the Carolinys."

Burnham took the shovel from the man and leaned it against the wall, then grabbed the wheelbarrow handles and rocked the wheel in the sand to get it moving. Henry walked up in time to open the barn lot gate for him. Without slowing, Burnham pushed the barrow down the path, followed by the two men, with Hall repeating the stories to Henry.

At the truck patch, Burnham dumped the load onto a pile, turned the barrow upside down under the shade of an oak tree and sat on it. Wiping his face with a bandana, he listened as Henry explained to Hall his worry about trying to find his old outfit.

"Suicide," Hall said. "Way I heerd it, there's Yankees ever whar. You'd git caught for sure and git to spend the rest of the war in some prison, that's iffen you don't git yore arse shot off."

"I don't 'magine it'd be prison for just the rest of the war," Henry said. "I heard stories 'fore I left that the Yankees intend destroyin' the south, hangin' officers and politicians. And throwin' foot soldiers like me in jail to rot the rest of our lives."

Henry's face set into a frown. He looked into Burnham's eyes for a long moment. "I'm months overdue now. Iffen I don't get back, I'm a deserter. We was followed on our marches by deserters—bummers they was called—men what didn't want to fight, scavengers hangin' around for the loot they could pick up after a battle. Our officers hung some when they was caught."

"Son, I can't wrap answers up for you like a neat Christmas package," Burnham said. "If Lee's army is bottled up like Mr. Hall heard, the war's close to over. Probably, this springtime will see the end to it. It really don't make no never mind. The Reb army can't touch you if they lost the war. Hell, there won't *be* a Reb army. We'll just have to wait and see what other news comes in."

"Gonna be a fine day, ain't it?"

Burnham snapped around at the voice behind him. Douglas Dummett was leaning against the trunk of the oak tree, weaving an extended fore-finger before eyes nearly swollen shut in his bloated face.

"Coulda got you if I was a Seminole," he said in a thick voice.

Dummett sat on the edge of the rocking chair, his elbows propped on his knees, hands cupped around the mug of hot coffee. Burnham leaned against the porch post, looking down at his friend's thinning, white hair, trying to hold back the bile of condemnation over his decrepit condition.

"I was looking for her...Leandra." Dummett voice slurred softly over the words. "It seemed that killing McGirt was no end to it, should have wiped the slate clean but didn't. After I got to drinking, I figured it wasn't fair. With him dead, she should be alive again." He paused to slurp some more coffee, spilling some on his hand as he looked up at Burnham. "So... I went hunting for her."

Pity began to overwhelm Burnham's anger. What the hell? He hadn't lost anything. The cotton was for Dummett, anyway. "Where did you go?" he asked.

Dummett shook his head slowly. "Hell, where didn't I go? I went to a lot of the places I'd found when I was hunting McGirt—mostly saloons. I went down to the 'glades for awhile, to the Indian villages. Always, everywhere I went, I felt she'd been there and left just before I got there. Then I found her."

Burnham was musing over the pictures in his mind of the drunken jour-ney and almost missed the statement.

"You what?"

"I found her, or at least she found me." His face screwed up from the pain of his memories. "I was humping a slut in some room over a cowman's saloon in Kissimmee when her man came in and beat the coon dog shit out of me. Woke up in the alley, head throbbing like a steam piston. Almost sober, I guess, when I looked up. There was—Leandra. Leaning over me. Tried to tell me she was Kate, but I knew better. A hawk was sitting on her shoulder."

Burnham could see it then, deep within the black eyes staring up at him. In the fireplace of Dummett's mind, the flames of thought had died to the cold embers of dead memories. The beating, the drinking, or the phantom nightmares of his treatment of the woman he'd loved—Burnham didn't know which had pushed Dummett to the edge, but he was there.

"So Kate ...Leandra...fetched you home?"

"Yep. She didn't like it much, me wanting to come over here, but I told her I'd come back long as she was there. On the way over here, I stopped at my summer house on the lagoon. Needed some rum, but here I am."

He jerked to his feet, spilling the rest of his coffee on his pants.

"I know—now I remember. The cotton. How's the cotton? Gonna get rich again offa that, we are."

Burnham took Dummett's hand firmly in his. He spoke with a soothing sadness. "The cotton's ready. We've been waiting on you, old friend."

The trip to St. Augustine was made in the *Osceola*. Aware the river might be patrolled by Yankee gunboats, Burnham decided to go through Mosquito Inlet. Outside, he sailed just beyond the breaking surf. Hugging the coastline was slower than the gulf stream, but they could run the small sailboat to the beach and escape by land if threatened. Late the next afternoon, they skirted Anastasia Island and entered the harbor to land at St. Augustine.

As they passed the old Huguenot cemetery, Dummett stopped and stared into its gloom. "Hello, Papa," he said. After a few moments, Burnham took Dummett by the elbow and guided him through the old city gates and along streets packed with milling people. Knots of men stood on corners gesturing in animated conversation. Burnham caught snatches as they passed.

"Some little town in Virginny...Courthouse of some kind."

"...think of Governor Milton killing hisself like that? Musta couldn't stand the thought of the Yankees winnin' the war. I don't give a damn who won, long's it's over."

"...Grant turnt our men loose like there hadn't even been no war."

"...lost two of my boys. But t'others'll be home soon."

Burnham felt a giddy faintness as he realized the meaning; somehow the war had ended. Henry was safe and Junior would soon be coming home. Safe.

He pulled Dummett through the clusters of people, soaking in the news, until he found the saloon where Dummett had assured him the Olivaros brothers would be found.

Inside, they pushed through the crowd to the bar. When Burnham asked about the Olivaros brothers, a harried bartender pointed to a table in the corner.

"Dummett," one of the men at the table shouted, slapping Dummett on the shoulder. "Sit and have youself a rum."

"My friend," Dummett yelled above the din as he pulled Burnham to the table. "This is my other friend, Captain Mills Burnham, keeper of the Canaveral Light."

"And a damn good light it done been, too," said the swarthy young man, pulling the chairs from under two men seated at the next table. Ignoring the shouts and curses from the dispossessed drinkers, he gestured for Burnham and Dummett to sit.

The young man grinned at his table companions, his teeth flashing brightly against his olive skin. "These other drunken sailors be my brothers," he said, pouring rum from a wickered bottle. He again slapped Dummett on the shoulder. "Where you done been, man. Hain't seen you in a coon's age."

Dummett leaned close to the man's ear. "We got a load of cotton for you to run to the Bahamas. Gonna ship it to England." He sat back and lifted the glass to his lips.

Olivaros looked around at his brothers, then burst out laughing and turned back to Dummett.

"Hey, man, the war be over. You can ship anything you want from right here. Hey, they been shipping cotton out of Savannah for weeks."

Dummett looked confused for a moment, then slammed his empty glass on the table for a refill, and continued as if the man hadn't spoken. "We can load you by dory from off the Cape," he said picking up the full glass. "You can have it in Nassau in a couple of days."

Olivaros stared at him for a moment, then cut his eyes over to Burnham.

"How much rum he done already have? Don't he hear what I just say?"

"We heard Savannah had been taken by the Federals," Burnham said.

"Yep," he grinned. "But Sherman done left there in February for South Carolina, hellbent on destroying the state what led the secession. Face it, the war done be over and Europe got more cotton than they need. Stuff's cheap like dirt now." Olivaros turned to his brothers and laughed again, "And we be done with the running business. We be fishermen again."

Burnham stood and helped Dummett to his feet. As they stepped away from the table, a man leaned over Olivaros. His voice carried to Burnham. "Who dat crazy old drunk was?"

Olivaros' words spilled from his mouth to cover the room. "Hey, man, a little respect here. That done be Dummett, the famous Injun killer."

The man raised up and stared at incredulously at Dummett's back. Then he began to laugh. "Naw. No way he be him."

The men were still laughing as Burnham guided Dummett from the saloon.

Chapter 21

Burnham stuffed the package of mail into the tote when he left the general store in Sand Point. The news of the war's end had spread down like a wave ahead of them. Each town along the Halifax and Hillsboro rivers had a carnival air as they passed through. The people had taken their fine clothes from musty chests, and now paraded along waterfronts that had been deserted for four years. Goods appeared on store shelves that had long been empty, as if they had been hidden in some dark storage waiting only the news of peace to see the light of day.

The people of Florida apparently suffered little mental anguish over the loss of the Confederacy, instead they felt intense elation in the ending of the black time in their lives. Burnham suspected it wouldn't be this way in other parts of the country, that people living in the states along the border between North and South might continue the bitterness of the war for years.

Sand Point was alive this early morning, with settlers from the region pouring into the village in wagons or on horseback. Tiny sails of shallow-draft boats crowded the Indian River, manned by boys who had just reached a military age but now had a license to live.

Dummett sat in the bow of the *Osceola* at the Sand Point dock, his eyes vacantly scanning the people passing before him. Burnham threw his tote in the boat and stepped aboard.

He sat with Dummett for awhile, enjoying the celebration, greeting people he hadn't seen for years as they wandered by, some already deep into their rum, others drunk on the revelry itself. Shots rang out, fired in the exuberance of the day. Spontaneous horse races were run down the sandy street, with no regard for winning, the running burning away long pent up frustrations and fears.

Burnham's thoughts turned back to his meeting with Samuel Howell before they left St. Augustine. Howell had been Paul Arnau's assistant. He had gone back to Washington at the war's outbreak but returned less than a month ago in anticipation of the reconstruction of the country. He was now officially the Customs Inspector for St. Augustine.

When Burnham told Howell of his dismantling the light mechanism and burying it, the customs inspector was vociferous in his praise for Burnham's care for government property, assuring Burnham of his understanding the events prompting the shutdown of the light. Then he explained the government's plans to build a new tower.

"Half a million dollars were appropriated just before the war," he told Burnham. "Now that peace has returned, it's vital that the seaboard be made safe again. The country must move forward in all its commerce. I'm sure construction will begin on the new tower within the year."

Now, sitting in the gently rocking boat, Burnham felt secure in his future. The position as lighthouse keeper was still his, with no stigma attached from it being out of service so long.

With the sun at its zenith, Burnham reluctantly shoved away from the dock and headed across the river to Dummett Cove.

Dummett seemed to come alive, his eyes becoming animated once again as they as they rounded Black Point and neared the cove.

"Guess since the federal government's going to build you that nice new tower, they might get around to dredging the Haulover Canal wider and deeper."

"It'd sure help us get our citrus out," Burnham answered. "I figure we're going to see steamboats on the river soon."

"And settlers. The reb soldiers up in the other states don't have a lot to come home to. I doubt a lot of them are going to take to the federal government again. We're going to see a lot of them move down this way."

Kate stood on the dock, watching intently as they arrived. Burnham had a momentary shock when he saw her, understanding a little better how Dummett might mistake her for Leandra. Although she was still quite young, her maturity was apparent to Burnham when he saw her frown for a moment while she studied father's face. Then she brightened as she read Dummett's mood.

Dummett leaped onto the dock and took her in his arms, squeezing her until she squealed.

He released her and looked toward the house.

"Where's the girls, Leandra?" he asked. "I need to tell them we're not going to be rich just yet. The cotton's not going to bring much now."

Kate looked sadly across his shoulder at Burnham. Then she laughed.

"Don't make no nevermind." She took Dummett's hand. "We'll make do. We always have," she said as she hugged the old man again.

Burnham spread the letters over the kitchen table as he read them. Some were months old, letters from their relatives in New York and Vermont, one from the Lighthouse Board, giving him the same news of plans for the new tower.

"And the war be over for sure?" Mary asked for the fourth time since Burnham's return.

"For sure, darling," Burnham answered for as many times, smiling at her excitement. "And Junior's going to be home soon."

He picked up the last letter, noting the U. S. Army postmark. He turned it over a couple of times, then slit it along its glued edge with his knife and opened the sheet of paper. He began to read aloud.

"*Dear Captain and Mrs. Burnham, I am sorry to inform you of the death on November 26, 1863, of...your son...Private Mills O. Burnham.*" He felt the familiar burning sting as tears overflowed his eyes. He rose and walked slowly around the table to take Mary into his arms as she seemed on the verge of collapsing. She burrowed her face into his shoulder as convulsive sobs wracked her body.

He held her for what seemed hours but was only minutes until she pulled herself away and wiped her face with her apron. Sitting at the table, she motioned Burnham back to his seat.

"Read the rest," she said with a quaking voice.

Burnham picked up the letter and brushed his eyes clear.

"*I was Chaplain at the hospital in Chattanooga where your son was brought after his capture. He was not wounded. Many boys on both sides were struck down by dysentery. Please be assured the army physicians did all in their power to save Mills, but to no avail. He passed as so many did. I was honored to tend him in his last moments, and can assure you he is now in the Lord's house. You have my deepest sympathy in your time of grief and my sorrow at the length of time it took to notify you of this sad event.*"

Burnham lay the letter aside. "It is signed by a Captain Glynn," he said.

Slowly, Mary lifted her reddened, swollen eyes to his. "November... '63? More'n a year past. He's been gone...all this time, and I thought he was—"

"Don't think on it like that. I see him as being still alive, only gone somewhere else. We don't have to lose him in our hearts."

"Yes, we must lose him, and we must do it now," she said, standing and smoothing her apron. "Ye don't need be pamperin' me none. Life begins, and life ends, and we have to let go when it's time. I done it before, and it's sure I'll be doin' it again. I'll be goin' over to tell Frances now."

Burnham picked up the letter again after she left. She's one of the strong ones, he thought. I'm not so strong.

He folded the letter and went outside, deciding to walk to the tower. He needed to be alone with his memories for awhile and the tower balcony seemed the best place for it.

Lend me the borry of s'more of that cane liquor," the Colonel said, dabbing at his lips with his red neckerchief. Burnham slid the clay rum jug across the table and watched the dapper little man crook his finger through the ring and swing the jug up across to the outside of his elbow. Closing one eye to get a better aim at the cup he held under the tilted jug's mouth, the Colonel concentrated, pouring a tentative stream at first then smiling broadly, satisfied he was hitting the cup.

"Damn good job, Henry." Dummett said, clapping his hands together in a slow parody of applause.

Henry Wilson raised his chin from his chest where it had been resting. "What job'd I do?" he slurred as he leaned toward Dummett and squinted his eyes.

"Not you, Henry. I was talkin' to ole Henry, here, this other'n." Dummett pointed toward the empty chair and looked around for Colonel Henry Titus. "Where—"

"He headed outside for the outhouse...outside," Burnham said retrieving the jug and swirling it. "A dead soldier," he muttered. He leaned around in his chair and set the jug on the floor next to two other empties. His head began to buzz from the effort and he rocked back upright, shaking his head slightly to clear the fog from his eyes. He snapped his fingers at his son-in-law.

"Henry, would you mind getting—"

"Damn good job, Henry," Dummett said, fixing his eyes on a sheet of paper lying on the table before him.

"What job'd I do?" Henry Titus asked, stepping back into the room. Shifting his polished malacca cane under his armpit, he fumbled with the buttons of his fly.

"Not you, Henry. I was talkin' to ole Henry Wilson here, this other'n." Dummett giggled. "Ain't we been through this before?" Then he glared at Titus. "Dammit, Henry Titus, I hate it when a cripple sneaks around when I ain't watchin' good."

Titus flopped into his chair, hooking the cane on the back. "And I hate it when a drunk ain't watchin' good when I'm sneakin' around." He looked at Burnham and grinned.

The thought drifted through the mist in Burnham's mind that Dummett seemed so like his old self—arrogant, cocksure, and in complete control of his mentality. Probably the rum, or maybe it was merely the relaxation of being with good friends. Whatever, Burnham was pleased to see no sign of strange behavior, if the good-natured banter could be thought of as normal behavior. He reached for the sheet of paper lying on the table in front of Dummett.

"Let's have a looksee now," he said.

Dummett snatched the paper away.

"Like hell. No way you gonna see this will."

Burnham pointed at the three papers folded in the middle of the table. "You saw ours. How we spozed to witness your will without we see it first?"

"You ain't witnessin' the will. You witnessin' the *signin'* of the will," Dummett said. He folded the paper in half, creasing it a couple of times between thumb and forefinger, then folded back the bottom.

"Hell," Titus said, reaching for it. "You gonna be thataway, I oughta not sign it. Give me it here."

"It don't make no never mind," Dummett said, leaning toward Burnham. "It'll be in my wallet if you was to ever need it." He leaned across the table toward Titus. "Hell, you Kansas jayhawker, I bet as many enemies you got, I'll be filin' your will for the Widow Titus at the courthouse long befo mine'll ever be needed."

"Don't have no enemy in the world." Titus snorted through his nose, pulled the pen from the inkwell and signed Dummett's will.

"Only cause you done killed them already." Dummett reached for the will and slid it across the table to Burnham. He crooked a thumb back at Titus. "I heard Old John Brown was Henry's enemy back in Kansas. Course, now his body's already molderin' in the grave where Henry tried to put him and couldn't."

"Can't nobody," Titus yelled, "prove ole Henry Titus ever had an enemy. I ain't scared of nobody."

Dummett nodded and spoke behind the back of his hand. "Man's scared of sumpin though. Sittin' all day on his hotel porch with a shotgun crost his knees like Ole Harvey Martin used to do—can't be too comfortable." He leaned closer to Burnham and whispered loudly, "Probably scared somebody's gonna come steal that lady's plume outta his hat."

Henry Wilson slammed the door open and stepped inside. Scrubbing the fingers of one hand through the red thatch on his chin, he spread the fingers of the other before the men in an empty gesture. "Ain't a jug left in the boat. We plumb out."

Titus sighed and shoved his chair back as he rose shakily to his feet.

"Guess I'll have to go get some of mine," he said.

"Dagnabbed Yankee, you said you was out," Dummett shouted. Burnham chuckled, then began to cough.

"That was then. This is now," Titus said, walking gingerly to the door. "Ya'll don't leave now, ya heah," he said in an theatrical southern drawl.

Dummett grinned crookedly at Burnham as he folded his will and placed it in his leather wallet.

Henry Wilson sat in his chair and slumped his arms onto the table. "Ain't that sumpin? We all wrote wills and I'm the onliest one with younguns to leave sumpin to and I ain't got nothin' hardly to leave 'em. Ya'll got lot's to leave but you ain't got no younguns. Who you leavin' yores to, Dummett?"

"Hell, son, I don't even own my groves by myself any more. Family owns half of it, brothers-in-law and all. I don't guess I got any heirlooms at all."

With the war's end, Burnham saw an influx of settlers into the Indian River country, mostly young men coming down from the southern states seeking a fresh start from conditions back home. Most had returned from the war to plantations ravaged by the warring armies, or simply from the devastation of neglect. Finding themselves unable to rebuild their losses without slave labor, some were either too proud to hire their former slaves or financially unable to.

But Burnham suspected that many were like that young fellow, Hardee, who came over to the Cape last week to buy orange stock from him. The young man had moved from Georgia and filed on a hundred sixty acres of high land on the west bank of the Indian River. Like so many other war veterans, he had found life intolerable under a reconstruction government foisted on him by what he now viewed as a foreign country.

The great wilderness was becoming spotted with the homesteads and cleared fields of dozens of families. As soon as the sun rose, men were out clearing their ground. The wind carried the thunking of axes across Merritt's Island to the Cape. To Burnham, whose ear was accustomed to only the cries of night birds and the crash of surf along the beach, the raucous sounds were an intrusion on his soul.

Many of the new settlers to invade the area were black, mostly former slaves looking to build new lives for themselves. Almost all of them had gone to Douglas Dummett for advice and help in setting up as squatters on land north of the Haulover Canal.

Colonel Thomas Osborn, a commissioner from the Freedmen's Bureau in Beaufort, South Carolina, came to the area to help the Negroes file homestead papers on their land. Within a week of his arrival, he had crossed verbal swords with Dummett over the obvious mixed parentage of Kate and her sisters. Dummett endured his subtle slurs until Osborn pointedly accused him of miscegenation, a crime in Florida. Dummett drove him from his property at gunpoint. "Made him and his crowd scatter like a covey of quail," he later told Burnham.

Although freedmen were only allowed forty acres each, Jackson and his son, Andrew, were two of the first to file on land north of the haulover canal. When time came for Jackson to leave the Cape, the memories of their thirty years of living and working together left a bittersweet feeling in Burnham. He was stretched tight between a selfish desire to hold onto the past represented by an old friend, and the understanding that the old friend might want to build something permanent and personal for his son.

By 1869, Andrew finished a house and had young citrus trees already producing on his land. He walked to Dummett Cove and proposed to Kate Dummett. At seventeen, she was a beauty, having developed into a duplicate of Leandra, the same tawny complexion enhanced by the startling green of her eyes.

She accepted Andrew and they were married in a simple service by a circuit preacher at Sand Point. Burnham happened to be in town that weekend and attended the service. Dummett was conspicuously absent.

After the wedding, Burnham sailed the short distance across to Dummett Cove, finding Dummett pacing incessantly in front of his sleeping shack, his eyes wild and sparking, screaming incoherent obscenities at the pigs in the nearby pen. The awareness that Burnham was there finally penetrated the mist of his mind and he stared hotly at Burnham.

"Can't trust none of 'em," he ranted, pulling long strands of dank, dead-looking hair through his dirty fingers. "Been hornswoggled by women all my life, but never again."

"How you been hornswoggled, and by who?"

"Leandra. Damn nigger's just like a whorish white woman—left with the first man to come along."

"Dummett, that was Kate, not Leandra. Leandra's dead. You gotta snap outta this and know what's happening. Your daughter's married to Andrew, and that's the way it should be. A fine boy—he'll do you proud as a son-in-law. You oughta be happy over this."

Dummett began rubbing his eye with the heel of his hand, jamming it hard into the socket as he ground it in a circle.

Burnham stepped over to him, laid a hand on his shoulder and began to massage the tight muscles.

"It's all right," he soothed. "Maybe Leandra's hiding from you. She's probably just mad at you for not going over to Kate's wedding."

The hand rubbing the eye froze in position for a moment, then fell to his side. Dummett seemed to go limp, as if life's energy had drained through his bare feet into the ground.

"That's it," he said. "She hasn't left at all."

A shudder passed through his body, and he jerked upright like a man waking from a dream. He walked over toward the house, yelling, "Leandra? Where are you?" He broke into a sprint and ran into the house.

Burnham followed slowly, realizing that Dummett was no longer aware of his presence. When Dummett came from the house, he stopped, looked wildly in all directions, then took off through the groves, calling as he went.

As Burnham pushed the *Osceola* away from the dock, he could still hear Dummett wandering far in the distance, searching and calling for Leandra to show herself.

Chapter 22

Dummett reached for the oil lantern, bumping it with his knuckles, then grabbing it as it nearly overturned. Carefully, he turned up the wick. The yellow light in the globe grew brighter but did little to clear his vision.

Dummett shook his head and blinked his eyes, wondering what the hell was happening to them. For the last couple of months his eyes had been blurring, but not the result of their constant watering. He was seeing a doubling at the edges of things, probably causing the mindsplitting headaches that damn near drove him to his knees. They began when he got Louisa's letter, dated in May of 1873.

Louisa and Mary had obviously been planning their escape for a long time. Early in 1866, they waited until Dummett was gone, then they left the house taking Anna with them. When Dummett returned and found them missing, Kate refused to tell him where they had gone, only that she'd chosen not to go with them. He later learned that they had carried their belongings in one of his canoes to Live Oak Hill where they caught a steamer for St. Augustine.

Now, after all these years, he received a letter from Louisa telling him of their marriages, her to a Minorcan and Mary to a white Yankee. They had both moved north, she wouldn't say where, but were now living as proper white women. They would never come back to Dummett Cove.

Hell, they were white, weren't they? Their mama always said so. Now he guessed they'd got what they always wanted, to be in some place where no one knew they were really niggers. Louisa told him Anna had gone somewhere into Georgia, she didn't know where.

Now Dummett sat in the dim light of the room, feeling the gloom and silence of the house. With Kate and the other girls gone, he was left alone with only Leandra to comfort him. But he couldn't find her except when he befogged his mind with rum. Then he wasn't sure she was really there.

Maybe it was a case of the lonelies. The lonelies, his mama had told him, could eat at a man worse than a chigger bite. With no way to scratch the lonelies, they could eat into you even when you surrounded yourself with people.

He rose shakily from the chair and walked to the door. Stepping into the sandspur patch that used to be his house yard, he felt his mind begin to buzz. He knew he was falling but couldn't catch his balance. As the light dimmed in his mind, a shrill whistle tore into its darkness.

He awoke near dawn, his face and hands afire with mosquito bites, his head carrying a dull throb of pain that ran down his neck into his shoulders. His mind was clear enough to know he needed help.

The Cape—he'd go to Burnham's place. They would take care of him. Miss Mary would know what was wrong. Probably a touch of the swamp fever from passing out on the porch of his summer camp.

He roused himself and staggered to the dock. Crawling into the small canoe, he pushed off and paddled slowly out of the cove.

Within an hour he was around Black Point and at the mouth of Banana Creek. He was guiding the canoe into a sweeping turn for the creek when he saw the panther.

Bathed in the early morning light, it stood on the bank as if it had been waiting for him. Its tawny fur lay back along smoothly rippling muscles that seemed to quiver in expectation. Dummett backwatered to a dead stop, wondering if the cat was an aberration, existing only in his fevered fantasy. He blinked his eyes in disbelief, half expecting the vision to vanish. It didn't.

The panther moved several yards along the bank of the creek, looking back at Dummett, its eyes seeming to burn into his with an invitation to enter the creek. Then, as if understanding that the man had no intention of entering the narrow creek, it stopped, turned and screamed, reaching forward with one heavy paw to rake the air toward Dummett. A deep booming that Dummett realized was the slamming throb of his own heart, seemed to beat a counterpoint cadence against the shrill cry of the beast. An intense burning began deep in Dummett's throat.

Surely he wasn't afraid of the animal. He had his rifle, and the knowledge of dozens he had killed. He decided to wait for the cat to leave. Their eyes locked in battle, neither man nor beast wavering the gaze. "Scat," he finally yelled, wincing at the pain this brought into his skull. "Git the hell away from my creek."

The panther moved fluidly back to its original spot and dropped to its belly, yellow eyes still intently staring at Dummett.

Dummett turned the canoe and headed for the middle of the river. Maybe he could convince the cat he was going somewhere else. When he finally stopped and turned back to look, he could see the cat splashing through the shallow creek to the south bank.

With a start, he realized the panther was stalking him. Impossible. Panthers don't stalk men. Oh, an extremely hungry panther might stalk a man, might even attack and kill a man if given the chance, especially a cornered cat. But in most confrontations with men, a panther would escape whenever possible. Several years ago, he had been tracking a cat in the 'glades. The animal had turned behind him and was on his trail a long time before Dummett finally sensed his presence. When he turned and ran at it, the cat vanished like smoke on a windy day. Later, when he finally cornered it on a hammock island, it turned at the deep water and charged headlong into his rifle fire.

Now, he knew it could be fatal to take the canoe into the creek where that panther was. The cat could easily stalk him and attack through the shallows, or get ahead and drop on him from a tree. He realized that his weakened condition put him at a disadvantage in a close meeting—a fatal disadvantage.

The only other way to the Cape was around Merritt's Island to the south, entering the Banana River across from the new village of Arlington. Maybe he could even stop there, at Captain Houston's place, for help.

Then he remembered Doc Whitfield. Hell, if he planned to go to the end of Merritt's Island, he'd pass right by Whitfield's plantation, Fairyland, and might as well stop there. Old Doc Whitfield would tend him. That's the thing to do, he decided.

As he began to paddle south, he could see the slim outline of the panther pacing along with him, staying even with him, while it glided through the underbrush almost like a phantom.

"I ate your brother's heart, you bastard," he yelled at the ghostly form striding through the filigree of shadows along the shore, always remaining even with the canoe. As if in answer to his shout, the panther seemed to drift upward, at times barely visible through the foliage, until suddenly it was loping along the jagged edge of the treetops, a tawny silhouette against the blue sky, its long tail swinging behind him in rhythm to its stride.

A large, red-shouldered hawk swooped down over the panther, braking with cupped wings, then landing on the panther's back. It settled its wings into place and the red glare of its eyes burned into Dummett's.

Dummett felt the whimper begin far down within him, from deep in his bowels, working its way up past the burning lump of fear clogging his throat, its sound touched with despair when it escaped his lips.

Burnham leaned against the railing of the tower balcony, eyes squinted against the early morning brightness. He shielded the bowl of his pipe from the wind as he studied the progress of a sailboat far to the south on the Banana River.

Running before the wind, the sailor had his jib and mainsail billowed out on opposite sides of the mast like a cormorant drying its spread wings. The boat was too far away to identify. Could be Isaiah Hall or one of his boys. Or maybe it was one of the new settlers coming to buy citrus stock.

Burnham turned his back to the wind and knocked the dottle from his pipe into his hand. He dumped it into the can at his feet and blew through the pipestem to clear it. Stepping to the lantern-room door, he paused to look again at the distant boat. He figured the visitor should arrive about midday.

"Getting to be crowded like a parade ground around here," he muttered, stepping into the lantern room. The huge Fresnel lens towered above him as he prepared to fill the lantern reservoir with mineral spirits. He paused and let his thoughts drift back to the building of the new tower in '68.

Pictures flashed into his mind like a stereoscope—the furious activity of the builders, like ants scurrying around a hill, the tower rising in sectioned spurts, finally tapering to an end a hundred sixty-five feet above the cane-field, ready to receive the new lens.

Burnham smiled at the recollection, lifted the heavy can of mineral spirits and began pouring.

After the crowd of builders left, peace settled over the Cape and he had eased back into the nightly routine. Henry Wilson was assistant keeper the first year of the new tower, but gave up the job when James Knight, a young apprentice from the Cape Hatteras Lighthouse, came down in 1869. Burnham made him chief assistant, freeing Henry to concentrate on managing the groves.

Within the year, young Knight had courted and won the hand of Burnham's daughter, Mary Louise. After their wedding, the Knight's moved into the new assistant keeper's house, identical to Burnham's own. The house was quickly filled with the sounds of babies.

Burnham smiled at the thought of all the newcomers and shook his head. Next thing you know, someone'll set up a store on the Cape. Merritt's Island already had a store with a small community growing up around it, just north of Dummett's place.

Back in 1870, Burnham had hired two new men, Rose and Kruger. These bachelors now lived in enclosed rooms on the third landing of the tower. With three assistants, Burnham took himself off the rotation schedule, taking a turn only occasionally to give the men a break in their routine, or when he felt the need to be alone under the stars, like he had last night. His concern over Dummett was depressing him and he needed the solitude to cleanse his soul.

He finished filling the reservoir and descended the staircase, counting the steps as he had habitually done since his first climb up the new tower, the count keeping his mind off the boring trip down. One hundred sixty-five steps—easy enough for a man like him in a healthy condition, but he knew the climb, up or down, could be a potential killer to many other men his age. Hell, fifty-five wasn't all that old. He could still work younger men, like Henry Wilson, into the ground.

As he crossed the quadrangle toward his house, the front door burst open and his three-year-old grandson, Thomas Knight, jumped from the porch and ran toward him, squealing in delight. Burnham scooped the boy into his arms and shivered with pride as the child's thin arms wrapped around his neck in a hug.

"Tell me another story, Grandpa."

Burnham set the boy on the ground and took one little hand in his. Together, they walked up on the porch. Burnham yelled through the still open door, "Grandma, I'm home." Then he lifted the boy onto the porch swing, sat beside him and began telling a story of the olden days.

An hour later, Burnham was feeding Frances' chickens when he heard the shout from the river. He swept his arm forward, scattering the cracked corn across the ground, then hung the bucket from a nail on the fence and began the long walk down to the dock. His long strides slowed for a second as he recognized Doc Whitfield. The old man was laborously climbing from his small boat, trying to balance himself and a small carpet valise while holding the boat's painter between his teeth. Burnham ran out onto the rickety, salt-stained boards of the dock and took the rope while greeting the old man.

"Spotted you coming early this morning," he said, flipping a double clove hitch around a post. "Made pretty good time for an old timer."

Whitfield set the valise at his feet and hauled a large bandanna from his waistband to mop his sweaty forehead. "The man's old but the boat ain't," he grumbled with a faint smile. He stuffed the bandanna through a gallus and stooped to pick up the valise

"Douglas Dummett died yesterday morning," he said, abruptly walking away, hunkered over against the whistling river breeze.

Burnham felt the half-smile freeze on his face, realizing the old man hadn't thrown out the punchline of the joke and dreading its absence. Burnham hurried to catch up. He walked in silence behind Whitfield until they reached the end of the dock.

"Then it's true—you're serious?" He leaned forward and took the valise from Whitfield. "Dummett is dead?"

They stepped into the shade of a large wateroak. Whitfield's chin quivered slightly as he again scrubbed his face with the bandanna.

"He comes in to my place three days ago," he said. "First I know, I'm hearing some shots fired down near my landing. Then Dummett comes running up the hill like Satan's chasing him."

Burnham motioned toward the house. "Let's go on up to Frances' house and get us some cool lemon juice. Then I guess we need to walk over to my house. Mary'll want to hear all this."

"No, I can't go that far. I'll be needing to get on back. Man my age don't need to be on this river at night."

"Malaria—the man was burning up with fever," Whitfield said, leaning forward in the kitchen chair to rest his elbows on the table. "And drunk to boot. I got him into the bed—didn't have much trouble there, he was so weak and wasted away."

Burnham sat stiffly across from him, holding tightly to Frances' hand, feeling the clamminess and not knowing if it was from her hand or his.

The empty feeling deep within his gut was being washed periodically by a cold shudder passing through his body, like a dog shaking water from his wet coat. He tried to control these shakes but, when pictures of a vulnerable and weak Dummett invaded his mind, the shiver would begin in spite of his efforts.

Whitfield was staring sharply at him.

"You all right, Captain?" He reached for his valise. "I got something that might make you—"

Burnham waved his free hand toward the doctor. "No, I'm fine. Just a little upset." He looked at his daughter when she squeezed his hand. Seeing her soft smile, he tried to relax.

"Well," Whitfield continued, "I pulled ever trick I knew to get his fever down—cold towels, body rubs...nothing worked. He just got hotter and hotter. Yelling constantly in his delirium. Crazy stuff."

Burnham reached for the glass of rum Frances had poured for him. "You probably didn't know. He's been off the deep end of the dock for a few years now. Didn't show it much around other people, usually only at home when he'd been drinking a lot."

"I'd heard rumors." Whitfield nodded his head thoughtfully. "Something about that dead wife of his. But what he was yelling weren't that. Kept saying he was being stalked by a panther with a hawk riding on its back. Claimed they'd followed him all the way to my place trying to kill him."

Burnham clenched his fist. "Leandra. His mind broke one time too many over her."

Whitfield looked quizically at him.

"Leandra," Burnham said. "The dead wife. He thought of her as a hawk."

"How do you think he got the malaria?" Frances broke in. "Could any of our family get—"

"Naw," Whitfield said, shrugging his shoulders. "Just keep your kids in the house at night. Dummett's probably been laying out drunk in the night air. Everyone knows night air ain't good for you, and the miasmas can get in you easier when you lay outside at night drunk on the ground."

Burnham nodded his head to that. "Well, he's done a lot of that."

Whitfield stood and walked over to the window, staring through the glass for a long moment. "After he died, I opened his head. Found a brain aneurysm, probably a flaw from his father. I know he died like that—and Dummett might have passed the aneurysm on to his children. I heard stories about his boy..."

Whitfield raised a finger as if to point at something outside. "I buried him in my lawn overlooking Honeymoon Lake. Prettiest view in this part of the world. Probably be laid next to him soon myself. I only hope my own passing will be a lot more peaceable."

He shook his head slowly and walked back to the table. Lifting his valise, he began taking articles from it.

"These are his personal effects," he said. "I figured you might get a chance to take them to his girl." He laid Dummett's pistol and holster on the table. "I kept his rifle. Didn't see as how she'd be wanting it anytime soon. Her man can pick it up if he's ever down my way."

Dummett's knife and scabbard were added to the pile, followed by a cracked, leather wallet. Burnham reached over, picked it up, and opened it. Inside, he could see the folded paper—Dummett's will. He closed it and put the wallet in his pocket.

"His ugly face was close enough for me to see his eyes, black and heavy like lead rifle balls." Burnham reached into the hearth and ignited a sliver of fat pine. Holding his long beard aside, he touched the flame carefully to the bowl of a briar pipe burnished the deep color of mahogany from his touch. He glanced at his three-year-old grandson sitting on a wooden stool before the hearth, staring at him in wide-eyed wonder. Drawing deeply on the pipe, he held the pause until the boy began to squirm.

"Is that when he shot ya, Grampa?"

Burnham nodded his head.

"His musket banged so loud it felt like my eardrums blew out. The wallop from the ball knocked me flat on my back."

"Did you cry, Grampa?"

The old man chuckled. "Me cry? Lord, no. But I sure made that Seminole cry. My aim was about three inches lower than his. Right between the eyes."

"Your Grampa shouldn't have been there in the first place, Hon. And you, young man, shouldn't be so close to the hearth. The sparks'll be settin' your britches afire." Mary pulled her grandson back a few inches and returned to her rocker. Burnham gazed fondly at the expressive Irish face topped by a bun of auburn-streaked white hair.

Every twenty seconds, the window on the south side of the sitting room glowed softly from the light revolving high in the tower above them. Leaning back in his chair, he listened to the wind blowing off the Atlantic, letting visions of the past dance through his mind.

"Grampa! The story."

Burnham smiled at the boy and focused his mind on the tale. "Well, I heard the screams of dying men, white men on the steamer and Indians on the bank." He rested his eyes sadly on his grandson. "Men on both sides died that day hoping their families could live in peace on this land."

The scene was vivid to Burnham now—the pain in his head, the flow of blood across his face, the battle sounds echoing across the space of forty years.

"We pulled the soldiers out of the water under cover of that gunsmoke. Then the steamer got us to safe water around the bend." He paused to relight his pipe, then continued, staring into the fire as he spoke.

"We never knew how many Seminoles died that day. No one dared to go back." Burnham pulled his attention back to his grandson. "That introduction to Florida almost made me miss the beauty of this land."

"Well, something opened your eyes," his wife said. "But this lad can hardly keep his open. Time for bed, Thomas. Come on, I'll be tuckin' you in."

Later, Mary came back into the sitting room and sat before the fire. "Do you suppose the doctor would be home by now?" she asked.

"Oh, he got there long before dark. His little boat can make that sail in six hours easy. Twenty-five miles? I've done it quicker." He reached over and laid his hand on her shoulder. "Were you so surprised when Doc Whitfield told us Dummett was dead?"

"I never expect death," she said. "It sneaks up even on those who're ready for it."

"I guess he welcomed it more than anyone I ever knew. Life sucked out all his juices and left him dry as a squeezed orange." Burnham stood and stretched to his full height. "I think I'll go up the tower now and relieve James. Probably do me good to be alone for a while."

He left the house and walked across the quadrangle to the base of the lighthouse rising above the dunes of Cape Canaveral. A tang of salty spray dampened his lips as he looked up along the monolith, seeing the vast canopy of stars spread above. Three fingers of light reached from the shaft in their circular sweep to the horizon.

He knew the climb to the top would be good for him. A man can lay a lot of ghosts to rest while leaning over the railing, smoking a pipe, and looking miles out to sea. He'd done it on thousands of nights.

The faint glow in the east marked the backdrop of purple clouds on the horizon, then exploded into bright yellow highlights dancing along the edges where the clouds caught the direct rays before they reached his eyes. His eyes shifted quickly, trying to anticipate the exact spot where the fiery arc would appear. Burnham felt the involuntary intake of breath that happened as it had always done.

The arc rose steadily, expanding into a globe, its roundness more apparent at this time of day than at any other. He turned his gaze inland, watching the first shadows appear on the roof of the wilderness, instant long sheets of darkness emphasizing the encroachment of light. The far edges of the shadows moved toward the east like a live creature, shortening rapidly in these first moments of the new day as the sun spread its life-giving energy across the land.

Burnham moved around to the inland side of the tower and rested his elbows on the balcony railing, his eyes searching, trying to penetrate the canopy of foliage still shading the forest floor. He could hear the first sounds of awakening. Cicadas rattling like Cuban castanets, with the warble of songbirds taking up the cadence as the animals began rituals established through eons, the making of life and the continuance of life in the midst of subtle change.

The night had done much to dispel the grief lying deeply in his soul. At first his thoughts of Douglas Dummett had been of the recent years, and the dulling of the lust for life within the man. But, as the night wore on, the grief was crowded out by memories of their earliest experiences and the lessons of life learned, each from the other and from nature.

Now, gazing over the river yet shrouded with mist, he knew that Dummett had been merely another creature of the forest, here for only a short time, struggling to make life, and to continue life, in the midst of subtle change.

But with man, the changes were not always so subtle. Some men, unwilling to live with the land and driven to own it, destroyed those who wished only to live by nature's design. Whether through warfare as against the Seminole or even its own kind, or the bigotry of society against the Negro, the destruction was violent and it was always total.

From somewhere below, a panther screamed, breaking his thoughts and reminding him again of Dummett. He took the worn leather wallet from his pocket and removed Dummett's will.

As he read, a soft joy flooded through him. In death, Dummett had finally done what he had been unable to do in life. He read the words again.

"...my three illegitimate children, which I hereby acknowledge as my blood, Louisa Dummett, Kate Dummett and Mary Dummett, they being children of Leandra Fernandez."

Burnham carefully folded the paper and returned it to the wallet. Dummett had set Leandra's soul at rest by cleansing his own.

A slight movement in the canefield below caught his attention. At first he saw nothing. Staring fixedly at one spot, he relaxed into a frozen position.

Then he saw it, near the edge of his vision. The panther was almost invisible, its tawny color blending harmoniously into the grass. It stood with one paw raised, its head lifted toward Burnham. Slowly Burnham shifted his eyes until they met the burning gaze of the big cat. They stared, each locked into the other, for several minutes. Then, the panther lowered its paw and mewled softly. In a heartbeat it was gone.

Burnham shook his head, unsure now if what he had witnessed was fantasy or reality. He looked to the north, toward Dummett Creek.

There he could see the vivid image of Douglas Dummett calling to his pack of hounds in the early morning mist, returning from hunting the coon and possum of his once broad acres. The speedy *Flying Fish* slipped eerily over the dark waters bearing Dummett as passenger, a man free at last from torment, while a ghostly crew of Negro slaves sang in time to the dip of noiseless oars.

Burnham walked slowly around the tower and opened the lantern room door, pausing for a moment to look again at the rising sun. Above it, Tommy Jumper's bashful star was easing into the protective light.

The clatter of pots from his home below reminded him that his family was also awakening.

He laughed. "Gonna be a fine day," he said aloud as he entered the lantern room to extinguish the light.

The End

The End

ABOUT THE AUTHOR

DON DAVID ARGO is a Professor of Mathematics at Brevard Community College in Cocoa, Florida, an award-winning writer, and is the president of the Space Coast Writers' Guild.

The Indian River area, including Cape Canaveral, fascinates him, and he is busily working on additional novels that explore the lives and times of early settlers in this region of Florida. Fueled by intriguing tidbits of historical information found in period newspapers and in libraries in the region, Don Argo isn't content to merely work from documents. An intrepid explorer of East Florida, he believes in "getting the lay of the land" firsthand.

He lives with his wife and children in Rockledge, Florida.

ABOUT THE AUTHOR

COVER ART

by

J. T. Glisson

The cover art for *Canaveral Light* is a product of the fertile mind and talents of J. T. Glisson, a resident of Evingston, Florida.

A native of Cross Creek, as a young man J. T. fell under the sway of his neighbor, noted author Marjorie Kinnan Rawlings. Rawlings' love of rural Florida found expression in a number of popular novels (*Cross Creek, The Yearling*), and she found a kindred spirit in Glisson. Together they took great delight in the small world of Cross Creek, and Rawlings encouraged the young man to pursue his artistic talents.

More than a visual artist, J. T. Glisson is also a talented wordsmith. In 1993, he found success with *The Creek*, a humorous look at Cross Creek and its inhabitants. He followed up with a one-man play, *Sigsby*, an Ocala attorney whose successes in the court room made him a legend.

J. T. and his wife, Pat, live in Evingston, just about five miles from the family homestead at Cross Creek. From this base, J. T. carries on an active schedule of painting, writing and public speaking.

The Print Shoppe

The Print Shoppe is the bookstore and gift shop of the Florida Historical Society and the Tebeau-Field Library of Florida History. Members of the Society and the Library receive a full 20% discount on all books and gifts purchased in *The Print Shoppe*. From the newest book on Florida history to exceedingly rare pictures, Florida art and out-of-print *floridiana*, the shelves of *The Print Shoppe* are easily accessible in person, by telephone or on the internet. If a book or other item is not in stock, we'll order it for you.

For telephone orders, call (321) 690-1971. For internet orders visit our website at www.florida-historical-soc.org or www.floridabooks.net or by simply sending us an e-mail at Theprintshoppe@aol.com

Mastercard and VISA are accepted for all purchases, including telephone and internet orders.

Visit us in person at The Tebeau-Field Library of Florida History, 435 Brevard Avenue, Historic Cocoa Village, FL 32922.